WAR AMONG THE RUINS

WAR AMONG
THE RUINS

Scott Washburn

Stellar Pheonix Books

Philadelphia, USA
Toronto, Canada

ISBN: 978-1-4196-7760-1
ISBN-10: 1-4196-7760-8

Stellar Pheonix Books
Philadelphia, Toronto

Printed and bound by BookSurge in the USA

Cover design by Jonathan Cresswell-Jones
Cover image of Saturn by John Spencer

DEDICATION

There are a lot of people I want to thank
for helping me with this book.
People like Donna and Barb and Mary and Andy
and The Chief, whose feedback and enthusiasm
for my work made the writing so enjoyable.
People like Jenny, proofreader extraordinare,
who was always ready to help.
And Jonathan, who writes so beautifully himself,
who would always manage to both encourage
and challenge me at the same time.

I want to thank all of them.

But the person I want to dedicate this book to is
my wife, Rosemary. She's the one who put up
with all this. When the lawn needed mowing or
the walls needed painting (they still do, I think)
she never begrudged me the time to write.
A true friend, now and forever.

PROLOGUE

Hradj'akbul leaned back in his padded grav-couch and regarded the two slaves copulating on the thick carpet. They were nearly exhausted and providing little amusement. He reached out with his mind and touched the pair. They immediately redoubled their efforts and he drank in the sensations of their actions. An interesting species, this one. When first encountered it had seemed they would be a valuable addition to the Race's possessions. It was a shame they were so intractable if not directly controlled....

A faint vibration shook the chamber as if in confirmation of Hradj'akbul's evaluation. The enemy bombardment was getting closer. The chamber was in a fortress deep beneath the surface, but the enemy seemed intent on splitting the planet open, if need be, to kill him and all the rest. At this point it was definitely a case of over-kill. The Homeworld's surface must be an ocean of lava by now. The real oceans boiled to steam. Even if the enemy were to cease now, it would make little difference. Hradj'akbul was already entombed. There would be no way out.

With a gurgling sigh he put out a tendril to grasp a goblet of his favorite wine. No point in saving the good stuff for later. There would be no later. As he brought it closer, the chamber shook again, much more violently. Some bit of debris dropped from the ceiling and landed directly in the goblet, splashing him with liquid.

He roared out a curse and hurled the goblet away to smash against the wall. He looked for a target to vent his rage upon and settled on the pair of slaves, still busy carrying out his last command. This time his mind touched the collars on their necks. In an instant they were shrieking and convulsing on the floor. A few moments later he felt their lives flicker out.

It was hardly a satisfying revenge, however, and gathering himself, he launched his thoughts upward, through the rock, through the lava and up into space. The enemy ships were there in countless numbers, but he could not get at them. They had those miserable shields protecting them. Once, years ago, it had been possible to take control of their minds and pit ship against ship, but no more. In frustration, he withdrew.

That was foolish. They can not only block my thoughts, they can trace them. Soon they will concentrate their fire here.

But it did not matter. He could die now or later, but he would surely die.

He looked again at the bodies of the slaves. He summoned another slave to remove them. That hardly mattered either, but he valued tidiness and old habits died hard.

"Well, well, having a bit of temper are we?"

Hradj'akbul regarded the newcomer to his chamber. Kredj'nusek floated in on his own grav-couch radiating an insufferable aura of smugness. *He'll die the same as I. Why did he have to be visiting here when the assault came? I can think of a hundred far more interesting people to share my last moments with.*

He did not bother to answer and his guest's couch came to a halt next to his. Without asking, Kredj'nusek helped himself to refreshments.

"Brikj'tegal is dead," he said without preamble.

"Indeed?"

"Dead and vaporized, I would imagine. The enemy isn't leaving anything to chance."

"We shall certainly be next."

"Perhaps. I was in communication with Brikj'tegal just before he died and he had something very interesting to tell me."

"Indeed?" Hradj'akbul was in no mood for guessing games. The chamber shook again and more debris rained down. It would not be long now.

"Yes. It seems that when he was in command of Third Conquest

Fleet, back at the start of this unfortunate war, he made a rather bold decision concerning military research that he did not bother to tell any of the rest of us about."

"Oh?"

"Yes. If things had gone differently, it could have turned out to be most embarrassing for him. Probably why he did not tell anyone else. As things stand however, he has given us a most delightful gift to take with us to the afterlife."

"Gift? What gift?"

Kredj'nusek popped a morsel into his mouth and then slowly focused all his eyes upon Hradj'akbul. That aura of smugness was back.

"Vengeance."

CHAPTER ONE

The League starship *Gilgamesh* emerged from hyperspace two hundred and fifty million kilometers from the F3 star Leavitte and thirty million from the naval base orbiting Leavitte IV. The small, old, *Hero* class cruiser sat there for a few moments, as if the recent exertion had exhausted her, and then swung her bow around and headed toward the base.

"Standard challenge from the picket satellites, Skipper," reported Lieutenant (j.g.) Svetlana Terletsky from the Com station.

"Acknowledge and give them our recognition code, Lieutenant," said Captain Harold Liu-Chen.

"Aye aye, sir."

"Not that we really need to," said Commander Jaqueline Ellsworth. "They could hardly mistake this old bucket for anyone else."

Liu-Chen quirked a smile at his executive officer. "Please, Jaq, let's make *Gilgie's* last trip a dignified one, shall we? She's given a lot of good years to the Fleet and deserves some respect."

"Yes, sir. And her captain does, too," said Lieutenant Commander Charles Florkowski, casting a frown at Ellsworth. "Are you sure about your decision, sir? The Navy needs men like you."

"Not for much longer, Chuck. The war should be over in a matter of weeks from what I hear. They'll have more captains than they know what to do with then. Better to retire now at three-quarters pay than be beached at half pay. Besides, it will be nice to get home while I've still got some time to enjoy my grandchildren." Liu-Chen looked thoughtful for a moment. "If they weren't going to scrap old *Gilgie*, I might think otherwise, but no, best we call it quits together." Florkowski nodded and smiled sadly.

"Sir, we are on course for Orbital Station LV-4b. ETA, two hours fourteen minutes," said the astrogator.

"Very good."

The quiet routine of the ship's bridge crew went on for several minutes before the captain spoke again.

"Why the long face, Jaq? In a few weeks you'll be aboard that shiny new destroyer that's waiting for you. Master of your own ship. That's what you've always wanted isn't it?"

"I suppose so, sir," she replied slowly. "But, as you say, the war will probably be over by then."

"Ah, so that's it. Stuck here in a backwater sector while the fighting is going on a thousand light years away. No chance to strike a blow against the Darj'Nang." Liu-Chen sighed. "Yes, I suppose I would have been disappointed when I was a young fire-eater like you. Hard to remember back that far, though."

"I'm not all that young anymore, sir," said Ellsworth.

"We have been doing an important job out here, too, Commander," said Florkowski, a little icily. "The pirates and outsiders have been getting a lot more aggressive with most of the fleet tied up against the Darj'Nang."

"That will come to an end quick enough when the war's over," replied Ellsworth. "I doubt very much the pirates will be as aggressive when there's a battle squadron based here instead of a few old cruisers and frigates. And the Traglarians and Beresferds might act brave when we're distracted elsewhere, but they know they're just small potatoes compared to the League. I spent almost two years in the Back of the Beyond on the most boring patrols you can imagine right after I graduated. I foresee many more years of that in the future."

"Cheer up, Jaq," said the Captain. "You're probably better off out here anyway. Most of the battle fleet will be going into reserve status—you don't need battleships to chase pirates—and it will be the cruiser and destroyer skippers who will be seeing the action from now on. And there's as much opportunity to earn medals out here as there is with the main fleet."

Ellsworth glanced at the impressive rows of ribbons on Liu-Chen's uniform tunic and nodded. But then he'd been out here for fifty standard years....

"There's more to our duty than just earning medals," said Florkowski. Ellsworth frowned at him in return.

"Steady as we go, people," said Liu-Chen.

"Still not packed, young ones? Make haste! Make haste!" chittered Lieutenant Chtak'Chr, Survey Officer of *LSS Gilgamesh*. "With all the hours you waste in complaint about our fine vessel, I would have expected you to already be waiting at the airlock in hopes of getting off!"

"Keep your shirt on, Chtak," said Ensign Rhada McClerndon. "Oops, too late for that, isn't it?" She gestured to the Lieutenant's fur-covered torso. "We don't dock for another half-hour and the Captain probably won't let us off this tub for hours after that."

"Tub? A fine thing to say about a ship which was defending your parents when they were but babes! Show respect for your elders!"

"Like you, Chtak?"

"I have long ago given up hope for that, Rhada. You have no more respect for my age than you do for my rank."

"Well, they do say that respect has to be earned... " said 2nd Lieutenant Gregory Sadgipour from where he was holding up one of the bulkheads.

"And how might I have earned your respect this last year, oh large human warrior?"

"Didn't say you hadn't," rumbled Sadgipour, who was easily three times the size of Chtak'Chr. "But we all know that Rhada is pure Navy and has higher standards than a poor jarhead like me."

"Well, you should have gone Navy then, Greg."

"I tried—as you well know—but they took one look at me and said I was a natural Marine." Sadgipour was from a high gravity world and he was nearly as wide as he was high. He *did* look rather formidable in battle armor.

Rhada chuckled, but then looked at Chtak'Chr with a more serious expression. "So, you never answered my question about what you are planning to do after you leave here."

"My plans are not finalized, but I believe I shall return to my home. There is a position open at the Science Academy and I am very tempted to take it."

"You like to teach, don't you, Chtak?" asked Sadgipour. "I would have thought ten months of trying to keep us in line would have cured you of that!"

The Kt'Ktrian native gave a strange clicking noise. The young humans knew that was his way of laughing. "You two have been quite a trial at times, I will not deny it. But after you, the students on Kt'Ktr will seem like perfect models of scholarly discipline."

"Which compared to us, they will be," said McClerndon.

"Yes, exactly so. Still, I do not regret a moment of it. You have provided me with considerable wisdom—even though you have rejected all that I have tried to offer you."

"Well, not entirely all," said Sadgipour with a grin. "I don't think Rhada will ever touch an untested plant again after her experience on Jadalap III."

"Thanks a lot, Greg," said McClerndon with a grimace. "You haven't had the wonderful learning experience of being covered with boils from head to foot!"

"And I never will—since I listened to Chtak."

"Once." said McClerndon. "What about what happened to you when..."

"Never mind," said Sadgipour hastily. "What will you be teaching, Chtak?"

"As I mentioned, I have not yet accepted the position. If I do, I imagine I will teach planetary sciences and xeno-biology."

"What? Not computers?" asked McClerndon in surprise. "I thought those were your specialty."

"Computer scientists are quite common on my world. But few of us have traveled afar. My experience in the fleet will make me very... unusual."

"And hence in demand?"

"Quite. But what about you fine examples of species *Homo Sapiens*? What will you do when you leave *Gilgamesh*?"

"Follow orders, of course," said Sadgipour. "I just wish I knew what the orders will be."

"Sent off to a Reple-Deple somewhere and wait for reassignment, of course. And with half the fleet being demobilized, they aren't going to be needing any replacements," said McClerndon grumpily. "No chance to fight in the war, and now no chance for anything else. It's not fair!"

"Well, at least we'll have a chance to get home for a while," said Sadgipour hopefully.

"Home! I joined up to get away from home! Greg, my home, Fenwha, is a planet whose entire surface area is swamp. My family makes its living by straining swamp mud for little crustaceans that some people like to eat for reasons I've never been able to fathom. I have no desire to go back there."

"Even just for a visit? What about your family?"

"Never mind about my family. Let's just say I don't want to go back."

"Oh. Well, I hope I get a chance for some leave. I'd like to see my folks. Say, maybe you could come visit with me."

"And get squashed down to half my present height by your gravity? No thanks!"

"Rhada, we do have anti-grav belts for off planet visitors! We're not that far behind the times. Heck, I may need one myself after this long away from home. One standard gee is feeling strangely normal these days."

McClerndon was frowning and then she looked over to where Chtak'Chr was regarding her. "Have you heard anything? You get to talk with the captain and the exec. I know the skipper is retiring and the exec is getting her own ship; what's likely to happen to the rest of us? I don't want my career to end before it's even begun!"

"I am not sure. I imagine your statement about the replacement depot is correct, although it is possible Commodore Shusterman may have some need for you here on the base. But do not be so despondent! It is true that much of the fleet will be demobilized once the last Darj'Nang strongholds are destroyed, but many of the people crewing those vessels have been fighting for ten years or more. Many of them will be anxious to return to their homes. The Navy might not have the glut of personnel that you seem to fear."

"Well, I sure hope not!" said McClerndon. "I'm too young to retire and half pay for an ensign is practically no pay at all. And I damn well don't intend to become a mud-shrimp fisher!"

"I think you have no reason to fear that, young one. Your skills would be valuable in other places besides the Navy."

"Skills? What skills?" moaned McClerndon. "I didn't go to that great, glittering Academy that the 'professionals' go to, you know. If I'd gotten a few more years experience it would be different, but right now all I know how to do is lay a photon cannon and get boils from alien plants!"

"You sell my teaching skills—and your own abilities short, Rhada. And I seem to recall that even your gunnery skills are noteworthy. You have won the Captain's gunnery competitions, what, three times now?"

"Four," said Greg.

Rhada just shrugged. "That's not really anything I learned, I'm just good at it. And you only need good gunners if you've got something to shoot at."

"I'm sure the Navy will still have things to shoot at, even after the war is over," said Chtak.

"And you should complain," snorted Sadgipour. "You've got a lot more marketable skills than I do. Marine junior officers aren't much good except for commanding Marines."

"And not even much good for that from what Lieutenant Quatrok has to say about 'em," snickered McClerndon.

"Thanks a lot, Rhada."

"Oh, hell, there's no point in trying to guess what's going to happen anyway, Greg. We're just prisoners of the system." She sighed and looked around the tiny junior officers wardroom. "I suppose we should heed the sage advice of Lieutenant Chtak'Chr and get ourselves packed."

"You know as soon as we do there'll be a delay that will keep us here for another week and we'll just have to unpack again," said Sadgipour.

"True, but at least it will give us something to..."

McClerndon's statement was cut off by the howl of the General Alarm. The three officers looked up in surprise.

"All personnel report to your stations immediately!" came a voice over the com.

Chtak'Chr could move with remarkable quickness when he went on all fours and was out the hatch first. The other two were right behind.

"What's happening?" demanded Captain Liu-Chen as he strode onto his bridge.

"I'm not certain, sir," said Commander Ellsworth as she vacated the command chair. "We were in contact with the station and getting our docking instructions when communications were suddenly cut off. Not just with the station, sir; we can't raise anyone at all."

"Equipment failure? Hardly reason to sound the alarm and put more stress on my old heart, Commander."

"It's more than that, sir," said Ellsworth, sounding a little hurt. "We're reading complete power failures in the station and all ships and small craft in orbit. There have also been explosions aboard the station and the frigates *Active* and *Daring*."

"Explosions? What sort of explosions?" asked the captain in a much more alert fashion.

"We can't say exactly, sir, but they read like containment failures on the fusion plants."

"On all three simultaneously?"

"Yes, sir..."

"Sir!" interrupted the sensor officer. "I'm reading multiple explosions on the planet's surface! I just got the readings on them now, but they must have happened about the same time as the other ones."

"Contact the base facilities on the surface. Maybe they know what's going on."

"I've been trying, sir," said Lieutenant Terletsky, who looked somewhat frazzled. "I can't contact anyone at all, sir!"

"Is it possible the problem is with us? A communications failure and false readings from the sensors?"

"It's possible, sir," said Ellsworth. "We have had some random equipment failures up here, but the diagnostics on the sensors and com system all read green."

"What kind of failures?" asked Liu-Chen, obviously concerned about his ship.

"Primary Fire Control is out, but the secondaries are still working. A number of other minor things so far, sir. Sick bay reports their diagnostic computer is not working. Damage Control says that their repair droids are all out, too. More reports are still coming in."

"I never trusted those droids to begin with," muttered the captain.

"Sir, I don't think the problem's just with us," said Ensign Snowden at the sensor station. "I've got a shuttle on the scope that appears to be out of control and heading for a crash on the planet. Five minutes until they hit the atmosphere."

"No distress beacon?"

"Nothing, sir," said Terletsky, "nothing at all."

"Helm, move us in closer. Engineering, stand by on the tractor beam."

"Aye aye, sir!"

The bridge crew watched nervously as *Gilgamesh* moved away from the silent space station and headed for the falling shuttle. A few minutes later the tractor beam reached out to grab it.

"We've got it, sir," reported Ellsworth. "Solid lock."

"Good. Bring it into the boat bay. Have a medical team ready. Mister Florkowski, go down there and report as soon as you have anything. Meanwhile, Helm, take us back to the station."

"Aye aye, sir."

Second Lieutenant Gregory Sadgipour stood next to Lieutenant Quatrok and watched the shuttle being pulled into the boat bay. There was a medical team standing there, along with the Second Officer and Sadgipour's squad of Marines. Sadgipour wasn't sure what the Marines were there for, especially since none of their small arms seemed to be working, but he knew better than to question orders. A docking cradle slid over and seized the shuttle and then pulled it to an airlock. Someone could be seen waving through the cockpit window. After a moment the light on the control panel blinked green and a technician opened the door. This revealed the door of the shuttle itself, which was still closed.

"Open it," commanded Lt. Commander Florkowski.

"Uh, it's not responding, sir. All the controls read dead. No power, sir."

"Then open it manually."

"Yes, sir." The technician opened up a panel on the outside of the shuttle and pulled out a small hand crank. He turned it a few times and the door began to slide open. When it was open a crack, voices could be heard from inside.

"Get us out of here! Please!"

The tech cranked faster and the door opened the rest of the way. Four people came bursting out. Once outside, they stood blinking while the medical people swarmed around them. One of the passengers was an officer and Florkowski zeroed in on him immediately.

"What happened, Lieutenant?" he asked.

"Not sure, sir. We were just heading up to the station when we lost power. No lights, no grav. I thought we were goners for sure. Thanks for picking us up." Florkowski frowned and then spotted the actual pilot of the shuttle.

"How about it, chief?"

"Dunno, sir. I've never seen anything like it. Total systems failure. Everything went out at once. Power, the backups, communications, everything."

Florkowski's frown deepened. He turned to the ranking medical technician. "Are they all right?"

"Seem to be, sir. All our hand scanners are out, so we're kind of guessing. But they seem okay."

Sadgipour didn't think the Second Officer's frown could possibly get any more severe than it was, but he was wrong. "Take them to Sick Bay and check them out." Then he turned to a boat bay technician. "Hook the shuttle up to an external power supply and see if you can download anything from the computer. Anything that might tell us what happened. I'll be on the bridge."

"Still no contact with the station or anyone else, sir," reported Terletsky.

"That is going to make docking rather tricky, sir," said Commander Ellsworth.

"I know. Get some people suited up and into the main airlock. They'll have to lock down the boarding tube by hand once we are in position."

"Yes, sir." Ellsworth gave the order and then looked back to the navigation monitor. *Gilgamesh* had returned to the station, and was slowly—very slowly—maneuvering in to dock. Normally, the ship would just need to get close and then mechanical grapples would have secured her and pulled her up to the boarding tube. This time, they had to do it all on their own and the margin for error was measured in centimeters. The navigation monitor was showing the boarding tube and the airlock. The helmsman was gently nudging them closer together. The docking mechanism had to match up exactly. Ellsworth could see the sweat on Ensign Bartlett's forehead as she made tiny adjustments. The ship's thrusters were not really designed for such small changes in velocity and attitude.

The com light on Ellsworth's panel came on. She answered it and then frowned.

"Captain, we've got a new problem. None of the vac suits seem to be functional. Power, recycling and com units are all dead."

"What the hell?" the captain looked up in shock.

"Not only that, sir, all the small craft are out, too. No power. Same as the shuttle we picked up."

"What is going on, Number One?" Liu-Chen looked at Ellsworth but all she could do was shrug.

"I wish I knew, sir."

Captain Liu-Chen was silent for nearly a minute. Then he pressed a button on his command chair.

"Lieutenant Chtak'Chr?" he said.

"I am here, Captain," came back the Survey Officer's voice.

"Are you aware of what has been happening?"

"Yes, sir, I have been following developments with great interest. Quite a lot of my own equipment is malfunctioning, too. I did not think you needed to be bothered with that at this time."

"Yes, quite," said the captain with a brief smile. "Lieutenant, we need to find out what is going wrong with our equipment. I want you to work with Commander Van Rossum in engineering to get this sorted out ASAP."

"Yes, sir. I shall begin at once."

"Commander Ellsworth, get down to the main airlock. We have got to complete the docking. Those vac suits are still airtight. Get some volunteers to help with the manual lockdown. They'll only have air for a couple of minutes, so they will have to work fast and then get back in the airlock."

"Uh, yes, sir. Do you think we should rush into this, sir? Maybe we should let Lieutenant Chtak'Chr have a chance to come up with a fix."

The captain frowned. "Ms. Terletsky, elapsed time since this all began?"

"One hour, twenty-one minutes, sir."

"Commander, there is no power, light, or life support aboard the station. There are probably casualties from the explosion. There is no way they can help themselves, so we have to assist them. I'll also remind you that there are two frigates, four merchant ships and at least twenty small craft in similar distress out there. We're facing a major disaster here and we don't have time to be cautious."

Ellsworth stared at her captain for another instant and then nodded.

"I'm on my way, sir."

CHAPTER TWO

"I think I found some!" exclaimed Ensign Rhada McClerndon.

Lieutenant Walter Kinney, the ship's supply officer, bounded over a pile of packing containers to stand beside her. He had a smile of anticipation on his face.

"What have you got?" he asked breathlessly.

"Functioning power cells, sir!"

"I knew there had to be some in here somewhere. They couldn't all be bad!" Rhada and several dozen others had been going through *Gilgamesh's* cavernous cargo hold looking for functional power cells. They had found a lot of bad ones, but this was the first batch of good ones. Normally Rhada would have complained about being assigned to such work—even though that was the inevitable lot of very junior officers—but this time it was obviously important. Whatever was causing all the problems was affecting most of the power cells on the ship, too.

"They're only at about two-thirds charged, sir," said Rhada, "but they work."

"Not surprising," said Kinney. "Look at the date on those cells: they've been in here nearly thirty years. Old Jessup never threw anything away as long as there was a cubic centimeter of space to put it in. Okay, these are all size two and three. Good, that will work for the vac suits. Ensign, get these up to the main airlock right away. The rest of you come over here. There could be some more and they're probably in this area."

Rhada picked up the carton of power cells she had spent the last hour looking for and grimaced. They were heavier than she had thought. She staggered over to a grav-sled and plunked the box down on it. She cursed when it failed to operate. *This thing out, too?* She sighed and was about to pick the box up again when a thought struck her. She bent over and opened the access panel for the power cells. Four type-three cells. Good. She popped them out and then picked out four cells from the box. She shoved them in place, replaced the cover and was delighted when the sled rose off the deck when she hit the button.

She guided it out of the cargo hold and headed down the passageway to the lift tubes. At least they were working! While she waited for a car, she wondered just what was going on. Half the ship's equipment seemed to be on the fritz and according to rumors, the station and the other ships in the system were in even worse shape. It didn't make any sense that she could figure. For everything—well, almost everything—to stop working at the same time sounded like some sort of sabotage to her. But who had done it and why? They were very far from where the war was being finished up so it seemed unlikely that the Darj'Nang could be responsible. The League had a few minor enemies along the frontier in this sector, but she did not see how any of them could have pulled this off, either.

The lift tube car arrived and she guided the sled into it. She pushed the button for "E" deck and a moment later the doors opened. She only had to go a few meters more to reach her destination. She immediately saw the Exec talking to a half dozen techs in vac suits. All of them had their helmets off.

"No good, ma'am," one of them was saying. "The ship keeps drifting. Unless we can hit the lockdown levers all at once, we risk bending the docking ring and then we're really screwed. And we just can't stay in there long enough to wait for the ship to get to the right position."

"Dammit! We have to keep trying!" said Commander Ellsworth angrily. "It's been nearly three hours and those folks are going to be running out of air soon!"

"Ma'am?" said Rhada nervously. The Exec swung around and fixed her in an angry stare.

"What?"

"I… I've got some functioning power cells here. Mr. Kinney sent…"

She didn't even have time to finish her statement before the Exec and two of the techs were pushing past her to grab the power cells. They began frantically pulling the dead cells out of their suits and pushing the fresh ones in.

"All right! I'm up!" shouted one of them. "Everything looks good, Commander!"

"Thank God," hissed Ellsworth. In another minute the techs all had their helmets fastened on and were crowding into the lock. All but one. For some reason his suit refused to work even with functioning power cells. He looked on forlornly as the door hissed shut behind his teammates. The Exec hit her com.

"Bridge! We just got some functioning power cells for the suits. We're going to try this again."

"Roger. Stand by."

Rhada stood there, uncertain what she ought to do, but not wanting to leave. For a few minutes nothing seemed to be happening, but then there were a few gentle bumps. Another long pause and then a more solid thump followed by some clunking and clanging from the airlock.

"All right, that's it!" cried the Exec, suddenly. "We are hard docked. Helm, none of the other clamps are in place, so keep a close eye on things and be ready to compensate with the thrusters. Get the medical and engineering teams up here, we're going in." She looked around and her eyes fell on Rhada again.

"D-do you want me here, ma'am, or should I go back down to Mr. Kinney?"

"Stick around, we may need those power cells aboard the station."

Other people started arriving and a moment later the inner door of the airlock hissed aside. Almost immediately, some of the vac-suited techs began passing people through, into the ship. There were about two dozen of them and they all seemed to be talking at once. Most of them appeared to be very relieved and basically unharmed. Commander Ellsworth shouted for quiet.

"What's the situation over there?" she bellowed.

"Complete power failure, ma'am," answered an ensign with engineering collar tabs. "There was quite a jolt and then the lights went out. None of the backups or emergency circuits are working, either. We managed to find a few of those chemical lights in the emergency kits, but nothing else was working."

"What about casualties?"

"Don't know ma'am. There was some sort of explosion and a lot of the station is cut off. People are generally congregating in areas with viewports to the outside so they can get light. Sorry, ma'am, but that's all I know—except that the air's getting pretty thick in there."

"All right, you should know the layout of the station pretty well, Ensign. You'll come with us. Chief, get the rest of them down to the enlisted mess and have the meds check them out. Everyone else follow me."

The exec led the way into the station, followed by the engineers. Rhada McClerndon shrugged and followed along, towing her grav-sled.

"Mr. Kinney, any luck?" asked Captain Harold Liu-Chen into the com.

"Sorry, sir. We've found two more crates of the size four and five power cells, but none of the big ones yet. We still have over half the hold to search though, so we might still find some."

"Damn it, we're running out of time."

"I'm sorry, sir, we're doing our best down here. Commander Jessup was a bit of a packrat, I'm afraid. All sorts of stuff that isn't on the manifest."

"Yes, that doesn't surprise me a bit. Well, keep at it." Liu-Chen closed the connection. He wished Jessup were still around—he had been a bit of a slob, but he would have known exactly what was in his cargo hold and where to find it. He sighed and then swiveled his chair to look at Commander Florkowski. "So what do you think, Chuck?"

"As you say, sir, we're running out of time. Or rather, all those other poor devils are running out of time."

Liu-Chen nodded and directed his attention to the main tactical display. Five hours. It had been five hours since this mess began. How long could the crews of those ships hold out? He had never heard of a situation where all the backups and emergency equipment failed. They were even finding that the breath masks in the survival packs here on *Gilgamesh* were failing as often as not. A spaceship had a lot of interior volume that held air. It should be enough to keep those crews alive for at least a few more hours, but there was no guarantee they would get any help at all, let alone in time. And the small craft, drifting out there, were probably in even worse shape.

Liu-Chen nervously drummed his fingers on the arm of his chair. His ship was still attached to the station and still taking on survivors. A large section of the station was cut off due to the explosion aboard, but they still had found over three hundred people. *Gilgamesh* was not a large ship and she was starting to get crowded. Unfortunately, there was not much they could do about it. She wasn't designed to land on a planet's surface, so the only way to get those people down to the planet was with the small craft. Also, the best hope for getting help out to those other ships was with the small craft. It would take far too long for *Gilgamesh* to try and dock with them.

Unfortunately, right now, none of the small craft were operational.

The shuttle they had rescued was completely useless. Even when hooked directly to the ship's power system, nothing on it worked. *Gilgie's* own small craft would work—except that their power cells were all dead. Unless Kinney could find some working ones soon, they were going to be facing a real mess.

Unless…

Liu-Chen hit the com button. "Commander van Rossum, come in, please."

"Van Rossum, here."

"Van, are you and Chtak making any headway?"

"Not really, sir. We're starting to see some patterns in the equipment failures, but nothing to give us any clues what to do about it."

"All right. I've got a new job for you," said Liu-Chen. "We have to get the shuttles and the cutter operational or a lot of people are going to run out of breath real soon. We've got a few hundred size four and five power cells. Can you adapt them to work in the small craft?"

"I… maybe. We'd have to hook a bunch of them up in parallel to do the job of the type tens we normally use. There'd be a lot of inefficiency there, sir. They wouldn't have near the endurance."

"We aren't talking about a cross-system trip here, Van. We just need to get some people down to the surface."

"Okay, I think we can do it. It's going to take time, though."

"Then I suggest you get on it immediately. It's important, Van."

"I'm on it, Skipper."

"Good."

Lieutenant Chtak'Chr watched Lt. Commander Van Rossum gather his people and leave Engineering with large bundles of tools and equipment. He twitched his whiskers in frustration and tried to pick up the thought train the captain's message had interrupted.

The equipment failures aboard *Gilgamesh* and the other ships and facilities in the system were unlike anything he had ever heard of: Simultaneous and complete failures of multiple unrelated systems, along with all back up and emergency systems. The reports of the failures in the fusion plants were especially puzzling. There were so many built-in safeguards to prevent that from ever happening—even with a complete loss of power—that he could not understand how it could have occurred.

Here aboard *Gilgamesh*, it was equally strange. Some systems and equipment had failed and others had not. Some of the failed equipment was operational once given a new power supply—and some was not. Chtak was hampered in his analysis because most of his own equipment—including all his reference material—was among the items that refused to work.

It was extremely puzzling. He picked up two power cells and looked at them. They were virtually identical. The labeling was a bit different, but the physical construction seemed the same.

But one worked and the other did not.

And the truly baffling thing was that the one that did not function was fully charged. He had found a working hand scanner and verified that the malfunctioning power cell was charged, and yet it would provide no power. The other cell worked just fine. Oddly, the working cell was much older than the dead one. The working one had been dug out of Lieutenant Kinney's cargo hold and had been manufactured almost forty years ago. The dead one was barely three years old. One would normally expect the older equipment to fail first.

Further study was needed, but he was handicapped by lack of tools and information. He needed the specifications for the failed and the working gear to make comparisons. Unfortunately, all those specifications were locked up in computers that were not working…

Just a moment. Lieutenant Kinney's inventory computer was still working. Perhaps the specifications might be there as well.

Chtak'Chr gathered up the power cells and headed for Kinney's office.

Rhada McClerndon watched as the vac-suited damage control people opened the door to the temporary airlock they had constructed. The team leader came over to Commander Ellsworth.

"All done, ma'am. We can get through to the next section now."

"Great job. Let's go."

Rhada blinked and tried not to yawn. She was getting very tired. She had been trailing along behind Ellsworth for nearly six hours now. From time to time, she handed out a power cell for some vital piece of equipment, but otherwise she felt pretty damn useless. The zero-g was unpleasant, too. She had never liked free-fall, but the artificial gravity on the station was out, just like everything else.

And it was terribly stuffy in here. They had set up blowers in *Gilgie's* airlock to force fresh air into the station, but it did not seem to be helping much. The DC people had done some welding on their lock and the place stank of burned metal.

She looked on as the rescue parties floated through the lock. Before she could follow, people started coming back out again. Station personnel stumbled or were half carried past her. They were looking pretty bad. The air must be even worse over in the next section.

The flow of people stopped and she started to move forward when she saw more coming through. She was startled when she saw the exec and a medic helping another man who was in the uniform of a commodore.

"Make way!" snarled the commander and then she did a double-take when she saw Rhada. "Ensign! Clear a space on that sled!"

Rhada jumped to obey and she quickly moved the half-empty carton of power cells to the back of the grav sled and resecured them. In a moment the commodore was placed gently down and a restraining strap put across him. The man looked pretty old to begin with, but with his pallid face and white hair, he looked like death itself right now.

But he wasn't dead. He was still breathing and the commander pulled out one of the precious breath masks and put it on him. They all stared at him for a moment and then his eyes fluttered open and he looked around in apparent confusion. Then he made a little waving motion with one hand and closed his eyes again.

"Ensign, take the commodore to sick bay. You go with him." The commander's second remark had been aimed at the medic. Rhada looked at him and he nodded. She activated the grav sled and started back toward the ship. The sled was quite versatile: it could act in anti-grav mode, or in this case magnetically latch on to the deck and crawl along like a ground vehicle.

The passageways were deserted, but the air got steadily fresher as they neared the ship. She was starting to realize how tired she was. To her surprise, the captain was waiting in *Gilgamesh's* airlock. He immediately went to the commodore, while Rhada negotiated the transition back to full gravity.

"Commodore Shusterman, are you all right, sir?" Shusterman opened his eyes and slowly took off the breath mask.

"Hello, Harry. Glad to see you. Forgive me for asking, but what the hell took you so long?" There was a deep breath between every few words.

"We've had some serious problems, sir. The station isn't the only thing to have systems failures. *Active* and *Daring* are both disabled. All of our small craft, the civilian vessels in orbit and the facilities dirtside. We came as quickly as we could, sir." There was a lengthy pause while the commodore digested this. All the while, Rhada slowly steered the grav sled through the throngs of people toward Sick Bay.

"How is that possible, Captain?" asked Shusterman, eventually.

"I don't know, sir. I have my survey officer working on it, but he doesn't have any answers yet."

"This does not sound like a coincidence, Harry. It could be the prelude for an attack. And you have the only ship capable of mounting a defense right now."

"I also have the only ship capable of mounting a rescue, sir. Do you want me to give up on the people who might still be alive on the station or on those other ships?"

"No, no, of course not. Keep at it, Harry, but don't forget to keep your eyes open."

"We'll do our best, sir, but we're being stretched pretty thin."

"You say there's trouble dirtside, too?"

"Yes, sir. Explosions in the power plants—just like you had here—and a complete communications blackout with our facilities and the major cities. We've started picking up individual communications, mostly out in the boondocks, but they're just confused people trying to figure out why the main communication and entertainment channels are all out. We've also picked up signals from some of the mining vessels out in the belt. A lot of ships in distress out there, it seems. I've had to tell them they are on their own for the time being."

"Have you gotten out a message to Sector Headquarters about this, Harry?"

"Can't, sir. The HyperCom station is down just like everything else."

"Damnation, what a mess," sighed the commodore. "What are you doing for the other ships here?"

"Nothing at the moment, I'm afraid. *Gilgamesh* is stuck attached to the station. I've got my engineers jury-rigging power supplies for my small craft, but until they're done, we can't do anything else."

Rhada brought the grav sled into Sick Bay. There were a lot of people in there, but the commodore got immediate attention.

"Commodore, I'll let the doctor look you over," said Liu-Chen. "I'm going back up to the bridge. If there is any change in the situation, I'll let you know immediately."

"Thanks, Harry. I'll come up myself as soon as I'm able."

The medics took Shusterman off the grav sled and put him on one of the beds. Rhada looked around, uncertain what to do next. Most of the people in Sick Bay did not look like they were too badly off, but any more they found on the station were likely to be worse. They could probably use her grav sled over on the station.

Rhada wearily turned the sled around and headed back the way she had come.

Lieutenant Chtak'Chr hopped up on to the uncomfortable human chair in Lieutenant Kinney's office. It was unoccupied at the moment. Everyone in Kinney's department was out in the hold, still sorting through mounds of items. He activated the computer terminal and was relieved to see that it was working. Chtak reached into his belt satchel and brought out one of the data cartridges from his own office and pushed it into the reader slot. He was frustrated, but only slightly surprised, when the computer informed him that it could detect no cartridge to be read. A few quick swaps proved all of his reference library to be useless. A feeling of frustration and even fear passed through him. What about all his records? The papers he had been working on? Several years of effort, were they all lost?

That is not important now. Lives are at stake and that is far more important. All right, what do we have here?

Chtak began going through the records already on the computer. Supply files going back decades scrolled up the screen. Thousands of different items. What was he looking for? He wasn't sure.

He picked up the two power cells he had been examining earlier. He typed in their respective item codes and found when they had been brought aboard the ship. The working one thirty-seven years ago, and the bad one only two. Was there any more information on these things? Chtak tried various inquiries and was finally rewarded with full specifications on both cells.

Let me see... they are both nearly identical, it seems. The same capacity, the same endurance, outer shell construction the same. Inner mechanism nearly identical, a small difference there, but nothing that could make any real difference. What about the power regulators? Hello... that's interesting...

Chtak'Chr swiveled his whiskers in growing amazement.

Second Lieutenant Gregory Sadgipour stood on tip-toes to see out the shuttle's window. The engineer in front of him was too darn tall. He gave up and settled back, only to bump into the large piece of equipment behind him.

"Careful, there, Lieutenant," said the engineer. "That's precious cargo. Can't afford to break it now." Sadgipour just shrugged. As big as he was, he was in no danger of damaging the large air-scrubber. Still, it was indeed 'precious cargo', maybe the only hope for the crews of the two crippled frigates.

One of those frigates, *LSS Daring*, was growing in the cockpit window now. The engineers had gotten the cutter and one of the shuttles operational. The cutter was dashing off to tractor and bring in the drifting small craft around the planet. This shuttle was hoping to succor the frigates. The next shuttle, when it was ready, would be heading for the stranded merchantmen, and when the last two were operational, they would begin ferrying people down to the planet.

"All right, ma'am, I'm going to try to latch on to that emergency airlock, right over there," said the coxswain who was piloting the shuttle.

"Okay, but make it quick," said Ensign Claritta Torres, who was in command of this mission.

The shuttle edged up to the airlock and then spun around to present its docking collar. Unlike *Gilgamesh*, the shuttles could latch right on to the skin of a ship and make a hard dock without difficulty. There was a small bump and a thump and then the coxswain announced they were fast.

Torres had the artificial gravity switched off and she pushed past Sadgipour and over the two air scrubbers to the rear airlock. She hit a few switches and the inner door opened. A few more seconds and the outer door opened revealing the door leading into the frigate. Just like the earlier shuttle, the door would not operate on its own and Greg found himself cranking it open by hand. It was difficult to get leverage in the zero-g, but he managed. The interior of the emergency lock was small and dark, but after only a moment, he could hear someone pounding on the inner door.

"Let's get this open," said Torres urgently. Greg found the manual crank and went to it with a will. In a few moments, the hatch was open and he could see a crowd of gasping, but happy-looking people on the other side.

"Thank God you're here!" shouted one of them.

"We're suffocating in here, we need air!"

Greg could believe them. The air that was filtering into the shuttle was extremely musty and foul.

"All right," said Torres, loudly, "stand back and let us get this air scrubber set up."

They did so reluctantly, but soon the engineers had the scrubber fastened to the deck and purring away. Some of the people put themselves in front of it and breathed deeply.

"How many of you are there?" asked Torres. A lieutenant pulled himself through the crowd to the front.

"There are about thirty of us here, Ensign. The fusion plant cut loose and took out a number of compartments amidships. There may be more people trapped aft of there." Greg frowned. The normal complement of a frigate was around a hundred.

"Where's your skipper"

"I don't know. He's not with us here. He may be aft...or he may have been in engineering. Look, Ensign, when can you take us off? Some of us are in a pretty bad way."

Ensign Torres looked uncomfortable. "Uh, I can't take anyone right now. I have to get this other scrubber to *Active*."

"What the hell do you mean?" exclaimed several people at once. "You're not going to leave us here!"

"I don't have much choice," said Torres warily. "I mean, I might be able to squeeze in a couple if they really need medical attention, but that's all."

The lieutenant didn't look happy. "What's the problem with *Active*? Why can't you just start shuttling us over to the station? I mean it was bad enough we had to wait ten hours for you to drag your sorry asses over here, but you are not leaving my people here any longer!"

"I'm sorry, sir," said Torres in increasing agitation. "The station, *Active*, and every other ship in orbit except for *Gilgamesh* is in the same shape as you. We came as quick as we could, but for the moment you are going to have to be happy with the scrubber. We'll be back as quick as we can."

There was a stunned silence among the crew of *Daring*.

"What the hell are you talking about, ensign?" said the lieutenant.

"It's true, sir. Everything has gone to hell in a handbasket. Now I'm sorry, but I have to get over to *Active* before they all choke."

"Like hell!" shouted someone. There was suddenly a rush of people heading for the shuttle's airlock. They were kicking and clawing as panic swept through them. Ensign Torres cringed back and Greg realized why Lieutenant Quatrock had included him in this mission. He pushed into the door and braced himself. The year in one standard gravity might have weakened his muscles, but he was still far stronger than a normal human and he was recently trained in zero-gee unarmed combat. A man came flying at him and in an instant he was flying the other way, clutching himself. He plowed into the scrambling throng, slowing them up. Another made it through, but Greg handled him as well. After two or three more, they gave up and huddled a few meters away, eyeing him with unconcealed fury. The lieutenant was screaming for order.

"What about the people in the stern of the ship?" he snarled. "This scrubber isn't going to help them!"

Torres tossed a bundle of tools and a vac suit at the man. "Maybe you can open a way aft."

"You've got to be kidding!"

"Look, I don't have any choice!" cried Torres, almost pleading. "Now I'm closing the hatch and going on to *Active*! We'll be back as soon as we can. I'm sorry!"

There was muttering and cursing from the mob, but Greg turned and cranked the airlock door closed as quickly as he could. In another minute the shuttle's lock was shut and they cast off.

"God!" hissed Torres. "I... I wasn't expecting that!"

"Me neither," admitted Greg. "I guess ten hours in the dark, not knowing if *anyone* was coming would be pretty awful."

"What the hell are they going to be like on *Active*? It will be nearly thirty more minutes before we can rendezvous with her."

Greg could see that Torres was shaken. He was pretty shaken himself. They turned the artificial gravity back on and sat there quivering slightly.

"Ensign, you might want to see this," said the coxswain after a while. Torres and Sadgipour went forward. Another frigate was floating in front of them.

"Looks like a worse explosion here than on *Daring*, ma'am."

There was a gaping hole in the upper part of the midships hull. There had been no evidence of an explosion at all from the outside of *Daring*.

"Hell," muttered Torres. "Well, come on. Find a lock and latch on. There's no time to spare."

In a commendably short time, they were attached to an emergency lock. Greg felt a twinge of anxiety when there was no pounding on the lock door as he worked the crank. It proved fully justified when they shone their lights inside and saw the drifting bodies.

They were too late.

CHAPTER THREE

Commander Jaqueline Ellsworth looked around the conference table at the tired and worried gaggle of officers. Her own captain was there, of course, along with all the department heads from *Gilgamesh*, but there was also Commodore Shusterman and several aides and the senior surviving officer from *LSS Daring*.

"Ladies and gentleman," said Shusterman, "you all know what a crisis we are facing here. We have far more demands on us than we can hope to fulfill with our current resources. We are going to have to come up with a set of priorities and then stick to them, no matter how painful it might seem."

"Sir, the situation on the planet must take priority," said the commodore's aide, Lieutenant Leslie Boshko. "There are millions of people down there without power, water, proper sanitation and very shortly, without food."

"The power situation is the key to it all," said Shusterman. "If we can get a few of the fusion plants up and running again, that would take care of a lot of the problems. Getting the food synthesizers running will be particularly critical."

"How about that, Van?" asked Captain Liu-Chen. "Any hope of repairing those plants?"

Van Rossum looked glum. "I don't know, sir. I haven't seen them, of course, but if they are like the ones on the station and the other ships, I rather doubt it—at least not quickly. Every one of them had a containment failure that blew the guts out of them. We'd be looking at weeks, if not months even if we had all the proper parts and facilities—which we don't."

"How the hell did that happen, Van?"

"I wish I knew, sir. The fusion plants have a dozen different back-ups and safety systems to prevent that from ever happening."

"Well, we have to do something," said the Commodore. "If the fusion plants can't be made operational quickly, we need alternate sources."

"Sir, in the early days of the colony here, they made considerable use of solar power," said Boshko. "Most of the outlying settlements still use it extensively, which is extremely fortunate. The most serious problems are in the larger cities." Ellsworth nodded to herself. Leavitte IV's population was about fifty million, but about half of that was concentrated in only six cities. There was no power and no communications in any of them. People were panicking already and heading out into the countryside. Police and emergency personnel were nearly helpless since their vehicles and weapons were mostly useless, too.

"Perhaps we can get some solar arrays in operation," suggested the Commodore. "At least to get the food plants and the emergency services back in operation."

"We do have a few small power generators in our stores, sir," said Liu-Chen. "We could ship them down to at least get the emergency services some power. Perhaps if we get a core area operational, we can slowly restore service to the rest of each city as we get solar panels or the fusion plants on line again."

"C-Captain?"

Ellsworth looked to where the Survey Officer, Lieutenant Chtak'Chr, was sitting rather uneasily in a conference chair that was not really contoured to his body shape.

"Yes, Lieutenant?"

"I-I am afraid there will be serious problems with your plan. Serious problems with any plan we come up with here."

"What do you mean, Lieutenant?" asked Shusterman rather sharply.

"S-sir, I believe I have discovered the cause for our recent misfortunes."

"You have? What?" said several voices in unison. Chtak'Chr seemed to cringe back slightly. Ellsworth had noted the Kt'Ktrian's nervous nature before. All these intense humans seemed to be intimidating him.

"I should perhaps clarify by saying that I believe I know the *immediate* cause of the systems failures rather than the *ultimate* cause..."

"Out with it, man!" said Shusterman impatiently.

"Y-yes, sir. They have been caused by a complete failure of the nanocircuitry chips in the various devices and equipment. I cannot explain why they failed, but there is no doubt that they have failed—all of them."

"All of them?" exclaimed Van Rossum.

"Yes, Commander, I believe so. Every device which has failed has made use of the nanocircuitry to some degree. Only those devices which employ the older molecular circuits are still in operation."

"But…but that's impossible. Why would they all fail at once?"

"I do not know. And until yesterday I would have agreed with you that it was impossible. But my findings—while far from conclusive—indicate that this is exactly what happened."

"Could it have been a defective batch of chips, Lieutenant?" asked Boshko.

"I do not believe so, sir. According to our supply officer's records, the failed equipment—at least here aboard *Gilgamesh*--was manufactured over a number of years and came from widely different places."

"But you say that none of the molecular circuitry was affected? Nor any of the actual software?" asked Ellsworth, speaking for the first time.

"Not that I have found, ma'am. You must understand that I have not been able to examine every piece of equipment on this ship, let alone in this star system, but as of now, every bit of the nanocircuitry I have seen has failed, while none of the molecular circuits have done so."

"Are you sure?" asked Van Rossum. "Quite a lot of my older equipment is down and I'd imagine they have the molecular circuits."

"I believe you will find that the problem with those items is with the power cells, Commander." Chtak'Chr paused and rummaged in the belt pouch he always seemed to have with him. "This was how I first stumbled on to the answer," he said, holding up two power cells. "These two cells are almost completely identical except for the regulator that controls the flow of power in and out of the cell. This older model has a regulator constructed with molecular circuits—it works. This other one is a newer cell. Its regulator has nanocircuits—it doesn't work."

"I'll be damned," breathed Van Rossum.

"Excuse me," said the Commodore. "I'm afraid I'm not all that conversant in computer hardware. Would you mind explaining this in a bit more detail, Lieutenant?"

"Certainly, Commodore, I'd be delighted." In spite of the serious situation, Jaq Ellsworth found herself biting back a grin. Chtak'Chr had gone into lecture mode and all his nervousness had vanished. He would talk to a midshipman or a Prime Minister with the same easy manner.

"Until about thirty years ago, all computer circuits were based at the molecular level. That is, the molecules of the circuit were what stored the data or did the computations. Magnetic fields or vibrational resonance, or sometimes both in unison, is what allowed the circuit to function. There were a number of different types, but they all worked in the same way.

"Then nano-circuitry was developed and all this moved to the subatomic level. It was a quantum improvement over the molecular circuits and within a few years, the older circuits were no longer produced. However, the basic architectures of computers and their software did not change greatly and the two types of circuitry could be used interchangeably. Because of this, many examples of the molecular circuits remained in service until the item wore out and had to be replaced."

"Like *Gilgamesh*," said Captain Liu-Chen.

"Indeed, sir. The ship has many items of older equipment, which seem to have been unaffected. Fortunately, these include the fusion plant, sublight and hyper drives. Other systems have failed, however. For example, the records show that the primary fire control system was upgraded about seven years ago. That system contains nanocircuitry and is not functioning."

Van Rossum was nodding. "That would explain the explosions on the fusion plants. All the safety features depended on realizing that something was wrong. If all the circuits died at the same time, none of the backups would have had time to be initiated. The power would have stopped flowing and the containment force fields would have shut down. The flow of fuel would have been cut off, too, so fusion would have ceased almost instantly. But that still leaves us with a super-hot, super-dense ball of plasma with nothing holding it in. It would have expanded explosively and that's what did the damage we see."

"Yes, Commander, that is almost certainly what happened," confirmed Chtak'Chr. "That is also why the air-tight emergency doors did not shut on *LSS Active* after the hull breach occurred. Even though there were both electrical and spring-loaded mechanisms to shut the doors, the pressure-drop sensors that were supposed to activate them were not functioning."

"So what you are telling us, Lieutenant," said Shusterman with a frown, "is that even if we manage to set up new power sources, most of the things dirtside are still not going to work."

"That is entirely possible, sir. There are very few devices or tools of any sort that do not contain some computer circuitry. Vehicles, communications devices, production facilities, even weapons all have them. Any that contain the nanocircuits will remain inoperable even with power restored."

"I can vouch for the weapons," said Lieutenant Quatrok. "All my Marines' plasma rifles are out along with a lot of our other gear. We've got a few older items that are still okay—once they get new... er... old power cells."

"This is bad," said the Commodore, shaking his head. "We'll have to replace all those circuits and that is going to take a great deal of time. Those people may not have that much time."

"And we will need to have the replacement circuits before we can even begin, Commodore," said Chtak'Chr.

"Well, surely we must have replacements in stores, Lieutenant!"

"I do not believe so, sir."

"What do you mean?"

"Whatever has caused this seems to have affected any and all nanocircuitry—even the replacements."

"Even if they weren't installed?" asked Van Rossum in amazement.

"I'm afraid so, sir," said Chatk'Chr. "Once again, I cannot claim to have examined every circuit, but I have tested over a hundred taken from both *Gilgamesh's* and the station's spare parts storage, and all exhibit the same lack of function."

"But how can that be possible? Unpowered chips in storage?"

"That I do not know, sir. What agency could have caused this is a great mystery to me. But the effects are undeniable."

"Effects?" prompted the Commodore.

"The nanocircuits operate at the sub-atomic level, as I mentioned, Commodore. The physical structure is a crystalline matrix of great complexity. The magnetic resonance and 'spin' of the subatomic particles is what makes the circuits work. Even when not installed, the circuits have an internal power supply, which maintains the alignment of the matrix and this gives them a recognizable 'signature'. My initial studies indicate that somehow these circuits have been rendered inert. There may even have been some actual chemical changes in the matrix, although I can't confirm this. The result, however, is quite evident: the circuit is useless and I can see no way of repairing them *in situ* as it were."

"This is very bad, sir," said Lieutenant Boshko, who seemed to have a better grasp of what Chtak'Chr was saying than his boss. ">From the sound of things, we will need to replace virtually every piece of equipment, both up here and down on the planet."

The Commodore was frowning, He looked back at Chtak'Chr. "And you say you have no idea how this could have happened?"

"I am afraid not, sir."

"Is there a possibility that there is some unsuspected 'life expectancy' to these chips?" asked Captain Liu-Chen. "That after thirty years, they simply die of old age?"

"Unlikely, sir. If that were true, they should 'die' in the same order they were made, rather than all at once."

"What about some sort of disruptive signal or radiation burst?" asked Boshko. "Perhaps some enemy set the thing off way outsystem and we didn't detect them."

"A possibility," said Chtak'Chr. "However, there is evidence against that. We were receiving telemetry signals from various picket satellites when the phenomena occurred. Satellites on opposite sides of the system-—many light hours apart—all went dead at the same instant. Any sort of signal or radiation would have been limited to lightspeed and should have affected the satellites at different times."

"Maybe some unknown emanation from hyperspace?" said Van Rossum, clearly grasping at straws.

"That, I cannot comment on, sir," said Chtak'Chr.

"All right, people," said the Commodore, "it seems that we aren't going to figure out the immediate cause right now. Personally, it reeks of sabotage to me, although if so, I cannot understand why there has been no follow up attack to take advantage of the situation. But whatever it is, we have to deal with the crisis at hand. As much as I hate to admit it, I don't believe we can adequately deal with it ourselves. We are going to need some outside help.

"Harry, I'm sending you off to the fleet base at Flemington. I don't like the idea of leaving us completely naked here, but *Gilgamesh* is the only hyper-capable ship we've got and it looks like there's no hope of getting the HyperCom station operational again. I'll give you a message to take to Admiral Barringsworth, but basically, I want you to bring back a fleet repair ship and whatever supplies and equipment they can spare. Make sure Barringsworth knows the gravity of the situation. People are going to start dying here without some serious help. Understand?"

"Uh… yes, sir…"

Ellsworth glanced at her captain and then at the other officers in the room. They all seemed to recognize what the Commodore seemed to be overlooking, but no one wanted to say it. Or perhaps they *couldn't* say it; the chill that had been creeping down her own spine seemed to have frozen her vocal cords. Finally, the Commodore noticed the nervous looks.

"Is there a problem, Harry?"

"Well, sir… that is…"

"Commodore," said Chtak'Chr, "I am afraid that things might not be as simple as that."

"What do you mean, Lieutenant?"

"Sir, there is no reason for us to believe that this phenomenon is limited to the Leavitte star system."

There was a long silence in the conference room. Jaq Ellsworth looked from face to face, watching the true meaning of Chtak's statement sink in.

"Oh my God…" whispered Shusterman.

Ensign Rhada McClerndon stumbled back to the bunk room and collapsed on her bunk. She let out a long, noisy sigh. Sixteen-hour days were the pits. She'd only endured a watch-and-watch schedule a few times before and she hated it. But there was so much work that needed to be done and everyone had to pitch in. She felt too tired to even move, but she only had four hours until she was on duty again. She needed to shower and eat and try to snatch a few hours sleep.

As she lay there, she slowly realized she wasn't alone. A small sound caused her to turn her head and she saw that Gregory Sadgipour was lying on his own bunk a few meters away. He had been so quiet she had not noticed him when she came in—which was quite a feat considering the size of the man. She could see that his eyes were open.

"Hi, Greg. I didn't see you. How are you doing?"

"Fine."

Rhada looked more closely. One-word answers were not Greg's usual style. He was just staring straight at the overhead. She propped herself on one elbow.

"Are you okay, Greg?"

"Fine."

Rhada swung herself around to a sitting position and stared at her friend. As the only other 'very junior' officer on the ship, she and Greg spent a lot of time together. This wasn't like him at all…

"Greg, what's wrong?—and don't tell me nothing."

"N… I don't know. This whole thing is just…"

Rhada wasn't sure what he meant, but then she suddenly guessed.

"You mean what happened out on the frigates?" He had said almost nothing about it, and she had been too busy to ask.

"Yeah. I guess so. Rhada, they were all dead. Everyone on *Active*. Half of them dead from decompression when the fusion plant blew, the other half ran out of air. I… I never saw anything like that before. It was kind of… kind of hard."

"I'm sure it was. We… we took quite a few bodies off the station, too." Other people had. The exec kept Rhada away from the worst of it.

"We even found a few people outside the ship in vac suits," continued Greg like he had not heard her. "Vac suits that didn't have working recycler units. They had to know they could only last a few minutes, but they wanted out so bad they went anyway. Damn, I wish we could have gotten there sooner!"

"You got there as soon as you could, Greg. You did everything possible."

"I guess. Torres is pretty shaken up about it, too. She was in command."

"I haven't talked to her."

"I keep seeing their faces. The ones on the ship, itself, weren't too bad. Oxygen deprivation probably snuck up on them slowly and it would have just been like falling asleep. But the ones in the suits… they were worse."

"I'm sorry, Greg." Rhada didn't know what to say. She'd never seen him like this.

"So what happens now?"

"I don't know," said Rhada. "There's a hell of a mess to clean up, I guess we just keep working."

"Right. Well, I better try to get some sleep."

"Yes, me, too. But I need a shower."

She pushed herself to her feet with a groan, But she had only taken a few steps when Chtak'Chr came into the compartment.

"Hi, Chtak! What's going on? You were in some high-powered meeting with the brass, weren't you?"

"Yes."

Rhada started. One-word answers were even more unusual from Chtak than they were from Greg.

"So what's happening?"

"*Gilgamesh* will be leaving for the fleet base on Flemington in two hours."

"Really? What, to get some help?"

"That is the intention, yes. We will be leaving the cutter and three of the four shuttles here to help with rescue operations."

"Well, I guess that makes sense," said Rhada. "But what's the situation? You must have found out something by now. What caused this? What are we going to do about it?"

Rhada had slowly learned to read some of Chtak's facial expressions and other body language, but she could not quite interpret what she was seeing now.

"I... I do not believe it would be appropriate for me to discuss anything with you at this time," he said.

"What? What do you mean?"

"If you'll excuse me, Ensign, I have work to do." The Kt'Ktrian turned and left the compartment. Rhada stared after him.

"Well, what the hell do you make of that?" she said in amazement.

"I don't know, Rhada," said Greg. "But I have a bad feeling about it."

CHAPTER FOUR

"Our heading is nominal, ma'am," said Lieutenant Pliskin from the hyperspace astrogation station. "ETA to Flemington is twelve hours, thirty-two minutes."

"Very good," said Commander Jaqueline Ellsworth. "Steady as she goes." She looked up as Lt. Commander Florkowski came on to the bridge. He came over to her and saluted.

"I relieve you, ma'am."

Ellsworth stood up from the command chair and returned the salute. "I stand relieved. You have the bridge. Nothing new to report."

"Very well." Florkowski sat down in the command chair and began asking the various stations for their status as though she weren't there. Ellsworth shook her head slightly and left the bridge. Florkowski was a twit. A reasonably competent twit, but still a twit. She usually got along with him well enough, but the three-week trip from Leavitte to Flemington was straining things more than usual. It had been obvious to Ellsworth from the day she came aboard that he had expected to be bumped up to the exec position when the previous first officer had been transferred, and resented the fact that she had been brought in instead. Well, that was just too damn bad. And he better get used to it, because it looked like they would all be stuck on this bucket for the foreseeable future.

She grimaced as that thought formed. For all her complaints about the war ending and lack of future opportunities, she had been desperately eager for her own command. That promised destroyer had beckoned like a new lover. Boundless potential, endless opportunities. But now. Now she feared that she would never set foot on *LSS Gatchall*. It was a numbing thought.

She reached the door to the captain's cabin and pushed the button next to it. "Come in," came the captain's voice over a small speaker. She opened the door and stepped inside. Captain Liu-Chen was sitting at his desk. He had the lights turned low and for some reason it made him look very old. His cabin was filled with pictures and holographs and all manner of bric-a-brac: the mementos of a naval career spanning over fifty standard years. With his white, thinning hair, he looked like a college professor instead of a naval officer.

"You asked to see me at the end of my watch, sir?"

"Yes, come in, Jaq. Have a seat." She took the one opposite the desk and sat expectantly.

"How are you doing, Jaq?"

"Me, sir? I'm fine." The question had taken her by surprise.

"Really? Then you are probably the only one on this ship who can say that."

"Sir?"

"Surely you've noticed the mood on the ship?"

"Well, it has been a bit grim, now that you mention it, sir. I was assuming it was because of all the casualties back at Leavitte."

"That's probably a part of it, yes," said Liu-Chen. "But our people aren't stupid, Jaq. They can think just the same as you or I. They are probably asking themselves the exact same questions we are: what are we going to find on Flemington?"

"I see," said Ellsworth. Naturally, they had made no official announcements about the possible magnitude of the disaster, but the captain was right: they weren't stupid. "What do you think we'll find, sir?"

"I wish I knew. I wish to God I knew!"

A new thought struck her. "Your family's on Flemington, isn't it, sir?"

"My wife," he said, nodding his head. "My daughter and two grandchildren, as well. My son is with the main battle fleet."

"I'm sure they are fine, sir."

Liu-Chen sighed and rubbed at his eyes. "I hope so. But Lieutenant Chtak'Chr's analysis is frightening. Why *should* it be confined to Leavitte? If it is some sort of sabotage, as the Commodore thinks, then what would be the point of just hitting some fairly minor frontier outpost?"

"Perhaps as a test? A trial run, sir?"

"Possibly. But if someone was clever enough to come up with something like this, I'd think they would be clever enough not to give up the element of surprise. If Flemington is okay, then we have warning and can be ready the next time."

"What if it isn't okay? What will we do then, sir?"

"I don't know." A long silence ensued. So long that Ellsworth was about to rise and try and excuse herself when the captain spoke again.

"Can I offer you something, Jaq?" He swung around and picked a bottle and two glasses off the sideboard and set them on his desk. Ellsworth was a little startled. The captain rarely drank that she had ever observed and he had never offered her a drink in his quarters before, either. Still, you didn't refuse the captain's hospitality...

"Thank you, sir."

Liu-Chen poured out two glasses. Ellsworth noticed that the bottle was less than half full before he poured. He gave her one of the glasses and picked up the other.

"To the Fleet," he said holding out his glass. Ellsworth carefully clinked her own glass against his and then took a sip. It was very good brandy. The captain took a somewhat larger gulp.

"Y'know, Jaq, I'm getting a bit old for this sort of thing," he said. She did not know how to respond, so she said nothing. "I was hoping to retire. With the war ending and old *Gilgie* heading for the breaker's yard, it seemed like the proper thing to do. And I'm tired. Fifty years in the Navy, going from one crisis to another has worn me out." Liu-Chen sighed and looked past Ellsworth.

"You're too young to really remember, but everyone today seems to think that the time before the war, before we ran into the Darj'Nang, was some sort of Golden Age. The League at peace, no worries. But it wasn't really true—at least not out here on the frontier. I'd been out here for over thirty years already—I'd just been given command of *Gilgamesh*—and it wasn't any Golden Age out here, no sir. I'd already fought more pirates and raiders and slavers and smugglers than I can count now. An ugly business sometimes, too, the slavers in particular. And there were never enough ships. The Star League was so huge and powerful no other star nation wanted to mess with us, but that didn't stop the small fry from nibbling around the edges, taking whatever they could get. We were stretched damn thin."

"We were terribly unprepared when the Darj'Nang attacked," agreed Ellsworth. "I had just started at the Academy when..."

"Yes, the Darj'Nang knocked us all back on our asses," nodded Liu-Chen, interrupting. "Of course, maybe it was just as well that we were so unprepared. Before we figured out their little mind-control tricks, they could take over our own ships. If we'd had a bigger fleet, they would have just turned it against us. But it was still a hell of a shock at the time! It was only the fact that we were so damn big—had so much room to fall back—that we survived at all. Even then it was a near run thing." He paused and took another drink from his glass. Another sigh.

"We pulled in everything we had to stop the Darj'Nang. Every ship in the Fleet that had a weapon. Stripped the frontiers bare. They installed the new thought-screen generators and sent us out. We rendezvoused off Dinwiddie. A hell of a sight to see. It wasn't much compared to the fleets we built later, I suppose, but the League had never seen anything like it before. So many ships. I don't think we realized just how strong we really were until that day. Glorious, what a glorious sight. Did I ever tell you about the Battle of Dinwiddie, Jaq?"

"No, sir, I don't believe you have." In fact, he had told her the story at least twice, but she wasn't about to say so. And it was a good story. He rambled on for the best part of an hour and the bottle was quite empty by the end of it, even though she had only let him refill her glass once.

"So we won," he said with remembered pride. "Sent the bastards packing. It may have taken another ten years to liberate the planets they had already taken, and another ten to wipe out the rest of their cursed slave-empire, but it was at Dinwiddie that the tide turned. And *Gilgie* and I were there."

Ellsworth nodded. She had read over the official reports, of course—hell, they became a major part of the Academy curriculum—and she had read *Gilgamesh's* logbook. She knew that *Gilgamesh*, obsolescent even then, had not taken a major part in the battle. She was back guarding the supply ships. She had gotten in a few licks when the enemy sent a suicide force against those ships, but that was all. Still, there weren't many ships or people left who could claim to have been there. Ellsworth's eyes flicked to one particular ribbon on the captain's tunic.

"Afterwards," continued Liu-Chen, "when we were sure the Darj'Nang offensive was stopped, we had to send some ships back to the frontier. The pirates and outies were already taking advantage of our absence to start raiding again. Did you know they offered me command of a new cruiser then and a place with the main fleet?"

"No, sir, I didn't know that."

"Well, they did. But they needed people and ships to come back out here, too. So I left the glory to others and stayed with old *Gilgie*. Never regretted it. It was an important job to hold the line out here, you know."

"Yes, sir."

"Held for a long time. I'm tired, Jaq, very tired."

"You should get some rest, sir."

"I wish I could. But worrying about what we'll find on Flemington… hard to sleep with those sorts of worries."

"Yes, sir."

"If this turns out to be as bad as it could… I'm going to need your help, Jaq."

"You have my full support, sir," said Ellsworth. She was getting worried. She'd never seen the captain like this before. The brandy was obviously affecting him, but there was more to it than that.

"I know I do, Jaq. You're a good officer. But the first officer of a ship is very important in setting the whole… mood of a ship. Just as important as the captain. I know you haven't been happy here on *Gilgamesh* and I know you got a raw deal before that…"

"I have no complaint on either score, sir," said Ellsworth.

"Yes, you've never really complained and I appreciate that. But you've also never really made the commitment to the ship or the crew, either. I mean the emotional commitment. You do your job, but you've never become a part of *Gilgamesh*."

She didn't know what to say to that. In a way it was probably true, but it was also a matter of her personal style. Captain Liu-Chen tried to be a father to his crew and that was fine. With the right crew and the right captain it could work. She had seen it work on other ships. But she was not a parent, either literally or figuratively. She did her job and she did it well and the crew could think about her as they liked.

"Well, it looks like I may become a permanent fixture here, sir, no matter how I feel about it."

"Yes, I suppose that may be possible. And if that's so, I am going to need you, Jaq. The ship will need you. And the League is going to need all of us." He stared at her with a gaze only slightly blurred by the brandy.

"I… I'll do my best, sir." No promises she couldn't keep—she'd learned that much over the years.

"I know you will. Well, thank you, Jaq."

"Thank you for the brandy, sir." She got up and left before he could start talking again. Outside his cabin she leaned against the bulkhead and breathed deeply for almost a minute. That had been as awkward as almost anything in her naval career. Was her captain losing it? Or was he just tired? Was she just tired? One question she could answer anyway. She straightened up and headed for her own quarters.

Lieutenant Chtak'Chr whistled in frustration as another computer search came up empty. The main computer on *Gigamesh* had been reformatted and expanded and just generally screwed around with (as these humans would say) so many times during its lifetime that there was almost no way of knowing for sure just what was in it. Chtak needed information. Information that was locked in a stack of dead computer cartridges littering his normally fastidious office. He was hoping against hope that he could find what he needed in the main computer's labyrinthine innards.

He may have been the one to alert the commodore and the captain to the immensity of the possible crisis, but he was still only coming to grips with it himself bit by bit. Measureless amounts of knowledge and data probably lost forever. There were backups and backups of backups. Thousands of duplicates of the information he needed—that other people would need—all useless now. He was just beginning another search when the buzzer on his door sounded.

"Come in," he said. He was not entirely surprised to see Rhada McClerndon and Gregory Sadgipour standing in his doorway.

"Hi, Chtak," said McClerndon. Sadgipour said nothing, but nodded. Chtak had seen little of the humans on the three-week trip from Leavitte to Flemington.

"Well, youngsters, come to see me again at last?"

"We knew you were busy and we didn't want to bother you," said McClerndon, almost shyly.

"You mean *I* didn't want to bother him," said Sadgipour. "You've been itching to bother him for weeks."

"You are not bothering me. I am glad to see you. How have you been these past days?"

"Busy. The Exec has every spare hand checking out every single bit of equipment on this ship and recording its condition."

"I fear you have me at least partially to blame for that, Rhada," said Chtak. "I need that information, too."

"What are you working on?"

"As you suspect, I am sure: the cause of our current difficulties."

"Yeah, we did sort of figure that," said McClerndon. "Have you found anything yet?"

Chtak hesitated. The captain had not made any general announcement regarding what had been discussed with the commodore. He and Commander Ellsworth had stressed to everyone present the importance of not alarming the crew with dire possibilities. Still, he had observed that everyone aboard seemed to be aware of the situation.

"Nothing of any significance." A safe and true answer.

"You must have found something!" blurted Sadgipour.

"Yeah, with all the nano-chips dying you must have some suspicions at least!" added McClerndon, confirming that the story had gotten to all the crew.

"Suspicions are always… suspect, Rhada. We cannot base actions—or fears—on suspicions."

"Don't try your little platitudes on us this time, Chtak!" said McClerndon. "We've got a right to know what's going on."

"Do you indeed? Heavens, and here I thought we were on board a military starship where the commanders decided what their crew had a right to know. How foolish of me."

Rhada subsided with a sheepish look, but to his surprise, Gregory did not.

"Chtak," he said with unusual intensity, "some people are saying that what happened on Leavitte may have happened other places, too. Maybe everywhere! I'm worried about my family."

"As well you might be," said Chtak. "As well might we all be." He glanced at Rhada, who avoided his eyes. "But at the moment we know nothing for sure except that Leavitte is in need of aid and thus we go to Flemington. Worry without facts is a waste of energy."

"But could it have happened?" persisted Sadgipour. "Could it have affected the whole Star League?"

Chtak regarded the two humans. He was quite fond of them although he could not have defined exactly why. He was fond of most humans and that was probably what had drawn him to the Navy. The humans had always tended to dominate the Star League and nearly three-quarters of the Navy personnel were humans. There were a few other races in the League, like the Dralnars and the Betadorfs who seemed to have the same sort of drive to explore and expand as the humans, but most were content to leave such things to others. Chtak had a great curiosity, like most of his people, but also had the wanderlust of the humans—a rarity on Kt'Ktr. But these humans' need-to-know exceeded even his own curiosity. Chtak saw a mystery or puzzle as something to solve for the mere pleasure of the solving. The humans *needed* to know the answer—even if no answer was possible. And lacking a real answer, they would cling desperately to any answer at all. McClernon and Sadgipour clearly 'needed' to know that the League was safe; that their families were safe. He felt a strange sense of guilt that he could not give them the answer they wanted.

"You know more about computers than anyone on this ship, Chtak. What do you think?" Sadgipour's voice had taken on a tone that he recognized as pleading—something he usually only did when trying to get out of an assignment.

"You want my opinion, is that it?"

"Yes!" said both in unison.

"Very well, then. I am of the opinion that both of you should spend your off duty hours sleeping or eating or studying instead of trying to wheedle me for information I do not possess."

"Chtak!"

"Time to drop-out?" asked the Captain.

"Five minutes, thirty seconds, sir."

Commander Jaqueline Ellsworth ran her eye around the bridge, looking for anything out of place. There was nothing. Captain Liu-Chen, for all his easy-going ways, ran a taut ship. All the stations were manned for re-emergence into normal space. This could never be considered entirely routine: there were far too many dangers for it ever to be routine. But this was an experienced crew and they had done it hundreds of times before.

But this time was unlike any other.

In spite of the officers' attempts to downplay the situation, every soul aboard was well aware that what they would discover five minutes from now would irrevocably influence the rest of their lives. No one dared say it, but they all knew it. Flemington was the headquarters for this whole sector and a number of the crew had families there. Most of them had made combat drop-outs, emerging from hyperspace with an enemy waiting. Those were tense, to be sure, but not like this.

Ellsworth checked over her status board. "All stations report ready, sir. Weapons are manned, secondary fire control on-line, shield is at full strength." Probably useless precautions, but why take chances?

"Sensors read clear, sir. Turbulence is holding at zero-point-two. Looks like clear sailing the rest of the way."

"Very well," said Liu-Chen. "Engineering stand by on the hyper generator."

"Standing by, sir," said van Rossum. "Capacitors at full charge, waiting for your command."

"Astrogation?"

"On course, sir. Picking up Flemington's gravity well at extreme range now. We're right in the groove for a zero-margin drop-out. Estimated distance from Flemington III will be one point two million kilometers."

Ellsworth glanced up at the main viewscreen. A multicolored swirl filled it. Hyperspace didn't actually look that way, of course, this was just a computer representation of it—and she was one of the very few people who knew that for a fact. For a moment her thoughts flipped back to her midshipman cruise where, on a dare, she had over-ridden the controls of a viewport and opened the shutters to look out with her own eyes. Big mistake. A rating found her curled up on the deck in convulsions. She'd been violently dizzy and nauseous for three days afterward and the butt of many a joke for months more.

"Emergence angle is nominal; three minutes."

The time ticked away and she could see the nervous shifting in seats all around her. She forced herself to absolute immobility. More just to prove to herself that she could do it than because anyone was watching her.

"Sensors still clear, sir."

Ellsworth frowned slightly. One possibility they had discussed was that they might find ships with disabled hyper generators hanging around the boundaries of star systems looking for help. There did not appear to be any here.

The seconds wound down rapidly and the tension wound up in direct proportion.

"Thirty seconds," said the Astrogator.

"Engage automatics," commanded Liu-Chen. A number of heads turned. The Captain loved to do the drop-outs manually. He prided himself on being able to hit the edge of the gravity-well boundaries and only once in the time Ellsworth had been aboard had they missed and had to go around again. But this time he was leaving it to the computer...

"Five... four... three... engaging hyper generator... now!"

The universe turned inside out and for the thousandth time Jaq Ellsworth had the amazing insight that the sensation was exactly what she had felt when looking out that viewport so many years ago. Then, an instant later, for the thousandth time, she had forgotten it again.

"Drop-out complete," groaned Lieutenant Pliskin.

"All stations report," commanded Liu-Chen.

It was an automatic command, given after every drop-out, but right now the only stations anyone was interested in were the sensors and communications. One glance at the display told the story.

"I'm not getting any energy readings from the orbital installations, sir," said Ensign Snowden in a voice devoid of emotion.

Lieutenant Terletsky looked up from her console and shook her head. "Nothing, sir. I'm sorry sir, it... it's just like Leavitte."

CHAPTER FIVE

The bridge crew of *LSS Gilgamesh* stared at their monitors, hoping against hope that what they were seeing was not real. Flemington was a far more developed world than Leavitte, with a population of over two billion. There were a hundred major cities and many more smaller ones. Dozens of large orbital habitats, factories and shipyards circled the planet. A major League naval base was there, too. Nearly seventy military and civilian vessels showed on the scope.

All were silent.

Or nearly so.

"Sir, I am picking up some transmissions from various points on the planet," said Lieutenant Terletsky. "I'm running them through the auto-scan now, but they seem to be like what we were picking up on Leavitte: folks out in the boondocks with older communicators trying to figure what's going on."

"They've had over three weeks," muttered Ellsworth. "You'd think it would have sunk in by now."

"Sensors, are you getting anything at all from the orbital facilities?" asked Captain Liu-Chen in a voice that could hardly be heard.

"No, sir, nothing. "Everything is d... not radiating any energy beyond normal background. I... wait a moment! Sir! There's a ship under power just coming around the planet!"

Everyone's head jerked up to look at the display. It showed the icon of an unidentified ship.

"Communications, signal that ship!"

"Aye, sir!"

The communications screen momentarily filled with static and then cleared. It showed a human male in a rather shabby suit that once might have been some sort of merchant captain's uniform. The expression on the chubby face was one of extreme relief.

"This is Captain Liu-Chen of the League starship *Gilgamesh*, please identify yourself."

"Oh, thank God!" gasped the man after the six-second com delay.

"Everyone's dead, Captain! Dead! On the stations and all those ships! I didn't know what to do! Thank God you've come!"

"Please identify yourself, sir," said Liu-Chen patiently.

"Deering. Talbot Deering. Master of the League merchant ship *Tassafaronga*. We dropped out four days ago, Captain, and found this. Do you know what's going on? Have you brought help? Those poor devils down on the planet need help."

Ellsworth quickly called up the merchant registry on one of her monitors and found the entry for Deering and his ship.

"Registered out of Parson's Planet, sir," she said to her captain. "Constructed almost ninety years ago. Obviously hasn't had a refit recently."

Liu-Chen nodded slightly. "Captain Deering, is your ship operating properly? And what cargo are you carrying?"

Deering looked slightly puzzled. "The ship is operating as well as it ever does. We had some stuff go on the fritz a few weeks back, but all the main systems are okay. We're carrying a load of glowwood. I was contracted to trade it for a cargo of general merchandise and then proceed to Norlendale. But... but we got here and found this mess and... well, we couldn't just leave!"

"I see. Have you made contact with anyone in authority?"

"Authority? There's no authority left that we've seen. Traffic control, the harbor master, even the base commander don't answer. We... we boarded the main passenger station yesterday and everyone... everyone..." the man trailed off.

"What about dirtside?"

"Lots of isolated signals from down there, but hardly any from the towers. It sounds like a real mess."

"I see," said Liu-Chen. Ellsworth could see the tension in her captain's face. "Thank you, Captain Deering. If you would please stand by, I'm sure we'll have some instructions for you later."

"Instructions? What the hell sort of instructions? I've only got a crew of twenty! What can we do? You're the professionals, you've got to do something!"

"We'll try, Captain, but we may need you to run messages for us."

Deering's expression was growing more and more alarmed. The pause was longer than the com lag could account for. "Surely there will be more ships coming to help! We'd be happy to take a message somewhere if we could, but more help is coming, right?"

"Yes, of course," said Liu-Chen. "Please stand by, Captain and we'll get back to you." He motioned to Terletsky to cut the connection. "Helm, ahead at half power. Astrogation, plot a rendezvous with the installation FL-1a."

"Aye, aye, sir."

The bridge crew sat in silence for several minutes. Eventually the Captain stirred. "So what do you think, Jaq?" he asked.

"An unpleasant situation, sir. It appears that Lieutenant Chtak'Chr's theories were correct."

"Yes. Well, for now, I intend to dock and see if we can find Admiral Barringsworth. We don't know that there are no survivors on those stations. They may have been able to come up with some manual fixes."

"Yes, sir," said Ellsworth. It was possible, she supposed, but after twenty-three days without power it would be a miracle to find anyone alive.

"Also," continued Liu-Chen, "Mister Snowden, do we have any functioning recon drones?"

"Yes, sir," replied Snowden. "We have two of them that are operational."

"Good. I'll be wanting to send them down for a look dirtside when we get closer."

"Very good, sir. I'll make sure they are ready."

It took over an hour to rendezvous with the station and then another to find a port they could dock at. Ensign Bartlett was becoming quite good at manual docking and he gently nudged the ship toward a hook-up. Meanwhile, the captain had ordered the recon drones dispatched.

"Send the first one to the main government tower in Flemington City," he said. "The other one can go to these coordinates."

"Aye, aye, sir."

Ellsworth noted the coordinates the captain had provided. They were for a small city in the planet's southern hemisphere. She watched her captain closely. All of his usual easy-going manner was gone. He wore the face of someone going into a desperate fight.

The drones descended, their cameras and sensors active. The drone sent to the small city had the shorter distance to travel and arrived first. Sensor scans were put up on the main screen, while the camera images appeared on several smaller ones. At the moment, all they were showing was clouds.

The cities on Flemington were of a model that was quite common in the League. Rather than sprawl out in a multitude of unconnected structures, there were only a few very large habitation towers, surrounded by many square kilometers of open park land. The towers could be enormous, usually several kilometers across and several high. A million or more people could live in a single tower. The interiors were open and spacious and with lift tubes and slidewalks, the inhabitants were only minutes from the outdoor parks. Ellsworth, herself, had grown up in such a place. But, like the orbital installations, they were highly dependent on their technology. And if that technology should fail....

"I'm not getting any significant power emanations, but there is a considerable heat source reading here, sir," said Snowden hopefully.

The drone broke through the clouds and revealed a snow-covered landscape. Ellsworth did a quick check and saw that Flemington had a sizable axial tilt. It was winter in the southern hemisphere.

"Oh, God..." hissed Svetlana Terletsky. The drone's cameras were now revealing the heat source Ensign Snowden had reported. A single, large housing tower was centered in the screen. A pall of black smoke drifted out of the smashed atrium windows at the top and was then blown away in the wind. The drone got closer and they could see black, scorched areas on other parts of the building.

"I... I thought those buildings were fireproof," said Snowden.

"No such thing, Ensign," said Van Rossum grimly from the engineering station. "Oh, the buildings themselves won't burn, but the stuff inside them sure will. My uncle was a fire-safety engineer and he was always complaining about how the safety regulations on fireproofing furniture and clothing and other consumer goods were never enforced. The fire suppression systems in the buildings were so efficient, nobody worried about it. But if the systems weren't working..."

"But with the power off, how could a fire get started?"

"Look at your outside air temperature readings, Ensign," said Lt. Commander Florkowski. The man's face had gone white and his eyes kept flicking between the screen and the captain.

"Minus two degrees, sir."

"No power, no heat. And it's damn cold outside," nodded Van Rossum. "Those buildings have good insulation, but after a week or two, the people would be getting cold. The only way to keep warm would be to burn something. It wouldn't take much for a fire to get out of hand. And once it did, that central atrium would act like a chimney. The place would have become a furnace."

"My God, what about the people?" asked Terletsky.

"They'd have to get out. Look at the IR readings. I bet this fire happened a week ago but the center of that tower still reads at over four hundred degrees."

"Out? Out where?"

The question just hung in the air. Ellsworth looked at her map. The city below them was called Bloomsburg. The next nearest tower was almost a hundred kilometers away. And it was two degrees below freezing outside.

The drone had continued to spiral down. Now they could begin to see smaller objects on the ground outside the tower. Some of them were snow-covered shrubs or benched or other features of the park. Others were bits of debris or items dragged out of the smoldering building.

But a lot of the objects were bodies.

Some were nearly covered by the snow, but other could be clearly seen. Men, women, children. Some scattered individually, others huddled in groups. Some looked like they had been burned. The infra-red scans showed that they were at the same temperature as the snow around them. Without orders, Snowden pulled the drone up to a higher altitude. The bodies shrank to mercifully indistinguishable spots. The IR scan now showed a few pockets of heat surrounding the tower at varying distances. The drone dropped toward one of them. After a minute, the image showed a group of people, maybe a hundred of them, clustered together around a fire. Several people were hauling in branches they had torn off trees and tossing them in the fire.

The bridge crew stared at them. Some were wearing appropriate clothing, but others were wrapped in blankets, huddling together for warmth. There were some empty boxes and scraps of debris piled together in a makeshift shelter. Most of the people seemed to have sunken into an apathetic misery.

Suddenly a boy looked up and spotted the drone. He shouted something and the others looked up as well. In an instant, the whole group was on its feet waving and screaming. It went on and on for minutes. Some of the people ran out of strength and collapsed, but continued to look skyward with expressions of hope.

Jaq Ellsworth shook herself and looked around. Everyone else seemed as frozen as the bodies they had seen earlier.

"Sir? What are we going to do, sir?"

Captain Harold Liu-Chen did not appear to hear her. He continued to stare at the screen. There was a slight jolt and the helmsman, who had commendably refused to be distracted by what was going on, reported that the docking was completed.

"Sir? What are your orders?"

The Captain blinked and shook his head. He slowly got to his feet. He looked very old.

"Send a party into the station and see if you can find Admiral Barringsworth. Send another party down in the shuttle to the main government tower in Flemington City. I'm going to my quarters, Jaq, you have the bridge." He turned and walked toward the hatch. Ellsworth watched him go.

"But sir, what about these people?" blurted Terletsky. The Captain didn't answer and the hatch slid closed behind him.

Ellsworth became aware that every eye was now focused on her. She found herself staring at Florkowski.

"This Bloomsberg place. This is where his wife lived, wasn't it?" she asked. Florkowski's head jerked stiffly and he blinked back tears.

"His daughter and grandchildren, too," he choked out.

"Oh, merciful God," whispered Van Rossum.

Ellsworth shook her head and slowly moved over and sat in the command chair. After a moment, she looked up.

"Commander Florkowski, take a party down in the shuttle to Flemington City, as the Captain ordered. I'll oversee the search of the station."

Florkowski nodded.

"But Commander, what about these people?" asked Terletsky in alarm. "We can't just leave them! And the Captain's family, they could still be alive down there!"

"An old woman and a mother with two young children," whispered Florkowski. "What chance would they have had in that mess?"

"But what about these others? We can't abandon them, sir!" Terletsky was on the verge of tears. The people continued to wave and silently shout in the monitor.

Jaq Ellsworth shook her head. "We have one shuttle that can carry twelve people, Lieutenant. There are thousands of people down there. And a dozen other cities in the winter zone. What the hell can we do? Ensign Snowden, recall the drone. Commander, carry out the Captain's orders."

The image in the monitor shrank swiftly enough that she could not see the reactions on the people's faces. She was profoundly grateful for that.

Second Lieutenant Gregory Sadgipour watched the top of the city tower growing through the shuttle window.

"A lot of people on the roof, sir," said the coxswain to Commander Florkowski. Greg craned his neck to look. The shuttle was settling in to land on one of the pads and there was a large crowd gathering to watch. They all seemed very excited and he was dreading what might happen when they learned that no immediate help was at hand. The memory of the panic on *LSS Daring* was still amazingly fresh in his mind, and the rumors that were circulating about what the recon drones had picked up were very frightening.

With a slight bump the shuttle was down. The hatch opened and immediately Greg and his four Marines spilled out. They were all in body armor and carrying heavy-duty stunners, which, though obsolete, were in full working order. He just hoped he would not need them. Looking around he could see at least two hundred people surrounding the landing pad. Even more were streaming toward the area from the tower's broad roof gardens. They all looked dirty and underfed and heartbreakingly hopeful at the sight of the shuttle. At least it was not winter on this part of Flemington, but a pillar of black smoke in the distance caught his eye for a moment. Then Commander Florkowski was out in front, shouting for quiet and asking to see whoever was in charge.

The thought occurred to Greg that maybe *nobody* was in charge, but after a lot of shouted answers, a woman pushed her way through the crowd, escorted by three men in police uniforms.

"Commander, I'm Darla Shandy, Governor Strothers' chief of staff. I must say I'm extremely happy to see you!" The woman did look truly pleased.

"Lieutenant Commander Charles Florkowski, ma'am. *LSS Gilgamesh*. My captain has sent me down here to make contact with the civil authorities. Is Governor Strothers here?"

"No, I'm afraid not. He wasn't in Government Center when we lost power. I've sent out several search parties to try and locate him, but so far we haven't found him. In the meantime, you can deal with me."

"Wait a minute, Darla!" exclaimed someone from the crowd. "Tom

Haskins is the majority leader from the Legislature, he should be in charge."

"Until the Governor is located, I have full authority to act in his name," said Shandy with a snap in her voice.

"He might not even be alive, Darla. Your authority ends with him."

Shandy shook her head and was clearly exasperated. "Then go get Haskins! In the meantime, I'll talk with the commander." The man in the crowd hurried off.

"Sorry about that, Commander. Now maybe you can fill me in with what's going on. We've been almost completely cut off for over three weeks. The fact that no one from elsewhere on the planet or in orbit has come to help forces me to assume that there has been some major disaster. You're from outsystem? What's the situation?"

Greg saw Florkowski glance around nervously. What was he going to tell these people? How would they react when he did?

"Ms. Shandy, can I speak to you inside the shuttle?" said Florkowski at last.

She looked surprised, but eventually nodded and followed him inside. This left Greg in charge of the security perimeter. The people had been happy and excited, but now they were looking uncertain and afraid. As he feared, they started asking him questions.

"Lieutenant, what's going on? When can expect some help?" A dozen people asked this or variations on this within a few seconds.

"I'm not exactly sure, but I'm sure help will be coming as soon as possible." He was surprised at how easily the lie came. To forestall any more questions, he asked one of his own.

"How have you people been making out here? You seem to be doing all right."

"So far, but it's a good thing you showed up when you did. Things are getting tight," answered one of the policemen who was wearing captain's insignia. "We've been hauling emergency rations up out of the storerooms—heluva hike, three kilometers straight up—and drinking water out of the storage cisterns on the level below the roof."

"I only see a couple thousand people here. Where is everyone else?"

"It was night when the power went out. Most people were home. Of those that were here, some went down and out instead of up. Others got trapped in lift tubes or wherever. Some of them are still trapped," he ended in a low voice.

"You are lucky to have all those rations," said Greg, trying to keep the conversation away from when help was coming. "What about the rest of the city?"

The policeman frowned. "It's pretty bad. You can see where one of the towers burned the other night," indicating the smoke. "A lot of people are out in the streets and the parks. We've had to barricade the entrances to this building. They're getting pretty desperate out there. We're going to need a lot of help here. How many ships are with you?"

Now what do I say?

Fortunately, Commander Florkowski and Ms. Shandy chose that moment to emerge from the shuttle. Shandy's face was pale and frozen. If Florkowski had told her the whole truth, she was handling it remarkably well.

"Captain Burkman," she said to the police officer. "I'm going up to the Commander's ship to make some arrangements. Please tell Mister Haskins what is happening when he gets here."

A few people shouted out questions or protests. Florkowski gave the police captain a working radio and then hustled Shandy and the Marines back into the shuttle. They lifted off immediately, leaving the crowd in stunned silence.

Ensign Rhada McClerndon pushed the floating body away from the hatch, taking care neither to push too hard, nor look at the person's face. She had deliberately darkened the faceplate of her vac helmet so the features of the bodies were less distinct in the glare of her suit lamps. Hopefully it also hid the tears on her face from the other team members.

This was bad. She had thought the station back at Leavitte had been bad, but this was far worse. Everyone was dead. They had found no survivors at all. Twenty-three days without the air recyclers was just too long. And this was a very large station. The normal contingent must have been several thousand and Rhada was convinced she had seen every one of them.

With the hatchway clear, Rhada used a handcrank to open it. The sign on the bulkhead said that this was Admiral Barringsworth's office. She could see at a glance that this part of the station was in the same condition as all the rest. But at least this was the objective. Maybe after this they could stop. Maybe she could go back to her quarters and scream for a few hours.

"Bridge, this is Ensign McClerndon," she said into her com. "We've reached the Admiral's office. The Exec said she wanted to be here."

"I'm on my way, Ensign," came back the First Officer. "I'll be there in two minutes. Stand by."

"Aye, aye, ma'am."

Commander Ellsworth appeared in considerably less than two minutes and pushed past her, through the open hatch. Rhada followed, drawn by a sense of duty rather than curiosity. She vaguely wondered if she would ever be curious again. The next compartment was the Admiral's outer office and, to her relief, it was unoccupied. All manner of small objects were drifting around, although the desks and larger pieces of furniture were anchored to the deck. The inner office door was shut, but slid open easily when the Commander pulled at it.

Ellsworth went through the door and Rhada followed. The Admiral's office had a series of large windows along one wall and light streamed in. There was a similar amount of drifting clutter, but this office was not unoccupied. Admiral Barringsworth was strapped into a chair that he had dogged to the deck by his desk. This time Rhada did look at the body's face. The man appeared to be sleeping. Eyes closed. A calm expression. His arms were floating a few centimeters above the desk. Fingers slightly curled as the body stiffened in death. An old fashioned stylus was still between his fingers. A number of sheets of paper were clipped down to the desk.

The Exec briefly examined the body, but then moved around so she could look at the papers. Rhada found herself drawn over to the desk as well. Ellsworth glanced briefly at her, but made no attempt to stop her from reading over her shoulder, while she was reading over the Admiral's shoulder.

The first two sheets held a long list of orders and contingencies for dealing with the emergency. Commands to the various ships in the system and recommendations to the civil authorities. Each one had been boldly crossed out. The third sheet was much different.

To whoever should find this:

It has been fourteen days since the unexplained systems failures struck this station and, apparently, the other ships, stations, and cities in this star system. We have been unable to contact anyone else and all attempts to restore power have been unsuccessful. The fact that there has been no sign of movement among the other ships or stations and no attempts at rescue fill me with the greatest foreboding. I have no explanation for what has happened. I do know, however, that the men and women under my command have behaved with the greatest courage and devotion to duty I have ever witnessed. There has been no panic and each person is a credit to the Fleet and to the League.

The air is very bad now and I doubt I will have the strength to write much more. If you can, please pass on my love to my wife and family. God bless the League.

Admiral Carter Barringsworth

The last few letters were shaky. Rhada thought they had been blurred somehow and then she realized it was her own tears that were causing the blur. She started when the Exec let out a long sigh.

"Well, that's that," she said.

"What do we do now, ma'am?" asked Rhada.

"I suppose we should keep looking for survivors just out of decency, but we are also going to have go through all the supply dumps to see if they have any more of those old power cells stashed away. Those things are going to be worth their weight in platinum before long."

"Yes, ma'am." Now it was her turn to sigh. The Exec peered at her through her darkened visor.

"But that can wait until the next watch, Ensign. You should get some rest while you..." The com suddenly came to life, interrupting the Exec.

"Commander Ellsworth! Please respond at once!"

"Ellsworth here, what is it?" Rhada recognized Lieutenant Terletsky's voice, but she had never heard her so agitated.

"Commander, you must return to the ship immediately!"

"What's happening?"

"Commander, the... I... Oh God, the Captain is dead!"

CHAPTER SIX

Captain Liu-Chen's cabin looked far too much like the Admiral's in Jaq Ellsworth's opinion. Right down to the body sitting in the chair. She was still gasping from the scramble back to the ship and the rush to get her vac suit off as she pushed past the crowd of onlookers.

"All right, back to your duties!" she snapped. "Anyone without business here clear out!"

She practically had to throw a blubbering ensign out of the compartment, but eventually just she, Florkowski, Doctor Abercrombie, and Chief Gossage, the Captain's Steward, remained.

"So what happened?" she asked.

"I came in about ten minutes ago to ask if the Captain would be needing anything and I found him like this, ma'am," said Gossage, clearly close to tears himself. "That's all there was to it. I took one look and then alerted the bridge."

"I see." She slowly walked around the Captain's desk. He was leaning far back in the chair with his face pointed toward the overhead. His eyes were closed and a neat round hole in his right temple was still slowly dripping blood. There was a somewhat bigger and messier hole in the left temple. His arms were slack and an old model gauss pistol was lying on the deck below his right hand. Ellsworth found that she was shaking slightly. She looked up at the others.

"Is there anything you can do, Doctor?"

"He's been dead about thirty minutes, ma'am," said Abercrombie. "I could probably preserve the body, but with that sort of head wound, it would not be doing anyone any kindness."

"I see," said Ellsworth with a small sigh. "There will have to be an official report and perhaps an inquiry. All of us may have to testify. I don't have any doubt that this was a suicide. Are the rest of you in agreement?" Each one nodded in turn, although Florkowski fixed his stare on her. His expression was of unconcealed hatred.

"Do we need a complete forensic investigation, or do you think our statements and a few holographs will be enough? I'll be honest with you, gentlemen, I've never had to deal with anything like this before."

"There will have to be an autopsy, but I think the holographs and our testimony should be sufficient, Commander," said the Doctor. "As you say: there's no doubt what happened."

"Only why," hissed Florkowski.

"That we may never know," said Ellsworth, returning Florkowski's stare. "Did he leave any message?"

"Just the written one on his desk there, ma'am," said the steward. "If there's anything else we haven't found it."

Ellsworth stepped over so she could read the hand-written note. It simply said that she was now in command and that he had sent a message to her computer with all the pertinent access codes. He directed her to carry out Commodore Shusterman's orders to the best of her ability. That was all. No message, no explanation… no apology. There should have been an apology. She felt a growing sense of anger at him leaving her in the lurch like this. *That was the coward's way out, Captain!* She silently raged at him. But the rows of ribbons on his tunic told the lie of it. He wasn't a coward. *Just tired. Very tired. So what the hell do I do now?*

She had wanted a command. Desperately wanted a command. But not like this. She wanted a ship that would be hers and hers alone… not one she inherited from a man who would always be the crew's captain no matter what she did.

"What… what do you want me to do, Commander?" asked the doctor. She paused for a long moment, looking at each of them in turn.

"Doctor, you will take care of the body and do your autopsy. Chief, examine the Captain's quarters for anything else unusual or out of place. But don't disturb things more than necessary. Commander…" she paused and looked at Florkowski. "Alert the department heads that I want a meeting in one hour."

"The Captain was going to have a meeting with that Ms. Shandy from the planet in an hour," said Florkowski.

"Well, then, we'll have the meeting in forty-five minutes and Ms. Shandy might have to wait a bit."

"Right."

Ellsworth noted the lack of any courtesy from Florkowski but she chose not to make an issue of it just at the moment. She could see that he was on the ragged edge and there was no point pushing him. "All right, carry on. I'll be in my cabin."

She turned and left the Captain's quarters. On the small cruiser her own quarters were not far off. It only took a few steps to notice that she wasn't alone. Florkowski was two paces behind her.

"Can I help you, Commander?" she asked without pausing.

"So you've finally got what you want. What are you going to do with it now that you've got it?"

She reached her door and stopped. "I certainly didn't want this, Commander. As for what I'm going to do, we'll discuss that in forty-three minutes."

"Oh, you wanted it all right," whispered Florkowski, standing far too close for comfort. "You were just aching for it. Everyone could see it."

"Maybe so, but I didn't want it this way. Captain Liu-Chen was a good officer..."

"You're damn right he was! A damn sight better than you! Better than you'll ever be! You're not worthy to sit in his chair, Ellsworth! If you'd given him half the support he deserved, this never would have happened!"

Ellsworth rocked back. What the hell was he talking about? She had done her duty and done it well... *'But you've also never really made the commitment to the ship or the crew, either.'* The Captain's words came back to her. Was Florkowski right? Had she let the Captain down when he most needed her help? The thought was numbing.

Florkowski was breathing hard and had his fists clenched. His pale blue eyes glittered with a frightening intensity. At that moment Ellsworth honestly didn't know if he intended to attack her physically—or what she'd do if he did. He wasn't that much taller than she, but considerably larger. They stared at each other for a dozen rapid heartbeats.

"Commander Florkowski," she said at last, "I know you were very fond of the Captain and you have my sympathy..."

"I don't want your damn sympathy!"

"Very well then, I withdraw it. But I am now the commanding officer of this ship. I intend to carry out his last order. Are you willing to help me do that or do you wish to be relieved?"

Florkowski stepped back a half pace and continued to glare at her.

After a few more seconds he turned and walked off without a word. Ellsworth watched him go. When he disappeared around a turn in the corridor she sagged and let out a long sigh. How much more of that sort of thing could she expect? Maybe a lot: this was Liu-Chen's crew, not hers. Shaking her head she punched in the entry code to her cabin. The door slid open, but she paused as a thought struck her.

Straightening up, she turned and went back the way she had just come, the door hissing shut behind her. She came to the Captain's cabin, and the door was still open. She looked in and saw that the Doctor had gone, presumably to fetch a stretcher for the body, but the steward was still there. He looked up as she entered.

"Ma'am?"

She suddenly felt very self-conscious, but she forced herself to keep going. She walked around the desk and then reached down to pick up the Captain's gauss pistol. She slid open the compartment and took out the power cell. It was one of the old ones they had found in the storage hold. She looked at Chief Gossage. He turned pale.

"He... about an hour ago he sent me down to Lieutenant Kinney, ma'am, to get a power cell. I didn't think anything of it. If I'd known what was going to happen, I never would have... Oh God, ma'am, I'm sorry!"

"It's not your fault, Chief," she said gently. Gossage was terribly distraught. He had probably worked for Liu-Chen for a long time, judging by the many hashmarks on his sleeve. She felt sorry for the man, but here was another one. Another crewman who would never really accept her as the captain. Her hand slid the power cell back into place with a soft click. Her eyes never left Gossage.

"I'm going to hang onto this for safekeeping, Chief," she said. He nodded, but seemed to be reading her unspoken thought: *Because it works and mine doesn't and God help me, I might just need it!*

She returned to her own cabin with the reassuring weight of the pistol in her pocket. She sat down at her desk and as she had expected, there was a message waiting for her from the Captain. She didn't want to read it right now, but there was no choice. Thirty-seven minutes left until she met with the officers—her officers now, whether they liked it or not—and she had to be ready.

It was a long, rambling message and she suspected that Chief Gossage might find another empty brandy bottle in his search of the quarters. He did apologize. Several times, in fact. And he made excuses. He had never seemed like the type to make excuses, but now he did.

I had devoted my whole life to defending the Star League, Jaq. My whole life. And I failed. The League is dead. You can see that can't you? A thousand worlds just like Flemington. Most of the people dying and the rest thrown back to a stone age, hunter-gathering society. And the Outies will be coming in to plunder what's left and there's nothing to stop them. Dead.

I don't know how we screwed up, but we did. Someone did this to us, I believe the Commodore is right on that. They did it to us and we couldn't stop them. My generation failed and the League is dead.

I don't mean to say that there's no hope, Jaq, but it will be up to you and the people of your generation to go on from here. I'm too old and tired to start over from scratch. That's up to you. Build a new League. A better League. Take care of my ship. God bless you.

She shook her head. What the hell was he expecting from her? The part about taking care of his ship, she might just be able to do. With a little luck. Well, maybe more than a little. But as for the rest of it... She was out of time. The officers would be waiting. She blanked the screen and left her quarters.

"People, you've all heard what has happened. I know many of you had served with Captain Liu-Chen for a long time and I offer my sincere condolences to all of you on this tragedy. I have assumed temporary command of *Gilgamesh* until such time as higher authority may confirm my position here or appoint another officer." Ellsworth looked around the conference room, judging the reactions of the people there. She had decided to throw in the part about 'temporary command' to try and defuse any possible resentment by the ship's old-timers. She could not tell if it was working, but at least there was no immediate outburst. Not that there should be: the regulations fully supported her, but you never knew... At the very least, Florkowski did not seem intent on making any trouble.

"Captain Liu-Chen's last instruction was for me to carry out Commodore Shusterman's orders. As you recall, those orders were to proceed to Flemington and bring back help to Leavitte. Obviously, there is no help to be had here. We must now consider how best to proceed. The final decision will be mine, but I would appreciate your input."

"Commander, you are not seriously considering returning to Leavitte, are you?" asked Doctor Abercrombie.

"Those are our orders, Doctor."

"But the situation has changed. As you pointed out, there is no help here, but the people of Flemington are in desperate need themselves. Surely our duty is to stay here and help them."

"The people of Leavitte are also in need, Doctor," said Commander Van Rossum.

"Leavitte has a population of only fifty million," said Abercrombie. "They have a much better chance of survival on their own. There are two *billion* people here! And they will be dying by the millions very shortly if they don't get help."

"I might remind you, Doctor," said Ellsworth, "that the population of the Star League as a whole is on the order of about ten trillion sentient beings. In all probability they all need help, too."

"I haven't forgotten it, Commander! It haunts my nightmares. But we are here and these people need our help. We must not desert them."

Ellsworth chewed on her lower lip. What Abercrombie said was true, but an even harder truth was that *Gilgamesh* could not hope to do anything significant here. There were just too many people and most were too dependent on high technology to survive without it. Nothing they and their single shuttle could do would stop the inevitable collapse of order and society on Flemington. A year from now that two billion would probably be slashed by ninety percent. And the survivors would be eating each other....

"Doctor, I share your concerns, but we cannot simply fail to return to Leavitte. Commodore Shusterman needs to know the situation here. And since he is the senior officer who we have contact with, we must follow his orders. It is even possible that he might elect to move his headquarters here."

"Yes, Doctor," said Florkowski, speaking for the first time, "and we all know how keen the Commander is about following orders." Ellsworth only cast a quick glance in his direction and no one else seemed to make anything special of the remark.

"Do you think that is possible, that he might relocate here?" asked Abercrombie.

"I couldn't even begin to speculate, Doctor," said Ellsworth, honestly. "But we do have to report back to him. However, we do not have to depart instantly. Is there anything we can do, before we leave, that would significantly help the people here on Flemington?"

"Perhaps we should ask this Ms. Shandy, Commander," suggested Van Rossum. "I'm sure she would have some valuable input."

Ellsworth frowned. It was inevitable that Shandy would do everything in her power to convince her to remain here, so she doubted it would be much use talking with her. Still, she had to meet with her eventually and perhaps some good could come from this.

"All right, let's bring her in."

Shandy looked far better than when Ellsworth had first seen her. A shower, clean clothes, hot food and a few hours' rest had done wonders. Even so, the woman was not smiling. It took a few minutes to bring her up to date, and she looked even less happy at the end of it.

"So you are just going to *abandon* us?" she asked incredulously.

"'Abandon' is a harsh word, Ms. Shandy," said Ellsworth. "I appreciate the seriousness of your situation here, but we have duties and responsibilities..."

"I have a responsibility to this entire world, Commander!" interrupted Shandy. "Two billion people! >From what I've been told about the nature of this catastrophe, there is little hope of help coming from outside and even less of us helping ourselves. You and your ship are our only chance. You can't leave us!"

"Ms. Shandy, it is entirely possible that Commodore Shusterman will order us back here, but we must report to him first."

"You can send that freighter," insisted Shandy. "There is no need for you to go yourself!"

"An interesting idea," admitted Ellsworth. In fact, it *was* an interesting idea and she kicked herself for not thinking of it earlier. Not so much because she wanted to do it, but to have a counter-argument ready. The simple fact was that Jaq Ellsworth desperately wanted to get back to Commodore Shusterman and get some new orders. *You wanted your own command, girl. Time to earn your keep. But I didn't want it like this! I wanted to be a destroyer skipper, not in charge of some doomed rescue effort. Two billion people! I'm not ready for this!* For an instant she completely sympathized with Captain Liu-Chen. It was too much for anyone...

As she sat there, the full weight of her predicament finally began to settle firmly on her shoulders. She could almost feel herself being squashed down—crushed under an impossible burden. For years she had been preparing herself for the command of a ship. She had taught herself, or learned from others, all the technical and practical information she thought she would need. She had never once thought about what she would be asked to do with her ship once she had it. She had always imagined she would be part of a fleet or task force. She'd always have clear orders. Anything unexpected that came along would be of a tactical nature. Tactics she could handle.

What the hell was she supposed to do now?

Build a new league. Liu-Chen's words returned to her, like a sentence of doom. *How? How can I do something like that?* The sheer impossibility of the task had her shaking.

"No..."

"Why not?"

Ellsworth started. She had not been responding to Shandy's suggestion at all, but now she realized everyone was staring at her. How long had she been dithering? Did her officers realize how uncertain she was? She couldn't allow that, she had to follow through.

"No," she repeated, getting control of her voice. "I'm sorry, Ms. Shandy, but we have to report back to Commodore Shusterman. I can't depend on the freighter for that. However, the freighter does have several small craft of its own. I'm sure we can make arrangements..."

"So you can run out on us!" exclaimed Shandy. "Commander, your duty is to help the people of the League. Well, there are League citizens only a few hundred kilometers away in desperate need of your help! Don't try to tell me that you have to travel a hundred light years to get permission to give that help!"

Ellsworth glanced around the compartment. Her officers' expressions were impossible to read. No one liked this situation...

"I'm sorry, but I have no choice. We'll be leaving in one week. Before we go we'll try to give you as much help as we can and set things up with the freighter captain. Hopefully we will be able to come back."

"Come back?" said Shandy, and her face took on an expression of raw fury. "Come back? After it's too late to do any good!" She got to her feet. "You are running away! You can call it anything you like, but that's what you are doing! May God forgive you, Commander— because I surely won't. Neither will the people of Flemington!" She turned and stormed out of the room.

A long silence ensued. Some people were still staring at her.

Others were looking down at the table. What were they thinking? *My first hour in command and I've already lost their confidence. But what the hell can I do?*

"Very well," she said after the silence became unbearable. "Doctor, I want you to put together a list of recommendations for actions we can take in the next week to help these people out. Commander Florkowski, every spare hand is to be put to work searching the supply dumps on the stations for usable equipment. This base has been here a long time. We might find all sorts of things."

The officers nodded their heads, but said nothing.

"Let's get to it, people."

Gregory Sadgipour reflected that he seemed to be spending an awful lot of time going places in this shuttle. *You're a Marine; Marines get to go on landing parties and boarding parties. It's your job, so shut up and do it.* Yes, concentrate on his job. He had been clinging to that thought for days. It was the only thing that was keeping him sane—if he really was still sane. How to judge? The universe was collapsing around him. What was sanity anymore?

What's happening at home?

He gritted his teeth and clenched his fists. He could not afford to think about that now! There was nothing he could do about his home or his family. They were five hundred light years away and impossibly out of reach. Don't think about them! The only reality was the here and now. He forced himself to think about his job.

He looked around, at the other occupants of the shuttle: Commanders Ellsworth and Florkowski, sitting as far apart as physically possible, the Captain's steward, Lieutenant Quatrock, an enlisted technician, four Marines, and himself.

And a large metal box, covered with a flag, which took up the center of the shuttle.

Greg kept glancing between Ellsworth and Florkowski. Scuttlebutt had it that the two had had a ferocious argument just a few hours ago. Now they were not speaking to each other at all. He shook his head slightly. Things were screwed up enough without the two ranking officers being at each other's throats.

"Commander, where do you want me to set us down?" asked the pilot from up front.

"Do you have any particular preference, Commander Florkowski?" asked Ellsworth. Her voice would not have thawed metallic hydrogen.

"His will called for him to be buried next to his wife," replied Florkowski in a tone just as frigid. "I suppose we should do it as close to the Bloomsburg tower as we can."

"All right. Chief," said Ellsworth to the pilot, "can you get us close to the tower without landing in anyone's lap?"

"I think so, ma'am. There's an area on the north side that looks pretty empty on the IR scan. Nothing within five hundred meters. It's snowing pretty hard right now, so we might not even be seen."

"All right, carry on. Lieutenant Quatrock, your people will keep any curious onlookers at a distance. No communications, no explanations. If they get too curious, they will be stunned, understood?"

"Yes, ma'am." Quatrock obviously didn't like his orders, and Greg didn't either. Even with a light stun, a person could easily freeze to death before they could recover. He shivered slightly in spite of the insulated parka he was wearing. A minute later the shuttle jolted slightly and it was down. The rear door swung open and a swirl of snow and icy air came inside.

Quatrock led the Marines outside and they set up a perimeter. The burned-out city tower loomed over them like a cliff, its top fading to near-invisibility in the falling snow. Dimly seen white mounds stretched off in the other directions. Greg hoped they were objects in the park rather than bodies.

He turned as the technician slowly steered the Captain's coffin through the hatch on an anti-grav lifter. Everyone else, except the pilot, followed. They went about twenty meters out from the shuttle until they found a level spot. The technician stopped the lifter and took up a hand tractor. At the Commander's direction, he began excavating. Snow, and then dirt, went flying off in a steady stream. The tech kept shifting position, but he skillfully kept the dirt all going into the same pile. It took about five minutes but eventually he turned off the tool and stepped back. Greg took a quick look to make sure that his security perimeter was still in place and then walked over to the grave.

The tech reactivated the lifter and moved it next to the hole. The Captain's steward carefully removed and folded the League flag. Then, using the hand tractor again, the tech lowered the coffin into the ground. When he was done, he stepped back. Commander Florkowski came forward holding a small book, from which he began reading. It was in a language Greg did not understand, but he could hear the emotion in Florkowski's voice. He found himself choking up.

"Why'd he do it?" he whispered to Lieutenant Quatrock. The cutting wind seemed to whip each word away as he said it. "Why'd he kill himself?"

"That's rubbish, Greg," said Quatrock through clenched teeth. "Don't you believe those stories, Marine; the Old Man died of a broken heart. I don't give a damn what any medical report says, that's the truth of it and anybody asks you, you tell 'em that!"

"Yes, sir."

Florkowski finished reading and the entire party assembled beside the grave. At his signal they all saluted, the troopers presenting arms. Greg supposed they should have fired volleys, but with the noiseless stunners it would have been slightly ridiculous. Even so, he found that he had tears freezing on his cheeks. Florkowski held the salute for a long time, but finally released them from this last duty. While the tech filled the grave, Florkowski returned to the shuttle and carried out the headstone. It was a stainless metal slab with the Captain's name, rank and a short service record deeply engraved into it. As the last of the dirt was being packed down, he set the headstone in place.

"Commander, I'm picking up some people headed this way. Range about three hundred meters." The voice of the pilot in his earphone startled Greg.

"Acknowledged," said Ellsworth, "we're coming back."

Slowly the party returned to the shuttle. Lieutenant Quatrock almost had to drag Florkowski away from the grave. Greg was the last one and he looked back. A few gray shapes could be seen approaching in the distance.

"Come on, Lieutenant," said Ellsworth.

Greg nodded, but instead of obeying, he unsealed his parka and took it off. The icy wind cut through his tunic like it wasn't there. He tossed the parka in the direction of the approaching shapes. He stood for a moment longer and then turned. The others were all standing there watching him. After a moment, the Exec began unsealing her parka, too. The others did so as well...

All that the shapes found was a fresh grave and a small pile of clothing next to a depression in the snow that the wind was rapidly filling.

* * *

Ensign Rhada McClerndon shuffled through the lock into the familiar and comforting confines of *LSS Gilgamesh*. She was tired and sore and utterly sick of her current existence. Long days crawling through cargo holds, storage facilities and supply dumps, finding decomposing bodies in unexpected places, had drained her completely. Even discovering that large cache of working power cells had not made her feel good. Right now all she wanted to do was sleep. She badly needed a shower, too, but she didn't have the energy. Greg would just have to put up with her stink.

She started walking aft, toward her quarters, when she stopped short. She could see a number of people around the entrance to one of the rec compartments. What was going on?

Oh hell, the Captain's funeral.

A party had gone dirtside to bury the Captain. There was a video hook-up and it was being piped through here. Rhada had liked Captain Liu-Chen, but she had not been aboard long enough to know him very well. She knew that others had served with him for many years and were shattered by his death. They would be clustered around the monitors, watching.

But just at the moment, the last thing Rhada wanted to see was another body. She had seen so many in the last few days. The funeral even seemed a bit hypocritical to her. On the various orbital facilities they were looting—sorry, searching—all they could do was push the bodies aside. No burials for those people. No coffins or flags or salutes for them. It wasn't right. One of the things that had attracted Rhada to the Navy in the first place was its reputation for always taking care of its own. It was hard to hold on to that idea when bodies were being treated like rubbish to be shoved into piles and ignored.

She stood in the passageway, hesitating. If she continued on, she would go right by the rec compartment and people would see her. She did not want to watch the funeral, but she didn't want the others to think she didn't care. It was ridiculous, she knew, but she suddenly needed to get away, get back to her quarters and burrow under the blankets.

Another moment of indecision and then she turned down a side passage that led outboard. She could bypass the center parts of the ship and reach her bunk that way. Yes. A few seconds took her into the less frequented parts of the ship. At the moment they seemed deserted. Or nearly so. Up ahead, she heard a thump and a bang and a low curse. At least someone else wasn't watching the funeral.

She turned a corner to head aft again and almost bumped into a man. Startled, she recoiled and was then surprised to see a half-dozen ratings carrying boxes and bundles and containers. They seemed very surprised to see her, too. In fact... Rhada didn't have a lot of experience, but she had learned to recognize the expression of a crew member who was *Up-to-Something*. Looking closer, she could see that they had the hatches to two of the ship's escape pods standing open and they were putting their burdens inside.

"What's going on here?" she demanded.

"Uh..." said one of them.

"Ur, that is..." said another.

"They're acting on my orders, Ensign," said another voice and Rhada was surprised to see Doctor Abercrombie, the ship's surgeon, come around the far bend of the corridor. She stared at the Doctor and he stared back at her. Something wasn't right here...

"It's all right, Ensign," said Abercrombie, "We're just sending a few emergency supplies down to the surface. Since the shuttle isn't available, we're using these pods."

"I... see, sir," said Rhada uncertainly. The Doctor held the rank of lieutenant-commander, so she wasn't in any position to challenge him on this, but she knew something was wrong... Escape pods were re-usable to an extent, but to use them to transport cargo was highly unusual.

"Go on about your business, Ensign."

"Yes, sir." She turned and retraced her steps. Rhada's communicator wasn't working--like most people's—but there was a com panel back around the corner. It would probably be a good idea to check in with the Bridge. She came to the panel and reached for the button, but suddenly a strong hand grabbed her arm and pulled her away. She twisted around to see a large man in a petty officer's uniform. He yanked her back into the corridor with the others.

"What are you doing?" she cried in outrage. "Let go of me!"

"Sorry, ma'am, but I think you better stay with us for a few minutes. Please don't yell, or I'll have to stop you." The way he said that last part sent a chill through her. She ceased struggling and just watched.

There seemed to be about a dozen of them, all enlisted ratings except for the Doctor. Each escape pod could hold twelve, and they seemed to be filling the extra space with supplies and equipment. The Doctor carefully loaded in a complicated looking object that probably came from his sick bay. What were they doing, looting the ship? She clenched her fists when she saw a container of power cells—maybe the very ones she had worked so hard to find.

She glanced around. The P.O. still had her by the arm, but his grip had loosened when she stopped resisting. She thought back to her unarmed combat training. If she were to twist like this, and kick like that… She hesitated. She had hated the combat training and was not any good at it. But they were nearly done loading. Now or never.

She twisted and kicked, but, as always, she was tentative rather than decisive and her blow was merely painful instead of crippling. Still, the P.O. let go of her with a curse of surprise. She leapt away from him and headed for the com panel. She nearly made it, but a hand grabbed the back of her collar and jerked her away with her fingers flailing centimeters from the com button.

"You bitch!" snarled the P.O. He pulled her back and then slammed her against the bulkhead with terrifying strength. The wind was knocked out of her and then he kicked her feet out and she fell to the deck. All thought of further resistance had fled already when a savage kick caught her in the side. Pain jolted through her and she gasped. Another kick and another. She couldn't breathe. *He's going to kill me…* The thought formed and panic surged up, but her body wouldn't respond.

"What are you doing?! Stop it!" shouted a distant voice. One more kick and then it stopped. She tried to get air into her lungs but she couldn't. There were lights sparkling in front of her eyes. Then, gentle hands turned her slightly and the Doctor was there. "What the hell, Johnston! You could have killed her!" he snapped over his shoulder.

Rhada's wandering gaze focused on the P.O. and his expression went from one of fury to embarrassment and then to true horror. He knelt down next to the Doctor.

"Oh shit! Oh shit! I… I'm sorry, Ensign! I didn't want to… " he moaned. "It's just that our families are down there! You can understand that, can't you? We have to get down to help them and I thought you were gonna try and stop us. I couldn't let you. You can understand that, can't you? I didn't want to hurt you, I didn't! She'll be okay, won't she, Doctor?" The man was babbling.

"Ensign, you have some broken ribs," said the Doctor quietly, "but you are not in any danger. I'll summon a medic just before we leave and you'll be fine. We'll be gone in a few more minutes, so just lie still."

She couldn't possibly do anything else, so she did as he told her. She could hear more thumps and bumps as they finished their loading. The P.O. was still there.

"I'm sorry, Ensign, but you understand, don't you?" he pleaded.

She gave her head a convulsive jerk and it seemed to please him greatly. He stood up and he was gone. After a few minutes the pain had lessened slightly, but she still lay there curled into a ball. She heard the doctor at the com panel and then he moved past her. "We're going now." Another few seconds and she heard the escape pod hatches slide shut and then the deck quivered slightly as they launched.

It seemed to take forever for anyone to find her.

"Is the ensign going to be all right?" asked Commander Ellsworth.

"She has two broken ribs and a number of bruises and a mild concussion," answered the assistant surgeon. "Certainly nothing life threatening, but she'll be pretty sore for a few days."

"God damn it. What they did was bad enough on its own, but to do this, too!"

"Ensign McClerndon said she thinks the crewman just lost control and that it really wasn't deliberate."

Ellsworth nodded her head grimly and looked around the conference room. The senior officers were all here—except for the senior medical officer, of course.

"Commander," said Florkowski, "we tracked the pods down to Flemington City. Their transponders have been disabled so we can't pinpoint them exactly, but we could send a party down in the shuttle and probably find them with no trouble."

"And do what?" asked Ellsworth. "Assuming they are still in the vicinity of the pods, they will have made contact with the locals, who will, no doubt, resist our efforts to reclaim our equipment and our personnel. And they are armed, isn't that correct, Lieutenant?"

Lieutenant Quatrock nodded unhappily. "Yes, ma'am. One of my men went with them and four stunners are missing from the armory. I'm sorry, ma'am, I was inexcusably negligent."

"We all were, Lieutenant. I should have seen this coming. But in any case, we can't go after them without expecting to meet resistance and at this point it's just not worth it."

"Surely you aren't going to let them go!" said Florkowski in amazement. "These… these *deserters* have to be caught!"

"And then what?" said Ellsworth icily. "Try them? Convict them? Hang them from the highest yardarm? The morale on this ship is bad enough as it is. We don't need something like this on top of it."

"But if we just ignore it, it will be even worse. Other will try the same thing and this will happen again!"

"We are not going to *let* it happen again. Commander Van Rossum, you will disable the manual controls on all the escape pods. Arrange it so the pods can only be activated with a direct command from the bridge."

"Uh, yes, ma'am. That… is against safety procedures, ma'am."

"I'm aware of that, but those are my orders."

"Yes, ma'am."

"Lieutenant Quatrock, you will place all of your people on security alert. I want armed sentries posted on the bridge, in engineering and in the hanger bay. You will arrange for periodic patrols through the ship. Anything unusual is to be reported, no matter how trivial—and I mean that for all of you." She swept her gaze around the room.

"Yes, ma'am, right away," said Quatrock.

"And this Ms. Shandy is still aboard," said Ellsworth. "I don't suppose she had anything to do with this little unauthorized 'shore leave'?"

"She was talking with Doctor Abercrombie a great deal," admitted Florkowski. "There's no telling what might have passed between them."

Ellsworth frowned. What a mess. She felt like she was losing control of the situation. "Lieutenant Kinney, do we know what was taken?"

"I'm trying to put together a list, ma'am, but some of the items were things we had salvaged from the stations and that will make it more difficult."

"There were a number of items taken from Sick Bay, ma'am," said Lieutenant Twiggs, the assistant surgeon. "I'm still going over it."

"I see. Well, we are pulling out of here in two days. Commander Florkowski, you will keep a close watch on all of our salvage parties and… " The communicator pinged, interrupting her. "Yes?"

"Commander, that merchant ship, the *Tassafaronga*, is breaking orbit."

"What? Send the display down here." A moment later the tactical display appeared on the large monitor. It showed the planet and the orbiting installations. *Gilgamesh* was docked to one station and almost directly opposite it was an icon rapidly moving away from the planet.

"Ma'am," said Ensign Snowden from the bridge, "about twenty minutes ago their orbit took them behind the planet from us. I... I should have noticed when they did not re-emerge on schedule, I'm sorry."

Ellsworth nodded. They had waited until the planet masked them from *Gilgamesh's* sensors and then headed straight out. They were over a million kilometers away and accelerating.

"Communications, signal *Tassafaronga*. Pipe it through here." A few moments later the screen blinked and Captain Deering was there on the screen.

"Captain, where are you going?" asked Ellsworth.

"Home, Commander!" said Deering after the com-lag. "We are going home! Don't try to stop us."

"Captain Deering, we require your assistance here." A feeling of panic coursed through her. The plans to help Flemington depended on the merchant ship and her small craft...

"And our own families need us at home! We're not fools, Commander, we can see what's going on."

"Captain, you can't leave!"

"Yes we can. We'll pick our own place to die! You can do the same. Good-bye, Commander." The connection was broken and Ellsworth found herself staring at the tactical display again. The icon for the merchant was moving more and more rapidly.

"Can we intercept them?" she asked finally.

"Not short of the gravity well boundary, ma'am," answered Lieutenant Pliskin from the bridge. "If they hyper out as soon as they cross the boundary, they'll have at least a twenty minute head start."

Too much. If they took a random course after that they would be far out of sensor range by the time *Gilgamesh* could follow. There would be no hope of catching them. Hell. What should she do? Things were falling apart. They had to get out of here.

"Commander Florkowski, recall all the salvage parties. Put Ms. Shandy in the shuttle and send her home. We will break orbit in one hour."

"Commander! We can't just leave!"

"Yes, we can. And that is exactly what we are going to do—while we still have a crew left to man the ship!"

CHAPTER SEVEN

Gregory Sadgipour sat on his bunk and watched the young woman lying a few meters away. Rhada McClerndon was staring at the overhead. It was the position she had favored for the two weeks since she had been released from Sick Bay. Greg was worried about her. She was his closest friend aboard the ship and now she seemed lost to him—just when he most needed a friend. He had liked her from the start. He was even a bit attracted to her. She was rather pretty for one of those incredibly skinny, stick-like low gee-ers. He had tried to get her to talk, but with little success. She had always been quiet—at least more quiet than he was—but now she was nearly mute. Her large, brown eyes stared at nothing. The beating she had taken had done something to her, it seemed. The physical damage had healed, but something inside her had not. Or at least that is what he told himself. But her silence was getting to him. And he really was worried; there had been two more suicides aboard the ship since they left Flemington.

"Rhada?"

"Hmmm?" She didn't even turn her head.

"I... I was going to go down to the lounge. You want to come?"

"I don't think so. Thanks anyway."

"Aw, c'mon. We're going to be arriving at Leavitte in less than an hour. No more easy watches; they'll be putting us all back to work. Last chance to unwind."

"I'll pass. You go ahead."

Greg sighed and shook his head. This wasn't working. Oh well. He got up and left the compartment and headed for the lounge. *Gilgamesh* was not a large ship and it did not take long to get there. The small size of the ship also meant that there was not the segregation of the officers and enlisted ranks that you might find on a larger vessel. There was a small wardroom for the officers, but the main lounge was open to everyone. At the moment, there were about two dozen people there, some talking, some watching a holovid, some over at the game equipment. Greg served himself a soft drink and sat down and watched some people playing null-ball. The one woman playing was really pretty good and Greg watched her with pleasure. For a few moments he was able to put his troubles out of his mind and just relax.

But it would not last. Soon he was worrying about Rhada and his family again. What was happening back at home? He kept taking inventory of all the things that made life possible and it was a dauntingly complex web of interdependencies. He came from a medium-sized town, which fortunately did not have those enormous housing towers that Flemington did. With two-point-five standard gravities, they did not tend to build very high. Still, there were a lot of food synthesizers in use, which required power. Crops were grown, too, but Greg didn't think the existing farms could supply the demand. Most of those farms depended on robotic equipment, too. And then the food had to be transported and stored and distributed. How did you do that without power? How could you coordinate it without communications? Solve one bottleneck and you found two more. The climate wasn't bad, at least no one would be freezing to death, but…

"No, I will not be quiet!" came an angry voice, startling Greg from his thinking. He looked around and saw a rating stand up from a chair and glare at two other people.

"Marty, knock it off! You're going to get in trouble!" hissed one of the others.

"Trouble? What the hell kind of trouble could I get into?" said the man even more loudly. "The whole damn universe is falling apart around us and you tell me I'm going to get in trouble! Well I got news for you: we're all in a lot of trouble already!"

Everyone in the lounge had turned to face the man and he glared right back at them. "We're all screwed, you know that don't you? Everyone's dying! Just like on Flemington! All of our families are dying!"

"Shut up, Marty! I'm warning you!" the other man got to his feet.

"Why? Can't you see it? It's over! The League is finished! The Fleet is finished! And us along with it! We should go to Ellsworth and demand that she let us go home! What's the point of going back to Leavitte now? Let's take the ship and go back to our homes!"

An embarrassed silence filled the compartment. What the man had just said was technically an incitement to mutiny. But everyone there had been thinking similar thoughts and they all seemed to know it.

Anxious gazes flicked around the room like targeting lasers.

"Maybe he's right," said the woman who had been doing so well in null-ball. A few other heads nodded. Greg tensed. A little griping was one thing, and he'd been prepared to ignore it, in spite of Quatrock's orders to report anything at all, but this was going too far. He got to his feet. A number of eyes focused on him.

"Let's calm down, everyone," he said in as confident a tone as he could muster. "Why don't you all just go about your business."

"Business?" exclaimed the man. "What business do we have now except to get home to our families? What's the point of marching around here saluting and pretending we still have a duty to perform? There's only one duty left: get home!"

"I think you've said enough, Mister... Goode," said Greg, reading the name tag on the man's tunic.

"You do? So what are you going to do? Call your other jarhead buddies and throw me in the brig?"

"I don't think I need any help if I want to do that, Mister Goode," said Greg. He was starting to get annoyed. Goode looked him up and down and seem to have second thoughts about a physical confrontation.

"So you're another one of Ellsworth's toadies, are you?" he demanded instead.

"That's the captain you're talking about..."

"She's no goddam captain!" shouted Goode. "Our captain's dead and there's no way in hell she can take his place!"

"Well at least she's still here, Mister Goode," said a new voice. Greg turned and was amazed to see Rhada standing in the hatchway. Her expression was one of cold fury. Her brown eyes were glittering now. "Which is more than can be said of that captain of yours!"

Goode looked outraged. A few of the other people there did so as well. "What the hell do you mean by that?"

"I just mean that when things got rough, your captain went off and left us! At least Commander Ellsworth is still here, still trying. Or are you just going to give up like he did? Give up and let them win?"

"Who? Let who win?"

"Them! Whoever did this to us! The computers didn't just all quit working by chance. Someone caused it to happen. You all know that! And if we quit then they win! I don't intend to quit." She looked around the room in defiance. More than one person dropped their eyes rather than meet her gaze.

"Y… you're crazy," stuttered Goode.

"Maybe I am. But I'd rather be crazy and die fighting than crawl under some rock. I joined the Navy because I heard some good things about it. I thought it might be something worth belonging to. Well, I'm not so sure now. I don't think I like sharing my space with a bunch of cowards."

"Cowards? Why you little… " Goode clenched his fists and stepped forward. Greg prepared to intercept him if he kept coming.

"Oh, that's right, I forgot," said Rhada. She didn't give a centimeter and her voice dripped with sarcasm. "The one thing that can get a rise out of people like you is if they think someone's going to try and stop them from running away. They're real brave then! You want to beat me up and desert? Well go ahead and give it a try!" She dropped into a combat stance.

Goode hesitated, but still had his fists clenched. Several other people seemed nearly as angry at Rhada's words as he was. Greg wasn't sure he could handle all of them…

"Attention all hands, attention all hands," blared the intercom suddenly and people jumped in surprise. "Stand by for transition to normal space. Repeat: stand by for transition to normal space."

The drop-out into the Leavitte system. Greg had forgotten about that. Everyone around him seemed to tense themselves and then that awful sensation clutched at Greg's head and stomach.

"Shit, I hate that," moaned someone. Greg shook his head to clear it. It took a few seconds for the effects to pass and that was enough to defuse the situation in the lounge. People were still glaring at each other, but they no longer looked like they wanted to fight. With a few sour looks and some low muttering, people began turning away. Goode stalked back to his seat. Greg pulled Rhada over to a chair and sat down.

And immediately sprang up again as an alarm began shrieking.

"General Quarters! General Quarters! All hands, man your battle stations! This is not a drill! Repeat: this is not a drill!"

Chairs scattered in all directions as people rushed for the exit.

"Drop-out in thirty seconds," said Lieutenant Pliskin. "All systems on automatic; readings are nominal."

"Very well," said Commander Ellsworth. She let out her breath in a long, silent sigh. Leavitte at last. The previous three weeks had been hell. The crew had been stumbling around like zombies and her best efforts had done nothing to pull them together. All the little tricks she had learned over the years had done nothing at all. Or only made things worse. She told herself that the other suicides were not her fault, but she was only half-convinced. But at least there had been no major disasters; the ship was here and still functioning. Maybe when she had a chance to talk to Commodore Shusterman they could come up with something to...

The universe turned inside out and the view screen was suddenly filled with stars.

"Transition completed," announced Pliskin. "Distance to Leavitte IV twenty-nine million kilometers."

"Good job, Lieutenant. Helm, take us ahead at..."

"Commander!" exclaimed Ensign Snowden at sensors. "I'm detecting multiple drive sources near the planet! Nuclear detonations and high energy discharges!"

What the hell?

"Confirmed, ma'am, somebody's shooting at somebody!"

"Analysis, quickly."

"Yes, ma'am."

"Commander, I'm picking up the beacon of *LSS Steadfast!*" reported Lieutenant Terletsky.

"*Steadfast?* That's a corvette, isn't it?"

"Yes, ma'am, an old corvette."

"Getting more information, now, ma'am," said Snowden. "A total of six ships: *Steadfast* and five others. Three seem to be in pursuit of *Steadfast*; the others are near the planet. I'll get this up on the display in a few seconds, ma'am."

"Very well. In the meantime, Commander Florkowski, clear the ship for action, please."

"Aye, ma'am." A moment later the battlestations siren howled through the ship.

Snowden finished updating the tactical display and Ellsworth ignored the noise and studied it. As he had said, three ships seemed to be in pursuit of the League corvette. They were about two million kilometers from the planet and heading outbound. Not exactly toward *Gilgamesh*, but not too far off the track. The data on the other ships was still sketchy, but none of them seemed terribly large. An idea began to take shape in her head.

"Helm, come to course two-two-eight by minus oh-one-seven; ahead at half power."

"Half power, ma'am?"

"Confirmed, half power."

"Aye, aye."

"Lieutenant Terletsky, can you put a com laser on *Steadfast* without those other ships picking it up?"

"I think so, ma'am. She's a little out in front of the others."

"Very well. Let them know we are here, give them our position, course and speed and ask them if they would be so kind as to lead their friends out in our direction."

"Yes, ma'am!"

Gilgamesh leapt forward at an easy acceleration. Ellsworth hoped the power output would be low enough that the enemy—whoever they were—would not detect them. If they could keep them unaware, perhaps she could give them a nasty surprise.

With the time lag involved, it was nearly five minutes before they received a reply from *Steadfast*. Terletsky put it up on the main viewer. A youngish man in the uniform of a lieutenant commander appeared.

"*Gilgamesh*, this is Commander Thomas Downs, *LSS Steadfast*. Very glad to see you! I've got a bit of a situation here and your assistance would be appreciated. I've got three Sarlangian ships on my tail; I'm sending along my sensor readings on them. If I'm understanding your message correctly, you want me to lead them out to you. Capital idea! We'll be changing course shortly. These bastards aren't much of a threat individually, but I don't think I can handle three at once. The two of us together should have no problems. Keep me informed of your movements so we can coordinate. I'll see you in a bit. Downs out."

Ellsworth sucked on her teeth. Sarlangians. Sarlangia was a single world 'empire' about forty light years away. Not too advanced technologically, but the ruler there was pretty aggressive. He bought ships and weapons wherever he could get them and made periodic trouble along the frontier. It seems he was after bigger game today. The sensor readings Commander Downs had sent gave her a pretty good idea what she was facing. Two 'cruisers' and a 'battlecruiser' were chasing *Steadfast*. Fortunately, the Sarlangian emperor was as egotistical as he was rapacious. His 'cruisers' were the size of League frigates and that 'battlecruiser' was no larger than a destroyer. Their weapons and electronics were probably second rate, too. There were two other ships still close to the planet. They looked like another 'cruiser' and some sort of transport. She could deal with them later.

But exactly how did she plan to 'deal with them'? They would probably run screaming in panic the instant they realized she was there. She did not really need to fight…

But suddenly she wanted to fight very much indeed.

"Lieutenant Terletsky, give me the 'all hands' circuit."

Rhada McClerndon finished pulling on her vac suit and then grabbed her helmet and dashed to her battle station. She was in charge of the Number Four photon cannon. Passing through the heavily armored pressure hatch, she reached her station and strapped herself into her seat. She quickly, but carefully flipped on a row of switches and watched the display screen on her panel come to life. The main targeting monitor came on in front of her and a number of possible targets appeared. They were still far out of range, however. She checked over the status monitors on the weapon. Everything looked nominal. She glanced around the small compartment and saw that her gun crew was all there. Able Spacer Martin Goode was at his post and he glanced at her sheepishly and then turned away. Rhada hit another switch and the two joysticks for the manual controls rose out of her chair arms. She grasped them and put the huge turret through a series of movements. She switched back to automatic and glanced over her board again. All the lights were green.

"Number Four mount manned and ready," she said into her com. The battery commander acknowledged.

Then she waited. She had been through countless drills and waiting was something she was used to. It could be hours before they got in range and her mount might never fire even if they did get close. She had been through three real 'actions' since she came aboard and her cannon had yet to fire a shot in anger. But the Number Four mount had seen plenty of action over the years. It had been destroying enemies of the League long before she was born. She glanced at the bulkhead beside her. A long and carefully painted list of 'kills' covered several square meters. The very first was a pirate vessel blasted apart almost ninety years earlier. The most recent was two years ago. Another pirate. Some things never changed. She had settled in for the wait when her com came to life.

"Attention all hands. This is Commander Ellsworth. We are closing on three Sarlangian vessels that are attacking one of our corvettes.

About an hour from now they are going to get one hell of a surprise. So stay sharp, everyone."

Rhada sucked in her breath. This might be the real thing. She found herself quivering. Not in fear, but in anticipation. A chance to hit back at someone—at anyone!

"It seems that these Sarlangians think we're down for the count," continued Ellsworth. "Let's prove them wrong! They've come here thinking to pick the bones of the League. Well, the League can still bite! We're still here! *Gilgamesh* is still on patrol and these bastards are going to find that out the hard way!"

A low growl seemed to fill the gunroom and Rhada realized she was one of the ones growling. Then one of her gunners gave a cheer and in an instant everyone doing it, too. Even Martin Goode. He saw her staring at him and gave her a lopsided smile and a nod of his head.

"Good luck to you all," said Ellsworth. "Good luck and good shooting!"

"Range to Target One two million, three hundred thousand kilometers. Still no sign that they've seen us," reported Lt. Commander Florkowski from the tactical station. "Photon cannons are tracking, plasma torpedoes are on stand-by."

"Very well. Helm, reduce power to one third," said Jaq Ellsworth. "Engineering, stand by to bring up the shield."

"Aye, aye, ma'am."

Ellsworth typed a few numbers into her own monitors, checked the results and nodded in satisfaction. Commander Downs had maneuvered *Steadfast* perfectly. He had stayed far enough from his pursuers that they had not been able to do him any serious damage, but close enough to keep them interested in the chase. In another few minutes the enemy ships would be unable to avoid action with *Gilgamesh*. But what should she do when they got in range? Put a few shots across their bows? Sting them a little bit? Or blow them to atoms? She was tapping her finger nervously on the arm of her chair when she looked up to see Chief Gossage, Captain Liu-Chen's steward standing there with her vac suit in his hands.

"I… uh… will you be needing this, ma'am?" he asked.

Ellsworth blinked. She had not moved into Liu-Chen's quarters and she had not made any use of Gossage's services so far. In fact, she had hardly given the man a thought. Now he was standing there expectantly. She glanced around and realized that the rest of the bridge crew all had their vac suits on.

"Yes, Chief, thank you." She got out of her chair and pulled the suit on over her uniform. She opted to forgo the plumbing connections this time. Hopefully this wouldn't take too long. In fact, she was going to make sure it wouldn't take long. With a start, Ellsworth realized she had made her decision. *Am I going to kill those people just so I won't need to pee in my suit?*

No, that wasn't the reason. In the old days it had been policy to just scare off raiders if they had not actually done any damage before they were caught. But that was before. Things were different now. The League wasn't going to be scaring people like in the past. Sharper lessons were going to be needed from now on.

"Range two million kilometers," said Florkowski.

"Disengage safety locks. Weapons are free," ordered Ellsworth.

"Aren't you going to give them a warning first?" asked Florkowski in surprise.

"The only warning they're going to get is when our photon cannons blow through the shield of that lead ship," answered Ellsworth.

"But the Captain… Captain Liu-Chen always…"

"Captain Liu-Chen is dead, Mister Florkowski. I'm in command of this vessel now. And those are my orders. If you have any problems following them, please let me know and I'll have someone take over for you."

Florkowski bristled. "That's not what I meant!"

"What did you mean?" Ellsworth realized this was no time to be pushing him, but she couldn't help herself. She was really coming to hate this son of a bitch. *I can't afford this right now! I can't afford to hate anyone in my crew—not even him. Ease up!*

"Nothing," growled Florkowski. "Weapons are free."

"Very well."

The range wound down. *Steadfast* was very close now. She was keeping herself on an almost exact line between *Gilgamesh* and her pursuers to help mask any drive signature from the cruiser. When she passed, it would be show time.

"Range one million kilometers, weapons have a good target lock."

"Engineering, once we fire bring up the shield immediately. Helm, go to full power at the same time."

"Aye, aye, ma'am."

Closer and closer still. Ellsworth put one of her smaller monitors on a visual display. She could actually see *Steadfast*... The corvette swelled enormously and then was gone as she flashed past.

"Stand by... Fire!"

Only four of the photon cannons could be brought to bear but they lashed out against the unsuspecting target.

"A hit! Two more!" exclaimed Ensign Snowden. "At least two blast-throughs! I'm reading air and debris, ma'am!"

Three hits. Good shooting at this range. Ellsworth watched her crew as they brought up the shields and increased the drive to full power. The Sarlangians were frozen by this sudden change of fortune and they maintained their course for a number of long and fatal seconds. The photon cannons fired again and scored two more hits before the enemy even reacted. Then the three ships peeled off in three different directions, but *Gilgamesh* was still closing on them rapidly. The target ship's acceleration had fallen significantly.

"Come left ten degrees. Maintain fire on Target One. Bring the plasma torpedoes to full power."

"Aye, ma'am."

This wasn't going to be pretty.

Rhada watched the targets getting closer and closer. Only the forward mounts had a shot right now, but in a few more moments number four mount would have a clear view of Target One. She grasped the joysticks and moved her targeting reticule as far to the left as it would go. The mount was still on automatic control, so her actions had no effect, but she went through the motions as if she were really aiming the turret. This was partly in case the automatic controls were knocked out and partly as a training exercise. Her actions would be compared with what the automatics did.

And right now she was determined to nail that sucker.

She could scarcely believe how wound up she was—how wound up everyone was. She had a natural skill for gunnery and her training scores were the highest on the ship. She intended to increase that score today. She wanted to kill those bastards! A small part of her mind was telling her that it was just the weeks of suppressed frustration and anger boiling over. She had needed to strike out at someone for what was happening, and these Sarlangians had had the extreme misfortune of putting themselves in her path. She realized this was true, but she didn't care.

The ship turned slightly and the enemy was moving into her field of fire. She adjusted her aim and waited as the enemy icon slid into her sights…

Fire! She pressed the trigger and in the same instant the cannon fired. A second later the target disappeared from the display. "We got him!" she shouted.

The compartment erupted in cheers.

"Target One destroyed!" exclaimed Ensign Snowden. Ellsworth saw the icon fade from the screen. That was one of the Sarlangian 'cruisers'. Now for their 'battle cruiser'.

"Shift fire to Target Two. Ready on the torpedoes," she commanded.

"Ma'am, they are signaling us," said Lieutenant Terletsky.

"Do not reply."

"Yes, ma'am."

Gilgamesh fired another salvo with her photon cannons and scored a hit on the battle cruiser. Now the Sarlangians finally returned the fire. A scattering of lasers flashed by or impacted on the shields, but they were not especially powerful and nothing penetrated. Then missiles began showing up on the sensors.

"Point defense on automatic," commanded Ellsworth. The enemy missiles were slow, but they carried nuclear weapons and could do considerable damage if they scored a direct hit. *Gilgamesh's* secondary weapons began to pick them off. More hits were scored on the enemy ship. The main photon cannons punched through the shields again and again.

"Range one hundred fifty thousand kilometers, torpedoes have a good lock," reported Florkowski.

"Stand by," said Ellsworth. The Sarlangian was entering optimum range for the plasma torpedoes. She waited another two heartbeats…

"Fire."

The twin launchers in *Gilgamesh's* bow spat out two balls of glowing plasma, one after the other. Traveling at three-quarters lightspeed, they hit their target in less than a second. The first hit collapsed the enemy's already weakened shields and the second blew the ship to even smaller pieces than the first 'cruiser'.

"Got him!" shouted Ensign Snowden. Several other people on the bridge cheered as well.

Jaq Ellsworth looked at the tactical readout. The third enemy ship was now past them and heading outbound at high speed. They could get a few shots off at them, but it was unlikely to accomplish much. *Steadfast* could still intercept them, but perhaps it would be good to leave at least one survivor to spread the warning that the League wasn't dead yet. Meanwhile, the other two Sarlangian ships were fleeing away from the planet.

"Helm come to one-nine-four by oh-four nine, ahead at maximum."

"Aye, aye, ma'am!"

"Lieutenant Terletsky, open a channel to *Steadfast*."

"You've got them, ma'am." Lt. Commander Downs appeared on the screen, grinning ear to ear.

"Nicely done, *Gilgamesh*!" he said.

"Thank you, Commander," answered Ellsworth with a considerable smile of her own. "Now I think we can go after those two ships near Leavitte IV. I'll handle the 'cruiser', and you can take the transport. They are deep enough in the gravity well that I think we can go for a capture this time. They should be pretty demoralized by now as it is."

"What about this other 'cruiser', ma'am?"

"Let him go. I think the emperor of Sarlangia ought to hear what that captain will have to say, don't you?"

"Yes, ma'am," said Downs with a chuckle. "I'll get us turned around as quick as I can and track down that transport."

"Very well; carry on, Commander."

Steadfast had an edge in acceleration over *Gilgamesh*, but she was heading the other direction. By the time she had turned around and caught up, they were nearly upon the fleeing enemy. It took almost an hour and with all the excitement Ellsworth was thinking about her vac suit's plumbing connection...

"Communications, signal the enemy warship."

It took a few attempts, but eventually the screen came to life and Ellsworth found herself staring at a greenish lump of scales and feathers. The Sarlangian appeared to be foaming at the mouth, but she didn't know if it was enraged or if they always did that.

"Captain..." she began.

"Why do you humans attack us!?" cried the creature. "We came here peacefully and you attack us! The Emperor will not tolerate this! Leave us alone!"

"Captain, we both know exactly why you came here. Surrender

your vessels or I will be forced to destroy them."

"Surrender!? I dare not! This is the Emperor's ship! What would he say when he learned of it?"

"Frankly, sir, I don't give a damn. Surrender at once."

"I cannot!"

"Very well. Tactical, lock weapons on that vessel."

"No! Do not fire! But the Emperor will kill me if I surrender to you."

"And I'll kill you if you don't! Now heave your ship to or I'll blow you out of space!"

The creature gave off a blubbering sigh and bowed its head.

CHAPTER EIGHT

"About a week after you left, a Sarlangian courier arrived," said Commodore Shusterman. "They came to complain that a lot of trade goods they had bought were no longer working. No doubt the same nano-circuitry problems we had suffered. We did our best to not let them know what a mess things were in, but there was no real way to conceal it. Obviously, they thought they could take advantage of the situation. Fortunately, a few weeks later *Steadfast* showed up and then you came back in the nick of time. That was an excellent job, by the way."

"Thank you, sir. I probably should have consulted with you before engaging them," said Jaq Ellsworth, "but I would have had to give up the element of surprise."

"Don't worry about it, Commander. You did exactly what I would have ordered you to. Considering you destroyed or captured half the Sarlangian Navy right there, I doubt they'll be bothering us again for a while."

"But there are plenty of other folks out there who could, sir," said Lieutenant Boshko, the Commodore's aide. "The word about what has happened to us is going to be spreading fast."

"Yes, unfortunately that is true. People are going to be wondering why all of our export items are failing. In addition, League ships out beyond the borders will have had the same problems as ours here. Two weeks ago a Dlerdanji trading vessel arrived with the crew off one of our merchant ships. All their systems failed but fortunately, they were safely docked at a Dlerdanji system when it happened and were rescued. That sort of thing is going to be happening all through the border regions and it won't take long for people to figure out why."

Ellsworth nodded. The Dlerdanji traders were all through this sector. Fortunately, they were not aggressive and scrupulously honest for the most part. Unfortunately, there were plenty of others out there who did not share those virtues.

"Were you able to get any help from the Dlerdanji, sir?"

"Some. They gave us a few emergency generators and communicators and other items. Those have been a great help dirtside. They said they would be back with more. We asked for a portable fusion plant, power distribution gear and food synthesizers. Hopefully they will be back in a few weeks."

"Pardon me for asking, sir, but how are we going to pay for all of that? Our usual trade items are mostly worthless, aren't they?"

"Yes, that's true. There are some things the Dlerdanji will accept that don't depend on nano-circuitry, but relatively few. For the moment they are extending us credit based on our suppression of piracy in this region. In the long term, however, I'm afraid we may have to give them some things we would rather not."

"Sir?" said Ellsworth, not entirely following him.

"They have expressed interest in our HyperCom system. I believe they would trade a great deal for that."

Ellsworth's eyes widened. The HyperCom, the League's faster-than-light communications system, was one of its most jealously guarded bits of technology. It had given the League an enormous advantage over its rivals and had been a major factor in making the huge, sprawling League possible. To give it away... Ellsworth glanced at the other two people in *Gilgamesh's* conference room, Commander Downs from *Steadfast*, and Lieutenant Boshko. It seemed as though they shared her uneasiness.

"But our HyperComs aren't even working, sir," she said for lack of any other inspiration.

"True, and it would take the Dlerdanji time and effort to adapt it to their own technology. They still want it badly." Shusterman paused and looked sharply at Jaq. "I know what you're thinking, Commander: do we have the authority to make such a decision? Believe me when I tell you I have been agonizing over that and related questions for most of the time you have been gone. We have some very tough decisions before us." Shusterman sighed.

"I read your report on what happened on Flemington—not just dirtside, but on *Gilgamesh* as well. An ugly situation all around and you handled it as well as was possible. Harry Liu-Chen's death is... hard. He and I go back a long way. He was as good a ship captain as you will ever find. Within his sphere of expertise he was superb. But he always had a reluctance to go beyond that. He valued order and familiar routine. When faced with a completely new challenge he would hesitate. I don't mean to speak ill of him, but his dilemma is now our own. We are faced with something totally unique. How do we deal with it? I don't just mean how do we feed the people of Leavitte, or keep the pirates and raiders in this sector at bay. What do we do about out responsibilities to the League as a whole?"

"Sir, you know my recommendation," said Boshko. "We should consolidate our position here at Leavitte first. With the help from the Dlerdanji and the outlying farmers and herders we have the immediate crisis under control. No one is going to starve here and we have the prospect of restoring limited manufacturing with time. To pull out and try to help Flemington or any of the larger worlds will just be throwing our limited resources into a bottomless pit. We'd be swallowed up and accomplish nothing."

"Yes, there are practical limits to what we can hope to accomplish," said the Commodore, "but there are other considerations besides food and power and manufacturing." He paused and touched the controls for the holographic display. A moment later, a star map shimmered into being above the conference table. It showed their small section of the Star League's frontier and one star glowed brighter than the rest.

"You can see our position here at Leavitte," continued Shusterman. "A subsector base, one of a dozen, subordinate to the sector fleet base at Flemington. Each subsector base is responsible for patrolling a section of this part of the frontier. We were fortunate to have *Gilgamesh* here when the disaster happened. That let us save a portion of our personnel and greatly helped our attempts to restore order on the planet. Unfortunately, I don't imagine the other bases were as lucky. Commander Downs and *Steadfast* only returned to their base at Neshanimy after it was too late."

Jaq glanced at Downs. She could imagine the horror he had discovered, but he let none of it show on his face. His eyes met hers and she looked away.

"I've gone through the records on your computer here, Commander Ellsworth, and according to the Naval Register there are several hundred warships and even larger numbers of naval auxiliaries which are old enough to have survived the way *Gilgamesh* and *Steadfast* did. Unfortunately, they are scattered all over the League and we have no way of knowing whether they did survive and no way to contact them. The records you have are not complete as far as refits go, so it is possible that many of those ships may have received new equipment which could have proved fatal to them. I'm hoping that there may be a few others in this sector. They may be still at their own subsector base or they may have gone back to Flemington just as you did.

"But the bottom line is that the Navy has been gutted. Maybe ninety-eight percent casualties or worse. Of course most of it was facing the Darj'Nang. I'm praying that those bastards were finished off before this disaster hit, because right now there isn't a working thought-screen generator anywhere in the League. But even if they are all dead, there are plenty of other dangers."

Shusterman touched the controls and the display expanded to show the entire League. At this scale only the more important stars could be picked out individually.

"We are lucky in this sector that there are only a few bordering powers of any note. The Traglarians and Beresferds could make some trouble for us, but are still pretty small fish. It's over here and here that the real threats are. The Vurnaglan Empire and the Quedansti are major powers and would love to take a chunk out of us. And right now there is damn little to stop them."

"But what could they want, sir?" asked Commander Downs. "With the disaster there would be little of value left to loot."

"There are the planets themselves, Commander," said Shusterman. "Fully habitable planets are rare. Over three-quarters of our colonies have been terraformed to some degree and at considerable expense. Right now they could just move in and take them. And there are the people of those planets." Shusterman's face became grim. "With no working defenses and the people in danger of starving, what sort of resistance could they offer? The invader could just set up fortified food distribution points and the population would have to submit or starve. They could be reduced to serfdom or outright slavery in very short order. And I don't have to remind you that the Quedansti hate our guts. I shudder to think what they might do out of malice now that they can.

"So while it is tempting to concentrate our efforts here at Leavitte, how long can we hold off the invaders? The sheer size of the League and logistical difficulties involved will make conquest slow, but sooner or later we will probably be overrun."

"So what do we do, sir?" asked Ellsworth.

"I wish I knew."

* * *

Lieutenant Svetlana Terletsky sat at her com station and tried to shake off her gloom. The battle of three days ago had been exciting and had done wonders for the morale of the crew but, unfortunately, the dire situation they were in could not be permanently corrected by blasting a couple of second rate raiding ships to dust. The crisis was the same as before and the crew was starting to slip back into its earlier state. Just on the way here to the bridge Terletsky had seen a man slumped in a chair in the lounge crying quietly. A dozen other people had been there and they had let him cry. How could you comfort anyone in a mess like this? She tried to immerse herself in her duty and not think about anything else, but it was hard. Right now there was not a great deal to distract her, anyway....

A light on her monitor blinked and she saw that there were a number of incoming signals. *That's odd...*

There were over a hundred separate signals and each was a short, compressed data burst. The signals were coded and she could not make any immediate sense of them. Intrigued, she ran them through her recognition routine. It took almost a minute—which was also intriguing—before a match was found.

Terletsky looked at what it was and then snorted in disgust. *Is that all? Why the hell haven't they deactivated those things?* She reached out to send the messages to the archive. She didn't even know why she was bothering, but routine died hard.

Her finger paused over the button. *Wait a minute...* Her finger moved to a different button.

"Lieutenant Chtak'Chr, respond please."

"Chtak! What's happened to you?" exclaimed Rhada McClerndon in dismay. She stared at her teacher and friend in growing alarm. The alien looked horrible. His usually sleek fur was discolored and matted. His whiskers were drooping and he looked to have lost a lot of weight. Ribs were showing despite his fur.

"I have been... working," responded Chtak'Chr. In spite of his haggard appearance his voice was as animated as ever.

"Working on what?" demanded Rhada.

"Our present dilemma... and other things."

"Have you forgotten to eat or something? You look terrible!"

"Thank you. No, I have been eating, although that is one of the problems I was working on. I'm afraid my rather poor appearance has been caused by something else."

"Like what?"

"Rhada, this situation goes far beyond a simple matter of our machines not working. The loss of basic knowledge may ultimately be the greatest tragedy. Virtually every scrap of knowledge from the last thirty years has been lost. All the records, all the scientific papers, everything. Even much of our earlier knowledge is in peril. Most of our records were transferred to the new computers and storage devices when they became available. No doubt the older records remain, but who knows where they might be? *Gilgamesh's* computers hold some of that information, but not all by any means. All of my work had been crippled by a lack of reference data."

"That doesn't explain why you look like this."

"I am getting to that. Patience. Much of the knowledge I need is locked inside my brain. In theory, everything I've ever read or learned is in there. It is just a matter of recalling it. With the help of Assistant Surgeon Twiggs, I have been recovering that information."

"Twiggs?" said Rhada in puzzlement. Then insight: "You've been taking some sort of drug?"

"Yes. There are drugs that can stimulate an almost total recall from memory. They have been quite effective, but the physical toll is considerable."

"It sure as hell is! Does Commander Ellsworth know you are doing this to yourself?"

"I may have forgotten to inform her..."

"I bet you did! Well, you are going to stop right now!"

"Oh, dear, I always thought a lieutenant outranked an ensign. Have I been wrong all this time? How embarrassing!"

"Rank has nothing to do with it! You're going to kill yourself!"

"Calm yourself. Lieutenant Twiggs is monitoring my health. But truth to tell, he has refused to allow me to continue for a few days until I can regain some strength."

"Well, I'm glad to hear that!"

"And if it will placate you in the slightest, my efforts have also been essential to my continued good health."

"What do you mean?"

"Do you recall why I am one of only two non-human species aboard this ship?"

"Physiological compatibility."

"Bravo, my teachings have not all been for naught. The League only put species with very similar physical needs on ships together. It simplifies the life support and subsistence situation enormously. My needs are almost identical with your own. However, I do require several chemicals and proteins in my diet which are not normally found in your foods. The synthesizer that was providing me with those substances is no longer working. Lieutenant Twiggs can provide them for me with an older synthesizer he has in sick bay—but he needed the exact chemical formulas."

"Good grief! Are you going to be okay?"

"Yes, fortunately, I could survive for some time without them, but I have successfully recalled the formulas and I should not be in any danger."

"Well, I'm certainly glad to hear that!"

"I am flattered by your concern for my well-being."

"You said that was just one thing you were working on. What else have you been doing?"

"As I said: I am recovering basic data. It is amazing how much I know that I did not know I knew. Still, it will probably be some time before I can..."

The com terminal on Chtak's desk pinged.

"Lieutenant Chtak'Chr, respond please."

"Chtak, here."

"Lieutenant, this is Lieutenant Terletsky. I've just picked up a series of signals and I thought you should know about them..."

"So, for the time being, I plan to keep you and *Gilgamesh* here, Commander," said Commodore Shusterman. "You can provide for our defense along with the Sarlangian ship you captured. Commander Downs is to take *Steadfast* and make a circuit of all the subsector bases within range and try and send any surviving ships here. If we can concentrate our forces it will give us a lot better chance at holding off any attacker."

"Sir," said Downs, "I'm concerned that any ships I encounter might not be willing to come here."

"Yes, that could be a major problem. The normal chain of command is shot to hell. With Admiral Barringsworth dead, the subsector commanders are on their own. I'm senior to all but four of them, but we don't even know which ones are alive. So any ships you encounter won't necessarily accept me as their legitimate commander."

"And each ship captain will feel compelled to defend his own home turf first," said Boshko.

"True again. But I still believe this to be important. At the very least it will let them know we are here and not doing too badly. If they run into trouble, they might head here as a refuge."

Jaq nodded her head. It seemed like a reasonable plan. And kept her and *Gilgamesh* here. She was going to have to talk with Shusterman about her ship and her crew and get some things settled, but right now probably wasn't the best…

"Commander Ellsworth," said the com suddenly, "Lieutenant Chtak'Chr is here and he wishes to speak to you. He says it is quite urgent."

Ellsworth looked to Shusterman. He shrugged. "May as well send him in, maybe he has some good news for a change." A moment later her Survey Officer came in. She was shocked at his appearance, but he gave her no chance to ask about it.

"Pardon me for interrupting, Commander, but I have an urgent need for the ship's cutter."

"The cutter? What for?"

"I must go out to the fifth planet for a short time. It is extremely urgent."

"Why? There's nothing out there."

"I believe there is. Something very important."

"What?"

"I… would rather not say just now, Commander. I have a theory, but I need to confirm some things—which I can only do if I have the cutter."

Again Ellsworth exchanged glances with Shusterman. The cutter was still performing important service on the planet. "You have my permission, Commander," he said.

"Very well, Lieutenant, but I'll require an explanation when you return."

"You will have it, Commander, I promise."

"Chtak, where the hell are we going?" demanded Rhada McClerndon from the cutter's control station.

"As I have told you several times, and as your navigation instruments are hopefully telling you, to the fifth planet of this star system."

"But why? I mean, I'm not complaining that you brought me along.

It's been so long since I've had a chance to pilot one of these things I was going to lose my small craft rating soon, but why all the way out here?"

"We are looking for something."

"We had already figured that much, Chtak," said Gregory Sadgipour from one of the passenger seats. "But after a three-hour flight, it better be something good."

"How have the two of you avoided being thrown in the brig for insubordination? The way you treat me is contrary to all of the Navy regulations I am familiar with. Or is it only me that you subject so?"

"Pretty much only you," admitted Sadgipour, glancing sheepishly at his two Marine troopers. "You're the only one who lets us get away with it."

"Greg! Don't tell him that! Now he knows!"

"Oh, darn."

Chtak clicked in amusement. He was glad to see the young humans in such good spirits. He knew they had been despondent, like most of the crew, for weeks. Indeed, he could understand their feelings. He had only maintained his own spirits with considerable effort.

"Okay, we're entering high orbit, Lieutenant Chtak'Chr, sir," said Rhada. "Where the bloody hell do you want us to go now? Sir."

"Take us down to a low orbit and prepare for a full sensor scan."

"And just what are we looking for?"

"There are a number of automated sensor probes on the surface. I wish to find a few of them."

"Can't we just signal them and ask for a response? If they're like most probes, they probably have automatic locational beacons you can activate."

"No!" said Chtak emphatically. "That is the one thing we must not do. We dare not signal them."

"Why not?"

"Will you trust me—or just this once simply follow orders?"

"Okay, okay!"

The cutter lost altitude quickly and was soon only a few hundred kilometers above the planet's surface.

"Commencing sensor sweep," announced Rhada. "I assume I'm looking for refined metals or energy sources?"

"Correct. There should be several hundred of them down there, so I hope it will not take that long to find some of them."

"I'm getting the horrible suspicion that once we do find some of those things we will be going down to that hellhole to retrieve them," said Sadgipour.

"You are very perceptive, Greg," said Chtak.

In fact, it took almost two hours just to find the first one. Rhada was getting frustrated by that time, but she shouted for joy when the sensors showed a positive result.

"It's down there; you want me to land, Chtak?"

"Yes. Please."

"It's on the night side. Weather's looking pretty rough, too. Guess I'm going to get my money's worth on this ride. Hang on, this is going to be bumpy."

The cutter's speed decreased and then it dipped down into the atmosphere. Rhada was correct: it was bumpy. The cutter jounced and jolted its way downward and then began a spiral that narrowed around the sensor contact on Rhada's screen.

"Okay, holding at... trying to hold at one hundred meters. Switching on floodlights. Damn, no place to land here, too many boulders. There's a flat spot about fifty meters over to the side. I'm going to have to set us down there. Sorry Greg."

"Thanks a bunch."

"I don't have any choice... shit!" The cutter lurched sharply and then recovered. "The wind's gusting over a hundred KPH. Either I land it over there or we go back up!"

"Take us down, Rhada," said Chtak gently.

"All right, hang on." Rhada swung the cutter's bow around so it was facing the wind and then slowly drifted to the side toward the 'flat' spot. She put the landing legs down and the extra drag they created buffeted the small vessel even more.

"Ten meters... five..." There was bump and a thud and the cutter leaned a bit to the side, but they were down.

"Whew! My flight instructor woulda been proud of me," said Rhada.

"Well done, Ensign," said Chtak. "Greg, I'm afraid it is up to you and your men now. I would go with you, but in my emaciated state, I believe I might well be blown away in the wind."

"Okay, now what exactly am I looking for?"

"It should be a metal object, roughly cylindrical and perhaps a meter and a half long. Unfortunately there is probably a spike on the end that is imbedded in the rock. You will need your tools to get it loose."

"And you just want me to bring it back here?"

"Yes. Please be careful—both with the probe and with yourselves."

"In that order?"

"Off with you, youngling."

Greg closed the faceplate on his vac suit helmet and led his men into the airlock. The atmosphere of the planet was primarily carbon dioxide with a large amount of methane and other unpleasant gases mixed in. Fortunately, the cutter had an airlock, unlike the smaller shuttles, so they should be able to keep the worst of it outside where it belonged. The trio crowded inside and shut the inner door. A few moments later Chtak and Rhada could dimly see them through the front viewport. In spite of the floodlights, visibility was terrible. The wind was driving the rain (water? ammonia?) almost horizontally.

"I'm going to tie a line to the cutter so we can find our way back," said Greg over the radio. He did so and then backed off a half dozen meters. "Which way?"

"A bit to your left," said Rhada comparing what she could see to her sensor readings. "No, your other left… that's it… a little more… back to the right now. Got it! Stay on that heading and you should go right to it."

"Okay, we're on our way." The three figures slowly vanished into the gloom. Their flashlights flickered a bit longer before disappearing as well. Rhada continued to track them on her sensor display.

"You're about halfway there, but you are veering too much to the right," she said.

"Can't help it, a lot of big boulders here, we have to go around." A few more minutes passed and the blips for the party nearly merged with the blip for the probe.

"You're right on top of it," said Rhada. "Look around."

"Nothing here that I can see," said Greg. "Just a bunch of rocks and…wait a second. Okay, we've got something here. I have to clear off some the dirt and gravel. Yes, definitely some metal, but this thing is nearly buried."

"Can you dig it out?" asked Chtak anxiously.

"We'll give it a try."

It took nearly an hour, with much grumbling and cursing, but eventually the party was reeling in its line and returning. Greg cradled the prize in his powerful arms.

"All right, we are in the lock. You want this inside?"

"Please."

The lock cycled and the inner door opened. Greg waddled inside and carefully placed his burden down where Chtak instructed him. It did not look like much. A dented and dirty metal cylinder with a bent spike on one end and a few knobby protrusions. Chtak treated it like pure gold and strapped it down with care.

"Phew!" exclaimed Rhada. "What's that smell?"

"The local atmosphere, I'm afraid," said Chtak, absently. He was already examining the probe with a hand scanner. Greg sneezed explosively three times in succession.

"Can we go home now, Chtak?" asked Greg. "I don't think this place agrees with me."

"I'm afraid not. We need at least one more of these."

"Another one?" said Rhada in dismay. "What for? What the hell's so important about that thing?"

"Find me another one and I may just tell you."

"Right," snorted Rhada. "Strap yourselves in. Going up."

The second contact only took twenty minutes to come. "Got another one, Chtak. Same metallic signature, but no energy readings this time. You still want it?"

"Indeed yes. That may be of significance, too."

"All right, down we go again. It doesn't look as rough in this area, but hang on anyway."

This time it was much easier. It was in daylight and the wind was calm. It only took Greg ten minutes to return with another probe.

"It does not appear damaged does it?" asked Chtak with great interest.

"Beats me," answered Greg between sneezes. "Looks in better shape than the first one. Can we go now?"

"I think so. Thank you very much for your efforts."

"Not so fast, Chtak. You promised us an explanation!" said Rhada. "Just what are those things?"

"An answer," said Chtak. "Perhaps an answer."

CHAPTER NINE

Commander Jaqueline Ellsworth looked at the thing lying on the conference table and wrinkled her nose at the faintly unpleasant smell it seemed to be exuding. The others in the conference room could obviously smell it, too. Commodore Shusterman motioned to her to begin.

"Well, Lieutenant, I believe you owe us an explanation," she said to Chtak'Chr. "What is this and why was it so important to bring it here?"

"Of course, Commander," replied the Survey Officer. "But before I answer you, I wish to warn you against getting any false hopes from what I tell you. I believe this to be a discovery of considerable significance, but it will not solve our immediate difficulties."

"Very well, your warning is noted. Now what is this?"

"It is a sensor probe from Leavitte V. As you might know, the fifth planet of this system was scheduled for terraforming, but the war forced that project to be put on hold. However, some initial work was done. Several bacteria strains were added to the atmosphere, along with some of the other preliminary steps. As part of that project, a number of sensor probes were placed at various locations on the planet's surface. These recorded and relayed information on the weather and climate back to Leavitte IV. This is one of those probes."

"I see," said Commodore Shusterman. "But I fail to see the great significance."

"The significance, Commodore, is that this probe was constructed with nano-circuitry—and it is still working."

"What!?" said a dozen voices from around the table.

"How?" demanded Shusterman.

"I have a theory, sir," said Chtak. "I must emphasize that it is just a theory, and again caution you against over-optimism. While this device is still functioning, it is unlikely there will be many other devices throughout the League that still are. The disaster remains as we feared. However, I do believe I know how the disaster was arranged."

"Arranged? You mean...?"

"Yes, Commodore, it was deliberate sabotage. Of that I am nearly certain. I also believe that it was sabotage undertaken by the Darj'Nang, although I am slightly less certain of that."

"And this probe tells you that?" asked Commander van Rossum.

"Yes, Commander. Fortunately, there are some records of the terraforming effort that have survived. Those, along with information from my... from other sources have allowed me to piece together this puzzle."

"I'm aware of those 'other sources', Lieutenant," said Ellsworth with a frown. "I don't want you consulting them again without my permission."

"Yes, ma'am. I'm sorry, but I didn't want to bother you," said Chtak.

"Next time, bother me."

"Yes, ma'am."

"So explain this 'puzzle', Lieutenant," said Shusterman.

"Yes, sir. This probe was manufactured twenty-two years ago; eight years after nano-circuitry became the standard and three years before the start of the war with the Darj'Nang. The probes were set in place and then left to perform their tasks automatically. Once a week they send their collected data back to Leavitte IV. It was those signals that our communications officer detected. They required no instructions or communications from their creators to do their jobs. It was that isolation that allowed this probe to survive. While it sent messages, it never received any and that was the key."

"The key to what?"

"Commodore, the current disaster was caused by an ASP. By an 'Aggressive Software Particle'. A deliberately constructed program with the purpose of destroying computer equipment. That ASP was spread throughout the League and it was designed to strike when and how it did. It passed from device to device, multiplying itself many-fold as it went. Only devices that were completely isolated could have avoided infection."

Jaq Ellsworth knew that her mouth was hanging open, but then everyone else's was, too, so it made no difference. The silence dragged on for at least fifteen seconds before Commander Van Rossum exploded.

"Lieutenant, that's impossible! We have safeguards—hundreds of safeguards—against any such thing!"

"Yes, that is true, but this particular ASP was of a type totally unlike anything ever created before. It was undetectable by our normal means and it was utterly deadly when it went into action."

"How do you know this?" demanded Shusterman. "You said this probe wasn't infected; how could it tell you about this 'ASP'?"

"The ASP itself was theorized by a Doctor Ejatsnardpul almost thirty years ago. I... remembered reading his article when I was in school. Doctor Ejatsnardpul was an Andlarian scientist who was involved in the original research that led to the nano-circuitry. The article was more of a theoretical exercise than a real warning, but he postulated that a certain set of commands executed within a circuit could set up a harmonic that would destroy it. The results would be entirely consistent with what we have seen happen here."

"That does not really prove anything, Lieutenant," said Van Rossum.

"By itself, no, you are right, Commander. But there is other evidence. We also recovered an additional probe. This was part of a second series that were placed on Leavitte V fifteen years ago—four years after the war had started and shortly before the terraforming project was halted. These probes were identical to the first and they were just as isolated as the first batch—and yet this probe has failed. All of its nano-circuitry has been destroyed, exactly like all the rest. Clearly this probe was infected *before* it was dispatched. This gives us a time frame in which the ASP infection occurred."

"I see," said Shusterman. "Sometime either shortly before the start of the war or in the first few years after it started."

"Yes, and one other item of considerable significance is that Andlara, Doctor Ejatsnardpul's home planet was overrun by the Darj'Nang during the war's opening stages. The Doctor must have been captured and enslaved along with the rest of his people."

"My God, and he was an Andlarian," hissed Shusterman.

"Yes," said Chtak grimly.

Ellsworth shuddered. The Darj'Nang's mental control affected different races to different degrees. Humans could be controlled directly, but they became near-zombies, obeying orders, but showing no initiative or imagination. And the effects wore off quickly. Other species, like the Andlarians, could be turned into loyal, obedient, enthusiastic slaves who would *eagerly* serve their masters—permanently. The League had discovered this the hard way when planets they were supposedly liberating turned out to be filled with people who would now fight to the death for the Darj'Nang. Andlara had been one of them...

"So you are suggesting that this Doctor Ejatsnardpul created the ASP for the Darj'Nang?"

"Him or some of his associates, Andlara had an outstanding research community."

"I still have trouble believing the League could be infected the way you propose, Lieutenant," said Van Rossum. "Surely someone would have noticed this ASP with such a long incubation period."

"Not necessarily, sir. The Doctor's article theorized that the ASP could embed itself in the hardware of the circuit itself, 'hibernating' and becoming virtually undetectable. >From time to time it would produce copies of itself and send them out with normal communications to infect other circuits. I don't have any details about how it would do this, or how it would remain undetected while in transit, Doctor Ejatsnardpul himself was only theorizing at that point, but if such a thing could be created the effects would be... well, they would be what we are seeing."

"But why such a long... incubation period?" asked the Commodore. "It sounds like this thing got far enough through the League to even be infecting those climate probes in only a few years. Why did they wait until they had already lost the war to activate it?"

"I don't know, sir," said Chtak. "I can only speculate on the thinking of the Darj'Nang. By its nature, the ASP would have to have the execution date built-in to it and changing it later would have been very difficult. Perhaps they wanted the long incubation period so that if the war went well for them they would have time to release some 'cure' for the ASP before their new conquests were all devastated by it. Perhaps they simply did not realize it would spread so quickly. But it would have spread very quickly, indeed. The nano-circuitry was designed to be in almost constant communication with other circuits. For example, Lieutenant Kinney can tell you that on more modern ships the inventory of items in the hold is automatic. The main computer periodically sends out a signal that prompts every item to answer back, giving an exact count. If even one infected item were put in the hold, it would infect the main computer the first time the inventory was taken and then the main computer would infect *all* the items the next time. In fact, I believe it would not have taken long for the ASP to have gotten back to the manufacturing facilities. After a while, the circuits would be *made* with the infection already inside them."

"Good God," muttered the Commodore. "Those bastards, those murdering, slaving bastards."

"Commodore," said Lieutenant Boshko, "this is a very interesting theory, and Lieutenant Chtak'Chr may be correct about the Darj'Nang having done this to us. But the critical thing is that there are still some working nano-circuits. We may have a chance to repair some of our devices and ultimately recover from this mess!"

Jaq Ellsworth glanced over at Chtak. His whiskers seemed to droop. In spite of his warning not to raise false hopes, his information seemed to be doing exactly that.

"Wouldn't these circuits just self-destruct as soon as they encountered the ASP again?" asked Van Rossum.

"I don't believe so, sir," said Chtak. "I have removed several circuits from this probe and had a variety of our working computers run signals through them without a problem. I am theorizing that the nature of the ASP irrevocably linked it with the nano-circuitry it infected. It could not actually be 'stored' anywhere else and so when the nano-circuits died, so did the ASP."

"Well, that's great! Then if we can get more circuits they should be safe to use," said Boshko.

"That may be so, sir, but getting the circuits will be extremely difficult. As I said, please do not raise your hopes too high. It may be possible to salvage a number of nano-circuits from devices like these probes. There are probably a number of such isolated devices throughout the League, but finding them will be a long and difficult process and it will only yield a limited number of circuits."

"But we can surely make more somehow!"

"How, sir? The factories that made the circuits were, themselves, dependent on the circuits. Except for the initial pilot plant—which I seriously doubt still exists—they will all be inoperable. Even the instructions for how to *make* the circuits have probably been lost. I do not wish to seem defeatist, sir, but the problems we face are enormous."

"Could we buy them from outside?"

"Doubtful, sir. No other culture has circuits of this sophistication and we only began issuing licenses for foreign manufacturers a few years ago. The prototypes and equipment we sold were doubtlessly already infected."

"I'm seeing why you told us not to get our hopes up, Lieutenant," growled Shusterman. "What about the old molecular circuits? Could we substitute them?"

"For some purposes, perhaps, sir. But I do not know of any manufacturing facilities in the League. They were superseded so long ago... Perhaps in some out of the way place."

"Could we buy *them* from foreign suppliers?"

"That could be our best option, sir," said Chtak. "Many other races have circuits with similar capabilities. A substitute might possibly be found."

"But that brings us back to the trade problem, Commodore," said Boshko. "Like we were discussing earlier: we don't have a great deal to trade in exchange. And once it's realized how badly crippled we are, a lot of outsiders may prefer conquest to helping us get back on our feet."

"Surely the *Dlerdanji* would be willing to help us out," said Van Rossum.

"They probably would," said Shusterman, "and we might be able to get enough from them to get back on our feet here. It is certainly worth a try. But I imagine it will take some time to work out the technical requirements and actually get the chips. If other powers get wind of what we are trying to do, they might even try to stop it. In any case we are going to have our backs to the wall for a long time."

"But, as you say, sir, it is worth a try," said Boshko. "The Dlerdanji should be coming back here in a few weeks. We should get our technical requirements ready and see if they would be willing to help."

"Yes, we will do that. Commander Van Rossum, Lieutenant Chtak'Chr, that will be your assignment."

"Yes, sir."

"As for the rest of us..."

Jaq Ellsworth listened as the meeting went on. She was impressed with how Shusterman kept the discussions to the point and gave out assignments. *Could I do this?* She was doubtful. Of course, Shusterman had a lot more years of experience. Still, she compared his performance with her own back on Flemington and she had to admit hers had left a lot to desire. She had a hell of a lot to learn.

As the meeting progressed, she felt a little better. There seemed to be some chance that they could buy what they needed to get a fresh start. But it was still going to be a mess. It wasn't like they could just go back to where they were before this disaster struck. They would have to rebuild a great deal of their industry to use the different circuits. It might be years before they could start building complicated things like starships. In the meantime the rest of the League would have collapsed completely and the outsiders would be sweeping through. Would they have the time to do it?

It was frustrating as hell. Equipment lying around all over the place and all of it was useless. And some of it was completely ready to use if they could replace the nano-circuits. She remembered longingly the five ships sitting in the repair docks at Flemington. Their fusion plants had been off-line so they had not even been damaged from a containment failure. Five ships, and one of them a battlecruiser! If they just had the damn chips to put in they would all be usable again. Replacing all the chips would be a hell of a job, it was true, but still a damn sight easier than building new ships from scratch!

But there wasn't much choice that she could see. Chtak was right that every factory that produced the nano-circuits was surely just as useless as those ships. For any to have survived they would have had to be completely isolated and out of communications for nearly twenty years. There would be no place like that. Why would there be? Planets communicated with ships and ships with planets. And there was the HyperCom, too. The Darj'Nang were too damn clever. Their ASP would have been spread everywhere by now. Everywhere except to the Back of Beyond… Ellsworth suddenly froze.

The Back of Beyond…? The phrase conjured up the image of her, a much younger her, staring for endless hours into a blank sensor display. It came back with remarkable clarity. *Wait a second…*

No. It was impossible. Wasn't it? That was so long ago and… An electric shock seemed to course through her.

Jaq looked around the conference room. Everyone was still discussing their plans. She suddenly had the feeling if she moved a muscle everyone would suddenly stop and look at her. Very slowly she activated her computer terminal and did a few quick inquiries. There wasn't much information on what she was looking for, but she had not expected much. And nothing she did find destroyed the ridiculous idea that was taking shape and growing in her head. Finally, it had swollen to a size that demanded she put it out on the table before her brain exploded.

"Commodore."

The conversation stopped and now everyone *was* looking at her.

"Yes, Commander?"

"I've had an… idea. Commander Van Rossum, Lieutenant Chtak, if we were to find a source for nano-chips, it would greatly speed our recovery efforts, would it not?"

"Yes, indeed. Almost all our equipment could be made functional again," said Chtak.

"Except for things that were actually damaged during the failure, like the fusion plants," added Van Rossum. "And it would be a considerable task to replace all those circuits, but still a lot better than trying to start over again!"

"Why do you ask, Commander?" said Shusterman. "You have a secret cache of these things salted away?" He was smiling, but there was an intense spark of interest in his eyes.

"Maybe I do, sir," said Ellsworth. *Here we go!*

"What do you mean?"

"Sir, are you familiar with the sector base on Tractenberg IIIc?"

"Not really; that's over in the Sagittarius Quadrant, isn't it?"

"Yes, sir. Here, let me call it up on the chart." Ellsworth activated the holographic display and brought up the star map they had been looking at earlier. The map of the Star League with a glowing blue edge to its borders hovered over the table. She typed in a few commands. Leavitte appeared and then another glowing speck, two thirds of the way around from there. The other speck was beyond the blue boundary line.

"That's Tractenberg," she said.

"What about it, Commander?"

"Shortly before the war with the Darj'Nang began we were building a full sector base on Tractenberg to support the League's expansion into this region. It had just barely become operational when the Darj'Nang came busting in on us. Tractenberg wasn't directly in their path, but they hit it anyway. Neither side was entirely sure of the geography of the other's space at that point, I guess. Anyway, they hit the base and destroyed the orbital facilities. But before they could take out the dirtside installations, a counterattack drove them off again. Our commander on the spot decided that the base was too exposed and damaged to try and hold, so he evacuated the personnel and pulled out before the Darj'Nang could attack again.

"But they didn't attack again. The main theater of the war was shifting further east and Tractenberg was too far away for anyone to worry about. I'm familiar with all this because one of my first assignments after graduation was aboard a light cruiser assigned with patrolling this region. We weren't interested in Tractenberg anymore, but the high command wanted to know if the enemy—or anyone else—was. We would do a silent drift-through about once every six months to see if there was any sign of activity. There never was. Some of the most boring duty I ever had, sir."

"I'm not sure I see what you are getting at, Commander," said Shusterman.

"What I'm getting at, sir, is that this was a full sector base and that it has been sitting there—completely abandoned and isolated—for almost twenty years. Since before Lieutenant Chtak'Chr's ASP was released!"

"You're suggesting the equipment there may still be intact, Commander?" asked Lieutenant Boshko excitedly.

"It is a possibility. The base was evacuated very rapidly and there was certainly no time to remove any significant equipment."

"But you said all the orbital facilities were destroyed. That would have taken care of almost all the really useful things, Commander. The factories and shipyards..."

"Not necessarily, Lieutenant. It was a Type IV base—believe me, I got real familiar with the specs on that base!—much of it was underground. And heavily fortified. I believe the preliminary surveys of that region had indicated a number of potentially dangerous neighbors so it was decided to go the full route with the base. There could be a lot of stuff down there that's still intact."

"After all this time?" asked Shusterman. "You were there a long while ago, Commander. A lot could happen between then and now."

"True, sir, but perhaps not that much. I met an old friend a few years back and he was telling me that his own ship had pulled that same duty just four years ago. We compared notes and it sounded like no has been there since the start of the war."

Shusterman frowned and shook his head. "You've thrown me a bit of a curve here, Commander! I presume you are suggesting we send an expedition there?"

"That was a thought I had, yes, sir."

"Commodore," said Van Rossum, "a Type IV base would normally have full manufacturing capabilities, including the machinery to produce nano-circuits."

"And a fully intact reference computer, sir!" said Chtak eagerly. "Twenty years out of date, to be sure, but that's still better than what we have now."

"Settle down, people. We have no clue what might still be there or what condition it may be in. Still, this is extremely interesting. But the only ship we have capable of making such an extended journey is *Gilgamesh*. That would leave us awfully exposed here while you were gone. And look at the distance: over six hundred light years. It would take almost four months just to get there. Probably a year before you could get back. I'm going to have to give this some serious thought. I think we have covered about everything else we needed to for now. Let's adjourn until tomorrow. Thank you, everyone."

They got to their feet and began filtering out of the compartment. Jaq went over to Chtak'Chr.

"That was a good job, Lieutenant. Well worth the use of the cutter."

"Thank you, ma'am. Do you think he'll send us to Tractenberg?"

Ellsworth tilted her head and raised an eyebrow.

"What choice does he have?"

CHAPTER TEN

"So what do you think of all this, Mr. Gossage," asked Jaq Ellsworth.

"All of what, ma'am?"

"This expedition. This voyage to the other side of nowhere. What does the crew think of it?"

The Chief stopped his packing and looked at her. They were standing in the Captain's cabin—her cabin. A clutter of half-filled storage containers surrounded them.

"They seem to be pretty excited about it, ma'am. It's given them some hope, I think."

"Hope. That's a nice word. We haven't heard it much lately."

"No, ma'am."

"But I was lying to you Mr. Gossage; what I really wanted to know was what you—and the crew—thinks about me moving into this cabin?"

"It is the captain's cabin and you're the captain now, ma'am."

"Yes, that's true—legally. But what's legal isn't always what's right. Or what people think is right. I know most of the crew thought the galaxy of Captain Liu-Chen. And some of them think I make a pretty poor substitute."

"It will take some getting used to, ma'am. He was the skipper for a long time. But I think you impressed a lot of people when you trashed those Sarlangians the way you did."

"Hmmm. You were steward for Captain Liu-Chen for a long time, too, weren't you?"

"Yes, ma'am, over fifteen years."

"Do you have any problem working for me, now? I certainly won't hold it against you if you do, so speak freely. In fact, I've never had a personal steward before, so I'm sure I could make out well enough."

Gossage stood motionless, still holding Liu-Chen's folded dress tunic above the open storage container. She could see that he was blushing slightly, which seemed very odd for a grizzled veteran like him.

"I... don't have a problem with it ma'am. I think we could work together—and I'm too old to start doing a real job again."

Jaq did a double-take and realized that Gossage was smiling, ever so slightly. A joke. He could joke with her. That was good.

"They call you "The Goose", don't they?" asked Ellsworth.

"Uh, yes, ma'am, but "Chief" would be fine. Really." His blush had deepened a bit and Jaq resolved to find out the whole story behind that nickname someday. Some other day.

"Okay, then, you've still got a job, Chief. I suppose I do need a steward as captain." She paused and looked at the man for a long moment. "I think I could really use a friend, too." He blinked in surprise and she instantly regretted her statement. It was a true statement, but it was too soon to be saying things like that.

"I'm at your service, ma'am," he said finally. Noncommittal, but that was okay, too.

"Well," she said, clearing her throat, "I have to go meet with the Commodore. Once you've put all this away, you can bring my gear from my old cabin. It's all packed."

"Yes, ma'am. I would have packed that for you, ma'am."

"I know, but old habits and all. I'm afraid I may try your patience for a while, Chief."

"I'll manage, ma'am."

Ellsworth smiled and left the cabin. It looked as though this might work. One thing anyway. The smile left her face as she thought of all the other things that might not work. *Including what's coming up.*

She reached the main conference room and went inside. It was empty. She checked the time and saw that she was a few minutes early. The Commodore wasn't up from dirtside yet. She sat down and called up the ship's roster on a screen. She wanted to review it again before Shusterman arrived. But her thoughts kept straying to the upcoming mission. It had been four weeks since she arrived back at Leavitte and the situation looked far better than she would have believed possible when she left. The Dlerdanji had come back with three packed cargo ships carrying the equipment for two fusion plants and the power distribution gear to go along with them. They had also brought communicators and food synthesizers and loads of basic tools and computers. A treasure throve. The one fusion plant was already being assembled in Leavitte's largest city. Shusterman had decided to send the second to Flemington. Order had largely been restored on Leavitte. Enough old air cars had been found to give the Marine battalion stationed there mobility and martial law was in effect. The people were living mostly off the large herds of a local cattle-like creature that had been driven into the cities. Once the food synthesizers were operating there would be a stable food supply—although the Dlerdanji synthesizers would only be able to provide a bland survival ration.

So the immediate crisis was being dealt with, but the bigger one remained. Ships from several other bordering planets—plus a number of unknowns--had come snooping about and it was obvious that they had not expected to encounter *Gilgamesh*. They left quickly when they realized Leavitte was not defenseless. She didn't want to think about what was happening on other League planets which had no garrison.

How long would it be before someone showed up who was too tough to scare off—and too tough to beat? As soon as Thom Downs and *Steadfast* returned from his circuit of subsector bases *Gilgamesh* would leave for Tractenberg, leaving Leavitte even more exposed to attack. It was a frightening and all too probable possibility. And an attacker wouldn't even have to come in with weapons blazing. If a major force of Traglarians, say, were to show up and announce they were there to help out the League during these difficult times, what could they do about it? Fight? And lose. Accept, and before long the Traglarians would be in control. And the Traglarians were far from the worst possibility. They might take over, but they would neither enslave nor exterminate the population. There were other groups out there who would gladly do either. Ellsworth sighed. What the hell were they going to do?

She looked up as Commodore Shusterman came in. She got to her feet. He had his aide, Lieutenant Boshko, and a man wearing the uniform of a lieutenant commander with him.

"Good morning, Commander," said Shusterman. "I'd like you to meet Commander Karl Bradley."

"Pleased to meet you, Commander," said Ellsworth. She extended her hand and he took it in a firm grasp. He was a bit taller than she and had a nice face, she thought. A shock of unruly brown hair and a strange, quirky smile lent him a mischievous look.

Shusterman gestured for them to be seated. "I've read your memo, Commander, and I agree that we need to do some shuffling and reassigning before we send you off to Tractenberg. The first thing, however, is your own status. I'm breveting you captain, effective immediately."

"I... uh, thank you, sir." Ellsworth hoped she didn't look as surprised as she felt.

"The brevet is just for form's sake. As far as anyone's concerned, you're a captain. I'm not sure why I'm even worrying about form at this point anyway. It's not like anyone 'higher up' is going to object."

"Yes, sir."

"As for this other matter with Commander Florkowski, I don't like doing it, but I can't argue with you. A captain has to have faith in his exec and vice versa. It is obvious that that sort of rapport does not exist between you and Florkowski and it seems unlikely that it will develop given time. Therefore, I'm assigning Commander Bradley as your first officer. I'll be breveting him to full commander, so there will be no seniority problems between him and Florkowski. Brad has been on my planning staff for two years and was scheduled to be rotated back to shipboard duty soon anyway. He's got a lot of shipboard experience and I think he'll do a good job on *Gilgamesh*."

"That sounds excellent, sir," said Ellsworth. "Welcome aboard, Commander." She smiled, partly in welcome, and partly in relief. She had sent Shusterman a memo telling him flatly that Charles Florkowski was not going to work as her executive officer. She hated doing it, but it had to be done. She was very happy that the Commodore was seeing things her way.

"Thank you, Captain," said Bradley with a smile. "I look forward to serving with you."

"Now what do you want to do about Florkowski, Commander? You have a number of empty slots in your T.O. already and with us fitting out that captured Sarlangian ship I don't have anyone else with that sort of experience to replace him. Do you want to keep him aboard or swap him for the most experienced lieutenant I can find you? Normally a transfer would be in order, but since he was never officially made the exec, it would not be impossible to keep him."

Ellsworth bit her lip. She would dearly like to get him off the ship, but there was no denying he was good at his job. And she did feel a little bit guilty about doing this to him. He had wanted the exec position as badly as she had wanted her own command. But she just did not trust him for that and that was answer enough. Still...

"If he's willing to stay on as second officer I could use him, sir," she said. "He's been on *Gilgamesh* a lot longer than me. He knows the ship and the crew very well. He could be an asset." *Or he could be a real pain in the assets. Well, it will be up to him.*

"All right, we'll give him the choice," said Shusterman. "Will you talk with him or do you want me to?"

"I'll do it, sir."

"If he turns it down, tell him I'll find him a dirtside assignment for the time being. Unfortunately, a shipboard assignment isn't going to be possible since he's clearly not ready for a command of his own and yet he actually outranks everyone I have on hand except Downs and Bradley here."

"I understand, sir."

"As for the rest of your crew, you were already under-strength even before the 'losses' you took at Flemington. I want to fill you up to as close to full strength as possible before you start out. You aren't going to be able to pick up any replacements en route and there's no telling what you'll run into on the way or once you are there.

"I'm using all of *Daring's* survivors as the core of the crew for the Sarlangian ship, so there's no help there. But there are a number of people from the station and dirtside we can probably spare. Some of them will be pretty green, I'm afraid, but you ought to be able to whip them into shape on the trip to Tractenberg."

"Yes, sir. Thank you, sir," said Ellsworth, nodding. It would be good to have the extra hands, and they also might help dilute the feeling of *Gilgamesh* still being Liu-Chen's ship.

"Also, I'm going to beef up your Marine contingent. You've got one platoon now and room for another. Are you satisfied with Lieutenant Quatrock?"

"Yes, sir, he's a good officer."

"Very well, I'll take a platoon with an officer who's junior to him and he can be in overall command. There is also a detachment of combat engineers dirtside and I'm going to steal a couple of them for you, too, although God knows we need them down there."

"Sir, is it possible to scare up some people with manufacturing experience? Assuming the facilities on Tractenberg are operational, we'll need someone who knows how to run them."

"Good point. Lieutenant, put out some feelers with our people and the local population and see who might be available."

"Yes, sir," said Boshko, making a note.

"Finally, we need to discuss your route to Tractenberg," continued Shusterman. He touched the display controls and once again a holographic map of the League appeared above the table. Leavitte and

Tractenberg were picked out and then a glowing line connected them together.

"A straight line route takes you along the edge of League space for most of the journey. Normally, that would be a good thing, but not this time. You will need to refuel at least twice along the way and I'm not hopeful that you'll find much at the League worlds."

Ellsworth nodded. Almost every planet with interstellar contact would have a fuel station in orbit. But without power for refrigeration, the liquid hydrogen in the storage tanks would slowly rise in temperature and eventually boil off through the safety relief valves. The tanks were well insulated and it would take months for that to happen, but by the time *Gilgamesh* could reach any of the potential fuel stops many months would have passed. Leavitte's own fuel dump had only been stabilized with the Dlerdanji's help at the last minute.

"You do have a cutter with fuel scoops available, so you could refuel from gas giants, but that is a lengthy process. We don't have the luxury of time to waste. Therefore, I think you will have to take an alternate route." Shusterman touched the controls again and the line bent in several spots and now showed a curving route that was mostly outside the League's boundaries.

"Your first stop would be Paramar. The Dlerdanji have a trading post there and we can get fuel from them. After that, things get tricky. You'll have to skirt the edge of Beresferd space and then make a stop at Freeport. I don't like it, but there isn't any place else even remotely as safe."

Ellsworth frowned. Freeport. She had never been there, but it was a hellhole from all she had heard. A safe haven for pirates and raiders and smugglers. But it was neutral ground, too. They would sell or trade anything there and the locals had sufficient naval force to make sure everyone stayed polite. Still, they would not be thrilled to see a League warship there...

"The Dlerdanji should fuel us without a problem, sir. How will we pay for it at Freeport? I doubt League credits will have much buying power by the time we get there."

"No, you are correct. We are going to have to put together some sort of cargo for you to trade with. There are things that have value without electronic parts. We are going to have to collect whatever we can. Make a note of that, Lieutenant."

"Yes, sir."

"But even with the stop at Freeport, you will arrive at Tractenberg with almost dry tanks. You'll probably have to do some fuel scooping there."

"Not a problem, sir. There is a gas giant in that system. In fact, the base is on a planet orbiting a gas giant. It may take some time to refuel, but I imagine we'll be there at least a couple of months sorting things out. But that brings up the next question: Assuming we get there and do find the base and there are working factories. What do we do then?"

"Yes, it's a good question. My initial reaction would be to have you cram your ship to the deckhead with every nano-chip you can produce and then hustle back here as fast as you can. Once you get back and let us know you are in business, we can send other ships to pick up more. And then we can get things working again here and start work at Flemington to get their factories and shipyards working. Then try to get a few of the intermediate bases back in operation so we have fueling stops between here and Tractenberg. That's my initial reaction. But then I think about the time it's going to take for you to get back and what could happen here while you are gone. It would be a nightmare for you to come back with the goods only to discover that we had been overrun here."

Shusterman shook his head. "And there are other League worlds much closer to Tractenberg. Maybe you should stop at one of those first. Get some other ships operational. But then it could be years before you can send anything here. I don't know, Captain. It's a hell of a problem. I think I'm just going to have to give you discretionary orders. Try to come back, but act as the situation dictates."

Great, thought Ellsworth with a chill. *Act as the situation dictates.* That left her with far more latitude than she would ever want.

"I'll write it up in more detail before you leave, Captain, but that's going to be the gist of it. You are going to have a hell of a job on your hands. But enough of that for now, Lieutenant, call up our personnel roster and let's fill out the Captain's crew...."

"So that's the situation, Commander: you can stay on here as Second Officer or you can transfer to a dirtside assignment."

"That's not much of a choice...Captain."

"Perhaps not, but it's the only one either of us are going to get." Jaq Ellsworth stared at Charles Florkowski from across her desk. She had explained the situation to him and laid out his choices. She was expecting an explosion. She had a Marine standing guard outside her door—just in case. But Florkowski did not seem like he was going to explode. In fact, he seemed strangely subdued. Maybe it was finally sinking in that he was no longer Captain Liu-Chen's fair-haired boy and that he was not holding a winning hand anymore. He did not seem at all happy, but he was keeping his anger in check.

"I'm sorry things didn't work out better between us, but I hope you can understand I need a first officer I can… work with." She had almost said: 'trust', but that wouldn't do. To have said she didn't trust him would have been to imply things that no officer should ever say to another. But even unsaid, they both knew it was there.

"I do understand the situation, Captain. Stay here in my old position or go dirtside and possibly never set foot on a ship again." There was bitterness in his voice and Ellsworth really couldn't blame him for that. In his place she would have been bitter, too. But she had briefly gone over some of the efficiency reports Liu-Chen had filed on the man and she was sure she was making the right decision. Florkowski had performed adequately, but it was pretty obvious Liu-Chen had doubts about moving him up to positions of higher responsibility. She would have to look at those reports more closely when she had the time. Florkowski was still frowning at her desktop.

"I think I'd like to stay aboard… ma'am," he said at last.

"Very well, that's the way it will be then. You've done some good work aboard *Gilgamesh*. I hope when we've had more time working together things might… improve."

"Yes, ma'am."

"That's all, Commander."

He got up and left. Ellsworth breathed a sigh of relief and took the gauss pistol out of her tunic pocket and put it into her desk drawer.

Gregory Sadgipour dismissed the platoon and turned away. It was his platoon now—at least in theory—and he was proud of it. Scared as hell, but proud, too. He saw his platoon sergeant walking across the ready room and intercepted him.

"Sarge?"

"Yes, sir?" said Sergeant John McGill, halting and turning to face him.

"I… uh, the men looked sharp today. Good job."

"Thank you, sir; we try."

"I'm looking forward to working with you—as the platoon leader, I mean. I know we've worked together before with Lieutenant Quatrock leading the platoon, but this will be a bit different, I guess."

"I suppose so, sir, but you can count on us to get the job done." McGill was smiling at him. He always smiled at him and Greg knew what he was thinking: 'Stay out of the way and everything will be fine, I don't need some young shavetail telling me how to run *my* platoon'. *But it's my platoon, dammit! I have a job to do, too!*

"Was there anything else, sir?"

"Uh, no, carry on."

"Yes, sir." McGill walked off. Greg sighed. With the second platoon of Marines on board, Lieutenant Quatrock was the acting 'company' commander and Greg had been given command of the first platoon. He really felt like he should be doing something active to lay claim to his command, but there wasn't much to do, really. McGill had the platoon running like a well-oiled machine. The only problem was with the weapons and there wasn't anything anyone could do about that. With that thought, Greg walked over to the armory and punched the access code to gain entry. The duty corporal nodded to him. The door slid back and he stepped inside.

All of the Marines' most modern weaponry was useless, but they had managed to scrounge up enough old weapons to arm everyone. Mostly old gauss rifles, but a lot of stunners, lasers, and even chemical slug throwers. One missile launcher and a bunch of miscellaneous grenades made up the rest of it. They were seriously short on scanners and detection gear, too. And all of the power armor was useless. He looked longingly at the rows of armored suits hanging in their racks. They still had them—plus all the weapons—in hopes that they could get the parts to reactivate them once they reached their destination.

"Quite a collection of relics, isn't it?"

Greg turned and saw that 2nd Lieutenant Doug Rawlins, commander of the newly assigned detachment of combat engineers, was standing there.

"Sure is. Hope we don't have to use them."

"What? Pass up a chance at combat? Why, us Marines would prefer not to use any weapons but our bare hands—or in our case our shovels, you know that!"

"Oh, right. How could I forget? How are you folks getting settled in, by the way?"

"Not too bad. The barracks is a little crowded, but at least there's light and running water. We had to fight the rest of the battalion to get the privilege of shipping out with you folks."

"I'll bet."

"Speaking of settling in…" Rawlins gave Greg a sly look. "What's the story with the ensign in the junior officers' berth with us?"

"You mean Rhada?' asked Greg, startled.

"That's the one. She is seriously cute, in case you haven't noticed. Is she spoken for?"

"Uh…" Greg was really startled now and he had no clue what to say.

"Actually, I guess I'm asking if *you* had her spoken for," continued Rawlins with a smile. "I've got no problem stealing her away from some Navy-type, but not from a fellow Marine—I do have a few principles!"

"She and I are friends… "

"Friends or *'friends'*?"

What kind of question was that? Did he mean were Rhada and he having sex? Were they in love? Greg knew that the customs and moral outlook varied enormously throughout the League, but he came from a place where you didn't ask questions like that. He knew that Rhada's home planet was pretty strait-laced, too. He had liked Rawlins when he met him, but he was having second thoughts now. And with a shock, he suddenly felt jealous that this stranger had set his sights on Rhada. Greg had not made any claim—had not said anything at all. But he liked Rhada a lot. And she was awfully cute—in a string-bean sort of way. The silence had gone on for several seconds.

"Well, if you figure it out, let me know, will you?" said Rawlins with a laugh. He turned and left Greg staring after him.

Captain Jaq Ellsworth walked the length and breadth of her ship. One last inspection before departure. She was sporting captain's tabs on her collar now and everyone seemed to be getting used to the fact that she was the skipper. Even Florkowski was not being a problem.

She paused as she came abreast the hatch leading to the Number Four photon cannon mount. Then she turned and entered. The people inside snapped to attention when they saw her. She ran her eyes over the gunners and their equipment. She stopped when she came to the mount commander.

"Everything in order, Ensign?" she asked.

"Yes, ma'am!"

Ellsworth smiled. She had taken a special interest in Ensign McClerndon since the incident with the deserters. The young woman seemed to have recovered from the assault, but she was keeping an eye on her. Her gaze drifted over to the bulkhead beside McClerndon's command station to the newly painted 'kill' record. Just two days ago Ellsworth had presided over the ceremonies awarding the kills made during the action against the Sarlangians. It was slightly ridiculous—even unfair—to award individual weapons mounts 'kills' when the whole ship was contributing to the victory, but this was a tradition that dated back centuries and Ellsworth wasn't about to tamper with it. And for a ship as old as *Gilgamesh*, it would all even out in the end. The Number Two torpedo launcher, the other recipient, had a list as long as this mount's and every other weapon did, too. Anyway, it was good for morale.

"Carry on, Ensign."

"Yes, ma'am!"

Ellsworth left the mount and continued aft. Everything was in good order. The ship seemed more crowded than she had ever seen it. They had their full roster of three hundred now, plus almost sixty Marines. Add in a few supercargo and the place was downright packed. After touring the Marines' barracks, she encountered Lieutenant Chtak'Chr and a man in civilian clothes manhandling a lifter filled with crates through the main airlock. The Survey Officer looked far better than he had a few weeks ago. His pelt was sleek and glossy again and he looked almost plump.

"Still bringing things aboard, Lieutenant? We're shoving off in less than an hour."

"Yes, Captain, I'm aware of that. This is the last load. Some items Mister Haussler thought we should bring."

"I see. I hope you can find somewhere to store them."

"We'll manage, ma'am."

"How are you doing, Mister Haussler? Everything to your satisfaction?"

"Perfectly, Captain," said the civilian engineer. "A bit crowded, but with more than the comforts of home. I'll make out fine."

"I'm afraid we won't have much for you to do for quite a while. I hope you can keep yourself amused."

"The Lieutenant and I will be refining our contingency plans. That should keep us busy."

Ellsworth nodded and continued on her tour. She hoped the civilian technicians could adapt to military shipboard life—and that they would have something to do at the end of their journey.

Eventually her tour brought her back on the bridge. "Everything is ready for departure, Captain," said Commander Bradley as he vacated the command chair.

"Excellent. Miss Terletsky, put me through to Commodore Shusterman."

"Aye, ma'am. On the screen."

The main monitor lit up and there was Shusterman. He was smiling. "So you are on your way at last."

"Yes, sir."

"I guess I won't burden you with any 'we're-all-counting-on-you-speeches' or anything like that."

"Thank you, sir," said Ellsworth sincerely. "We'll do our best to get the job done and get back here as soon as we can."

"Can't ask for more. Good luck, Captain."

"Thank you, sir. *Gilgamesh*, requesting permission to undock and break orbit."

"Permission granted, *Gilgamesh*. Good luck and Godspeed."

Ellsworth nodded and then broke the connection.

"Helm, detach us from the station," she commanded.

"Aye, ma'am. Detaching…now." There was a slight jolt. "Activating thrusters. Moving away from the station at one meter per second squared." A minute went by and Jaq could see the station receding in the monitor.

We have passed the safety margin, ma'am," announced Ensign Bartlett. "We are free to maneuver."

"Very well. All ahead two-thirds."

"Aye, ma'am. Ahead at two-thirds power."

Gilgamesh's normal space drive clutched at the fabric of space and thrust the ship forward. The station dwindled quickly.

"Come to course one-three-five, by oh-two-eight," said Ellsworth.

"Aye, ma'am, turning to starboard."

"We're on our way," she whispered.

* * *

Two hours later *LSS Gilgamesh* passed the gravity well boundary and shortly after that transited to hyperspace. The ship and her crew had begun their quest.

CHAPTER ELEVEN

Captain Jaqueline Ellsworth stretched on the sofa and stifled a yawn. She had not intended to take a nap, but upon checking the time she saw she had slept for nearly an hour. She swung her legs around so she was sitting up and retrieved the book she had been reading from where it had fallen on the deck. Liu-Chen had an amazing collection of old paper books and she had not had them packed away with the rest of his things. She stood up and crossed over to her desk and touched a button.

"Bridge, Bradley," came the voice of her First Officer.

"Time to drop out, Brad?"

"Forty-two minutes, ma'am."

"Good. I'll be there shortly."

"Do you plan to go to GQ, ma'am?"

"Yes, I do."

"Very, good, we'll be ready."

Ellsworth closed the connection. Forty-two minutes until they reached Freeport. Forty-two minutes after two and a half months in hyper. It would be good to see the stars again. The stop at Paramar to refuel had been very brief and seemed like a very long time ago. At least that had gone smoothly enough. She hoped this stop would be as easy. *No chance of that. We're really going to have to be on our toes!*

She heard the door to her cabin slide open and saw Chief Gossage come in with a cup of coffee for her. It did not surprise her a bit. He always seemed to know what she wanted before she did herself.

"Thanks, Chief." She took a sip and smiled. "Perfect."

"Always aim to please, ma'am."

"And you always do. Don't see how I got along without a steward before."

"I'm sure you managed, ma'am."

"Ever been to Freeport, Chief?"

"Once, a long time ago, ma'am. Hell of a place then and it's probably worse now."

"So I've heard. Think we'll have any trouble getting fuel this time?"

"Dunno, ma'am. They say they'll sell anything to anyone who's got the money. But they've never liked the League and they've probably heard about our troubles. They might want to make more trouble for us just out of orneriness."

"They might at that. We'll have to be careful." She took another sip and then set it down. "Well, I have to go to the bridge. Better leave that here since we'll be going to GQ."

"I can put that in a battlecup for you, ma'am."

"Would you? That would be great. I'll get my vac suit while you're doing that."

She pulled her suit out of its locker and Gossage was back in an instant with the coffee in a secure, no-spill cup for her.

"Thanks. See you later."

She walked out of her quarters and acknowledged the salute of the Marine sentry. She reflected that she didn't really need the sentry anymore. The spirit of the ship was much improved and there had been no trouble. Florkowski was moody at times, but that was all. She hoped he was adjusting to the situation. She was half tempted to tell Quatrock to forget about the sentry on her door, but then there wasn't much for the Marines to do on a long trip like this, so he'd probably ask to keep the post anyway.

A few moments later she arrived on the bridge and stowed her vac suit in the container attached to her chair and clipped the cup into a holder. Bradley got up and moved over to the tactical station. "Dropout in twenty-nine minutes, ma'am," he said. She settled into her chair and checked over the status of the various stations. Everything was in order as she expected. The only thing to do on this trip had been to train and that was what they had done. Drill and drill and drill some more. There had been some grumbling at first—Liu-Chen had never let her drill as much as she wanted—but they had gotten used to it. The new crew members had been mostly assimilated by this time and it was a smoothly running team now. Ellsworth hardly ever thought about that shiny new destroyer anymore. And Bradley was working out better than she could have hoped. He was skilled and efficient and she genuinely liked the man.

The minutes went by as *Gilgamesh* hurtled toward the Freeport system. At the ten-minute mark Ellsworth had the ship cleared for action. "All stations report at GQ-Two, ma'am," said Bradley after a bit. The ship was at battle stations, but the weapons were not charged, nor were the shields up—that would have been taken as an unfriendly gesture by Freeport's guardians.

"Elapsed time?"

"Six minutes, twelve seconds."

"Sometime before this trip is over I want us to crack that six minute mark, Commander," said Ellsworth.

"We'll do it, ma'am. Three minutes to drop-out."

The last seconds passed and Ellsworth felt that familiar wrench and the viewscreen was suddenly filled with stars. It was good to be somewhere again. But then the stars vanished as the main tactical display filled the screen. It showed dozens of contacts.

"We are being challenged by the sentry ships, Captain," said Lieutenant Terletsky.

"Give them the standard reply and request docking instructions."

This was done and their course given to them without comment. Maybe this wouldn't be so bad after all. *Gilgamesh* headed for the orbital station. It was a two-hour trip from the gravity well boundary and as they drew nearer, they could see that there were at least a hundred other vessels docked or floating nearby. Many were merchant vessels—probably armed merchant vessels, but a lot were warships. Warships from a dozen different builders, and now owned by anyone's guess. Not many legitimate warships came to Freeport.

"Looks like business is good," said Ellsworth.

"Skipper, take a look at the sensor readings on that cruiser over there," said Commander Bradley, looking up from his readouts. He switched the data to her monitor. The ship was one of a group clustered to one side of the station. It was a pretty typical small warship that you found out beyond the League's borders.

"What about it, Commander?"

"Compare it with our own database." More information appeared and she suddenly realized what her Exec was getting at.

"Norman Wolfe's ship?"

"Ninety-eight percent match on the sensor profile, ma'am," confirmed Bradley.

"Damn, and we can't do a thing about it."

"Not unless you want to have an 'accidental' weapons malfunction, ma'am," said Bradley with a grim smile.

"Any other time, I'd think about it, but we can't afford trouble right now." Ellsworth was frowning. The ship in question belonged to a notorious mercenary (or pirate or raider, depending on who've you talked to) who had been a thorn in the side of the League Navy for years. Ellsworth herself had been on a ship that had almost caught him years ago.

"Seems like he's picked up some friends, too," continued Bradley. "You suppose all those ships are with him?" Ellsworth looked at the readings on the other ships floating near the cruiser. There were a dozen destroyer and frigate-sized vessels and one larger one that looked like a small battleship.

"I guess business has been good for Captain Wolfe, too. Assuming he's even still in command—or alive. Job security in that sort of activity isn't exactly the best."

None of the orbiting vessels seemed to notice the old League cruiser passing by them and *Gilgamesh* was soon docked at the station. It was a much easier docking than they had been doing lately and Ensign Bartlett said so.

"Incoming message from station security, ma'am," said Lieutenant Terletsky.

The screen lit up with the image of a man in a Freeport uniform. "Hello, *Gilgamesh*. Welcome to Freeport. May I ask what business you have here?"

"Fueling," said Ellsworth.

"Ah. Then I must inform you that pending information on the... situation within the League, you have no credit here. All transactions must be in cash or other recognized forms of exchange."

"We were expecting that... Lieutenant. We have brought items to trade."

"Excellent. Ah... just what *is* going on in the League, Captain? We get the most incredible rumors here, you know."

"I'm afraid I'm not at liberty to discuss that."

"Of course. Well, I'll transfer all the pertinent safety and security regulations. Enjoy your stay on Freeport."

"Thank you." The screen blanked.

"Commander Bradley, I want you to re-emphasize to the crew that no one is to say *anything* about what's going on back home to *anyone* while we are here. Nor are they to discuss our current mission."

"Yes, ma'am."

"Miss Terletsky, hook us into the station com system and try to contact the League Consulate."

"Yes, ma'am," said Terletsky, but a moment later she looked up in surprise. "Captain, the League Consul is trying to contact you."

Ellsworth's eyebrows shot up. "Very well, put him through."

The screen came to life again, this time with a harried-looking man in civilian clothes that were two years out of date in the League. He stared at her expectantly.

"Captain...?"

"Captain Jaqueline Ellsworth, the League cruiser *Gilgamesh*, at your service, sir."

"Thank goodness," sighed the man. "I'm Donald Brown, League Consul on Freeport. Captain, I need to talk to you immediately. This line isn't secure, so it will have to be in person."

"Very well, sir. Do you want to come here, or shall we meet in the Consulate?"

"I think it might be better if you come here, Captain. Bring a few of your officers; we have a lot to discuss. Oh, it might also be better if you don't come in uniform."

"I understand, sir," said Ellsworth. "We'll be there in about an hour."

Brown looked away for a moment. "Could we make it two hours, Captain?"

It seemed a little odd that he wanted to postpone a meeting he seemed so eager to have, but she shrugged. "That would be fine, sir. We'll see you then." She signed off.

"Brad, you have the bridge. I'll take Mister Florkowski and Ensign McClerndon with me. And two Marines as escort. I believe the station regs only permit stunners so have them ready to issue."

"Aye, aye, ma'am. Are you sure this is safe?"

"We should be okay. The Freeporters can't afford to have customers assaulted in the corridors. Since we've got some time, make contact with a fuel dealer and see how much it's going to cost us to fill up. Also check with Lieutenant Kinney and see if you can get a rough estimate on the value of our trade goods. We can probably get more help on that from Consul Brown's office, too."

"Yes, ma'am, right away."

An hour and a half later, Jaq walked down to the main airlock. She had been a little chagrined to find that all her own civvies were even more out of date than the clothes Donald Brown had been wearing. *I need to get out more often.* She felt a little better when she saw the rest of the party. Florkowski's clothes looked about as bad as Brown's; McClerndon was wearing a totally non-descript jumpsuit, and the two Marines… well, the less said the better.

She had decided on bringing Florkowski because she wanted to have another bridge officer along and she wanted Bradley to remain on the ship. Besides, Florkowski had been performing well lately and she was hoping that a show of confidence on her part like this might improve things between them. She was including McClerndon just because she liked the girl. She had the potential to become a good officer and some additional seasoning would do her good. Not that the old career standards meant anything anymore…

"All ready?"

"Yes, ma'am," said all four in unison.

"Again, I want to remind you not to say anything about conditions back in the League and especially, nothing about our current mission. Hopefully in these clothes no one will pay us any mind."

Their anonymity lasted until they had left the airlock.

The customs officer asked them a dozen questions about the League beyond the scope of his own duty before they were all checked through, and he wasn't happy that he wasn't getting any answers. Then, they were immediately accosted by a small crowd as soon as they entered the public corridor.

"Are you the captain of that ship?" shouted one man. The question was directed at all of them. Jaq kept moving.

"Captain, I represent Interfacts News! Can you give us some information on what's happening inside the Star League?" said another as he pushed past his rivals.

"We've heard that everything has collapsed in the League! Can you verify that?"

"Captain! We have a right to know what's going on!"

"Keep moving," muttered Ellsworth.

They pushed their way through the crowd and down the corridor. Fortunately the League Consulate was not far and they all breathed a sigh of relief when they shut the door behind them.

"God!" exclaimed Florkowski in disgust. "Are we going to face that every time we leave the ship?"

"I hope not," said Ellsworth. She looked up as a woman crossed the lobby toward them.

"Captain Ellsworth?" she asked.

"Yes."

"The Consul is waiting for you. Please come this way."

They followed her down a corridor. Ellsworth looked around and was slightly surprised at the opulence of the place. Until she had started this journey she had never even thought about the League having a consulate here. They reached a smaller waiting area and detached their Marine escort. Just before they got to Brown's office, the woman stopped and looked at her.

"Please, do you have any word from Callgarey?" she asked in a whisper.

"No, I'm sorry," said Ellsworth. The woman's face fell and then she ushered them through the door. Donald Brown got up from his chair as they entered.

"Captain, it's good to meet you in person." He offered his hand and she took it.

"Good to meet you, sir. These are Commander Florkowski and Ensign McCerndon." More shaking of hands and then he had them in chairs facing his desk. His office was tastefully decorated. She noticed the holo of what she assumed were his wife and teenage daughter.

"Captain, I'm hoping you have some information for me about conditions in the League. We've been hearing some incredible things and the regular courier has not arrived. There's been no reliable word at all. Can you tell me what's happened?"

"I'm afraid that I can, sir, and it's not good."

"Bad?"

"Worse. A catastrophe, sir. I hardly know where to begin, but please brace yourself." Ellsworth launched into the story of the sabotaged nano-circuits and what had happened on places like Leavitte and Flemington. She tried to spare him the more grisly details, but she did not try to sugar-coat it either. Minute by minute, Brown's face turned paler and paler.

"There's no chance that this was just limited to certain areas, Captain? I know that a lot of our own equipment failed at that same time, but... everywhere?"

"We can't know for sure, sir, but all the evidence we have indicates that the entire League has been affected."

"My God..." Brown just shook his head. "I was coming to fear it was bad, but..." He shook his head again. "So what brought you here,

Captain?" he asked, getting control of himself after a moment. "From the sound of this you have more urgent things to do than check in on this particular black hole."

"We stopped to get fuel, sir. I'm hoping you can help arrange that. We know our money's no good, so we brought trade goods."

"Certainly. But where are you headed after this? Obviously you are on your way somewhere else, where?"

"I'm afraid I can't tell you that, sir. We're under orders from Commodore Shusterman and it's top secret."

"Captain, you are the first League ship to come through here in four months and probably the last for God knows how long. I think I have a right to know where you are headed."

"Sorry, sir."

"Captain, I'm a grade three consul and that outranks a commodore, now please tell me."

"Sir, it wouldn't matter if you were President of the Grand Senate, I still wouldn't tell you while we are on this station. I'm sorry, sir, but that's how it is."

Brown looked angry, but then he settled his expression and stared at her again. "All right, I won't press you. Anyway, you'll have to tell me sooner or later, because I'll be coming with you."

"What? I'm sorry, sir, but that's impossible!"

"Captain, I'm requesting and requiring transport for myself, my staff and our families. Thirty-four people all told."

"Sir, I can't..."

"Yes, you can, Captain. I insist."

Ellsworth glanced around in alarm. Was he serious? "Sir, I have no room on my ship."

"Then make room. We are coming with you."

"You don't even know where we are going!"

"Only because you refuse to tell me. Assuming you are not just deserting, Captain, I have to assume you will be returning to League space eventually. That will be far better than staying here."

"But... but it could be months or even years before we get to anyplace safe to let you off," pleaded Ellsworth. This was crazy! "Surely you would be better off chartering a flight with some neutral merchant ship."

"What with, Captain?" demanded Brown. "As you've already found out, League credits are worthless here now. The Consulate is broke."

"There must be some other arrangement, sir. We are heading out on a very important and probably very dangerous mission. I can't take you along!"

Brown sat and stared at her again. This was getting unnerving. "Captain, I could plead with you; get down on my knees and beg with you if it would do any good. But I think I may have a better argument. I'll admit that I expected you to object to providing us transport and I arranged the timing of this meeting just in case. There is something I want to show to you. If you would please follow me."

Brown got up and Ellsworth, Florkowski and McClerndon did the same in puzzlement. The Consul led the way out of his office. They picked up the two Marines and then left the consulate by a back door. To her relief, there was no one waiting to shout questions at them.

"Where are we going, sir?"

"My turn to keep secrets, Captain. We'll be there soon enough."

They went down more corridors and then came to a wider, commercial section. Hundreds of people wandered past the shops and eateries. There was a bewildering variety of alien species, many of which Ellsworth had never seen before, but the majority were humans. Humans were the dominant species in the sprawling Star League, but some estimates said there were actually more humans living beyond its borders than within. There had always been wanderers and free spirits and dreamers who ranged ahead of the slow outward expansion of the League. There were also religious or political dissidents who could not find what they were looking for on the inside. And there were exiles fleeing troubles, too; for the League was no utopia, either. They had all gone forth, looking for something. Sometimes finding it among the alien races who were already out there, and sometimes not. They settled worlds and hoped the ever-expanding League would not catch up with them for many generations. They plowed their fields and fought their wars and held no love for where they had come from. And there were the misfits, too. Criminals and pirates, freebooters and mercenaries. People who could not fit in or obey the laws of the League. People drawn to the troubles and opportunities among the Outies.

Examples of every type were all around them now. Jaq spotted a group in quasi-uniforms that might well have come from Captain Wolfe's ship, or perhaps some other ship entirely. They were being earnestly followed by a man in a loincloth who was urging them to give up their violent ways and follow the path of the One True God. Merchants, walking in step, dickering over prices. Provocatively dressed men and women hawked merchandise of another kind. They detoured around a pair of acrobats who were performing for coins thrown from the watching crowd. A teenage girl with a tray of candied meats tried to lure customers into her family's restaurant. It was almost like a carnival. Almost.

They turned down another corridor and the mood changed. These shops and vendors sold drugs that were illegal in the League. Or weapons that were illegal almost everywhere. Others offered risky bio-upgrades. Many storefronts had only a name on them and if you had to ask what they sold, you didn't belong there in the first place. Brown led them to a door with the name "Maurder's" in glowing letters above it. Two gruff-looking guards were standing outside. They scrutinized the newcomers carefully, but made no move to stop them from entering.

Inside there was a crowd of people and a murmur of voices. There was a raised stage on the far side of the large compartment. Rows of seats, mostly filled, were up close and more people were standing farther to the rear. There were a number of people up on the stage and they were... what were they... ?

Ellsworth stopped short and a shudder of horror went down her spine.

It was a slave auction.

Several dozen men and women in short white smocks were standing at the rear of the platform. One was near the front with two men standing on either side of him. A third man was near the front taking bids from the crowd. As she watched with wide eyes, the bidding ended and the man in white was taken out through a side door and disappeared.

"Consul, what the hell is this?" hissed Ellsworth, finding her voice.

"Exactly what it looks like, Captain." He led them to an empty spot behind the last row of seats. The auctioneer was calling for the crowd's attention.

"Ladies and Gentlemen! These next lots will be of special interest! The former crew of the League merchant ship *Poquessing* are up for sale to cover unpaid debts. By order of the Freeport Chief Justice!"

There was an outburst of cheers, jeers and catcalls.

"Just in time for the main event," said Brown, grimly. "Your arrival here was fortuitously timed, Captain—if I can use that term for something as awful as this." The two burly overseers grabbed one of the waiting men in white and hustled him to the front. He moved in a clumsy fashion like he was drugged and he probably was. He, and all the others, had metal collars around their necks.

"Lot Number One, an engineer," said the auctioneer. "Twenty-two years of starship experience. A master powertech rating and submaster on hyper generators. An excellent buy! Will someone start the bidding at a thousand? Yes, I have a thousand, do I hear two?"

Ellsworth shook her head as the bidding went on. "What is this?" she demanded of Brown.

"It's why I want out of here, Captain!" snarled the Consul. "I had two main jobs in this hellhole. One was to assist League merchants and to keep commerce running smoothly. The other was to rescue people from this. I was authorized to buy or ransom League citizens who had been captured by pirates or raiders who would otherwise have been sold into slavery. I've been here four years, Captain, and I've saved over five hundred. But now I can't save any more and I'm trying to save myself and my family."

"My God," gasped Florkowski. McClerndon was watching with an expression of raw horror.

"These poor devils were on a League merchant ship which was docked to the station," explained Brown. "Four months ago all their systems failed and their fusion plant exploded. It wrecked their ship and destroyed most of their cargo. Worst of all, it did considerable damage to that part of the station. These were the survivors and they had nothing of value left to pay for the damage with. I tried to intercede and for a while it looked like I could save them. But then rumors of the disaster in the League started coming in and League credits plummeted in value. They're nearly worthless now. I have nothing to pay for them with."

"Surely we can do something!" exclaimed Florkowski.

"There's nothing, Commander. We have no friends here at all, you know. Most of the Outies hate us with a passion. They're enjoying this. We've been too big and too strong and too arrogant for too long. They think it's payback time. Owning a 'Leaguer' slave is becoming a status symbol."

Ellsworth swallowed numbly as the engineer was sold for thirty thousand Freeport dollars, a sizable sum. An astrogator was next. Jaq had no clue if these people would end up doing the jobs they were trained for, but it was possible. Slavery was an all-too common fact beyond the borders of the League. It was rarely employed on a mass scale since machines could do brute labor more efficiently, but for specialized tasks and domestic chores, slaves were often preferred. A sentient being was more versatile and adaptable than any machine. If you could 'acquire' them fully trained and educated, they were usually cheaper than a machine, too. And with modern technology, it was easy to assure the obedience of a slave as well. Ellsworth noted the collars on the necks of captives. They were probably far more than simple metal rings.

"Captain, I again make my plea for transport," said Brown. "The consulate is leased from the station owners. We get our supplies from local merchants. We are paid up for a few more months, but then our credit is exhausted. We have no source of money and from what you tell me there will be no help from the League. We can't get out of here on our own and with the current mood no one is going to offer us employment. No one stays on Freeport for free. We'll accumulate debts and when enough time has gone by...I've already had personal enemies tell me they plan to be here to bid on my wife and daughter when they go on the block! You must help us!"

"Yes... yes, of course," said Ellsworth in a daze. "We'll find room somehow."

"Thank you, Captain," sighed Brown. "With all my heart I thank you. Now let's get out of here."

"But what about these people?' demanded Florkowski. "We can't just leave them!"

"Unless your cargo is worth a lot more than I think it is, there's nothing we can do, Commander," said Brown, "I'm sorry."

Ellsworth pulled out her communicator. "Commander Bradley, do you have those figures on the fuel costs yet?"

"It looks like it will run us around a hundred thousand local dollars for a full load, Skipper. If we want to fuel here again on the way back, that will be another hundred thousand."

"And what about the value of our cargo?"

"One buyer made an offer of a quarter million based on our manifest. I'm still waiting for offers from two more. The consulate trade officer is helping us out, but frankly, ma'am, I think these folks are cheating us."

"You're probably right. Okay, thanks, I'll get back to you." She looked up to see Florkowski and McClerndon looking at her expectantly. She looked over to the auction block. A new person was being shoved into place. A young woman.

"Lot Number Three, a power room technician, second class," said the auctioneer. "I'm sure many of you have need for a good power tech, but just in case you don't, this offering is well suited for... other duties." He made a gesture and the woman's smock was pulled off. She wasn't wearing anything underneath. There were hoots and cheers from the mostly male audience. In spite of being drugged the woman cringed away but was thrust forward again.

"Now that's more like it!" shouted one man.

"Just the way I like my Leaguers!"

"Serves 'em right! 'Bottom rail on top' now, eh?"

"I wouldn't mind being on top of that rail!" Another roar of laughter.

"Captain, we have to do something!" hissed Florkowski in Ellsworth's ear. She shook her head and turned away, fists clenched.

"We can't. We have to buy that fuel and we have to have money to buy more on the way back." She knew what she was saying was true, but it did not make it any easier. She had sworn an oath to stop this sort of thing! It burned inside her to be so helpless.

"We don't need all the money, Captain!" insisted Florkowski. "We have a little to spare, maybe we could buy..."

"We could buy one or two, Commander—and leave us with no contingency funds. Which one do you suggest we bid on?" she gestured at the seventeen remaining people. That icy glare that she had not seen on his face for quite a while was back again. He turned and stalked out.

"Come on, Captain," said Brown. "I'm sorry you had to see this."

She nodded and started to turn away. Then she noticed that Ensign McClerndon had not moved, She was still staring at the naked young woman—a girl about her own age, really. The bidding was up to over forty thousand now. A group of uniformed men near the front seemed to be the main bidders. The auctioneer was making her turn around and take various poses to the delight of the onlookers.

"Rhada, we have to go," she said gently. McClerndon did not appear to hear her. She took a step toward the platform and her hand was coming up. Ellsworth grabbed her shoulder and spun her around.

"Rhada! There's nothing we can do for her! If you try to interfere—

or bid without any money—then tomorrow you'll be the one up on that block!"

McClerndon finally seemed to hear her. Her light brown complexion turned a sickly gray. She cast one last, terrified look at the woman and then bolted from the room.

"Fueling is complete, Captain," said Commander Karl Bradley.

"Very good, Brad," said Ellsworth. "And Commander Florkowski, a well done to you and Lieutenant Kinney on transferring the first half of the cargo to the buyer."

"Thank you, ma'am," said Florkowski. Jaq stared at the man for a moment. He had been furious about their inability to intercede at the slave auction and she couldn't blame him for that one bit. But he seemed to have settled down again and she was glad to see that. She wasn't sure how Ensign McClerndon was handling things.

"All right, we are ready to get out of here. The only thing left to do is get Consul Brown and his people on board. He doesn't think it is a good idea to let the locals know this is going to happen until the last minute and I agree with him. So starting around 2300 hours, we are going to get a string of 'visitors' to the ship. The plan is that by 0400 they will all be aboard and we can pull out. Our docking fees are paid and flight plan filed, so hopefully it will be smooth sailing. Brad, how are the accommodations for our guests coming?" Bradley frowned.

"Well, ma'am, the 'guest list' is up to forty-two now and I'm running out of places to put bodies. If any more League citizens show up on Brown's doorstep, I don't know what we are going to do. All the recreation spaces are filled and I may have to start setting up cots in the corridors or the mess hall."

"What about the cargo space that's opened up now?"

"I can fit a few in there and Commander Van Rossum is modifying the ventilation to make it more comfortable. Actually that brings up an idea Commander Florkowski had a little while ago."

"Oh?"

"Yes, ma'am, he suggested that we sell all of our cargo now and put a deposit on another load of fuel. That clears out more space in the hold and guarantees us the fuel when we come back."

Ellsworth nodded as she pondered this possibility. It was a good idea, really. If they were going to return to Leavitte through non-League space then they had no choice but to stop here again. If they decided on staying inside the League then their cargo would have little real value on any world they might stop at. And assuming they had the nano-chips, those would be a thousand times more valuable anyway. And by fixing the price now, they might avoid being cheated later if anti-League feelings continued to grow.

"All right, I agree. Good thinking, Commander Florkowski. Can you and Lieutenant Kinney make the arrangements with that buyer and transfer the rest of the cargo?"

"Yes, ma'am, I'll get right on it."

"Good."

Six hours later the first of the refugees started coming aboard. They looked profoundly grateful and Jaq was relieved that they had commendably little baggage. She still didn't know what the hell she was going to do with a bunch of civilians on a voyage that could well last a year or more. At least Tractenberg IIIc had a reasonable environment; maybe they could build some temporary barracks dirtside once they got there. For that matter, if the base was intact they might have more living space than they could ever need. Yes, that was a good possibility...

"Captain?"

She looked up to see Lieutenant Kinney standing there. His face was pale and he was clearly upset.

"What's wrong, Lieutenant?"

"Ma'am, we... we sold the cargo like you ordered. Then we took the credit voucher to the fuel dealer. Commander Florkowski told us to wait outside so we did. We waited and waited but he didn't come out. So we went in to find him and they told us he had gone out another door."

A chill went through her.

"And he didn't pay for any fuel, either, ma'am!"

"Did you try to find him?" she asked in growing alarm.

"Yes, ma'am, we searched all through that area, but he was gone!"

CHAPTER TWELVE

Captain Jaq Ellsworth leaned back in her chair and sighed. She listened to the barely audible hum of the hyperdrive as it pushed *Gilgamesh* through the weird un-space that surrounded it. With a frown she closed the computer files on her terminal.

It all seemed so obvious now.

She had just finished reading the files on Lieutenant Commander Charles Florkowski. All of them. The files she should have read months ago. The files that might have warned her and maybe prevented this latest fiasco.

Florkowski was gone. Deserted. Absconded with a hundred and twenty-five thousand Freeport dollars. They had searched for him, of course. They had contacted the station security. They even gave him the benefit of the doubt and assumed he had been abducted. But he had not been, and it soon became obvious that he had no intention of coming back to the ship. And with the refugees coming aboard and their departure hour set, they had had to leave him behind.

She sighed again. It wasn't a total disaster. Losing the money was an irritant, but it wasn't fatal. If their mission was a success, they could load a far more valuable cargo at Tractenberg. And if it wasn't, they could still scoop fuel from gas giants. It would take them a lot longer to get back, but if their mission failed it probably made little difference in the long run anyway.

"This was my fault, dammit," she said to the empty room. "But you're to blame, too, Liu-Chen. You knew. You knew and you didn't do anything. I was stupid, but you were negligent!"

No, that wasn't entirely fair, either. Liu-Chen surely knew there was a problem, but it didn't really become evident until you read it all at one sitting: A half-dozen efficiency reports spread over fourteen years stating: 'Has trouble working as a team member'; 'Exhibits hostility toward superiors when under stress'; 'Shows tendency to disagree with orders.' And then the psych evaluations: 'slight symptoms of paranoia'; 'Neurotic tendencies'; 'Trouble dealing with stress.' Recommendations for psych treatment with no evidence that any treatment was done. Spread out over a period of years, interspersed with more reports of good performance, it would have been easy to miss.

Or to ignore. Or cover up. Or brush under the rug.

Florkowski had clearly been devoted to Liu-Chen and she had no doubt the Captain had liked Florkowski. So he had coddled him and helped him along and never wrote a report that would have landed him in real trouble. But it was obvious Liu-Chen knew there was trouble. When the former first officer had left *Gilgamesh*, he could have made a case to promote Florkowski. Most captains would have. But he had not. He knew Florkowski wasn't fit for the job, so he had let them bring in Ellsworth instead. How Florkowski had felt about it was obvious. Liu-Chen was trying to be kind to an officer he had liked, but it wasn't any kindness. Not in the long run. He should have eased Florkowski into a shore assignment. Made sure he got the psych treatments. He could have become a good staff officer for someone instead of a deserter.

But Liu-Chen's death had clearly pushed Florkowski to the breaking point. It had just taken a few extra months for him to finally snap.

Of course, if Liu-Chen had gotten him a staff assignment Florkowski would probably be dead now: Suffocated on some crippled space station when the disaster hit. Ellsworth snorted. "Should have, could have!" she spat. "It's all air out the lock now."

No, Florkowski was gone and there was no point worrying about it. His desertion was not that big a problem in itself and she had to admit she was glad to see the last of him. At the very least it gave them one more cabin. She glanced around her own cabin. She was back in the one she had originally started with. Bradley was in Florkowski's cabin and Consul Brown, his wife and daughter were in Liu-Chen's. It was a little irritating, but it really made the most sense. Chief Gossage had not been pleased though....

The quartering problem was not as bad as she had feared. The refugees were so grateful to be off Freeport that they were accepting their Spartan accommodations far more readily than she had expected. She wondered how long that would last.

It was still four weeks to Tractenberg.

* * *

Rhada McClerndon sat in the small observation blister and stared at the inside of the closed shutters. Hyperspace lay on the other side and no one could look out. It was a small, uncomfortable place with the shutters closed, but she still found it preferable to the crowded madhouse that the rest of the ship had become. It was one of the few places where she could have any privacy. And she needed privacy. She closed her eyes and she could see that woman on the auction block again. *What's happened to her? She's probably being raped at this very moment and no one can help her.* Rhada shuddered.

She jumped slightly when she heard the pressure door hiss open behind her, but she relaxed when she saw that it was Greg Sadgipour. He closed the door behind him and sat down next to her.

"Hi," he said.

"Hi."

"I was looking for you."

"You found me."

"How are you doing?"

"Fine."

He stared at her. "No you're not. I heard about what happened on the station. Rhada, talk to me. Please."

She stared back at him and then turned away. "I don't understand," she said. "I don't understand how you can look an intelligent being in the eyes and then make a slave out of them. It's so wrong I go crazy just thinking about it."

"It's an ugly thing," said Greg.

"I... I was talking with Chtak about it for a little bit. He said that unless there is a strong and sustained morale outrage against it, you can never eradicate slavery. Without that, slavery is almost always economically viable and very profitable. Profitable! Making profits of thinking beings! It makes me sick, Greg."

"I'm sorry, Rhada. I wish we could have done something."

"I keep seeing that one woman, but she's just one. What's happening everywhere else? I couldn't believe how angry all the Outies seemed to be with us. With no 'moral outrage' to counter it, what will they do with all of us?"

"It's up to us to prevent them from doing anything. They're taking advantage of the situation now, but once we find that base and get the factories working again, we can stop them."

"I hope so. You really think there's a chance?"

"Sure there is."

"Optimist."

"Always."

They sat in silence for a long while. Rhada was glad that he was there with her. She liked Greg a lot. The fact that he was here with her and that he cared made her like him even more.

"So how are things going otherwise?" he asked. "I see Doug Rawlins is still following you around. Is he...?"

"Still trying to get into my pants?" said Rhada with a sudden grin. "He's tried once or twice, but I've redirected him towards 'Ritta Torres. I think she'll welcome his attention more than me."

Greg was blushing and his mouth was hanging open. Rhada laughed. It was a genuine laugh and it felt very good. "Greg, the look on your face! Don't boys try to get into the girls' pants back on your planet?"

"I... uh, they don't... I mean they don't talk about it that way."

"Oh dear, I've shocked you. Poor Greg."

"I'm not shocked," he protested. "It's just that..."

"Oh, you're shocked all right," said Rhada, still smiling. "You're not used to me talking like a deckhand, right?"

"Uh... well, right. You never usually... And from what I'd heard about your planet it didn't sound... normal."

"Then I'm afraid I'll have to destroy another illusion. Fenwha is a fake, Greg. Everyone hears about this fairy tale place with crystal palaces and knights and ladies faire and they believe it. Because they want to believe it—and because the rulers of Fenwha want everyone to believe it. I've told you about Fenwha, but you still don't believe it. Greg, I'm no lady faire. My world's a swamp. There are three spots of real dry ground on the whole planet. The rulers have their crystal palaces there. Everyone else lives in the swamp and farms mud shrimp. Those are the only export and the lords in their palaces have a complete monopoly on their export. I was shocked to find what a kilo of mud shrimp goes for on the Core Worlds—not that they call them mud shrimp there! The lords get rich and they pay the farmers a pittance. But none of the tourists ever get down into the swamps."

"I didn't know," said Greg.

"You're not supposed to. The farmers are all in debt to the lords and have no hope of ever getting out. It's serfdom, Greg."

"The League doesn't permit...!"

"The League doesn't care about two-bit worlds like Fenwha. Not as long as the shrimp supply keeps coming. So things are a bit...rougher down in the swamp. Fenwha lords might not try to get into their ladies' pants, but the boys down in the swamps sure try it with the girls—and they rarely take no for an answer. One of the reasons I got the hell out of there."

"I see," said Greg who looked very thoughtful. They were silent again.

"So you haven't... haven't let anyone get into your p-pants?"

"Oh, Greg, you can't even say it!" said Rhada laughing again. He was blushing fiercely. "I'm sorry, I shouldn't be teasing you like this. But no, I haven't."

She looked at Greg and she was suddenly filled with affection for him. He had always been a good friend. And she realized she wanted a friend very much indeed. Her hand reached out and touched his.

"But then the right man has never tried," she whispered. His eyes got very wide. She leaned over and kissed him. His lips were softer than she had expected. He smiled at her in astonishment.

"Rhada, I..."

"Don't say anything," she shushed.

She leaned against him and he put his arm around her shoulder.

LSS Gilgamesh squirted back into normal space ten million kilometers from the gas giant Tractenberg III. The long journey was nearly over, but the massive planet—so large as to nearly qualify as a brown dwarf—had its own gravity well boundary and forced the ship's anxious crew to wait just a little bit longer.

"Good grief, what a mess," exclaimed Ensign Bartlett from his helm station.

"It is a bit cluttered, isn't it?" said Jaq Ellsworth in amusement.

"Yes, ma'am. I'd been studying the charts, but it never quite sank in until now. Sure hope we can find a way through."

"I'm sure you'll do fine, Ensign. All ahead two-thirds."

"Aye, aye, ma'am."

Jaq looked at 'the mess' that Bartlett had been talking about and smiled slightly. Tractenberg III had an unusually rich collection of moons and rings. The planet itself was huge, nearly three hundred thousand kilometers in diameter. It had a spectacular set of rings that began a mere ten thousand kilometers above the cloud-tops and stretched another two hundred thousand kilometers out from there. Beyond the rings was a family of over fifty moons, a dozen of them terrestrial-sized. Some of their orbits were quite eccentric and because of their gravitation 'stirring' of this cosmic stew, there were rogue bits of debris all over the place. Collisions were frequent and sometimes spectacular. It was all inherently unstable and astronomers had argued for years how it had come about—and how long it might last.

"Strange place to find a habitable planet," observed Commander Bradley. "You'd think it would get pounded a bit too often."

"I believe there's some evidence the planet may have formed elsewhere and only been captured by the gas giant's gravity relatively recently," said Jaq. "That might account for the bizarre orbits, too."

"Why'd the League pick this place to build a base?"

"No doubt some staff-puke's 'brilliant idea'. Probably got a promotion for it, too."

"There's an awful lot of debris, too, ma'am," said Ensign Snowden at sensors. "Scattered metal readings all over the place and a tremendous lot in the rings themselves."

"Yes, we picked that up on our patrols years ago," said Ellsworth. "It's mostly debris from the battle, ensign. The orbital stations and a lot of ships got blown to smithereens. Most of the wreckage seems to have ended up in the rings. There was a lot of metal in those rings anyway. They're not just ice like you usually find. There were some mining facilities exploiting them before the Darj'Nang attacked."

"Well, we're here. What's our first move, Skipper?" asked Bradley.

"Assuming Mister Bartlett can get us into orbit without colliding with anything, we'll send down the recon drones for a look-see. Our charts give us the base's location, but things may have changed a bit due to the bombardment—and twenty years of time."

Ensign Bartlett proved equal to the task and a few hours later *Gilgamesh* slipped into orbit around Tractenberg IIIc. The drones were sent down and the next day their findings were being discussed in the ship's conference room.

"The remains of the base are just as we were expecting them, ma'am," said Ensign Snowden, pointing to the image on the monitor. "Most of it was constructed beneath this mountain and you can see that it is basically undisturbed. There were several nuclear detonations nearby, but there is no significant cratering near the main part of the base. There was quite a lot of direct energy fire, too and most of the surface installations have been wrecked."

"What's that large structure off to the east?" asked Ellsworth.

"There was a sizable presence of civilians working for the Navy here before the war and that is the remains of the housing tower. A nuke went off pretty close and collapsed most of it, I would guess. We are picking up some sporadic energy readings from there, so apparently some of the automatic systems survived."

"What sort of readings are you getting from the base?"

"That's a lot better shielded, ma'am. Both from the mountain above it and from its own construction. Getting readings through all that is difficult. However, we have been picking up a strong, low-level emission that is consistent with a fusion plant in standby mode. We can't be certain, but it looks as though something is still working down there."

"Jackpot," said Bradley with a huge grin.

"We can hope, Commander," said Ellsworth with a substantial grin of her own. Her sense of relief that this had not been a wild goose chase was like a boulder being taken off her shoulders. "Okay, it's down there. How do we get in?"

"The main entrance was on the east side, directly opposite the housing tower," said Snowden. "Unfortunately, that appears to be completely buried under debris. I don't know if we can get in that way. However, there is a secondary entrance on the south side that is in better shape." He touched the controls and the image zoomed in on a small valley at the foot of the mountain. "You can just make out the blast doors, right there. There was a considerable landslide—probably caused by the nukes—and the door is partially buried. I'm no expert, but it looks like we should be able to dig our way in."

"How about that, Lieutenant?" said Ellsworth to Lieutenant Rawlins. "You think you can get through that?"

"With time, there's no doubt, ma'am," said the combat engineer. "I'll need to take a closer look to give you a real estimate, but it probably shouldn't take more than a few days for the excavation. Getting through the door itself is another matter. Those things were built to take nukes and direct photon fire. If we have to cut, it might take a while."

"Lieutenant Chtak'Chr, Do you think we'll be able to get those doors open?"

"Impossible to say, Captain, replied the Survey Officer. "We have a number of standard access codes we can try, but that assumes we can connect to the local system and that the door mechanism is working and that it has power. A lot of assumptions, ma'am, but we'll try everything before we start cutting."

"Very well. Lieutenant Quatrock, do you see any special security hazards?"

"No, ma'am. Aside from those energy readings, there is nothing unusual. Sensors show considerable numbers of animals in the vicinity, but the records say they are mostly herbivores. The only predators on the planet won't bother a person. The only other sign of activity is a number of agro-robots that seem to be still farming a few plots about a hundred klicks to the east. On automatic, I guess."

"Interesting," said Ellsworth. "They might be worth salvaging later. All right! I am desperately trying not to get my hopes too high, people, but this is all looking very good. We'll be sending down the initial survey team in six hours, so make all your final preparations."

The cutter dropped out of *Gilgamesh's* boat bay and headed for the planet. Rhada McClerndon sat in the co-pilot's seat and watched Ensign Claritta Torres do her stuff. She was a little envious of Torres' piloting skills, but the woman had two more years of experience and seemed to get tapped for small craft duty much more often than her. *Yeah, but she can't hit the broad side of an asteroid with a photon cannon, either.*

There was some buffeting as the cutter entered the upper atmosphere, but Torres compensated and the ride down was as smooth as you could ask for. They broke through a light cloud cover and headed for their objective.

"I think that's the mountain," said Rhada, pointing through the forward canopy.

"Yup, I think you're right," agreed Torres.

"*Gilgamesh*, we have the target in sight," said Rhada into her com.

"Acknowledged, keep us informed."

The cutter continued to shed velocity and Torres put them into a tight spiral, directly over the mountain. Eventually, they were hovering a few thousand meters overhead.

"I can see where that door is supposed to be. I'll take us lower." They descended further and before long they could see the top part of the armored door, set into the hillside and partially buried under fallen rock. Unfortunately, the level ground in front of the door was a jumble of boulders.

"Lieutenant Quatrock, I can't land very close to the door, but there is some level ground about two hundred meters further south."

"Sounds good," said Quatrock, who was in command of the landing party. "Set us down there."

"Right, commencing landing." The cutter drifted to the side and then slowly settled to the ground. "Okay folks, welcome to OZ!" said Torres as she shut down the engines.

Rhada unstrapped from her seat and looked into the passenger compartment. They had a full load. Two squads of Marines commanded by Quatrock and Greg; Rawlins and two of his engineers, Chtak and a half-dozen spacers and quite a bit of equipment. Quatrock cracked the airlock and they began to pile out. Greg motioned to her.

"Stay inside until we've secured the area, okay?" he said.

"Why, Mister Sadgipour, are you concerned for my safety? How touching."

"You know I am," he said earnestly. She smiled and gave him a peck on the cheek. He glanced around in embarrassment, but nobody seemed to have noticed. She didn't care if they did. She did as he asked, but it only took ten minutes before he commed to report that everything was all right.

"Okay for me to come out?"

"Sure, not that there's much to see."

"We've come all this way, there better be something to see!" She turned to Torres. "Permission to leave the ship, ma'am?"

"Okay, but come back and spell me for a while, I'd like to take a look, too."

"Sure thing. See you later."

Rhada went through the open airlock and hopped down onto the ground. The cutter was in a small valley that had not really been noticeable from above. Hillocks blocked off a direct view of the door to the north and the open land to the south. She could see pairs of Marines on both ridges, but the rest of the party was off to the north. She walked in that direction. The gravity seemed about normal, and she knew the oxygen content was actually a little higher than normal. She topped the rise, nodding to one of the Marines, and then stopped to take in the view.

The mountain wasn't really much of a mountain, but it rose to about a thousand meters in a fairly gently slope. Directly ahead, however, was a cliff face and set into it was the armored blast door leading to the base. As their recon had suggested, a considerable rockslide had come down the slope, partially burying the door and spilling out into the paved area in front of the door. The paving led off to the east through another small valley. She guessed the road must have led to the housing tower. Looking closer, she could see several vehicles crushed under the rocks. She spotted Greg and went down the hill to meet him. He was standing with Quatrock and Rawlins.

"So what do you think, Lieutenant?" Quatrock was asking the engineer. "Can you dig it out?"

"Absolutely. If we had heavy equipment, we could do it in half an hour. With what we've got, it will probably take a day or two. The only problem is the possibility of more slides when we start to dig. Those rocks up there might not be stable. So to start off, I'm going to set off a few charges and see if that brings anything more down. Once I'm satisfied, we can get to work with the hand tractors."

Rhada nodded to Greg, but he was in his 'on duty' mode and not talkative. So she walked over to Chtak instead. "Finding anything interesting?" she asked.

"The sensor readings are still unclear," he said in a distracted way. "There is definitely power in there. I have sent out a few exploratory signals to try and contact the base computer system, but with no response."

"Is that safe?"

"As I've explained, the Darj'Nang ASP is dead. There is no chance of infecting the base's computers now."

"That's not what I meant. The last information any of these computers might have had was that the base was under attack. It might be in some sort of high-security, defensive mode."

"Oh. I had not considered that. I will have to proceed more carefully."

Rhada smiled and shook her head. She left Chtak to his musings. She wandered for a bit, but there was not a lot to see. There were some forests off to the south, but they were at least a few kilometers away and she couldn't get that far from the cutter. She liked forests and it had been a long time since she had been in one. Maybe later. The vegetation in this vicinity was mostly just low brush and rather dreary. After a while, she remembered her promise to Torres and went back to the cutter. She monitored communications and tried to stay awake. It was amazing to be here, at their goal, and still be bored. It would certainly be more interesting when they got inside the base. It better be.

She looked up as Torres came back in and sat down. "Not that much to look at is there?" she asked.

"Not when everyone is so fixated on that damn door," said Torres with a grin.

"Oh? Couldn't get Doug's attention, eh? Figuring on sneaking off somewhere with him?"

"I'd thought about it," she smirked, "but all those rocks and thorn bushes doesn't look too comfortable. Anyway, Doug's in engineer-land and wouldn't notice me even if I took my clothes off."

"He seems to notice you a lot even with them on. How are you two doing?"

"Just fine. Doug's a lot of fun. You ought to give him a try sometime, Rhada. I don't mind sharing and I know he wouldn't mind being shared!"

"No thanks, I've got someone else in mind."

"Greg? He's a dear, isn't he? But I didn't think he'd started to notice girls yet."

"Oh, he's noticed them. He just isn't quite so obvious as some people I could mention."

"Doug is a little aggressive, I'll admit, but that's okay, I..."

The communicator beeped urgently, startling them both. Rhada grabbed it. "McClerndon here."

"Ensign, this is an emergency recall. Get everyone aboard and then get back up here!" It was Lieutenant Terletsky.

"What's happening?" blurted Rhada. Torres was already warming up the engines.

"We've got a dozen unidentified ships heading this way fast. Now get moving! Captain's orders!"

"Right! Lieutenant Quatrock, respond please..."

But before she could get an answer, Torres suddenly shouted and pointed out the front canopy.

"Rhada! Look!"

Greg and Quatrock had already heard the recall signal and were calling in the landing party when all hell broke loose.

"Lieutenant! Post Three, I've got..." The message had been on the tactical circuit and was suddenly cut off. Post three was one of the sentries on the far ridge, beyond the cutter. Almost immediately, the two nearer sentries began firing at some unseen target off to the south.

"Marines! Form on me!" shouted Quatrock as he sprinted toward the high ground. Greg was on his heels, an antique laser pistol in hand. There were more shouts over the tactical circuit.

"Hostiles coming in from the south…"

"Holy shit! Look at them all!"

"Watch out! Ahh!"

As Greg neared the top to the slope, he saw one of the two men posted there topple over clutching at his chest. He reached the top and skidded to a stop. The valley below was swarming with gray-green shapes. They were long and low to the ground and moved with horrible speed. They were hard to see clearly, but in a flash a long-ago training holo identified the things for him.

Skraknars!

He couldn't believe it and for a moment he stood there, dumbfounded. The Skraknars were one of a dozen or so slave races used as soldiers by the Darj'Nang. He had never seen one and had never expected to see one. What were they doing here?

But there was no more time to wonder. A shower of… something rained around them. Projectiles of some sort and two thumped into the front of his body armor and stuck there. Arrows? No, shorter than that. Bolts. Two more Marines fell. He fired into the mass of enemies, but could not tell if his shot had hit anything. He crouched down to get some cover.

Then he looked at the cutter.

The things were swarming over it. And into it, through the open lock.

"Rhada!" The shout was torn from him. He fired into the enemy again and again. The other Marines were firing, too, but it didn't seem to be having any effect! There were just too many of them.

"*Gilgamesh!*" shouted Quatrock into the com. "We are under attack! We need immediate support!"

"Impossible!" came the garbled reply. "We are under attack and are breaking orbit now!"

Greg looked around in near-panic. Both squads had rallied on the ridge line and the rest of the landing party was assembled behind them. But half the Marines were down and the valley below was filled with Skraknars. There was no hope of reaching the cutter. And they were moving towards the open flanks… They couldn't stay here, either. But he couldn't leave Rhada!

"Fall back!" shouted Quatrock suddenly.

The other Marines obeyed immediately, falling back in alternate pairs, one covering the other. Some tossed grenades down the slope before they moved and the explosions echoed off the cliffs. But Greg hesitated. Rhada was still in the cutter.

"Greg! Come on! Move!" screamed Quatrock.

And then he fell. He tumbled backwards and came to rest face up, a bolt protruding from his left eye. The visor on his combat helmet was still open.

Greg stared in horror and another bolt hit his armor. And another. The enemy was coming on. He had to move.

He turned and fled down the slope. But Rhada was still in the cutter!

CHAPTER THIRTEEN

"Well, Commander, I believe your friends have spotted us."

Charles Florkowski just nodded in reply. He was learning not to engage 'Commodore' Norman Wolfe in any unnecessary conversation. The man seemed to enjoy baiting him and there was no point in giving him any additional opportunities to do so.

Instead, he looked at the blip blinking on the tactical display. It was *Gilgamesh*, no doubt of that. Even without the sensor readings to confirm it, there would have been no doubt—who else could it be? He had been alternately hoping for and dreading this moment for the last four weeks. Now that it was happening he could not define what he was feeling.

It still seemed like some sort of nightmare and he could scarcely believe he was really here, aboard the mercenary battleship, *Vindicator*. In a few minutes, when that bitch Ellsworth saw that it was he who had brought the mercs here, she would probably think he had been planning this all along. It would be just like her to think the worst of him. Just like always.

But she would be wrong. Florkowski had not planned this, had not even thought of it, before the instant the merc had approached him in the bar to offer him a job. No, he had only wanted to get away from her, away from all the people who had once been his friends before she and Shusterman turned them against him. And even that had not been planned. No thought of leaving *Gilgamesh* had even entered his mind-—not until the very moment the clerk at the merchant's office had asked him how to make out the credit voucher. It was when his mouth had said: "Make it out to 'Cash,'" that he suddenly realized what he was going to do.

Oh, he had known for a long time that he was going to have to leave. He had not known how or when, but he had known it. He'd known it from the moment that bastard Shusterman had forced Ellsworth on Liu-Chen as First Officer. Liu-Chen had not wanted her, he knew that. He had all but promised the position to him. He wanted him there, beside him. Liu-Chen had trusted him, had know how valuable he was to the ship and the League. Liu-Chen was a great man and could recognize greatness in others.

But the others had all been against them. They had hated and feared Liu-Chen and cheated him out of his own promotions. And when they saw that he had liked Charles Florkowski they had set their sights to destroy him as well. They had lied and made up fake efficiency and psych reports to discredit him. It had all been very clever. He had not really caught on until Ellsworth came aboard. Before that, he'd just thought it was the inevitable competition and backbiting you found in any large organization. But when Ellsworth became First Officer, then he knew.

But there had not been anything he could do about it. Liu-Chen was too good an officer—too loyal to the League—to lodge a formal complaint. And he was too honest to get rid of Ellsworth using the same methods that were being used against him. So they had put up with her and her martinet ways. And when they got the news that *Gilgamesh* was to be decommissioned, it had seemed like the opportunity to get away from their enemies. Liu-Chen was going to a well-earned retirement and he had hinted to Florkowski that he would call in some old favors to get him a decent posting with some honorable people far away from Shusterman and Ellsworth.

But it had all gone out the airlock when this disaster happened. He could halfway suspect that it was all some ploy of Shusterman's to increase his own power—to create his own little empire—except the man wasn't half clever enough to pull it off. In any case, there would be no new posting for him and he'd be stuck with Ellsworth as his superior. But at least Liu-Chen would still be there.

But they had gotten rid of Liu-Chen, too. That had obviously always been their goal. Wear him down and force him to retire if they could. Wear him down and kill him if that didn't work. He closed his eyes and he could still see Liu-Chen's body lying in his chair. He could also see the look of fake surprise on Ellsworth face when she came in. She might not have pulled the trigger, but she had killed him! And then she dared to try and say she was sorry! Liar!

It might have been then that he had known he could not serve under her for any longer. Then, or when she turned her back on the people of Flemington. She was a coward as well as a murderer and he would not serve her. He went through the motions, but he knew he had to get out.

He wasn't quite sure why he did not leave the ship when they brought in Bradley to replace him. He had expected them to try a trick like that. But to have left the ship would have been to put himself in Shusterman's clutches and that was unacceptable, too. At least he still had a few friends on *Gilgamesh*.

Then on Freeport, at the slave market, that was the last straw. Ellsworth refused to do anything to help those people. To help that poor girl. He could not stand it any more. He had to get out and when the opportunity fell into his lap, he grabbed it without a second thought.

They had tried to catch him, of course, to bring him back and punish him, but he had outwitted them. Then he was free. He had money and skills and he could do anything he wanted. It wasn't until that merc officer had sat down at the table opposite him that he finally realized what it was that he wanted.

Revenge.

"The target is signaling us, sir," said *Vindicator's* Com Officer, startling Florkowski out of his memories.

"Put it on the monitor," said Wolfe with a grin of anticipation. A moment later Ellsworth appeared on the screen. She looked worried. She had good reason to be worried! Florkowski was outside the arc of the camera pickup so she couldn't see him yet. He felt a strange empty feeling in the pit of his stomach.

"Approaching ships, identify yourselves," she demanded in that irritating voice of hers. "You are violating League territory."

"Ah, Captain Ellsworth," said Wolfe in a smooth, silky voice, "so good to meet you, although I'm not sure I like your tone."

"Identify yourselves," she demanded again.

"Oh, forgive me, I sometimes forget that not everyone knows me on sight. The vanity of fame, I'm afraid. I am Commodore Norman Wolfe of Wolfe's Free Mercenaries. I already know who you are."

"What are you doing here? This is League territory."

"Is it indeed? Heavens, my charts must be out of date. They don't show this 'League' you are talking about. There's just this huge empty space on the charts with an 'Up for Grabs' label on it."

"This is Star League territory and you are in violation...!"

"Oh, it's the *Star* League you mean! How silly of me! But, Captain, I'm afraid it's your information that's out of date. I have it on very good authority that the Star League doesn't exist anymore. Folded up shop completely. We heard there was a 'Going Out of Business' sale here in Tractenberg and we decided to pick up a few bargains.

So I'm laying claim to this system and everything in it and I'd be obliged if you would remove yourself from *my* territory."

"The Star League still exists and this is its territory, Wolfe!" snapped Ellsworth.

"Not according to my associate here. He says the League is dead, isn't that right, Commander?" Wolfe touched a control and Florkowski knew that the camera angle had expanded to include him. He couldn't move or say a word. He just stared at Ellsworth. She was staring back with a look of shock far more genuine than what she had shown in Liu-Chen's cabin. She blinked and opened and closed her mouth several times.

"You bastard!" she spat.

"Oh dear, I do hope you weren't addressing me," said Wolfe. "My feelings bruise so easily. But as you can see, we know the full story, Captain. Now, you can also see the full story: I have twelve ships and you have only one. Clear out. Now." All the silk had left his voice.

Ellsworth's face had gone from shock to fury. "I'll see you both in hell first!" she snarled.

"No doubt, but I'm afraid you will get there quite a bit before the rest of us. Tactical, signal the squadron to open fire. Captain Allen, you may fire at will." Ellsworth disappeared from the screen.

"The target's shields are coming up and they are taking evasive action, sir," said Wolfe's 'flag captain'. "We'll be in laser range in fifteen seconds."

But Ellsworth wasn't waiting for Wolfe to fire the first shot. As old as she was, *Gilgamesh* still had better weapons and her photon cannons lashed out. Ton-for-ton she was superior to any of the mercenaries' ships. But there were a lot more tons on the mercs' side. *Vindicator* alone out-massed her six-to-one.

"A hit on *SnickerSnick*, sir. Moderate damage."

"The bitch!" growled Wolfe. All his easy-going tone had vanished. "Going after our weaklings!"

Florkowski nodded to himself. Wolfe had been hoping that *Gilgamesh* would fire at the huge and threatening *Vindicator*, which could handle the cruiser's fire far better than the smaller ships. But Ellsworth wasn't falling for that. As much as he hated her he had to admit she was an excellent combat officer. He had warned Wolfe about that, but he had brushed it off.

"Entering extreme laser range. Commencing fire."

Wolfe's ships opened fire and half-a-hundred lasers reached out for *Gilgamesh*. Individually they were not terribly powerful weapons, but in mass, they could quickly hammer down a shield. Florkowski looked on and honestly could not say which side he was rooting for.

"We're hitting them, sir," said Captain Allen. They were still over a light second away, but closing the range fast. *Gilgamesh* fled toward the gas giant that was a looming presence in the background blocking off a quarter of the sky, but it was still a long way off. Florkowski doubted that they would even get that far before being overwhelmed. Ellsworth fired again and damaged another one of the smaller ships. Wolfe cursed.

"If we can take this Captain Ellsworth alive, I'm going to enjoy having her as my guest."

"Still scoring on them, sir. Reading some debris now. We're hurting them."

"Good. Pour it on, Captain." But a moment later *Gilgamesh's* icon disappeared from the display.

"They've gone around the moon, sir," reported the sensor operator. "I can't get a direct read on them from here."

"Playing hard to get, is she? Communications, tell Captain Hardunna to take his squadron left. I'll go right. And have the corvettes swing out wide to expand our sensor arc."

"Aye aye, sir."

Florkowski watched as Wolfe's force opened out. It was the logical move, but he should have had his corvettes in flanking positions to begin with. As skilled and legendary a ship commander as Wolfe may have been, Florkowski was coming to suspect he didn't have much experience in larger operations. Minutes passed and the mercenaries closed on the moon. Then *Gilgamesh* reappeared on the display. Twice, in fact.

"Reading two contacts now, sir. Hard to get a fix on either; they are jamming."

It was true, there were now two identical sensor contacts about two hundred thousand kilometers ahead. One was heading to pass above the gas giant's rings and veering slightly right, while the other was moving to pass below and to the left. Both of them were blurred and wobbly on the screen.

"A decoy, I assume, Commander," said Wolfe turning to face Florkowski. "And some rather annoying countermeasures."

"Yes, sir. The ship carries a half dozen of them and old as they are, they are still quite good. With your sensors you will have to close to within about a hundred thousand klicks to burn through their ECM and determine which is which."

Wolfe glanced back to the display. They were still overtaking *Gilgamesh*, but not as rapidly as the cruiser accelerated. The mercenaries' lasers stabbed at both contacts but did not appear to be scoring any hits.

"Tell Hardunna to go low. I'll go high. All the lighter ships are to go to maximum acceleration and overtake."

"Aye, aye, sir."

Vindicator was a bit of a pig and was soon falling behind the other ships. Her course took her very close to the moon *Gilgamesh* had been orbiting. As they passed, the sensor operator spoke up.

"Sir, I've got a fix on a shuttle or some sort of landing boat down there. Engines are powered up, but it's just sitting there."

"Weapons, can you get a lock?" asked Wolfe.

"Yes, sir."

"Commodore, is it really necessary to destroy it?" asked Florkowski in alarm. "Those people can't possible pose a threat."

"No, but they could pose a nuisance and they'll be much less of a nuisance without that boat. Weapons, destroy the target."

Stewart Paalova crouched motionless between the two boulders and peered through the branches of the ooula bush with the patience of a seasoned hunter. The Skraks could detect motion very readily and he did not want to give himself away. Certainly not to a party as big as this one!

He was still stunned by the huge number of Skraks he had seen. At least a thousand of them. There had never been that many before, not in all the years he had been alive. Their hunting and raiding parties rarely numbered more than a dozen and usually less. None of the elders back at the city were going to believe him when he told them about this!

Or maybe they would. They had seen and heard the space vehicle come down and they had immediately dispatched the scouts to find out what was happening. They knew something unusual was going on, so perhaps they would believe him after all. Several loud explosions from beyond the hill made him twitch slightly. There was a fight going on over there using modern weapons, but who was winning? He had tracked the Skraks as closely as he had dared and he had gotten to this position in time to see them launch their attack.

The two sentries had been human and that was information of enormous value in its own right. But they had been incredibly sloppy and careless. The Skraks had gotten within a few hundred meters without being seen and then loosed a volley with their murderous crossbows. Amazingly, one of the sentries had stayed on his feet despite a dozen bolts sticking out of his chest. He had fired his weapon once before a second volley felled him, too. Then the Skraks had gone over the hill in a gray-green wave. Their long, snake-like bodies moved with great speed on their multiple pairs of legs. There had been more firing. A lot more firing, and flashes of light; clearly there were more than a few humans.

But the battle was still going on and Stewart could not see it. He glanced around carefully to see how best to shift his position. He really needed to get up to the next ridge, but there were still a few Skraks close by and he was going to have to be very careful. He gripped his spear and was preparing to crawl away when a large group of Skraks reappeared on the ridgeline. Fifty or so were in a dense clump, coming down the hill in his direction. As they got closer he could see that there were two taller figures in their midst.

Prisoners. Damn.

They stopped only thirty meters away and Stewart was hardly breathing. He stopped breathing entirely when he realized the two prisoners were women. Two terrified, rather battered looking women stood there in the midst of the Skraks. One was quite tall and had blond hair. The other was only a bit shorter and was much darker. They were both wearing uniforms that Stewart recognized as belonging to the legendary Star League Navy. The Star League! Incredible! He had heard the stories that the elders had told about the League, seen some of the pictures, but he had scarcely believed them. Clearly, *someone* had built the massive ruins on this planet and not that long ago, but he could give little credence to those tall tales. To have proof that the League actually existed—still existed apparently—left Stewart stunned.

He came back to reality when there was a hissing command from one of the Skraks and they suddenly swarmed at the women, knocking them to the ground. He gripped his spear tighter. Were they being killed? No, the screams and shrieks were going on far too long for that. They would have been dead in seconds if that had been the Skraks' intent. The screams died down to whimpers and squeals and then, abruptly, the women were back on their feet. But now their uniforms were gone. The Skraks had stripped them naked. Stewart looked on with interest, in spite of himself. They were both very pretty. And very frightened. The Skraks had tied their hands behind their backs and looped nooses around their necks. There was another command and they began tugging and prodding their captives forward. They jabbed them with their spears and then several Skraks broke long branches off the bushes and used them as switches. The women were soon yelping in pain and trotting along to stay ahead of their tormentors. Within a minute, the entire party had disappeared over a rise in the ground.

Stewart lay there in total indecision. What to do? Follow the captives? Part of him wanted to do that very much, but there was not much point in it. He couldn't hope to free them on his own, and he knew where they were going, anyway. He inched back out of his hiding place and got to his knees. The firing was more distant now. Could he do any good over there? Not against the huge number of Skraks. He really should go back to the city and let people know what he had seen here. It was important. He flinched as a much larger explosion shook the ground. He looked and saw a large cloud of smoke rising up over in the direction of the gate. The firing was still going on, but it was fading.

Stewart sucked on his teeth. He knew the land around the mountain like the inside of his own bedroom. If there were more people over there and they had to retreat, where would they go? Up the mountain? Not too likely, they would be exposed and the Skraks would run them down in short order. The only other way to go would be down the old road. On level ground a man could run as fast as a Skrak. They might be able to stay ahead of them. But eventually, they would be cornered. Stewart quickly calculated. If he cut across country he could get ahead of those humans if they stuck to the curving road. Yes. That might do some good. And he desperately wanted to meet these people from the Star League.

He got to his feet and started off at a brisk trot.

"Is this everyone?" shouted Gregory Sadgipour.

"I think so, sir," said Sergeant McGill in a calmer voice. "Anyone not here now has bought the farm for sure." Greg winced in pain and the Sergeant realized what he had said. "I'm sorry, sir."

"Can we hold them here?" said Greg, getting control of himself.

"I don't think so, sir. There are just too many avenues of approach to cover for the firepower we have, and when the gauss rifles run out of ammo, they'll overrun us in a blink."

Greg looked around in desperation. They were backed up against the blast doors and taking cover in the jumble of rocks at its base. He looked to have about a dozen Marines left, plus the engineers, a few Navy ratings and Lieutenant Chtak. Climbing the cliff behind them was out of the question. The only way out seemed to be down that road. A few of the Skraknars were moving in that direction, but the way still seemed open. Directly to the front the enemy was slipping between the rocks and getting closer and closer. Off to his right, he could catch glimpses of shapes moving up the mountainside to get above them. McGill was right: they couldn't stay here.

"All right, Sergeant, we are going to head down that road. Put half the men on overwatch to cover the rest. I'll stay with them and fall back when you've gotten the rest started."

"An awful lot of open ground there, sir," said McGill doubtfully. "And those critters move too damn fast. I think maybe I should stay here with a few steady lads until the rest of you have gotten out."

"Sergeant..."

"Hey, if you two can quite arguing about who's gonna play Horatius, I think I've got a better idea." Greg started as Doug Rawlins stumbled into their cluster of rocks. He looked unusually pale and then Greg noticed the bolt through his upper arm.

"Are you all right?"

"Never better. But I won't stay that way long if we don't get out of here." He paused and looked at Greg intently. "What about the girls?"

Greg shook his head and blinked back his tears.

"Shit, shit, shit!" said Rawlins with feeling, shaking his head in turn. But then he got control of himself. "If you can get us moving, I think I can cover our retreat—at least for a few minutes."

"How?"

Rawlins held up a small device that Greg recognized as a detonator for a demolition charge. "I haven't just been standing around scratching my ass all afternoon, you know. It's placed up there and ready to go. If you could arrange for some of the Skraknars to be standing here instead of us, that would be grand."

Greg's brain raced furiously. It seemed as good a plan as any. "All right! All hands, prepare to fall back!"

With McGill to help, the word was passed and on Greg's command they moved. The Marines laid down as much fire as they could and expended the last of their grenades and one of the precious rockets from the launcher. The others all scrambled out of their cover and headed for the road. Then the Marines leapfrogged after them, pausing to fire at intervals. More enemy bolts fell among them, but they were poorly aimed and no one was hurt.

Fifty, a hundred, two hundred meters and they were out of the rocks and on the road. Greg spotted a Skraknar on the slope to his right, but before he could shoot, Chtak hit it with his stunner. A rather amazing shot considering the distance. Greg crouched down next to Rawlins and snapped a shot back in the direction they had come. He could glimpse a slithering carpet of gray-green shapes in the rocks where they had been.

"Fire in the hole!" shouted Rawlins and he pushed the button on the detonator. A geyser of smoke erupted from the mountainside and a moment later the concussion slammed into them. Greg looked again and rocks were flying through the air and tumbling down the hillside. The bang from the initial explosion turned into the roaring crash of a landslide. Clouds of dust joined the smoke and filled the small valley.

"Kind of overdid it, didn't you?" said Greg to Rawlins.

"I like explosions. That's why I became an engineer."

"All right!" shouted McGill. "Let's move!"

Greg pulled Rawlins to his feet and they scrambled down the road. They had covered perhaps half a kilometer when there was a brilliant flash from behind that sent his shadow stretching out in front of him. Another large explosion almost knocked him off his feet, but he kept moving. He glanced over his shoulder to see a pillar of smoke rising in the distance. The cutter.

He choked off a sob and forced his feet to keep moving.

"They're continuing to close, ma'am," said Ensign Snowden. "They'll probably I.D. the decoy drone any second."

"Understood," said Ellsworth. She took a deep breath and gripped the arms of her chair. The enemy was catching up with them. Their smaller ships had a higher acceleration and they had all started out with a substantial initial vector. But she had managed to divide their forces with a decoy drone. Half of them were pursuing *Gilgamesh* 'below' the gas giant's rings and the other half, including the battleship, were following the decoy above. In a moment, the ruse would be found out, but at least the other half would be out of the fight for a while. The rings were thin, but still far too dense to fire through.

"All right, if they are going to see through it, let's not keep them waiting. Commence fire on Target Eight."

"Aye, ma'am," said Bradley from the tactical station. *Gilgamesh* stopped her evasive action and fired a salvo at one of the pursuing destroyers. The range was much shorter now and they scored several hits. Almost immediately the enemy's fire focused in on them as their exact position was revealed. The ship shook and lurched as the lasers clawed at the shields. But with only half the enemy force able to fire, they were able to hold—for the moment.

But what should she do now? Even half of Wolfe's squadron was enough to beat her. And he had Florkowski with him. That searing thought forced its way into her tactical deliberations. Florkowski! That miserable son of a bitch! She had been flabbergasted when she saw him there on Wolfe's ship. For an instant she thought perhaps the mercenaries had kidnapped him and used drugs to force the knowledge of *Gilgamesh's* mission from him. But then she saw that icy stare—the same icy stare she had grown to hate—directed at her and she knew the truth. The traitor! Anger and hatred boiled inside her, but there was a chilling sense of fear—and guilt—there, too. She had made the same mistake as Liu-Chen: given him the benefit of the doubt. One word, just one different word to Shusterman four months earlier would have prevented this! It was her fault and she knew it.

The ship shook again and she forced the thoughts of Florkowski out of her mind. She had to decide what to do. The shields were weakening. In another few minutes they would be past the rings and the other half of the enemy would soon have a shot at her again. But not for long, She noted with satisfaction that the decoy had drawn those ships sufficiently off her track that they would have to go around the gas giant the opposite way she was. The only other choice they had was to run head-on into the planet and she couldn't hope they would be that stu...

Could that work? An idea was forming. They wouldn't be that stupid, but maybe she should be. She began drawing vectors in on her tactical plot. Maybe. Maybe it could work. *Gilgamesh* was angling to pass around one edge of the gas giant. They would pass very close to it and should gain a precious few minutes reprieve from the enemy's fire as they went around, just as they had earlier used the moon to block the enemy's fire. Yes, it might work, but they were going to need a little privacy to make it work.

"Brad, concentrate fire on that corvette, the one way out on the flank."

"Ma'am? That's at maximum range, there are better targets…"

"I know, but please do it."

"Aye, aye, shifting fire."

"Ensign Snowden, prepare two more decoys. I'm transferring the courses and speeds I want."

"Two, ma'am? Yes ma'am."

"Commander van Rossum, in a few minutes I am going to require emergency power to the shields and then shortly after that everything the engines have left."

"Yes, ma'am, I'll be ready. And this old girl has got a lot left to give us!"

Ellsworth smiled at her engineer, then ship shook again and this time she knew it wasn't just the shields. "Blast-through aft," reported Bradley, "Damage to secondary turret twelve and sensor cluster eight."

"The other enemy squadron has cleared the rings, ma'am."

The next few minutes were going to be bad. With all the enemy ships concentrating on them the shields just couldn't handle it. The ship quivered and groaned and the damage reports flowed in. If they lost something vital now, it would be all over.

But their luck held and the huge bulk of the planet shielded them from half the enemy fire again. Now, a few more minutes and the other group would be blocked too. All except that damn corvette.

"Commander, I need the target suppressed."

"Trying ma'am, the range is extreme and they are evading and…Bingo!"

The photon cannons had finally found their mark. The small target's shield and drive failed and the ship coasted, utterly defenseless.

"Finish the job, Commander," said Ellsworth.

"Ma'am? They're out of the fight…"

"They can still see us, Commander. We can't afford any spying eyes right now."

"Aye, ma'am, I understand."

A few moments later *Gilgamesh* fired again. Without the ability to change course, the target was a sitting duck, even at this range. A half-dozen hits were scored and the corvette exploded into fragments. Just a few more seconds now...

Gilgamesh curved around the planet and was lost to the remaining enemy's view.

"Helm come right to oh-two-eight by oh-three-three, ahead full."

"Aye aye, ma'am," said Ensign Bartlett. He carried out her orders and then looked back at her in surprise. "Ma'am, that course will take us..."

"I know, ensign, I know. Mister Snowden, launch the drones."

"Aye, aye, ma'am, drones away."

Ellsworth keyed on a visual display on one of her smaller monitors. The orange-brown bulk of the gas giant filled one edge of the screen. The night side terminator line was sharply etched and approaching fast. It was also slowly drifting across the center of the monitor...

"Skipper, are you doing what I think you are?" asked Bradley.

"Yup. Van, standby to cut power to the drive and put everything into the shields. Miss Terletsky, sound the acceleration warning. Tell all hands to strap themselves in."

The planet was swelling larger and larger. There were several flickers of light from the night side. *Lightning, good! Maybe it will cover our ionization trail.* She checked their course. It was just about right...

"Cut the drive! Full power to the shields!"

Gilgamesh was now hurtling for the gas giant's upper atmosphere at a frightening velocity. Seconds later the ship started to quiver as the shield began batting aside air molecules.

"Hang on, everyone, this is going to get a little rough," said Ellsworth.

Chtak'Chr paused beside the others and panted rapidly, his tongue hanging out the side of his mouth. At times like this he wished he could perspire the way the humans did, in spite of the nasty smell it made. It was difficult to talk and disperse heat at the same time. Although considering the circumstances, it might have been better if the humans had the same difficulty.

"Would someone mind explaining how the bloody hell those things managed to sneak up on us like that?" demanded Lieutenant Rawlins from where he was sitting. "Were the sentries asleep of something?"

"Sir, the men were on full alert," said Sergeant McGill stiffly.

"Really? Then how did a zillion enemy soldiers just stroll into our area unannounced like that?"

"They were on full alert," insisted McGill.

Chtak glanced rapidly around the gully the landing party was sheltering in. The road was just a few meters away and soon they would have to get moving again. They had covered nearly four kilometers at a fast trot and they had to rest a bit. Rawlins, wounded as he was, was starting to lag badly. Unfortunately, his temper wasn't. He cursed as the Marine medic tried to extract the bolt in his arm.

"Alert, were they? No more alert than the squids up on *Gilgamesh*! All those scanners running and no one noticed anything? That wasn't a few infiltrators, that was a whole army!"

"Lieutenant," said Chtak between pants, "the Skraknars have been engineered for stealth. They can alter their skin color to match the surroundings. They can also mask their infra-red signatures with an ingenious system of bio-heat exchangers that allow them to heat or cool their skin temperatures to become invisible on IR scans. They cannot keep that up indefinitely, but for more than long enough to have avoided detection in this attack."

"Yeah, and since they weren't carrying any energy weapons we couldn't spot any emissions," added Gregory. "Our motion sensors might have gotten them except they're all on the fritz. So lighten up, Doug."

"Easy for you to say," he said through clenched teeth as the medic pulled out the bolt.

"May I see that?" asked Chtak. The medic handed it to him and then finished patching up Rawlins' arm. Chtak examined the projectile closely. It was very well made and he noted that the point was a hardened piece of durasteel. With enough force behind it, such a weapon could pierce most body armor.

"There you are, Lieutenant," said the medic. "I hope that didn't hurt… too much."

"Can you walk, Doug?" asked Gregory. "We have to keep moving." Chtak looked closely at the young Marine. He was holding up well after the death of Rhada McClerndon, but he was clearly shaken. The loss of that human had caused Chtak, himself more pain than he would have believed possible. She had such potential. And she had been a good friend. He would mourn and light the ritual offerings later when there was time, but even now it hurt badly. Gregory had been even closer to the woman. Chtak did not think they had mated yet, but that had clearly been in the offing—if tragedy had not intervened. Then he thought of the other dead. There would be many to mourn—if any survived to do so.

Rawlins levered himself to his feet with an assist from the medic. "Yeah, I can walk. As long as I have to. Let's get going."

They were climbing the short slope back to the road when Chtak noticed the Skraknar on the opposite side. Chtak had always known that his own reflexes were much faster than the humans, but it had not become so evident before this current crisis. Chtak had his stunner out and aimed before any of the humans even moved. The Skraknar was very fast, too, but he shot it before it could bring its crossbow to bear. The humans jumped and then hastily looked around. Fortunately the Skraknar seemed to be alone.

"Nice shot, Chtak!" exclaimed Gregory.

"Thank you. We better move, they seem to be catching up again."

The party headed down the road at a jog that would have been easy a few hours earlier, but now it was quite an effort. Chtak had to alternately hop and run on all fours to keep up. It was an awkward pace for him. The backpack full of his instruments further hindered him, but he did not even consider abandoning it.

A half-hour later the road was turning to the north and the damaged housing tower could be seen in the distance. They were surprised when a dark shadow rapidly moved across the building and then rushed in their direction. Looking up, Chtak could see the sun disappearing behind the enormous black disk of the gas giant. The moon they were on was tidally 'locked' so that one side always faced the gas giant. This was the side the base was on. The orbital period was a bit over twenty-six standard hours and once each day the gas giant would eclipse the sun, bringing darkness at noon. The gleaming disk of the planet's rings provided some illumination, but it really was quite dark.

"How long will this last?" asked Sergeant McGill.

"One hour, twelve minutes," replied Chtak.

"Well then I suggest we get moving since our Mark One eyeballs will be even less effective at spotting those buggers now," said McGill. They pushed themselves for another twenty minutes and then had to stop for a break.

"Where now?" asked Rawlins.

"Maybe we can find a spot to hole up in the housing tower over there," suggested Gregory.

"Maybe, sir. But maybe that's where the Skraks came from. Maybe they've just been herding us in this direction on purpose."

"That's an ugly thought."

"Yes, sir."

"Well make up your mind soon," gasped Rawlins.

Chtak suddenly smelled something. An odor that was... human. Or almost. Not at all like what his companions smelled like, but certainly not one of the Skraknars. He noted the wind direction and looked to a clump of bushes on a slight rise beside the road. Yes. His eyes had adjusted to the dark now and he could make out a shape that was not part of the bush.

"Gregory, there is a human watching us in that bush. Twelve meters, bearing about ninety degrees," he whispered, and Gregory stiffened suddenly. "I could stun him if you think that wise."

"A human? You're sure?"

"Yes."

"Get ready with your stunner."

"I am ready."

"Okay. Hey you! Over in the bush! We see you, so don't make any sudden moves! Come out here with your hands up!"

"Very subtle, Greg," said Chtak.

"Hey, it worked, didn't it?"

Indeed it had. To his surprise the human stood up and came forward. Its hands were up and he could see that one held a spear in a non-threatening position. As it got closer Chtak could see that it was a young male dressed in a vest, shorts and boots. A long knife hung from a belt and he had a small bag hanging from his shoulder. He was very tall and muscular.

"Who are you?" asked Gregory.

"My... my name is Stewart Paalova," said the man. "Are... are you from the Star League?"

"Yes. Where are you from?"

"Here. This is my home."

"Well, you've got some charming neighbors!" said Rawlins testily.

"The Skraks? Yes, they are very dangerous. I have never seen them in such numbers. We should get to shelter quickly."

"Shelter? Where?" demanded Greg.

"There, in the city." He pointed to the housing tower.

"Can we get in there?"

"Yes. But the main gate is too far. The Skraks are very close behind you."

The whole party looked back down the road. They had not seen or heard anything...

"Then where...?" asked Greg anxiously.

"Follow me."

"Captain Hardunna is reporting that *Looterfiend* has been destroyed and he has lost sight of the enemy, sir," reported *Vindicator's* Com Officer.

"Damnation!" roared Commodore Wolfe. "When I get my hands on that bitch Ellsworth I'll be keeping the Sick Bay busy repairing her for a month!"

Charles Florkowski watched the tirade impassively. He was used to them now. The first one had been quite a surprise, but they had become almost routine after four weeks. At first, Florkowski had been very impressed with the Commodore. He had seemed calm and professional. He had managed to assemble a very powerful force of mercenaries and hold them together and that was never an easy feat. The man definitely had a strong charisma and he had used it skillfully on those around him. Including Florkowski.

Just like with his desertion, Florkowski had had no notion of joining up with Wolfe's mercenaries. It had just happened. The merc officer had sat down with him in the bar and started talking. 'I understand you are off that League cruiser,' he had said. 'You have efficient information sources,' Florkowski had replied. 'The Leagies asked Station Security for help in finding you. We have our sources.' 'I see.' 'My commander would like to have a few words with you. He's willing to pay.'

It had turned into more than a few words. He had a long, long talk with Norman Wolfe. He found himself giving up all sorts of information to him. What was going on in the League, how defenseless they were. He had not actually paid him anything, but suddenly he just didn't give a damn anymore. His whole life devoted to the League and they had betrayed him and driven him out. He didn't owe them a damn thing! But Wolfe was friendly. He flattered him and reminded Florkowski that he too had been driven out by those arrogant League bastards long ago. He had quite a lot to drink. Somehow he had ended up on Wolfe's flagship. He had been promised a command of his own. He hadn't planned it this way, but it had seemed like a good thing. At first, anyway.

The next day Wolfe was making plans for a major raid into the League. Not against Leavitte where that bastard Shusterman was—Florkowski would have welcomed that—but against another world. A world with a big population and no defenses. To his horror, Wolfe was planning it primarily as a slave raid. They would grab anything else of value they could find, but he intended to cram in as many people as he could catch and sell them as slaves while the prices were still high. It would be easy, too: they would just pretend to be a rescue fleet. When the people crowded around to get food or supplies they could just pick the young, pretty ones for 'evacuation' and fill their holds.

Florkowski couldn't allow this. He had to distract Wolfe from this somehow.

Then he thought of Ellsworth and her 'mission.'

It had worked perfectly. Wolfe had fallen for it completely: A story about a lost treasure. A base full of League technology ripe for the picking. And a lone League cruiser all that was in the way. Florkowski had breathed a huge sigh of relief when the fleet set sail for Tractenberg.

"We should be picking them up again any second," said the sensor officer.

"We had better," said Wolfe, regaining control after his rant.

And a few moments later they did. Twice. Once again, one contact was above the rings and the other below. Both were headed outbound at very high acceleration. Ellsworth must be redlining *Gilgamesh's* engines to pull that many gees. Those old drives couldn't take much of that.

"Two contacts again, sir. They are jamming and I can't get a fix on either. I'm sorry, sir."

"All right, the same as before. Hardunna goes low and we'll go high. We can still catch them long before they get out of the gravity well. All ships, maximum acceleration and pursuit vectors."

"Aye aye, sir."

Vindicator and her escorts skimmed over the top of the planet's rings. The lighter ships were well out in front, but still far astern of *Gilgamesh*—if that was *Gilgamesh*. Florkowski frowned. How had Ellsworth picked up that much distance on her pursuers? She had only been about a hundred thousand klicks ahead of Captain Hardunna's ships when she shook off contact. Now she was two hundred thousand out in front again. She had cut the planet closer and would have picked up a bit of a gravity assist, but not that much. Florkowski looked at the sensor display, but there was nothing there to give him any clue. Well, in another ten minutes they would know for sure.

The planet's rings were falling behind when Hardunna's lead ship burned through the jamming of the one contact and confirmed that it was a drone.

"Excellent!" chortled Wolfe. "Looks like we get to make the kill. Sadly, it probably will just be a kill. I rather doubt we'll be able to arrange a capture. This Captain Ellsworth doesn't seem like one to surrender, does she, Commander?"

"You are probably correct, Commodore."

"Yes, and I doubt she wants to fall into your hands, either, eh, Commander? Although she should be far more worried about falling into mine!" Wolfe laughed loudly as if it was a huge joke. A few of the bridge crew chuckled nervously. Florkowski forced a small smile.

"As you say, sir." Wolfe cocked an eyebrow at him and gave him a piercing stare. He had the uncomfortable feeling the man could see right through him. Florkowski turned and studied the display in front of him very deliberately.

The range fell and fell. *Vindicator* was far behind by this point, but her escorts were nearly close enough. Florkoswki imagined Ellsworth would turn and fight once she realized she couldn't get away. She could put up a good show against the three destroyers and two frigates that were tailing her, but then *Vindicator* and Hardunna's force would catch up and it would be over. It was a sad notion. *Gilgamesh* had been part of his life for so long and in a few minutes she would be gone forever. The last link with his old life...

"*Hardacre* is getting a lock, sir," said Captain Allen. The display updated with the new information and suddenly the bridge was very quiet.

Another drone.

"Where is she?!" roared Wolfe.

"I... she must have cut power and drifted, sir," stuttered the sensor operator nervously.

"And avoided all of our active scans? How?"

"I don't know, sir. We should have picked them up. I can't see how we could have missed them..." The man was sweating and Florkowski realized he was playing for his life.

"Commodore." Florkowski stood up.

"What?" Wolfe wheeled to face him.

"The only place they could have gone where we would have missed them would be either the gas giant's atmosphere or into the rings," said Florkowski. The sensor operator gave him a grateful look.

"Yes, sir, the target was very close to the planet, they could have used atmospheric braking and then done a power down."

Wolfe looked like he was going to explode again, but he shut it off and was suddenly cool and calculating again. The transition was as frightening as the earlier outburst.

"Good. That's just what I wanted them to do. Communications, signal all ships to come about. Take up patrol positions outside the planet's rings and keep a sharp lookout. There's no chance they can get away now. We just have to wait and we'll find them eventually. And when we do we'll have them." A shark-like smile was growing on Wolfe's face.

"The only way Captain Ellsworth and her crew will be leaving this system… is in chains."

CHAPTER FOURTEEN

Gregory Sadgipour splashed through the shallow water of the narrow creek, awkwardly supporting Doug Rawlins' stumbling body. The engineer was clearly reaching the end of his strength after his wounding and the long retreat in front of the Skraknars. The gravity of this planet was just about standard, which meant that everything was very light for Greg, even after his time away from his high-gravity home. But even so, he was nearly exhausted, too. The rest of his party was strung out along the creek bed, following their newly acquired guide.

That guide now stopped for a moment and motioned for quiet. He appeared to be listening for something. The man was large, but he moved with an easy grace and a near-silence that Greg had to admire.

"Has anyone given any thought to the fact that if there are Darj'Nang underlings around here there could be some of the big boys themselves?" said Rawlins, none too quietly. "How do we know ol' Daniel Boone up there isn't working for them?" Greg started. He had not thought of that at all.

"Calm yourself, Lieutenant," said Chtak from behind them. "If any of the Darj'Nang overlords were present, we would not be having this conversation; they could have taken control of our minds long ago. I have to believe that the Skraknars we have encountered are survivors from the original attack on this base."

"But *Gilgamesh* said they were under attack, too. If not the Darj'Nang, then who?"

"I can only speculate Outies or other intruders. Hopefully we will be able to reestablish contact with the ship soon."

"And what about our guide?" asked Greg.

"Obviously the evacuation was not as complete as the records show."

The guide waved them on and they continued forward. The remains of the housing tower were looming over them now. It was not nearly as big as the structures he had seen on Flemington, but it was still easily three hundred meters high. As he looked up, daylight swept across the tower and them—the sun had come out from behind the gas giant.

"Only a little farther," said the guide quietly.

"Thank God for that," muttered Rawlins.

The guide's word was good and after only another minute or so they came to a metal door set into a rock wall. A small pipe emerged from the wall beside the door and was feeding the stream they were standing in. Their guide took the haft of his spear and rapped on the door. Half a minute went by and nothing happened. Greg looked back along their path. He wasn't sure, but he thought he saw something moving a few hundred meters away. He looked around. They were in a dead end. That door better open soon...

The guide rapped again. "C'mon, Blaire! Open up!" he shouted. "It's me, Stewart!"

A small observation slit beside the door squeaked open. "Hi, Stu," came a muffled voice, "back early? Just a sec and I'll... who the hell are they?!"

"I found some guests, now open the door will you? I've got half the Skraks in creation on my tail!"

There was a thump and a clang and then the very heavy steel door swung open. Another young man, about the same age as their guide, was standing there, staring at them with wide eyes. To Greg's surprise and envy, the man had a plasma rifle slung over his shoulder.

"Please, everyone come inside quickly, we need to get the door shut," said Stewart. They followed his request and filed through the door. The second man flinched back noticeably when Chtak passed him. When they were all in, the door was pushed shut and locked. Greg looked around and they were in a narrow service corridor of some sort. Pipes and conduits were on both sides and above them. Lights glowed at intervals along its length.

"Keep a close watch, Blaire," said Stewart. "I don't know if the Skraks will follow this far, but if they do, be ready to toast them."

"Right," said the other man with an eager grin. He unlimbered the plasma rifle and peered out the view slit.

"Mister... uh, Paalova," said Greg. "Just who are you people and what are you doing here?"

"Greg, can it wait until we get somewhere where we can sit—or preferably lie—down?" asked Rawlins.

"Oh. Sorry."

"Yes, let's go upstairs and then we can talk," said Stewart. "Blaire, can you send a signal ahead? The elders are going to want to see our guests."

"Sure thing."

Stewart led them along the corridor and eventually came to an elevator. It wasn't large enough to take everyone at once so Greg and Rawlins and half the others went with their guide and Chtak agreed to bring the rest on the next trip. "Just press the button for 'lobby'," said Stewart. Greg shook his head. The abrupt transition from fleeing for their lives to 'press the button for lobby' was a bit hard to handle. And Rhada was dead. The thought came slamming back into him as the doors shut and they were carried upward. It almost hammered him to the floor, it was so numbing. She was really dead. He had loved her and now she was dead. Could he have prevented it? It wasn't fair! They'd had no time at all…

"Greg? Greg, let's go."

He blinked. The elevator doors had opened and he was still standing there, halfway supporting Rawlins. He shuffled forward into the 'lobby'.

Apparently the sentry down below had not gotten the word about their arrival through to everyone, because in an instant there were several dozen astonished people gaping at them as they left the elevator cab.

"Stewart! What is this?" exclaimed one of them, an older woman.

"I found some people outside."

"And we followed him home," said Rawlins. "Can I sit down somewhere, please?"

The woman who had spoken first parted the crowd like a prophet and ushered them to some seats and summoned a doctor all in an instant. A moment later she brought Chtak and the rest of the party over when they appeared in the elevator. Greg collapsed into a chair and looked around. The 'lobby' overlooked the central atrium of the housing tower. He could see that when the eastern side of the tower had partially collapsed, the atrium skylights had been destroyed. But a new set had been built, perhaps a hundred meters up, enclosing the central space again. Numerous balconies looked down from the higher levels. Those balconies seemed to be filling with excited people as the news spread. The appearance of these people came as a surprise after the rough, outdoor look of their guide. They were all clean and well-fed and dressed in adequate clothes. They looked like people you could find in any city of the League—not like the survivors of a devastating attack from space.

"Are you really from the Star League?" asked one of the onlookers. The question opened the floodgates and a hundred more were asked in a few seconds. Greg didn't know who to try and answer first. But after a moment the crowd parted again and a middle-aged man with silver hair at his temples walked quickly up to where they were sitting. With a groan, Greg got to his feet. The crowd quieted.

"Lieutenant? I'm Hakata Carmichael. I'm the… well, I guess 'mayor' would be the proper term; we don't go much for titles around here. Anyway, I'm the elected leader of the people of this city. Welcome." He held out his hand.

Greg took it. "Mister Carmichael, I'm Gregory Sadgipour, Star League Marines, assigned to *LSS Gilgamesh*. Pleased to meet you." It hadn't quite sunk in yet, but Greg realized that he was now in command of the expedition. Quatrock was dead—*my fault. That was my fault, too*—and though both Chtak and Rawlins outranked him, he was a line combat officer and they weren't.

"You really are from the Star League?" asked Carmichael anxiously. "The League really still exists? We haven't lost the war?" Greg wasn't quite sure what to say about that. Considering the recent disaster it would be a stretch to say that they had won the war, but he guessed the Darj'Nang had come off even worse.

"Well, I suppose you could almost call it a draw," he said finally. "The League has pretty well wiped out the Darj'Nang, but we've been badly smashed up ourselves." There, that was sort of true. There was an excited stir among the watchers.

"The Darj'Nang are destroyed?" asked one "Really?"

"As far as we know. The situation is a bit complicated. But who are you people? We didn't expect to find anyone here at all." Carmichael's face became grim.

"I guess Admiral Cunningham didn't get out with the other evacuees after all then?"

"Admiral Cunningham…?"

"Admiral Cunningham was the commander of the garrison in this system," said Chtak. "He did make it out with the convoy, but there was no record of anyone being left behind."

"That son of a bitch," said Carmichael quietly, shaking his head. "He knew we were here when he left and he never told anyone. All the ships were packed and time was short and there were still people trapped in the tower here. He had to pull out, he had no choice, but he knew he was leaving people behind. Trying to cover his own sorry ass, no doubt, but that was Cunningham all over."

"So you were all left behind?" asked Greg.

"Yes, I guess there were about two thousand of us all told. Some people were trapped under the east side of the tower and had to be dug out and a lot of others had been in the outlying settlements and there were personnel from the base. It was a hell of a mess. The Darj'Nang had come in with a fairly small force, but they had their damn mind control. The war was about six months old and we'd been warned about that, but we had no way to counter it. I assume you folks discovered a way?"

"Yes," said Chtak, "a thought-screen generator was developed about six months after the attack here." Greg did not add that every one of those things was now junk.

"That's good. So anyway, they came in here and started taking control of the ship crews and the people on the orbital stations. We fought back as well as we could, but it was hard and eventually all the orbital installations were knocked out and our ships had to fall back. The Darj'Nang came into orbit and started taking out the ground defenses, both with fire and with their mind control. It was pretty grim with Marines fighting Marines and no one knowing who they could trust and the 'Nangs blasting us from orbit. But then our ships put together a counterattack and they got lucky. They managed to destroy the enemy command ship and take out all the overlords. After that, the rest of them fell back.

"We pulled things back together as well as we could, but it seemed certain that the 'Nangs would come back again, so Cunningham made the decision to evacuate. And with all the confusion a lot of us got left behind."

"And you've been living here ever since?" asked Greg.

"For a while we hid out in the badlands. We figured it would be our only hope of survival when the 'Nangs returned. But when they didn't we came back here. Well, most of us did, there are still some folks out in the wilds who won't. We fixed up the tower and tried to put together some semblance of a society."

"It appears that you have succeeded quite well, sir," said Chtak. "Your people seem to be in good health and in good order."

"But what about the Skraknars who attacked us?" asked Rawlins. A woman had arrived with a medical kit and was examining his wound.

"Hakata," said Stewart from where he was standing, "there was a huge party of Skraks that attacked them. I estimate at least a thousand."

"A thousand?!" exclaimed several people. "There can't be that many!"

"Are you certain, Stu?" asked Carmichael with a deep frown.

"I counted over a hundred in just one column, sir. And there were at least eight columns." The young man spoke with a quiet certainty that seemed to impress the onlookers. But a few still argued that the number was impossibly high.

"Hak," said another older man, "even if Stewart counted each one twice—and I'm not saying he did—that's still ten times more Skraks than we've seen in almost twenty years. This is bad."

"During the initial attack, the Darj'Nang sent down some assault troops," explained Carmichael. "We didn't even know about it until later. There could not have been more than a hundred or so, and apparently they landed quite some distance away. After we had come back here and were starting to get things in order, they suddenly attacked. As I said, there were only a hundred of them, but they took us by surprise and nearly wiped us out. We lost close to half our number. But we killed almost all of them. The survivors retreated. They kept sniping at us until all their ammo and energy charges were gone. Since then, they've only come out in small numbers. We had no idea their numbers had grown so much."

"Yes," said Chtak, "you probably knew little about the Skraknars at that point. Since then we've learned that they lay eggs in sizable numbers and their young reach maturity in only five standard years. They can increase their numbers with alarming rapidity."

"But they only have relatively primitive weapons now, it seems," said Greg. "Just as we were attacked on the ground, we got word that our ship was under attack in orbit. Could the Skraks have been responsible?"

Carmichael frowned. "That seems very unlikely, Lieutenant. If they had warships still in the system, surely they would have attacked us here long before now."

"Yes. Perhaps you are right, Chtak. Maybe it's Outies. I guess all we can do is wait to hear something from *Gilgamesh*." Greg glanced around the assembly. "You still seem to have some modern weaponry, sir. When I saw Mister Paalova with his spear, I was afraid your technology had... deteriorated."

"No, we have all the comforts of home here," said Carmichael with evident pride. "In fact, it is home. We have power and food and medical facilities and our children are educated and clothed. But we send our young scouts out without the fancy weapons on purpose. Partly to keep them cautious, but mostly to make sure the Skraks don't get their hands on any modern stuff. We've fortified the tower sufficiently that they can't get in here with what they've got. If they captured a few plasma rifles, we wouldn't be nearly so secure. But Lieutenant, you haven't told us what you are doing here. If you didn't know we were here, it obviously isn't a rescue party."

"No, sir, I'm afraid not. We were coming here to see if the ground installations had survived. As I mentioned, we've been hurt pretty badly by the war. The technology in that base is now better than anything we have and we were hoping to salvage it." It wasn't exactly the whole truth, but it summed things up pretty well. Details could come later. He was alarmed when he saw Carmichael shaking his head.

"Well, if that's the case then I don't have very good news for you, Lieutenant."

"The base has been destroyed?" Greg's face showed his dismay.

"No, I don't think it has. But unless you can whistle up that ship of yours and some heavy duty weaponry, there's no way you are going to get inside that base."

Jaq Ellsworth floated into the darkened conference room and pushed herself over to one of the large windows. She hated freefall, but they couldn't risk using the artificial gravity. Its emanations were detectable at too great a distance and they did not dare to be detected now.

Gilgamesh was in hiding.

Jaq looked out the window and saw one of the most amazing sights she had ever seen in her twenty years in space. The sky was filled with millions of brilliant white objects. 'Above' and 'below' they were numerous, but black space could be seen beyond them. To the sides, the numbers became so great that they all merged into a solid band of white. By pressing her nose against the window and peering aft, she could see one edge of the enormous gas giant.

They were in the rings.

They had managed to break contact with the enemy forces and taken refuge here. The passage through the gas giant's atmosphere had nearly collapsed the shields, but it had allow them to shed most of their velocity far faster than the ship's drive could have accomplished. It had strained the gee nullifiers beyond their abilities, too. Several very long minutes at a perceived ten gravities had been rough. She was still sore where her safety straps had bitten into her. But then they had shot clear and another minute with the drive at emergency power had left them drifting slowly, a few kilometers from the inside edge of the ring. A couple of small thruster burns and they had been inside. Then they shut down the fusion plant and almost all the other systems, drifted, and held their collective breaths. The enemy, intent on the fleeing decoys, had charged past them without a second look.

But they were looking now. The eleven remaining enemy ships were cruising around the rings with active sensors blazing. So far, they had not even come close. Six hours had passed.

A faint clang made Ellsworth glance up. Something had banged into them. That was happening all the time now. The ship was being subjected to a gentle—and sometimes not so gentle—bombardment by the debris that made up the rings. The relative velocities were low so the damage was slight, but *Gilgamesh* was going to need a new paint job when this was over.

Another noise made her glance over her shoulder. Her staff was floating into the room. Ellsworth touched the controls and shutters slid over the windows. Then she turned on the lights. They couldn't risk even a stray beam of light reaching their enemies. Almost humorously, everyone was taking position by the chairs fixed to the deck. There was no need to sit down, but old habits died hard.

"All right, everyone, let's get down to business," she said. "First of all, my compliments to all hands. That was an excellent job during the battle. Please pass on my thanks to all of your people." There were a number of murmured responses. "Now, the first order of business is the repairs. What sort of shape are we in, Van?"

Commander Van Rossum was their chief engineer and also in charge of damage control. He awkwardly tried to hold his pad in one hand and keep from drifting away with the other. "I've done a complete survey and we are not in too bad shape, Skipper. They never managed to completely knock our shields down, so all their fire was buffered to some degree. We didn't take any really heavy hits and the armor absorbed a lot of what did get through. As a result, most of the damage was to surface mounted equipment. Two of the main photon cannon mounts were damaged, but I think they can both be repaired. Three of the secondaries were hit and I think only one is beyond fixing. About a dozen sensor cluster are gone. We can replace those, but we'll only have a few left in supply afterwards. Three shield emitters are out. They are going to be the trickiest, but I'm hopeful. A few dozen miscellaneous hull breaches and other minor damage makes up the list. It could have been a lot worse."

"How long for the repairs?"

"That's the bad news: at least three weeks."

Ellsworth was surprised. That was far longer than she had expected. "You're not pulling one of these 'promise-it-in-three-and-deliver-in-two-miracle-worker' routines are you, Van?"

"Sorry, Skipper, wish I was," chuckled the engineer grimly. "No, the repairs are going to be a major pain. Have you checked the outside radiation readings lately?"

"No, I haven't."

"Well, do that the next time you're on the bridge and you'll under-stand. That gas giant is hot. Hot enough to fry a man in a suit in less than an hour. A fatal dose in spite of all we can do to shield them. We're safe enough inside here, but outside work is going to be hell. I'm having to use some of the old remotes and use my men only for fast, must-do jobs. The surgeon will only allow a twenty minute exposure once a week and I'll go through my available people damn quick at that rate."

"I see," she said. "I hadn't realized." Maybe this had not been such a good idea after all. "Doctor, how are the casualties?"

"We had a half-dozen minor injuries from the actual fighting. I should have all of them fit for duty in a day or two," said Doctor Twiggs. "On the other hand, I've got two dozen people with injuries from our ride through the gas giant, including three of the civilians. That was pretty rough, ma'am. A number of broken bones and a few of them will be on the sick list for a week or more."

"But no fatalities or critical injuries?"

"No, ma'am, we were lucky."

"Lucky. Yeah, I guess we were."

"But some of the civilians are complaining about the zero-g, ma'am. They don't like it."

"Well, I warned Consul Brown not to come with us. Tell him I expect him to keep his own people in line."

"Yes, ma'am."

"Brad, how is everything else?"

"Life support is fine, supplies are no problem, except for fuel. We're down to under ten percent and with the cutter gone we haven't got a lot of options except to gather ice and crack it for aytch-two. Fortunately, there's plenty of ice around. Our batteries are at ninety-three percent and we should be able to go for a month or so on them without having to fire up the fusion plant, although if we start cracking ice, that figure will go down. Of course, our ability to gather ice or fire up the main fusion plant is going to depend on the tactical situation."

Ellsworth frowned. "Yes, the tactical situation. Let's talk about that." She didn't really want to talk about that because the situation stank. But it wouldn't stink any less by not talking about it.

"We've managed to break contact and for the time being we have the initiative. All the enemy can do is try to find us, but barring them getting lucky, we can choose when and where we make our next move." There, that put a positive face on an inherently impossible situation…

"What are the chances of them getting lucky, ma'am?" asked Bradley. "Right now, with the fusion plant off-line, it would take us nearly twenty minutes to bring our systems up. If they caught us like that we'd be cold meat."

"How about that, ensign?" said Ellsworth to Ensign Snowden, the sensor officer. He suddenly looked a little nervous—and very young.

"I've been looking at the problem from both sides, ma'am. What would I do if I was trying to find us and how I would go about making us harder to find. So far, I'd rather be us than them—at least as far as the detection issue goes."

"Glad to hear that," said Ellsworth with a small grin.

"Shut down as we are, they'd have to get within a few hundred kilometers to pick up any trace of energy emissions from our batteries. They know we have to be somewhere inside the rings, but that leaves an awful lot of space to search. Allowing for the average thickness of the rings, we've got over a trillion cubic kilometers to hide in. An active sensor scan could possibly pick us up at a longer distance, but the debris in the rings is also working in our favor. The ring particles range in size from dust up to rocks bigger than *Gilgamesh*. Plus all that metallic wreckage we detected earlier. If we could find some big rock to snuggle up to, ma'am, they'd have to be very, very lucky to spot us."

"Thank you, Ensign, that's good to know." Ellsworth was pleased with the report and impressed with Snowden's thoroughness. Maybe a brevet promotion to Lieutenant (j.g.) would be in order at some point. "In any case," she continued, "the enemy has not been making any serious attempt to find us yet. They have taken up positions around the periphery of the ring and above and below it in an attempt to prevent us from escaping. Frankly, they are doing a lousy job of even that. With our three remaining decoys and even a tiny bit of luck, we could make it to the gravity well boundary and hyper out before they could hope to stop us. If getting away was our goal."

"Is it, Skipper?" asked Bradley.

"No. It's not. We came here to take possession of that base and that is what we are going to do."

"Forgive me for asking, ma'am," said Van Rossum, "but how can we do that against the force against us? We're rather hopelessly outnumbered, aren't we?"

"For a stand-up fight, we probably are. One-on-one we can beat any ship they have except that battleship. The rest of them can only beat us if they gang up. It's going to be my job to see that they don't do that. If we can ambush a few of them individually we can cut down the odds. And the great weakness of our opponents is that they are mercenaries. They are here looking for profit. Getting their ships shot up is not part of their plans. We've already destroyed one ship and that has probably gotten them seriously pissed. If we can trash a few more of them, Mister Wolfe may start having troubles holding his little fleet together."

"Once we reveal ourselves by attacking it will be very hard to break contact and go back to hiding, ma'am," said Snowden.

"Yes, that is the trick, isn't it? We'll have to proceed carefully. Fortunately, according to Commander van Rossum, we have three weeks to make our plans before we can even try."

"Captain, what about the party we sent down to the planet?" asked Lieutenant Terletsky.

Ellsworth frowned. "Yes, that's another entire issue. We've had no further signals from them since they reported they were under attack. That is not too surprising. They knew we were also under attack, so they would not be sending any signals that might reveal their position until they heard from us first."

"But who could have been attacking them, Skipper?" asked Bradley. "The mercs didn't have the time to land anyone at that point. It had to have been someone already down there."

"I don't know. The situation is far more complicated than we had expected. At this point, the first thing we have to do is make contact with our ground team. A direct broadcast is out of the question, of course, since it would reveal our position. Lieutenant Terletsky, you'll have to use a remote transmitter to relay our message. The enemy will be sure to destroy them soon after they transmit, so we may need quite a few of them."

"Yes, ma'am. We have a number on hand and they are simple enough that we could fabricate more if need be. We'll have to push them out with enough velocity to put them in a different orbit and then when they are far enough away we can activate them. Since the moon our people are on is always facing in toward us, they should receive it with no problem."

"But how will they respond? We don't want them giving their own position away."

"We'll have to warn them, ma'am. They can set up some remote transmitter of their own and then signal out to the ring on a schedule we'll have to give them. We should be able to receive their signal okay out here. Of course, the enemy will certainly destroy their transmitters, too, so I don't know how long we can keep this up."

"I don't know either, but this at least gives us something to work on while the repairs are under way. All right, I think we all have enough to keep us busy. Let's get to it."

There were a number of 'aye, aye, ma'ams' and her staff began floating out of the compartment. "Commander Bradley, would you stay a moment," she said.

"Sure, Skipper." She waited until everyone else had left and the door was shut. Then she let out a long sigh.

"Well, I certainly screwed this up, didn't I?"

"Skipper, there's no way you could have known what he was going to do."

"Perhaps not, but it's still my responsibility. Brad, I always wanted my own command. I always thought I could do a better job than the people over me, and that attitude got me in trouble a few times. That's why I was still a commander with eighteen years of experience in the middle of a desperate war, instead of a captain. So now I have my own command and I've screwed up bigger than anyone else in history!"

"Skipper, you haven't…"

"Yes, I have. This was the one chance we had to rescue the situation the League has fallen into. We had to get that base. And now we've lost it and it's entirely my fault. Ten trillion people counting on us and I screwed it up. There's no way we can win against Wolfe, you know that as well as I."

"Not in a direct fight, no. But your idea of ambushing a few of them could still work. We fight a guerrilla war against them."

"Guerrilla wars take time, Brad. We haven't got time. Florkowski didn't convince Wolfe to come here just to destroy a single League cruiser. He must have told him about the base and all the great stuff he would find there. Wolfe's going to send his own people down there and get into the base and take anything of value and destroy anything he can't cart off. Even if we can survive out here, the whole point of our mission will have been lost."

Bradley stared at her, but said nothing.

"What am I going to do, Brad?"

"I don't know, ma'am, I don't know."

"Well, ladies and gentlemen, we have run our quarry to ground and we will soon reap the rewards I have promised you," said Commodore Norman Wolfe to his ship commanders.

"It had damn well better be worth it, Wolfe," growled Captain D'arstang. "I've got several large holes in my ship that need to be repaired."

"Yes, and I've lost a main laser and two sensor clusters," said Captain Leonov.

"Not to mention poor Carstairs and *Looterfiend*."

"Please!" said Wolfe. "Let's remain focused on our goal rather than the cost we have to pay to reach it. I assure you that goal is well worth the price." He glanced over in Florkowski's direction and his look seemed to say: 'It better be, for your sake'. Charles Florkowski kept a neutral expression and met his gaze evenly. But inside he was nervous. Wolfe was far more unstable than he had believed at first. He had not actually killed any of his own crew during his frequent rages, but it was evident that he was quite capable of doing so. The whole mood of the ship told you that.

And the fact that this conference of his ship commanders was taking place via communicator rather than in person was further confirmation. The only people in the conference room, besides Wolfe, were the senior officers of his flagship. The rest looked out of com screens. While the tactical situation made it sensible to keep the commanders on their ships, in the whole time Florkowski had been aboard, none of the other commanders had ever visited *Vindicator*. There was a tangible feeling that no one wanted to get within arm's reach of Norman Wolfe. As long as they stayed on their own ships, they were safe. But if they came here...

"So what is so damn valuable down there, anyway, Commodore?" asked Captain Sheila Jurgens. "An old League base, you tell us. Okay, I wouldn't mind picking up a few implosion torpedoes or replacing my lasers with photon cannons, but this was a hell of a trip just for a refit. And we've still got that cruiser to deal with."

"The cruiser is of no importance," said Wolfe, brushing it off and simultaneously contradicting his earlier statements that he would not let Ellsworth escape him. "If the opportunity arises to capture or destroy it, that is fine, but the real prize is the base."

"How so?"

"Oh, my dear Captain Jurgens. All my dear captains! You have so little vision! How fortunate for you that I am here to guide you."

"Cut the crap, Wolfe," said D'arstang. "What's the deal with the base?"

"The deal with the base is this: it is the key to the entire Star League! We have merely to grasp it and the whole League must bow before us!"

"Like hell! You're out of your mind, Wolfe!"

"Oh so little faith! You cut me to the quick, Alphonso! You have all seen the interview of our new friend, Commander Florkowski. You know that the Star League is in a state of collapse because of the failure of all their nano-circuitry. They are helpless and ripe for plucking."

"So let's go pluck them!" exclaimed Leonov. "I thought that's what we were going to do."

"Ah, but what is there to pluck, Captain? Cities full of useless equipment and hungry people? We could make a few easy dollars by rounding up a couple of thousand slaves and selling them, but in the long run that's a losing proposition. All the other pirates and raiders and small powers will be doing the same thing. Leaguer slaves will be six for a dollar after a while. No, I have a better plan."

"What?" said several of the captains simultaneously.

"That base contains manufacturing facilities that can make working nano-chips. That is why that League cruiser was here. They hope to get their ships and machines working again. It was the only hope they had and now we control it! What would those League worlds give us to have those chips? What could we make them give us? Loot? Slaves? Or perhaps… complete dominion!"

"What? You *are* crazy, Wolfe!" said D'arstang. Florkowski noticed that Captain D'arstang was the one most willing to challenge Wolfe. He commanded Wolfe's old ship, the cruiser *Fenris*, and seemed to be the unofficial leader of all the other captains.

"Gently, Alphonso, gently," soothed Wolfe, but Florkowski could see the gleam of anger in his eye. "And gently is how we will take control of the League: one hungry world at a time. We will show up with holds full of the chips that can save them from starvation and destruction. We can restore their power, reactivate their food synthesizers. Put their defenses back in order to hold off other raiders. And all we ask in return is that they put us in charge. What choice would they have but to accept?" A chill went through Florkowski. It wouldn't be as simple as Wolfe was saying. They would still have to repair the fusion plants. But still. A desperate world might agree to almost anything.

"Until they were back on their feet! Then they'd outnumber us a million to one and they would just wipe us out!"

"Only if we were careless. I don't intend to be careless." Wolfe turned to one of his staff officers. "Carol, that base down there will have other manufacturing facilities beside chip construction, won't it?"

"I would imagine so, sir," said Commander Carol Nista, *Vindicator's* chief engineer. "A base like that should have fabricators capable of producing just about anything."

"Do you suppose it could produce an item like this?" Wolfe reached down and picked up a metal ring about twenty centimeters in diameter and two centimeters thick. It had several small glowing lights on it.

Florkowski recognized it as a slave collar. A very sophisticated one. Most collars would include a locator beacon so a slave could not hide if they ran away. Others could access the nerve signals flowing through the slave's spinal cord, allowing the master to paralyze the wearer—or punish them with terrible pain. Often the two features would be combined to allow the master to restrict where the slave was allowed to go. If they tried to go somewhere they didn't belong, the collar would prevent them. The most sophisticated ones of all could analyze the brain waves of the wearer. In most species the attempt to perform a violent act would produce a distinctive set of waves. The collar could recognize them and immobilize the slave before they could hurt anyone—their masters or themselves. A person fitted with such a collar would be almost completely helpless. Even removing it would be impossible without the proper tools and access codes. The collar would kill the wearer if it was tried.

"I would imagine we could adapt the fabricators to produce those, yes, sir," said Nista.

"Good. Very good. Once we take over the base, get right on it. I think we'll probably be needing a few... billion of them."

There was a mutter of astonishment from the captains. Even D'arstang seemed impressed. "Yes, Alphonso, think of it," cooed Wolfe. "An entire world yours to command. Every person on it; every man, every woman, yours to control. Interested?"

The hungry look on D'arstang's face made it evident that he was very interested. Florkowski shuddered.

"And once we have one world working for us we'll have the resources to take the next and the next." Wolfe laughed loudly. "By the time we're done, every man-jack in our fleet might have his own world to rule!"

"But we still need to take control of the base," pointed out Jurgens. "The Leaguies sent a party down there already. We better get our own people down there before they beat us to the punch."

"An excellent point, Captain," said Wolfe. "I will be moving *Vindicator* into close orbit very shortly and I will be sending down my troops to secure the area."

"Not so fast, Wolfe!" said Leonov. "I want some of my people there, too!" The other captains voiced similar views.

"Of course, of course!" said Wolfe congenially. "I'd expect a boat from each one of your ships. Send some technicians and engineers as well as troops. We probably have some work to do to get inside and get the base operating. So here's what we shall do..."

An hour later Charles Florkowski left the meeting and walked slowly back to his quarters. They were very nice quarters. Much nicer than he had on *Gilgamesh*. Wolfe had picked *Vindicator* up as a prize in one of his earlier contracts and it was a lavishly appointed vessel. But Wolfe only had half the men he needed to crew it. There were plenty of empty staterooms and the officers had their pick.

He was still numb from Wolfe's briefing. He had led Wolfe here in hopes of avenging himself on Ellsworth and Shusterman and diverting Wolfe from his plans for a slave raid into the League. But now it could be much worse than he ever feared. He knew Wolfe's dream of a slave empire was insane and would never actually work. Other powers, with far more resources at their disposal, would come rolling over everything before Wolfe could get very far. But how much suffering would Wolfe inflict in the meantime? The thought of whole worlds collared and enslaved made him feel sick.

He reached his cabin and punched the entry button. The door slid open and he stepped inside. The lights had already been on when he entered--and that wasn't right. They would automatically go off when the suite was unoccupied. Florkowski was becoming extremely alert to such things. He very cautiously looked around the living space, but there didn't seem to be anything out of place. The windows showed a spectacular view of the gas giant and its rings. He slowly walked over to the door to his sleeping cabin and looked inside. A woman in an orange jumpsuit was sitting on his bed, looking at a book reader. When she saw him she sprang to attention.

"Who are you?" demanded Florkowski. "What are you doing here?"

"I have been assigned to you tonight, master," she said.

Florkowski stared at her in confusion. Master? What the hell was this? But before he could ask, the woman unzipped her jumpsuit and shrugged it off so it fell in a pile around her ankles. She wasn't wearing anything else except for a collar just like Wolfe had been showing off. "How can I serve you, master?" she asked.

My God, she's a slave! Florkowski was stunned. He had seen a few other women—and a couple of men—in those orange jumpsuits, but he had assumed they were stewards or something. His mind was racing as he stared at the woman. She was very pretty. In fact she reminded him of... Florkowski had to grab the edge of the door frame to keep from falling when he recognized her.

She was the woman from the slave market on Freeport!

In a flash of memory he realized just what sort of uniforms those men who had been bidding on her were wearing. They were some of Wolfe's men and they had bought her for their ship. And now she was standing in his cabin, offering herself to him!

While he was standing there in amazement and horror the woman sat down on the bed and kicked away the jumpsuit. She looked at him expectantly. "How can I serve you, master?" she asked again.

"Don't call me that!" blurted Florkowski, finding his voice.

"Yes, m... yes, sir." She cringed slightly. She'd only been here five weeks and she was already acting like a slave! What had they done to her? He looked closer and could see a number of faint bruises on her body.

"P-put your clothes back on!" he stuttered. The woman looked puzzled, but did as she was told. He felt relief when she had covered herself.

"Why... why haven't I seen you before?" he asked for lack of anything better to say.

"I am assigned to the senior officers in rotation," she said. "Until this week, your name was not on the list." Florkowski frowned. Was this some nasty trick of Wolfe's to annoy him? Or had the bureaucracy just caught up to the fact that he was aboard? Whatever, he had no intention on making use of this recreational facility!

"You...I don't require your services, miss. You can take the night off. Go back to your quarters and get some sleep. You probably need it."

To his surprise, all the color left the woman's face and she seemed terrified. "Please, master! Don't send me away! Please! I beg you!" She was on the verge of tears.

"Why? Surely you don't want to do this, do you?" What was wrong with her?

"Please, master," she wept. "If the person I'm assigned to doesn't want me, I have to report to the crew lounge. Then anyone who wants can have me."

Florkowski growled. Those bastards! What a way to make a slave eager to please! Satisfy one person or get gang-raped by a dozen others. What a choice!

"Please don't send me away!"

"No, no, of course, I won't send you away," said Florkowski gently. The woman's face brightened in hope. "You can stay in here and sleep on the bed. I'll be fine on the sofa out there." The woman didn't quite look as though she believed what he was saying, but she nodded her head and smiled.

"What's your name?" he asked.

"Clara."

Clara what? Had they already stolen her last name? "My name is Charles. Good night, Clara."

"Good night, sir."

He went back into the living compartment and lay down on the sofa. It would be comfortable enough. He turned off the lights and stared at the view through the window. What a mess he had gotten himself into. But it was Ellsworth's fault. She had driven him to this. It should be her that was suffering instead of that poor girl in there. He froze as he heard a faint sound. Was she…? Yes, there was no doubt that the woman in his cabin was crying. Poor kid. What a nightmare for her.

After a while he sat up. Then he stood up and walked slowly to the door and peered in. Clara was curled up on the bed crying softly.

"Clara? Are you all right?" Stupid question. She was a slave on a ship full of mercenaries, how could she possibly be all right? The woman just buried her face in the pillow. He was filled with pity and anguish for the woman. If Ellsworth had just let him bid on her!

Without really thinking, he crossed the room and lay down next to her. He put out his hand to touch her shoulder.

"I'm sorry," he whispered.

She turned and pressed her face against his chest and wept. He gently put his arms around her.

"Why can't we get into the base?" demanded Gregory Sadgipour.

Hakata Carmichael shrugged his shoulders. "I don't know for sure that you can't, but I know that we can't—and we've tried."

"What's stopping you? The closed blast door? There must be some equipment around that can get through it!"

"Oh, it's not the door. We don't need to use the door. There's a tunnel that leads directly from here into the base. We could just walk in if it weren't for the droids."

"Droids?"

"The base security droids. I told you about the chaos things were in down here when the Darj'Nang overlords started taking control of people. They started shutting down defense equipment and attacking people who haven't been taken over—I guess the overlords can only control so many people at one time."

"Yes," said Chtak, interrupting, "there is a limit to how many creatures they can control at once. The number is fairly high, but there is a limit. That is probably how the counterattack against their ship succeeded: they were totally occupied elsewhere."

"Well, whatever. Things were a mess down here. Someone—I don't know who—activated the base security droids and ordered them to shoot to kill anyone trying to enter the base. They are still down there and they are still on watch."

"And you can't deactivate them? Or get around them?"

"The only way I know to deactivate them is with a plasma rifle, Lieutenant. We've tried that, but there are just too many droids and they are too deadly. We lost three people in our one attempt."

"How many droids?"

"I don't know for sure. We went down there years ago and blew up one of them, but at least two dozen more appeared and chased us all the way back here. The ones of us they didn't kill."

"You were fortunate to have any escape, Mister Carmichael," said Chtak. "That model of droid is very capable."

"Yeah, they probably could have gotten us all, but they seem to have a programmed defensive zone. Anything entering it will be attacked and anything firing at the droids will be attacked. But if you just run, they break off their pursuit pretty quickly."

"So you can't get in at all?"

"Not into the main part. Some of the outlying compartments are outside the defensive zones. A lot of storerooms and such, which has been lucky for us. We've got enough power cells to last for a century. But we can't get into the main part. Not the armory, not the manufacturing facilities and not the control center or power station. All the really important stuff is in there."

"Chtak, is there any chance of deactivating those things?" asked Greg.

"Perhaps. I will have to see what can be come up with."

"Well, I wish you better luck than we had, Lieutenant," said Carmichael.

"Hakata, forget about the damn base," said one of the men. "What are we going to do about all those Skraks? These folks seem to have stirred something up and I don't like it a bit!"

"Calm down, Roger," said Carmichael. "They still can't get in here. We're going to have to be a lot more careful with our hunting parties in the future, but there's no call to panic." He turned to Greg. "We have a working food synthesizer here, but we supplement that with meat from the local animals. We also have a farm about a hundred klicks away, and we grow vegetables here in the city."

"Yes, we spotted the farm from orbit. Why so far away?"

"We didn't want to do anything to attract attention to us here in the tower in case the Darj'Nang returned. We still have a few functioning air cars so we can bring the harvest here. The tower itself is fortified on the lower two levels to make sure the Skraks can't get in."

"A few dozen can't get in," said the man named Roger. "We might not be so lucky against a thousand!"

"All the lower entrances are sealed, the windows covered over and obstacles to prevent climbing are in place. The Skraks would need heavy weapons to burn their way in. What more can we do?"

"I don't know, but I'm still worried, Hakata. And how many weapons did they get from these folks? Did you leave any of your people behind?"

Greg winced. They had left people behind. One very important person...

"We lost eleven people to the Skraks," he said sadly. "They were all armed, but not with anything very heavy. No plasma rifles, fortunately, and we still have our one rocket launcher. Let me see, there were eight Marines. Lieutenant Quatrock had a gauss pistol, Jenkins, Schmidt and Romero had gauss rifles..."

"Schmidt had a laser rifle, sir," said Sergeant McGill.

"That's right. Walsh and Dunkin had the laser rifles, too. Preston and Chaswell had the heavy stunners and Weston had that slugthrower monstrosity she was so attached to. All the spacers had hand stunners." *One very special spacer had a stunner. I wonder if she even got a chance to use it?*

"What about the two naval officers the Skraks took prisoner?" asked Stewart Paalova.

Gregory Sadgipour was on his feet without any memory of having stood up. Doug Rawlins was next to him, trailing a piece of medical gauze that the startled woman doctor was still holding.

"Prisoners? What prisoners?"

"Two officers?"

"A tall blonde?" demanded Rawlins.

"A darker brunette?" exclaimed Greg.

"Uh, yes, two women," said Stewart awkwardly from the corner the two foaming Marines had backed him into. "I saw the Skraks take them away. A few minutes before the big explosion that destroyed your vehicle."

"Where did they go? Why didn't you tell us this before?"

"I would imagine they took them to the caves. That's where the Skraks live. And I didn't mention it because we had other things to worry about at the time."

"Where are these caves? Can you lead us there?" Greg was already putting his gear on. All thought of the base had been banished. Rhada was still alive! His fatigue was gone. He could run a hundred kilometers without a pause. Let's get going!

"Whoa! Settle down, young fellow!" said Carmichael. "You aren't going anywhere in this condition. And I couldn't let you go to those caves in any condition."

"What? Why not?"

"Son, I'm sorry about your friends, but you may as well forget about them. Nobody has ever come out of those caves."

CHAPTER FIFTEEN

Rhada McClerndon huddled in the dark, on a cold stone floor, and shivered uncontrollably. She was cold and she was in pain. The sweat from the rapid pace her captors had set was now drying on her skin and she was cold. Her feet were cut and bruised from scrambling over rocks and brambles. There were innumerable welts on her back from her captors' whips. Her hands were tied painfully behind her and the noose around her neck was nearly choking her. She was blindfolded. The only thing that was keeping her from going totally insane was the presence of Claritta Torres. She could feel the other woman beside her and she pressed her shoulder against the reassuringly warm flesh.

She still could not believe this was happening. The time from when 'Ritta had shouted inside the cutter until now was a mad jumble of terrifying images. First, that wave of creatures swarming toward the cutter with such terrible speed. Then Torres screaming at her to get the airlock shut. Her frantic scramble to get there, only to be bowled over by the attackers as they poured inside. She had tried to get her stunner out, but dozens of clawed hands had grabbed her and taken her weapon and dragged her out of the cutter. Then she and Torres were hustled over the hill, past the horribly shredded body of one of the Marines, and into the next valley.

Then they had stripped them. That was perhaps the most terrifying moment of the whole ordeal. She had no clue what was going to happen and she screamed and struggled as they tore the clothes off her. They had searched through the remains of their clothing and their equipment very carefully. Then they had bound them and leashed them and driven them off like cattle. Kilometer after kilometer they had gone at a brisk trot. If they fell, they were whipped and tugged back to their feet. Rhada thought they were moving west, around the mountain, but she wasn't sure. They finally allowed them to rest, but when they started again they were blindfolded with scraps of their own uniforms. She had fallen a lot more often and they had whipped her again and again.

And now they were here. Wherever here was. She was fairly certain they were inside a cave or cavern. The sounds echoed around her and it was dark and damp and cold. She sat and shivered.

"What... what are those things?" she whispered.

"I think they're Skraknars," answered Torres. "Darj'Nang soldiers."

Darj'Nang? But they were all dead! Or they were supposed to be. Rhada tried to remember the briefings on the Darj'Nang forces she had received. There had been a lot about their ships and weapons, but not much about their ground forces. Skraknars, Skraknars, she couldn't remember...

She stiffened as she heard movement close by. She flinched when something touched her face and removed the blindfold. She found herself staring into the face of one of their captors. Another one had removed Torres' blindfold. The creatures were sort of like thick-bodied snakes with lots of arms and legs. Maybe two meters long, but over half of that was a thin tail and a thin neck. To her surprise, she now realized that she was actually larger than any one of them. They probably massed less than fifty kilos. Two pairs of short, powerful legs supported the lower bodies. Then the bodies curved upward and sprouted two pairs of short arms. She had seen some of them using the lower pair of arms as legs when they moved quickly, but the upper pair seemed to be strictly for manipulation. The head was large, but rather flat and wide. A large mouth with a lot of sharp-looking teeth narrowed to a pointed snout. Two bulbous eyes projected from either side of the skull. A pair of those eyes was now staring into hers. She cringed back.

There was a lot of hissing between the creatures and then she and Torres were pulled to their feet. Rhada winced at how sore hers were. She had a moment to glance around and confirm that she was, indeed, inside a cave and then they were moving again. Her leg muscles had stiffened while she was sitting and they shrieked in pain. A whimper forced its way out of her mouth.

"Hang in there, kid," whispered Torres. "The others will find us soon."

The others. What had happened to the others? What had happened to Greg? Surely they would come to look for them. But the ship had been under attack, too. What did that mean? Would there be a rescue party at all?

She almost stumbled and a sudden lash on the back of her legs reminded her to keep her mind on the immediate business. They were hustled up a long tunnel and then turned into a passage on their left. There were other openings along the way and every niche and ledge seemed to be filled with these creatures. Hundreds of them. There were torches or fires at intervals to provide some light, but it was terribly dim and she stubbed her aching feet on unseen rocks. Then they entered a larger chamber. She looked up and saw that the roof was dozens or perhaps hundreds of meters over their heads. A few pale beams of sunlight glowed high above.

There were more of the things here. They were dragged over to a group of them and flung to their knees. One of the creatures, who was considerably larger than the rest, looked down on them from a rock ledge.

"Looks like the head honcho," muttered Torres, but she was rewarded with a lash for breaking her silence. The creature regarded them for a long time. Minutes dragged by with no sound. Rhada was acutely aware of her nudity. Being naked didn't bother her in its own right. Poor Greg—*Greg! Greg! Where are you?*—Greg would have been shocked to learn that the shrimp farmers on Fenwha routinely worked in nothing more than their boots to save their precious clothing from the wear and tear of the swamps. But to be naked in the hands of an enemy—that was different. She felt horribly exposed and vulnerable. Their captors did not seem to wear anything either except for a set of leather belts and harnesses which they hung weapons and equipment on. The silence went on and on. What was going on here? How long were they...

"Ssslavess."

Rhada looked up at the big creature in surprise. The voice has been hissing and difficult to understand, but there was no doubt it had been speaking in their language!

"Sslaves," it said again, "you will answer my quesstionss."

"We are not slaves!" said Claritta Torres, firmly. "We are officers in the Star League Navy and we demand to be treated..."

She was cut off as a torrent of whip strokes rained down on her. She crouched down and tried to protect herself as much as she could with bound arms. Rhada looked on helplessly. Finally the beating stopped.

"You are slaves of the Great Masters, as are we all," said the creature. "You will obey and serve them as do we. Now you will answer my questions."

"Ensign Claritta Torres, serial number PQ12748…"

More blows. Torres was nearly prone on the floor and Rhada could see the tears of pain on her cheeks but she still had a fierce gleam of defiance in her eyes.

"You will answer my questions."

"No!"

Several more strokes hit her, but then at a hiss from the big one the beating stopped, More hissing and several of the creatures scuttled out of the chamber.

"'Ritta, are you all right?" whispered Rhada.

"Fine, kid. Just hang tough and don't give these lizards a thing. They obviously think we're hot stuff and won't do anything too extreme." Another blow silenced her again. Several minutes went by and then there was noise behind them. A number of the creatures were coming into the chamber. And in their midst were…what? They came closer and there was a swarm of what seemed to be miniature versions of their captors. A meter long or maybe a bit more. They appeared to be all claws and teeth and they snarled and hissed and snapped at everything around them. There were at least twenty of them. Several of the big creatures were herding them with long sticks. They stopped them a few meters away.

"What are those?" asked Rhada, shrinking back.

"Young ones, I think," said Torres. Her confident tone was gone. "These things hatch from eggs and for the first year or so the young ones are just savage little beasts."

"Now, sslaves, you will obey. You will answer. If not, then you are of no use except as food."

"Ensign Claritta Torres, serial number PQ1274839-01."

"Ritta, I think they mean business," said Rhada in near panic. The creatures were edging closer in spite of the sticks of their keepers.

One of their captors grabbed Torres' leash and pulled her towards the hideous little things.

"You will answer," said the big one.

"Go to hell!" said Torres.

The big one hissed a command and Rhada had one frozen instant to realize that Claritta had horribly miscalculated her status, before the creatures swarmed over her.

"Ritta! *Ritta!*" shrieked Rhada.

Rhada's screams went on far longer than Torres'.

"No! No! Stop them! We'll talk! We'll talk! Ritta! No! Please stop them!"

But there was no stopping them. Torres disappeared under a wave of snapping, snarling death. With her hands tied she could do nothing to protect herself. A bloody leg flailed for an instant above the swarm only to be seized in a set of jaws and pulled downward, out of sight again.

Rhada screamed and screamed and screamed.

The mass of creatures parted for a moment and she could see that Torres' body had been ripped open. Two of the things were having a tug of war with a length of intestines. Then they closed in again and the horror was hidden. Another creature suddenly darted off with a large piece of bloody flesh in its jaws, another in pursuit. The creatures were all covered in blood.

"No! No! *No!*"

Rhada was yanked around by her leash until she was facing the big one again, but she was still screaming.

"Now you will answer my questions."

Rhada had not even heard it. "No! No! No! Ritta! No!"

"Then you will die also."

They started dragging her around again when she realized what the thing had been saying.

"No! Stop! I'll talk! I'll talk! I'll talk! Please, no!" she shrieked hysterically.

They stopped and dragged her back in front of it again.

"You will obey. You will answer my questions."

"Yes, yes!" she sobbed.

"Good. You are a good slave. You come here on a space ship?"

"Yes."

"What kind?"

"A cruiser. *Hero* class."

"How many crew does it carry?"

"Three hundred." Not exactly true, she dimly realized; with all the Marines and the civilians there were almost four hundred aboard, but the creature accepted her answer.

It asked her more questions about the ship's armament and capabilities. She rattled off the answers and tried not to listen to the horrible chomping and slurping sounds coming from behind her.

"How many other ships are with you?"

"None, we came alone."

"Why did you come here?"

"To… to see if anyone was still here. We were scouting." *Don't tell them about the base!* She still had enough sanity to remember that. The creature paused a long time and she feared it knew she wasn't telling it everything.

"How does the war go? Do you win or lose?"

What to tell them? How would they react to learn that their 'Great Masters' were all dead? Probably not very well…

"We neither win nor lose."

"The war goes on?"

"Yes."

"Good. That is good." The thing hissed another order and Rhada was dragged to her feet. In spite of her fear, she looked to where Ritta had been. There was nothing left except some bones and some bloody scraps of flesh. A tangle of blond hair was to one side, still attached to a piece of scalp. Two of the creatures were lapping at a small pool of blood.

"No, Ritta, no…" she whimpered as she was led away.

They took her along more tunnels. She had no idea if it was the same route they had come on. Finally, they came to a small chamber. Her leash was run through a metal ring set in the stone and then tied to another ring a few meters away. She had just enough slack to lie down. As soon as the things left her, she collapsed.

"No, no, no…" She was soon crying uncontrollably. She was alone! They had killed Ritta! It couldn't be true, but it was. She sobbed harder and then she was coughing and choking. Before she was able to prepare, her stomach suddenly emptied itself. The vomit gushed out of her mouth and nose and splattered all over her. Again and again her stomach heaved until there was nothing at all left to bring up. Finally, all she could do was lay there, panting. Her throat and nose burned, but she had nothing to wash out her mouth with.

With another sob, she rolled away from the pool of vomit and fell into an exhausted sleep.

Rhada woke from a nightmare to find herself in a worse one. All the memories from yesterday flooded back into her. Ritta was dead. And she was a prisoner. A slave. *No, I'm not! I'm not a slave!* She rolled over with a groan and sat up. It wasn't easy with her hands tied. She was shivering with cold. Her hands and feet were like ice. Then she noticed that she wasn't alone. Two of the creatures, the

Skraknars, were lying by a small fire inside a ring of rocks a few meters away. At her movement both heads swiveled to stare at her. They got up and moved over to her with that strange, flowing motion. They moved so that one was on either side. They looked nearly identical, but the one was a little smaller and had a yellowish tinge to its skin. They both carried the long wooden switches they had been using to beat her with.

"Awake?" said the yellowish one.

"Yes, I'm awake. You speak my language?"

"Yes. The Great Masters teach Sslaskatar, our leader, and he teach me. I am Sspau, Elder Clutchmistress. This is Sspara, Junior Clutchmistress."

"My name is Rhada..."

A quick stroke from the switch made Rhada yelp.

"You are slave. No name! Now you are only slave here. No need for name. Later, when there are more slaves, then we give name!"

Anger flared up in her. "My name is Rhada!" she insisted. They could not take that from her!

Another stroke, this time from the other one. It hit her again and she flinched away, but she was up against the rock wall and she couldn't escape. Her hands were behind her and she couldn't protect herself. Three more times the stinging lash hit her. On her shoulder and then her belly. The last one was across her breasts and suddenly the yellow one hissed a command and the beating stopped. Rhada huddled against the wall and tried not to sob.

The yellow one moved closer and Rhada cringed as the thing's hands reached out to touch her. They were cool but dry. The clawed fingers moved along her torso and then stopped on her breasts.

"Glands? For feeding young?"

"Y-yes."

"Functional?"

"I...yes, I guess so. Only when I have a baby. I have not had one yet."

The thing's hands left her breasts and moved down her belly.

"Egg sssac?" hissed the other one.

"No, young born alive," said the yellow one, "correct?"

"Yes."

"Re-pro-duc-tive organs here?" Rhada clenched her teeth as the hands continued to explore.

"Yes."

"Have young?"

"No, I've never had a…"

"Can have young? Functional? Yes?"

"Yes."

"Good. We catch a mate for you and you have young."

Rhada stared at them in horror. A mate? Have young? Did they think she was some sort of cattle that they could breed? She stared into those cold, unblinking eyes and she realized that that was exactly what she was to them. Cattle. A slave. She shook her head. *No…*

The two creatures moved away from her and she sighed in relief. The larger one picked up something and tossed it at her. It landed just in front of her. It was a large strip of raw meat.

"Eat." Rhada stared at it. She suddenly realized that she was very hungry. And terribly thirsty. The inside of her throat was raw. How long since she last ate? She didn't even know what time it was; what day it was. But the strip of meat was raw. Where had it come from? Her stomach heaved slightly at the thought of Ritta Torres.

"I… I can't eat this," she said. The creature flowed over to her. It had the switch.

"Why?"

"I can't eat with my hands tied. And I can't eat raw meat. It will make me sick. Please, may I have some water?" Her mouth was parched.

The creature hissed at the other one and a conversation went back and forth for nearly a minute. Finally, the big one came over and untied Rhada's hands. She could hardly move them. Her shoulders screamed in agony as she flopped her limp arms in front of her and waited for the circulation to return. The Skraknar picked up the meat and took it over to the fire. Then it returned with a skin full of water.

"Drink."

Rhada fumbled around with her tingling hands and managed to pick up the skin and bring it to her mouth. The water burned going down, but it was so good. She drank and drank. When she had her fill, she put a little water on her hands and tried to scrub the dried vomit off herself.

Shortly, the creature tossed the meat back to her again. It was at least partially cooked and it smelled amazingly good. But what kind of meat was it? She glanced around in the dim light and finally spotted what looked like a haunch from one of the antelope-like herbivores that seemed so common on the planet. Relieved, she bit into the meat and wolfed it down in a few minutes. Finished, she washed herself a little more and watched the two Skraknars. They were cooking their own meal over the fire. As she watched, another one of the creatures scuttled in. It was carrying a large bundle of wood which it put down in a pile next to the fire. It hissed and sputtered with the other two for a while and all three gestured in her direction several times. Then the newcomer left.

"That one wanted to know when slaves will gather wood instead of him," said the yellow one to her. "I tell him soon. You finished now?" She was about to say yes when a sudden rumbling in her belly told her she had something else she needed to take care of. With a number of gesticulations and words she managed to explain what the problem was. The creatures untied her leash from the ring and led her over to a pit in the floor of the cave and indicated she should use that. She managed to, even with both of them staring at her the whole time.

"Good. Do this way. Make no more stinks," said the yellow one pointing to where Rhada had vomited. Somewhat to Rhada's surprise, the Skraknars had no real odor that she could detect. A deliberate modification for combat?

"Now, we test you, slave. Leave hands unbound. No tricks!"

Test? What sort of test? But Rhada had no more time to wonder because the yellow one pulled on her leash and the other one smacked her with the switch and they were moving. It was easier walking with her arms free, but all her muscles were sore, as were her feet. Fortunately, they did not go too far. They entered another large chamber, she didn't think it was the same one as before. Hundreds of Skraknars were there and they were conducting weapons training. Some had swords and others had spears and they all had shields. Some had a pair of swords and others had two spears in their multiple sets of arms. Others were practicing with the crossbows. A few of them looked over to her when she was brought in, but their 'drill sergeants' hissed at them and directed their attentions back to their duty. She stopped in shock when she saw several groups studying weapons that had obviously come from her own shore party. Two gauss rifles, a stunner and some more she couldn't see clearly. Had anyone escaped? She shuddered. But then a tug on her leash pulled her away.

Rhada's two captors led her to a clear, level spot where a post had been set in the floor. It was about a meter high and they fastened her leash to a ring set in the top of it. Then they moved away, leaving her standing there. What was going to happen now?

"Run," said the yellow one. Rhada hesitated and was rewarded with a slash of the creature's switch. She yelped and started trotting. She only had about three meters of slack on the leash so she had to go in a fairly tight circle around the post.

"Faster." Another stroke as she passed the yellow one. She picked up her pace, but that did not seem to satisfy them. Faster and faster she went until she was running as fast as she could in that tight circle. But they kept whipping her! She couldn't go any faster, dammit! For as cold as she had been earlier, she was now soon dripping with sweat and gasping for breath.

She stumbled and fell, bruising her knees and hands. They beat her until she got up and ran again. Around and around she went. She fell again and they beat her. She ran and they beat her. The fire on her back was matched by the fire in her lungs as she tried to draw in enough air to keep her aching legs moving.

Finally, she collapsed and could not move again in spite of the whips. Her captors eventually concluded that she really could not run any more and stopped. They tossed her the water skin and then crouched down to watch her. She lay there gasping and sobbing for a long while. Why were they doing this to her? Eventually she was able to crawl to the water skin and drink.

They let her rest for a long time. The pains slowly subsided and she sat up. The other Skraknars were still practicing with their weapons. From time to time some of them would come over to stare at her and exchange hisses with Rhada's two captors. Eventually those two got up and slid over to her. They unfastened her leash from the post and led her away to another chamber. Here there were small wicker baskets filled with black stones.

"Lift," commanded the yellow one. Rhada shrugged and grabbed hold of sides of the basket and lifted it up. It was only fifteen kilos or so, not too bad.

"Down." She set it down.

"Now, two." She was a little puzzled, but then got the idea. She set one basket on top of another and then lifted both together. Thirty kilos, that was a lot harder. She strained and managed to lift both off the ground.

"Here," said the yellow one. It was gesturing to the far side of the chamber. Rhada shuffled over there with her burden and then set them down.

"Now, three." Three? She couldn't do three!

"I don't think I can…" A whip stroke by the other one convinced her to try.

She put three of the baskets on top of each other. It was hard to keep them from tipping over. She grasped the sides of the bottom basket and heaved with all her strength. She staggered to her feet, swaying slightly with her burden.

"Here."

Step by step she struggled to the far side of the chamber. She almost fell when the big one whipped her, but finally she made it and dropped the baskets down.

"Four," said the yellow one.

"I can't!" she said in exasperation. But the whips forced her to try. She gingerly stacked four baskets and then tried to lift them. Sixty kilos, about her own weight. The stack moved slightly and then toppled over on top of her. She was buried under an avalanche of black stones. She pulled herself out from under and the two Skraknars forced her to collect all the stones and put them back in the baskets.

After that, they had her pick up a single basket and carry it back and forth across the chamber without stopping. They whipped her if she slowed down. Back and forth, back and forth until she collapsed again. Then, after another long rest, they made her do it with two baskets. She was nearing exhaustion and could not go for long. She lay on the ground in a near stupor and could not move despite the whipping. Why were they doing this to her?

They let her rest a long time and she actually dozed off for a while. Then they woke her and gave her some water and then led her away again. They went into a tunnel that led steeply down. After a few minutes it ended in an underground lake.

"Wash. You stink," said the yellow one.

She tentatively stepped into the water. It was like ice. But the thought of being clean—and the threat of the whips—made her take a few more steps until the water was up to her knees. She bent over and splashed freezing water over herself and then scrubbed vigorously. There was no soap, of course, but it was still better than nothing. She ran her hands over her body, wincing at all the welts on her back. She went in a little deeper and bent over to get her hair wet. She scrubbed at it with her hands. She splashed more water on her and was shivering. She decided that was as good as it was going to get and moved toward the shore.

"What is that?" demanded the yellow one. It had the switch and it was pointing at Rhada's head. For a moment she was confused and then she realized it meant her hair.

"My hair," she answered.

"What for?" Rhada suddenly had the horrible feeling that if she did not come up with a good answer they might cut it all off.

"It helps keep me warm." Maybe that would satisfy them.

"Not much to keep all warm."

"I… humans lose most of their heat through their heads. The hair is insulation." The creature was silent. Then the switch dropped lower.

"Why there?"

Rhada was suddenly furious. They had beaten her and put her through these pointless exercises all day long and now they were asking these stupid questions. To hell with all of them!

"It reduces chafing during mating!" she snarled. She fully expected to get another whipping for her tone, but to her surprise, the creature simply tugged on her leash and said: "Come."

They led her back up the tunnel. Rhada stumbled several times with her fatigue. Eventually they were back in the small chamber she had awakened in. They let her use the pit again and then they tied her leash through the metal rings. They charred another strip of meat for her.

"Rest," said the yellow one.

"Please, why did you do those things to me today?" asked Rhada. The yellow one stood still for several seconds and Rhada prepared to ward off the switch. But she wasn't whipped this time.

"We test you. See how strong. How long you go. Now no tricks. Tomorrow you shall work. Work hard. Good slave."

Rhada shook her head and then huddled in a ball on the floor and wept herself to sleep.

CHAPTER SIXTEEN

Chtak'Chr roused himself from the uncomfortable human bed and checked the time. He had slept for nearly eight uneasy hours and he needed to be up and about. He went out into the hallway and peered into the room Gregory had been assigned. He was relieved to see the young human still in the bed. His own sleep had been restless because he had kept one ear cocked to make sure Greg stayed where he belonged. While he rejoiced at the news that Rhada and Lieutenant Torres were still alive, he needed to prevent Greg from rushing off on some ill-planned rescue mission.

It had not been easy. Mayor Carmichael's warning that the Skraknar caves were far too dangerous to enter had not deterred Greg or Lieutenant Rawlins in the slightest. In fact, all the Marines had been eager to go immediately. It had taken all of Chtak's charm and persuasiveness to talk them out of bolting off. He feared he would not be as successful today. Of course, he wanted the captives rescued very much himself, but his natural caution urged a more thoughtful plan than just charging in there, guns blazing. As he stood there, Greg stirred and then sat upright in the bed and looked around in alarm. Then he seemed to remember where he was and relaxed slightly.

"Did you sleep well, Gregory?" asked Chtak congenially.

"All right, I guess," said the human as he swung his legs out of the bed and stood up. "But we are going after Rhada and Torres today, Chtak. Don't try and talk me out of it!"

"Of course not. But we do need to make some plans. And I would certainly vote for some breakfast first."

Greg even allowed himself to be talked into a hot shower, but he wasted no time in getting dressed, fed and assembled in the lobby with the whole team. Mayor Carmichael was there waiting for him. Greg went right up to him.

"Sir, do you have any maps of that area we can use? Or any diagrams of the caves themselves? I won't turn down a guide if you can provide one, but I understand that this isn't your fight."

Carmichael looked nervous. "Lieutenant, is there any way I can talk you out of this insanity? You're just going to get yourself and all your people killed. And it will all be for nothing."

"I'm sorry, sir, but those are my people in there and I will not abandon them. We'll have a better chance with your help, but with it or without it, we're going."

Carmichael sighed. "I was afraid you were going to say that and I admire your bravery. I don't like doing this, but you've forced my hand." Carmichael stepped back and the crowd opened out and there were a half dozen men with heavy stunners aimed at them.

"Please! Don't anyone try anything foolish! They'll just stun all of you if you try anything!"

Chtak glanced around rapidly. In addition to the six men in front of them, there were two more on a balcony above them. Any two of them could stun their entire party with a wide-beam shot.

"What the hell is this?" snarled Greg.

"I'm just trying to save you from doing something very foolish, Lieutenant," said Carmichael. "Now please put down your weapons. Any sudden moves and we'll just stun all of you. You'll wake up in about six hours with a hell of a headache. I don't think any of us want that."

Greg looked desperate and Chtak feared he wasn't going to be reasonable. "Gregory, I believe we should do as they ask us," he said.

"And give up on Rhada?" he asked angrily.

"I don't like it either, but they have us at a complete disadvantage. To try and resist now will just cost us six hours that we cannot afford to waste."

Greg still looked like he was going to argue, but Chtak slowly took out his own stunner and tossed it toward Carmichael.

"What do we do, sir?" asked Sergeant McGill.

Greg had an expression of raw fury on his face, but he unbuckled his gun belt and tossed it out, too. "Put down your weapons," he commanded through clenched teeth.

A few minutes later all of their weapons had been collected and they were sitting around a large table with Mayor Carmichael. A few men with stunners were standing at a respectful distance.

"Sorry I had to do that, Lieutenant, but you didn't look like you were going to listen to reason."

"So now what happens?" asked Greg. "Are we your prisoners?"

"Now don't be like that, Lieutenant. We were doing you a big favor whether you'll admit it or not. If we let you head out to those caves you'd all be dead before tonight. I couldn't let you do that to yourselves and I couldn't take the risk with the safety of my own people."

"Your safety? How were we threatening your safety?"

Carmichael sighed. "I had already told you about the first big attack by the Skraks when we were nearly wiped out. Well, after we drove them off, we didn't see anything more of them for a long while. We started to hope that maybe they'd all been killed or just run off somewhere. But four or five years later people out on hunting parties started disappearing. After a while we realized that it was the Skraks who were responsible. We got a lot more careful and we managed to ambush one of their own hunting parties. We tracked the survivors back to the caves. There's a huge complex of caverns on the west side of the mountain.

"We tried to seal the entrance with explosives, but there were too many other entrances and they always seemed to find a way to get out. Finally, we got fed up with it and decided to go in there and wipe them out. There were a dozen Marine survivors from the original garrison with us. Captain Golatz was in command. He had a bigger party than yours, Lieutenant, and better armed, too. He went into those caves and he didn't come back. And we were practically under siege here for the next two years because of the weapons the Skraks captured from them. That was twelve years ago. From what we've seen, there are a hell of a lot more Skraks now than there were back then. It would just be suicide to go in there, son. And I can't let you endanger my people by giving the Skraks any more modern weapons than you already have. I'm sorry."

"But we have to do something, damn it!" exclaimed Greg. "If the Skraks keep growing in number eventually they'll be able to overrun you, modern weapons or not!"

"He's got a point there, Hakata," said one of the onlookers. "maybe we should try to do something while we still can."

"Mister Carmichael," said Chtak, "how many people live in the city here?"

"Our population is around twenty-five hundred. A lot of them are pretty young, though."

"And about how many are capable of fighting if it came to that?"

"Oh, maybe five or six hundred, I'd guess. Maybe a few more if they really had to."

"I see. And how many modern weapons do you have for your people?"

"Well, that's the problem. We only have twenty or thirty all told. If I could give every person a real weapon then maybe it would be a reasonable idea to try and clean out the caves. As it is, we wouldn't stand a chance."

"Suppose we could get more weapons. Would you be willing to try then?"

"Maybe. But where are you going to get more weapons? Unless your ship comes back, but then you'd have your own Marines anyway."

"I was thinking that perhaps we could get the weapons from the base, sir."

"With those droids standing guard? Do all of you folks have a death wish or something?"

"With your permission, I would like to see if it is possible to deactivate the droids. I think it is at least worth a try. But we will require some assistance."

Carmichael frowned. "Well, I suppose it wouldn't hurt to look at the possibility. What would you need from us?"

"If you have a plan of the base, that will be very helpful. A guide would be appreciated, too."

"I would be willing to guide them, sir," said Stewart Paalova from the sidelines. "I know the area very well."

"Yes, I know you do," said Carmichael with a frown. "Far better than you are supposed to, I might add! Someday you and your friends are going to get your backsides fried by one of those droids down there! All right, I have a plan in my office, if you'd like to have a look at it."

"Thank you, sir," said Chtak, "I'd be very interested in seeing that."

Carmichael led them through a number of corridors until they reached his office. It could have been the office of any mid-level administrator anywhere in the Star League. They sat down and he activated a display with a plan of the base.

"We only have the non-classified stuff in our computers here, but that still shows the basic layout of the place."

Chtak and Greg studied the plan. It was far more detailed than the one they had on *Gilgamesh*. The base was laid out in a series of concentric circles. The center circle contained the main fusion plant, the control center, the Marine armory, the infirmary, and the officers' living quarters. Out from there were the manufacturing plants, two reserve fusion plants and materials storerooms. The next ring was more storerooms and living quarters. Beyond that there were a scattering of other chambers for a variety of functions. There were five main passageways that radiated outward from the central core, like the spokes of a wheel. One led to the housing tower and another led to the door on the south side that they had hoped to enter by. The other three went out in different directions and Carmichael confirmed that they were all deeply buried.

"The droids' patrol zone seems to be limited to the inner three rings," he said. "We've never seen them beyond those points—except when they're chasing one of us."

"If we were to go down the main corridor from the city to the first big intersection, is that where we'd find them?"

"Yes, there's always one there at that intersection."

"Just one?"

"Yes, but plenty more will come running in seconds if there's any trouble."

"What do you think, Chtak?" asked Greg. "You think you can shut those things down?"

"I can try. The trick will be to avoid being killed during the attempt. Or afterwards if the attempt fails."

"Do those things shoot on sight?"

"Not exactly," said Carmichael. "You can get within sighting range of one of them; get to within about a hundred meters and they won't do anything. But cross that line and they will start to shoot. Or if you try shooting at them from any range, they'll respond."

"I see," said Chtak. He zoomed the display to look at the area around the intersection in more detail. "I see several storage rooms off the corridor that are still in the 'safe' zone. Can we get into them?"

"Yes, but they've been pretty well cleaned out of anything useful."

"There also seem to be a number of service corridors all through this area. Are they passable?"

"Yes, it's a regular warren back there. We can get to most of the outer areas by using them. They allow us to bypass the droids in the main corridors."

"I don't suppose any of those might lead us to the central areas?"

"Sorry, there's no direct connection without crossing one of the main corridors—and that's where the droids are waiting."

"All right, I am willing to attempt this," said Chtak. "We can set up in this room, and if my attempt fails, we will have a route of retreat. Is that satisfactory with you, Mister Carmichael?"

"I suppose so. I can send young Paalova along with you. He knows the area as well as anyone. When will you go?"

"Immediately. I see no point in waiting." He glanced at Greg and he knew that 'immediately' was the only answer he would be willing to accept.

An hour later they were walking warily down a dimly lit corridor.

"It's just up ahead," said Stewart Paalova. "There, you can see it."

Chtak stopped and looked where the young human was pointing. In the distance he could see the droid. It looked vaguely like the upper half of a suit of powered battle armor, but instead of legs it was mounted on an anti-grav sled. It was sitting motionless at the intersection of the corridors. There were also three small lumps about halfway between it and them.

"What are those?" asked Greg.

"They last fellows to try something like this," said Paalova.

"Great." They all peered at the droid for a minute of more, trying to spot something—anything—that might give a clue to how to proceed.

"Those things have been on patrol for twenty years," whispered Greg. "I don't suppose we can hope they'll just run out of power or fall apart for lack of maintenance, can we?"

"Unlikely, Greg," said Chtak. "I imagine they routinely recharge their power cells and there is probably an automated maintenance unit somewhere. Although I'm not sure where all the power would come from ultimately."

"The main fusion plant fires up about once a year, I think," said Paalova.

"Yes, that would do it. They could charge up all the batteries and capacitors periodically. Obviously the whole base is on some sort of automatic routine."

"Okay, so what do we do?"

"Here is the storage room we saw on the plans. Let's get inside." They quickly did so and Chtak began to unpack his knapsack.

"Got enough stuff there, do you, Chtak?" asked Greg.

"I believe in being prepared, youngling."

He laid out his equipment and quickly sorted out what he would need. "Greg, would you set this directional antenna out in the hall-way there. Aim it at the droid, please."

"Right." The human picked up the indicated device and returned a moment later to say that it was done. "What are you going to do?"

"In simple terms, I am going to try and access the command routines of the droid and put it into a standby mode and then shut it down completely. I have a number of codes I can use in my attempt to do this. Unfortunately, the computer I'm forced to use is probably less capable than what is in that droid."

"Will you be able to shut all of them down?"

"That I do not know. Very well, I am ready to proceed. Mister Paalova, would you be so kind as to keep watch on the droid and let us know if it does anything?" The young man took his post by the door and signaled that he was ready.

Chtak pressed several buttons on his computer and studied the results on the small screen. "Well, it has rejected the first set of codes. Any activity, Mister Paalova?"

"No, it's just sitting there."

"All right, I'll try another. No, another rejection. Anything?"

"No."

"Again. Hello, this is interesting. I believe I have gotten through and actually made contact with it. Very good. Now if I can just access the command routines and order it to… Oh dear, what's happening here?"

"Uh, sir…" came the voice of Paalova.

"This is interesting. It's accessing my own computer in return." Chtak saw Gregory rush over to the door. "Now what is it doing…?"

"Chtak! It's moving!"

"Amazing! It's completely scrambled my own computer. I had no idea it had such a capable…"

"Chtak! It's coming this way!"

"Is it? Oh dear."

Greg and Paalova were shutting the heavy door. "We've got to get out of here, Chtak!" shouted Greg. He finished with the door and dashed over to help stuff the equipment back into the knapsack.

"This way! Quickly!" hissed Paalova. He had gone over to another door in the far wall and was holding it open.

They were halfway across the compartment when the door leading to the corridor exploded. Chtak nearly fell, but it was handy to be able go on all fours and by doing so he actually beat Greg to the other door. He looked back in time to see the droid moving through the smoke and into the compartment. Greg was two meters away and the droid was swiveling its weapons to bear on him.

Chtak lunged. Not to get out of Greg's way, but to get directly in his path. The Marine tripped over him and fell through the door-— just as a plasma bolt tore through the space he had just occupied. It hit the opposite wall, but fortunately the tough material absorbed the energy and simply melted in one spot instead of exploding in fragments. Paalova slammed the door shut behind them and the three scrambled down the passageway as fast as they could. Chtak looked back, but the other door did not explode. Apparently the droid had given up the chase.

"Well, that did not work very well," said Chtak when they stopped to catch their breath.

"No shit," said Greg between gasps. Chtak looked at him sharply. Greg did not usually use that sort of language. "So what do we do now?"

"We go back to the city and think of something else."

"Chtak, if we can't get into the base, I am going after Rhada. I will not leave her there even if I have to go alone and armed with nothing but a spear!"

"You will abandon your command, Lieutenant?"

"Damn you! This is Rhada we're talking about! You care about her, too!"

"I do. And about Ensign Torres as well. But we will not help them by throwing our lives away. Now please stop talking nonsense."

Greg frowned but said nothing more. Paalova had been watching the whole exchange with interest. After a short rest, he led them through a bewildering maze of tunnels and service corridors that led, eventually, back to the main passageway. From there it was a short walk back to the city. Mayor Carmichael was waiting for them.

"Didn't work, did it?" he said.

"No."

"Not surprised. But at least you all made it back in one piece. But I'm glad you're back now, I was just getting ready to send someone to find you."

"Why? What's happening?" asked Greg.

"I'm hoping maybe you can tell me. Our lookouts up in the tower have spotted a number of small craft landing over near the south gate; the same area you landed in."

"Maybe *Gilgamesh* is back," said Greg excitedly.

"You said a number, sir," said Chtak. "How many?"

"It was hard to tell, but the lookouts said maybe eight or ten. That sound like your folks?"

Chtak and Greg exchanged looks.

"I'm afraid not," said Chtak. "With the loss of the cutter, our ship would have only three shuttles left. Whoever these newcomers are, they aren't ours."

Charles Florkowski stepped out of the shuttlecraft and took a deep breath. The air was good. And it was nice to be outside for the first time in many months. It was not so nice to be surrounded by a crowd of swaggering, sweating, smelly mercenaries. And it was quite a crowd, maybe three hundred people, all told, most of them heavily armed and looking for something to shoot.

But the only thing to shoot had already been rather thoroughly shot. He walked over to a blackened crater in the ground. A few twisted pieces of metal were scattered about here and there. Nothing much left to tell what it had been.

But he knew what it had been: The cutter from *LSS Gilgamesh*.

He had been aboard the cutter hundreds of times and he could remember every detail of it, even that funny screeching noise the one turbine made. They had tried any number of times to fix that but with no success. It always screeched. But not anymore.

Had anyone been aboard when this happened? Or had *Gilgamesh* warned them to get out and make a run for it? If there were people aboard, did he know them? Probably. There were only a few of the new people that he didn't know. If there had been anyone aboard they were now dead.

Because of him.

Revenge had seemed such a simple thing. Get here and foil Shusterman's and Ellsworth's great plan. That would be revenge. Maybe even kill Ellsworth as an added bonus. But people were dying that he had not planned on. Maybe some people he had liked. A flicker of guilt took shape inside him, but he quickly stamped it out. There couldn't be any guilt, because that implied blame. And there couldn't be any blame because that implied that Charles Florkowski might be at fault. And that was simply unacceptable.

He looked up as several mercs began talking excitedly on a rise of ground to the north. A crowd began to gather and Florkowski walked in that direction.

"What the hell do you suppose did that?" one of them was saying when he got closer.

"Sure wasn't from the laser shot. It's not burned at all," said another.

"Hey, there's another one over here!" came a shout from fifty meters away. Enough of the crowd dispersed that Florkowski could get a look at what they were talking about. When he saw it his stomach heaved.

It had been a person. Man or woman he couldn't tell. The body had been ripped to pieces. By what he couldn't begin to guess. Inscets and scavengers were already working on the remains.

At least the mercs seemed to have been impressed by the bodies. They stopped wandering about and got themselves sorted out into a semblance of a defensive perimeter with pickets placed and sensors activated. But the bulk of them were heading for the door. Three hundred meters to the north he could just see the top of a huge metal door. It was nearly buried in a rockslide. He headed in that direction. He spotted Commander Nista, who Wolfe had put in charge of the engineering operation to get into the base. She was looking things over and conferring with several of her people.

"Some of this slide is very recent, ma'am. Not more than a day old, I would guess," said one of them.

"Maybe the Leaguies were trying to hide it from us," said Nista.

"Maybe," agreed the other, "but in any case, we've got a hell of job to dig this out."

"Well, the sooner we get started, the sooner we'll get inside," said Nista.

"Yes, ma'am, but I estimate at least a week to clear out these rocks. We haven't got much in the way of excavating equipment. We're just going to have to use lifters to move one rock at a time."

"Fine, but get started. The Commodore doesn't like to be kept waiting."

"I know, ma'am, I know." The man waved a sketchy salute and headed toward the rocks. Florkowski followed along. As he neared the edge of the slide, there was some more excited talk. He got closer and saw what the excitement was.

"Look at this thing, will you?"

"Strange looking critter. Never saw anything like it."

"Me neither. It must have gotten caught in the slide."

"Unlucky or real dumb, I guess."

The mercs laughed and then moved off. Florkowski stared at the mangled body in shocked silence. He wasn't surprised that Wolfe's men did not recognize it. They were from a part of space far from the great war between the Star League and the Darj'Nang. They wouldn't know what they were looking at. But Charles Florkowski knew what it was. *A Skraknar. What the hell is that doing here?*

He was still staring at it and wondering if he should inform any of his 'comrades' about it when his communicator beeped.

"Florkowski here."

"Ah, Commander, I trust you are enjoying your little walk in the park?" It was Wolfe.

"It's very pleasant, sir."

"Good. How do you think the work will proceed?"

"Your engineers think it will take about a week to clear the rocks from in front of the door. I'm no engineer, but it seems like a reasonable estimate to me."

"Good. I just wanted to let you know that our friend Captain Ellsworth is still around." Florkowski stiffened. What did he mean? Had they found *Gilgamesh*?

"Yes, we're picking up a signal being broadcast toward you on the planet. I imagine it is from some remote transmitter. I can't believe she'd give herself away so easily."

"No, sir, that doesn't seem likely."

"So glad you agree. The message is in code. I don't suppose you brought along any of the decryption keys when you left your old ship, did you?"

"I'm afraid not, sir."

"Pity. Well, we can't break it, but it is obvious they are trying to make contact with their shore party. We shall have to see if she gets any answer."

"What if there is an answer from them, sir?"

"Then we'll have to... deal with them."

Rhada McClerndon worked the bellows on the forge. Up and down, up and down, again and again. She could feel the heat increasing as the coal fire flared up. Finally, Sstrac, the weaponsmith, signaled that he was satisfied and she could stop for a moment. But

Sspara would not allow her to rest. Not yet. She tugged on her leash and she had to follow her to the chamber where the coal was stored. Rhada had only been vaguely aware of what coal was before she had to start hauling it. She didn't know where the Skraknars were getting the coal, but obviously they were digging it up somewhere and bringing it here to store. Once here, it was her responsibility to haul it to the forge. Sspara had her hoist a basket onto her shoulder and then trudge back to the forge and set it in place. There was now enough coal to last a day or more. She was pleased that Sspara had not used the switch on her even once during this trip.

Still no rest. Now it was back to work the bellows again. Sstrac was forging a sword blade from some scrap metal they had salvaged from somewhere. Great mounds of scrap metal lay at one end of the chamber. The blade went into the fire and then to the anvil and then to the quenching barrel and then back to the fire, again and again. Sstrac was the largest and strongest Skraknar she had yet seen. His four arms allowed him to wield two hammers in unison and still manipulate the tongs that held the hot metal.

After lots of heating and hammering, Sstrac was satisfied with his work and then it was over to the grinding wheel. Rhada took hold of the crank and turned the wheel briskly while the weaponsmith put an edge on his blade. It took quite a while and Rhada was sweating and gasping for breath before he was done.

But when it was done, it was time to rest. Sspara led her aside and allowed her to sit and have a drink. The Skraknars seemed to have spurts of intense activity followed by lengthy rests. They would go almost nonstop for what seemed like two or three hours and then rest for an hour or more. Rhada didn't mind the lengthy breaks, but those long stretches without one were hard on her.

She thought that this was her third day among the Skraknars, but she wasn't sure. In the dark caverns, it was impossible to judge the passage of time. There had been that horrible first day when Ritta was killed. And then there had been yesterday when she was trained to work here at the forge—not that it required much training to work the bellows or turn the crank or haul the coal. And now this was another day. Or so she guessed.

She winced as she shifted position slightly. The bruises and welts on her back still hurt. They had not beaten her nearly as much yesterday and hardly at all today. The work was simple enough that she wasn't likely to make a mistake and as long as she kept pumping or cranking or hauling as much as they demanded, they spared her the lash. Yesterday both Sspau and Sspara had watched over her. Today it was only Sspara. That wasn't necessarily good, though. Sspara seemed more ready to use the lash than the other one and she was definitely stronger.

But Rhada was tired. The pace was grueling and each morning she woke up with her muscles in terrible pain from the previous day's activity. She was so stiff at first that she was whipped again and again until she could get moving properly. They fed her, but it did not seem like enough to sustain this activity. Maybe she should ask for more. And it was hard to sleep at night despite her exhaustion. She got so cold. She would wake up shivering.

And she was a slave.

It was hard to accept, but there was no real way to deny it. She was doing work for her captors. She was helping them make weapons to use against her own kind. She was doing it in order to avoid being punished—or eaten alive—but she was doing it.

This is the way it starts. Fear makes you do something. And then something more. And it keeps going until you do exactly what they want without question. Each step seems like the best thing to do at the time, but before long it becomes a habit. And then they don't even need the whip anymore...

She shook herself. That was what was happening after only three days. But what else could she do? The image of Ritta Torres being ripped apart was always fresh in her mind. *I'm a coward! At least she had the courage to defy them!* But she died for it. Would she have done the same thing if she knew they would really kill her like that? If it had been Rhada who was torn to pieces before Ritta's eyes, would she be the one groveling here instead of her?

A slave. The one thing she swore she'd never be and now she was. She had sworn that and fled her own world to avoid another sort of slavery. Joined the Navy to escape it. But she had still ended up here in the end. A naked animal, trained to work the bellows and turn the crank and haul coal to the forge.

And have young. Have little slave babies to work for the masters in turn. That thought terrified her most of all. But they would have to catch a mate for her before that could happen. And the fact that they had not caught anyone else from the shore party yet was hopeful. But only a little hopeful. No one had come to rescue her yet. Surely they would if they could. But the ship had been under attack, too.

What did that mean? Maybe no one would come. Maybe they were all dead. Or maybe she would look up sometime and see someone else being dragged in here as a slave to work alongside her. Or mate with her...

To escape that terrible thought she looked over to the forge and the armory that lay beyond. She had been surprised to see the forge although she knew she should have expected it from all the equipment the Skraknars were carrying. It all had to come from somewhere. She had to remind herself that these were intelligent creatures who could use modern weapons and equipment when it was available. And they obviously knew how to make simpler gear when it wasn't.

And they were certainly making a lot of it. There were hundreds of swords and spears and shields hanging on racks. Also hundreds of those strange crossbows and thousands of bolts. What were they all for? Each of the Skraknar warriors she had seen carried its own weapons with it. All of these were extras apparently. What were they for?

"You look at weapons," said Sspara suddenly. "Why? No tricks! You never touch them!"

"I was just wondering what you need so many for. All of you already have weapons, I thought."

Sspara hissed. It was a strange sound that they used frequently and she was getting the idea that it was some sort of exclamation rather than an actual word. A snort of disgust maybe? Or a laugh? They were already starting to teach her some of their language. Just simple things like 'get up' or 'work' or 'come' or 'go'. She didn't think she'd ever be able to speak it herself, but they didn't want her to speak--just to listen and obey.

Now Sspara commanded her to 'get up and 'come'. She was sorry she had said anything because the rest period wasn't over. She was led down another passage she had never been in before. It led to the largest part of the cavern she had yet seen. A huge space with some light coming in from above. She was a little startled to see Sspau lying on a rock at the entrance. Sspara exchanged a few words with her and then led Rhada into the chamber.

"Weapons for these," she said and gestured.

Rhada followed the pointing arm and gasped. The chamber was filled with hundreds—thousands—of small spherical objects—eggs! Thousands of eggs. There were a multitude of small 'nests' made from cut grass and each nest had a dozen eggs in it. They were about twenty centimeters in diameter and seemed to be a pale yellow although with the poor light she couldn't really be sure.

"When these hatch, we have enough warriors to take this world for our masters," said Sspara. "Human city will fall to us."

"City?" said Rhada in surprise. "What city?"

Sspara focused both her eyes on her and stared intently. "Truth? You not know of other humans?"

"No, we didn't think there would be anyone here at all!" Rhada was shaking her head, her brain spinning. A human city? What did that mean?

But she had no time to ask any more questions because a half dozen Skraknars suddenly appeared and began hissing and sputtering with Sspara. Almost immediately they were tugging at her leash and hurrying her along. Sspau brought up the rear and used the switch on her. Rhada hurried as fast as she could, wondering what was happening now.

They took her to the first big chamber where the leader, Sslaskatar, was. They threw her down in front of him and a shudder of fear coursed through her. Whatever this was, she didn't think it was good.

"Sslave, you have lied to me," he said.

"No..." Involuntarily she glanced to the spot where Ritta had died.

"More ships have landed where the first one did. Many more. Humans swarm about in numbers greater than you claimed for your ship's crew. You lied."

"No, I did not..." A dozen quick strokes from Sspau and Sspara beat her down and silenced her before Sslaskatar stopped them.

"You say you did not lie. Then who are these newcomers?"

"J-just before you captured me our ship radioed that they were under attack in space," said Rhada desperately. "I do not know by who or why. These new ships may come from whoever attacked my ship. That is all I know."

Sslaskatar regarded her for a long time before speaking again. "Very well, we shall see. These new ones are too many and too well armed to attack yet. But we shall watch them and see what they do. If I find that you have lied then you will die."

They dragged her away and back to her sleeping chamber. She was a little surprised that they did not take her back to the forge. They tied her to the ring and Sspara left. Sspau settled down next to the fire and threw a few sticks into it.

"I hope you not lie, slave," she said. "Waste to kill good slave. You first female we catch in very long time. Long ago we catch others, but too few of us to keep slaves then. All killed. Now many more of us. We keep slaves."

"Why? Why do you want slaves?"

"For the Great Masters. Someday they come again. Claim this world. We have all in order: warriors to fight, slaves to work. Good."

Rhada huddled against the rock. All the Darj'Nang were dead. They would never come back to this planet. But these creatures were still devoted to them. They would do what they had been trained to do even if it made no sense. She had the image of thousands of years passing and new cities teeming with Skraknars filling the planet. And countless thousands of humans toiling endlessly in fields and mines to prepare the world for the Great Masters who would never come.

She curled up in a ball and wept silently. *Greg, Greg, where are you? Why haven't you come to find me? Please come and find me! Somebody, please come and find me!*

"It's from *Gilgamesh*! No doubt about it!" exclaimed Able Spacer Kara Dougan, who was the party's communications tech. "A compressed data burst in our standard code."

Greg and Chtak looked anxiously over her shoulder as she started the decryption routine on her small computer. They had no sooner gotten to the top of the tower to talk with the lookouts about the small craft that had been landing when they were called back down to Carmichael's office by the word of an incoming message.

"Thank God they're all right!" exclaimed Greg.

"We can hope they are all right," said Chtak. "The capacity for your species to engage in wishful thinking never ceases to amaze me, young one."

When the message was decoded, it proved to be a long one. Greg's enthusiasm was properly dampened by the time he had reached the end of it.

"Well, this is truly an awkward situation," said Chtak.

"The capacity of your species for understatement never ceases to amaze me, Chtak," said Greg.

"Bad news?" asked Mayor Carmichael. Greg looked up. He had not even heard the man come into the room.

"Bad enough," said Greg. "The newcomers are a band of mercenaries. They are probably here to loot the base and anything else they can grab. A nasty bunch of customers from what our captain tells us in her message. They have her badly outnumbered up in space and us badly outnumbered down here. Mister Carmichael, you were telling me that you had some emergency procedures in place in case the Darj'Nang came back. You might want to think about putting them into effect. Just because these new folks are humans, I wouldn't expect them to treat you very well if they find you."

"Yes, we have quarters and supplies down below in the sub-basements and ways to hide the passages to get down to them. And there are tunnels to let us get out if we have to. Do you think I should start moving my people down there?"

"Yes, I do."

"I'll get right on it. It's been a while since we had an evacuation drill, but my people still know what to do." The man left.

"So what do you think, Chtak?" asked Greg.

"I am not a tactician, Gregory, and I do not see any immediate solution to this dilemma."

"It sounds like the ship is safe for the moment and we'll have to set up a remote transmitter to get a message back out to them like they suggest. But beyond that, I don't know what we can do. Eight or ten boatloads of mercs is way more than we can handle down here—especially with them having fire support they can call in from orbit."

"And I see no hope of *Gilgamesh* defeating such odds to remove that support," said Chtak.

"No, damn it. So the mercs will blast their way into the base and we can't stop them."

"Of course, they will encounter the droids," said Chtak.

"True. That will probably surprise them, but it sounds like they have the firepower to take them out eventually and then they can just walk in and strip the place. So even if we lay low until they've gone, we've lost the whole reason we came here in the first place. And meanwhile, we still can't do anything to help Rhada," he ended bitterly.

Chtak went over to Charmichael's computer display and called up the diagram of the base they had been looking at earlier. Greg followed him over and sat down.

"What are you looking for?"

"Inspiration."

Greg looked for a few minutes without really seeing and then got up.

"Miss Dougan, we need to set up a remote transmitter to get a signal back to the ship. Can you check with the locals about getting the equipment and getting it placed? We'd better set up more than one of them and put them as far from here as we can manage. I imagine the mercs will get around to checking this place out eventually, but there's no point in bringing them right to us."

"Yes, sir, right away." The woman left and he sat back down. What a mess! Droids and Mercs and Skraks, oh shit! What the hell were they going to do now? He glanced over at Stewart Paalova, who had been trailing them all day. The young man was leaning against the wall and looking back at him.

"The Star League really needs the contents of this base so desperately?" he asked.

"More than you know. It was probably our last real hope."

"As I understand it, the biggest problem is the mercenary ships out in space. If you could eliminate them, the other problems would become far easier, correct?"

"I guess so," said Greg. "If we had *Gilgamesh* up there instead of the merc ships, we could take out their ground forces pretty easily. And then we'd have the stuff to take out the droids, get the base—and rescue Rhada."

"The woman is special to you?"

"Very. Doug's pretty taken with Claritta, too."

"I am sorry. Had I known, I might have tried to rescue them—not that I could have succeeded."

Greg laughed grimly. "Air out the lock now. We're not going to be able to do any of this—unless Captain Ellsworth can pull off a miracle."

"But the enemy ships are the key," said Paalova, half to himself. "It is a shame we cannot…" he trailed off.

"Can't what?"

Paalova straightened up and walked over to the display Chtak was studying. "May I?" he asked.

Chtak moved aside and Paalova zoomed the display out and then back in again in a different region. He pointed to a large circular object near one edge. "Would this be enough to even the odds?"

Greg and Chtak stared at what he was pointing at. They looked up in surprise.

"It would sure go a long way towards evening the odds!" exclaimed Greg. "Is it still there? Does it still work?"

"It is still there. It was never hit during the bombardment. Whether it still works, I do not know. There is no way to enter from the outside except along this access tunnel from the core area."

"Then we'd still have to get past the droids," said Greg glumly.

"Then we will get past them!" said Chtak loudly. Greg stared at his friend in surprise. The alien's fir was bristling and his whiskers were twitching. Greg wasn't sure, but he thought that for the first time ever he was seeing Chtak truly angry.

"These... these *mercenaries* come here looking for loot and personal gain. They would destroy the hopes of trillions of people for profit! We cannot permit that! We *will* not permit that! We will find a way to stop them!"

Greg was amazed. He had never seen his friend like this before. Suddenly the comical little creature seemed almost... dangerous.

"Okay. I'm with you. How?"

"Quiet, I'm thinking..."

CHAPTER SEVENTEEN

Captain Jaqueline Ellsworth stared at the message on her monitor. It was from the party down on Tractenberg IIIc. They were still alive and that was a great relief. Or at least some of them were alive. Lieutenant Quatrock was dead along with eight others and two of them—including Rhada McClerndon—had been captured. Captured by Skraknars of all things! She had never even considered the possibility that there might be Darj'Nang forces on the planet. On all those deadly dull patrols so many years ago, they had not detected any trace of activity. And the Skraknars weren't the only surprises down there. A whole group of stranded colonists were there, too. Throw in a band of rapacious mercenaries and a few rampaging security droids and it was enough to give a person ulcers.

She looked up as Karl Bradley floated into her office. He pulled himself down to a chair and strapped himself in.

"Have you read this?" she asked, indicating the message.

"Yes, ma'am. Sounds like they've got an even bigger mess down there than we do up here—as hard as that is to believe."

Ellsworth massaged her temples with her fingers. Five days. It had been five days since this nightmare began. *Gilgamesh* was still in hiding and the enemy was not making any serious attempts to find them. They were destroying their transmitters as quickly as they could after they went into operation, but that was all. The repairs were proceeding slowly, but satisfactorily. Now it seemed as though the shore party was in hiding, too. But at least they were among friends.

"What do you think of this idea they are proposing?"

"I don't know, ma'am. It sounds hellaciously complicated and if it fails at any point they would be in real trouble."

"Yes, and it will have no chance at all with Wolfe's flagship hanging right over them. As soon as they went into action, they would detect it quickly enough to stop them. What they are going to need is a major diversion."

"I assume you mean us, Skipper."

"Who else? We're all there is up here. The trick is going to be to hold them off long enough to let the dirtside people pull off their stunt."

"It's a hell of a risk, Skipper. Once we commit ourselves there will be no turning back. We might still be able to run depending on what the mercs do, but that will be the only other thing we can do if this doesn't work."

"Yes, but since our only other options are to wait until Wolfe has stolen the prize—or just run now and be done with it—I don't see that we have much choice. We're all expendable at this point."

"No, we're not, Skipper. That's the problem."

Ellsworth looked at him and laughed. "No, I guess we aren't, are we? If we could pull this off by sacrificing ourselves, it would be worth it under normal circumstances. But unless we survive and still be hyper-capable we can't get the chips to where they are needed. Double jeopardy. But still, we have to try. By doing nothing we lose automatically."

"Yes, ma'am. So what do we do?"

"Well, the first thing is to tell Lieutenant Sadgipour not to do anything rash before we give him the go-ahead."

"You think he might? He seemed pretty level-headed to me, ma'am."

"Yes, he is, normally. But then normally his girlfriend isn't in the hands of a bunch of Skraknars."

"His girl...? My God, I didn't realize."

"Yes," said Ellsworth grimly. "To be honest, I'm pretty fond of Ensign McClerndon myself. It kills me to think of her in those things' hands. But unfortunately, rescuing our people has about the lowest priority in a long list of high-priority tasks."

"Yes, ma'am."

"Next, we need to pin down Van on the repairs. We need to be able to move and fight and I don't think we can wait two more weeks to get ready. The mercs aren't going to wait that long. I may have to override the doctor's restriction and allow longer exposures for our repair people."

"Kind of rough on them, Skipper."

"I know. We'll ask for volunteers first. Make sure they know the risks—and what's at stake."

"Right."

"Finally, the two of us have to figure out just how to pull off the diversion they are going to need down there."

"Skipper, the only way to divert those bastards is to engage them in battle—at ten to one odds."

"I know. Kind of challenging, isn't it? But we've got at least a week to plan for it. They never gave us that much time in the tactical sims at the Academy. This will be a piece of cake, Brad."

"Oh, yes, ma'am, a real piece of cake."

"I estimate the digging will be completed in another two days, sir," said Commander Nista.

"You told me a week, Commander," said Commodore Wolfe, testily. "It has been a week. Now you tell me two more days. We are all running out of patience."

"I'm sorry, sir, but our people are not being terribly diligent about the work.... "

"Now you want to blame others. I'm becoming disappointed in you, Commander." The woman looking out of the communications screen frowned and seemed angry. Charles Florkowski had noticed that Wolfe's people all seemed more willing to stand up for themselves when they were not in the same room with him. Unfortunately, Florkowski was in the same room with him. There was nothing for him to do down on the planet until they got the door open anyway. Besides, he had other reasons for wanting to be aboard.

"Commodore, you know that my authority over the other crews is limited," said Nista. "They keep wandering off to shoot at those antelope things or go look over that ruined tower. If I turn my back for a minute, half my excavation crew has disappeared. They don't like this sort of work, sir."

"Yes, Commander. I'll have a word with the other captains to keep their people under a tighter rein. Meanwhile, I suggest you don't turn your back for a minute. I want this completed as soon as possible."

"Yes, sir." The image disappeared.

Wolfe leaned back in his chair and swiveled to face his staff. "Stupid bastards," he growled. "If they can't shoot it or drink it or rape it they lose interest. No vision. But then if they had vision, they might not want to follow me, so I suppose I can live with it." He chuckled at his own joke. Then his expression became serious again and he focused on Florkowski.

"Meanwhile, Commander, your former captain continues to make a nuisance of herself."

"She has a way of doing that, sir."

"Yes. Those communication units she keeps launching are very annoying. My men are getting tired of destroying them."

"Since there is no way we can prevent her from launching more, would it make sense to just ignore them instead of destroying them, sir?"

"Perhaps, but then we are conceding the round to her and I don't like doing that. And if we force her to keep launching replacements, perhaps she'll get careless."

"A good point, sir," said Florkowski. He didn't think it made any real difference one way or the other. As long as *Gilgamesh* was out there, she would continue to be a threat. A threat Wolfe did not seem to appreciate properly, in his opinion.

"And it is a good thing I did not allow you to talk me out of destroying their landing boat, Commander. Those people down there are nearly as irritating as Ellsworth. I'm convinced they are hiding out in that housing tower in spite of the fact my men can't seem to find anything there. I'd be tempted to just blast the place and be done with it, but they have not irritated me quite enough for that—yet."

"There is evidence that people had been living there, sir. For a long time."

"Yes, and that is another puzzle. You told me this planet was uninhabited. And yet there are clearly people living here. What else haven't you told me, Commander?"

Florkowski thought nervously about the Skraknars. He had not told anyone about them. "This information about the inhabitants comes as a surprise to me, sir," he said, trying hard not to sound nervous. "I'm certain Captain Ellsworth was not expecting it, either."

"Perhaps. Well, in any case, neither Captain Ellsworth nor these mysterious colonists will keep us from our prize. In another few days we'll have the door uncovered and then we can get in there."

"Have you given any thought about how we'll get the door open, sir?"

"If it won't open, I suppose we'll have to cut it." The expression on Wolfe's face showed that he obviously had not thought about it at all.

"That looked to be a heavily reinforced blast door, sir. It may take more than just standard cutting torches to get through it."

"Hmm, yes. I'll have to give this some thought. Thank you, Commander."

"Yes, sir." He was obviously dismissed, so Florkowski rose and left the compartment. He went back to his quarters and was surprised—and delighted—to find Clara there.

"You're early, Clara. Not that I'm complaining."

"Yes, the Chief Steward told me to be here. I don't know why, but I'm not complaining either." She smiled.

Florkowski smiled, too, but inside he was frowning. This was the third time he had seen Clara in only a week. That seemed too frequent for the 'rotation' she was on. Was Wolfe up to something? Probably, but let him play his game. If he could save this poor girl from one more night of abuse he wasn't going to complain.

"Have you eaten?" he asked.

"No, not yet."

"I'll have something brought here."

"That would be wonderful, Charles." He smiled again at the use of his first name. At least he had broken her of the habit of calling him 'master'. It sickened him when she had slipped a few times and called him that. They sat down, she on a chair and he on the sofa facing her. Except for the first night when they had held each other, he had been careful not to get too close to her. She could not entirely hide those tiny flinches.

They stared at each other and the silence dragged on. He wasn't sure what to say to her. 'How was your week, Clara?' 'Oh, fine, Charles, I've only been raped eight times so far, not bad at all.' No, normal small talk just wouldn't work.

"Where... where are you from originally, Clara?" That seemed safe enough.

"Oh, I'm from Odinwald, and you?"

"Franklinton. I've never been to Odinwald."

"It's pretty much like everywhere else, I guess," she said. "That's one reason I went for the merchant service: get out and see the universe." Her expression darkened. "Never thought I'd end up like this, though. Of course, from what I hear about what's happening in the League, maybe I'm lucky at that. If I'd stayed home I might be dead now. Not that I'd call this living—except for these times with you." She smiled again.

"I'm really sorry this has happened to you." Sorry, what the hell good was sorry now? A thought suddenly materialized in his head.

"Clara, I have some money. It's mostly in a bank back on Freeport, but maybe I can see about... about..."

"Buying me? Setting me free?" Her expression was skeptical. "Don't raise my hopes, Charles. It would hurt worse than... than what I have to do now. False hope is worse than no hope at all."

"I can't promise anything..."

"Then don't." She was quiet for a while and he didn't know what to say. Where was the damn food? He needed a distraction.

"The worst of it..." she paused and blushed slightly. "The worst of it is not what I have to do or what they do to me. The worst of it is that they *can* do it to me. There's nothing—nothing at all—to restrain them. I've been thinking about it; how we all take for granted the rule of law. The laws protect us even when we aren't thinking about them. People can break the law and hurt other people, but they have to do it in secret and they have to fear getting caught. Here, there is no law. They can do anything they like and only the victim has to fear. It's the helplessness that's worst."

Florkowski was surprised in spite of himself. He knew Clara had been a power tech and that was not a job for stupid people. But he had let himself forget that. She was obviously an intelligent and thoughtful woman. And they had turned her into a slave.

"I'm sorry."

Clara got up from the chair and came over to the sofa and sat down with her feet tucked under her. She was less than a meter away from him.

"Don't be. You didn't do this to me. And you are doing the only kindness anyone can do for me now."

She leaned closer and rested her head on his shoulder.

"Captain Ellsworth is suggesting we coordinate our actions with *Gilgamesh's* up in space," said Gregory Sadgipour. "She would keep them busy up there while we do our stuff down here."

"It seems like a good suggestion, Greg," said Chtak. "The weak spot in our plan was always the danger of the mercenaries getting direct fire support from orbit."

"Now wait a second, both of you," said Hakata Carmichael. "I haven't approved any of this cockamamie scheme of yours. And don't think you are going to use any of my people—or our weapons—without my approval."

Greg looked up in surprise. He and Chtak and Doug Rawlins had been hammering out details for days. Stewart Paalova had been supplying information on request and volunteering it unasked. Carmichael had been, too. What did he mean now?

"Sir, the help of you and your people is vital to saving the base and this whole situation," said Chtak.

"I'm aware of that. But in all this talk, you haven't given me one good reason for helping you at all. We were surviving just fine before you showed up. And after these mercenaries get what they want, I expect they'll move on and leave us in peace. It seems to me that just keeping a low profile is in our best interest. This plan of yours could get a lot of us—or all of us—killed for no good reason."

"Helping save the League is 'no good reason'?" asked Greg in amazement.

"Lieutenant, for close to twenty years we here all assumed that the League was already gone. Now you come here and tell us that it's not completely dead and you need our help to save what's left. Well, I don't recall the League giving us any help these last twenty years. Why should we stick our necks out now and lose everything for something that left us here on our own? And just so you folks can have access to some better weaponry. You said the Darj'Nang are dead, what do you need all this fancy gear for anyway?"

Greg hesitated. He had never actually gotten around to telling these people about the crisis with the nano-chips. They were probably thinking that the war had so devastated the League that most of the factories had been destroyed and a lot of technology had been lost. Would it hurt or help their case to tell them the whole truth now?

"Mister Carmichael," said Chtak, "I think this action is very much in your long-term benefit. These mercenaries may well stay around for some time. The base is enormous and they will require a lot of time to loot it properly. How long can you hope to avoid detection here? If they find you, I can assure you they will not treat you well."

"We can evacuate until they are gone."

"And you will come back to a tower stripped bare. No power, no food synthesizer. Life would be very different for you."

"At least we'd be alive! With your plan we could all end up dead!"

"Hakata, if they stripped everything from here we would have to go out and hunt and farm. How would we handle all those Skraks if we had to do that?" asked Paalova.

"We'd manage, Stewart."

"Would you?" asked Chtak. "Right now there are a thousand Skraks—at least. Five years from now there could be ten thousand. Ten years from now there could be fifty thousand. How long before they overwhelm you? You need what's in that base as much as we do."

Carmichael frowned but looked unconvinced. "Then maybe the best thing is to evacuate now and try to move as much equipment as we can. We could set up a new city thousands of kilometers away."

Greg was beginning to panic. They had to go through with this. It was the only hope for the League, the only hope for Rhada. "Mister Carmichael, you can't…!"

"Mister Carmichael," said Chtak, interrupting Greg with a touch to his arm. "You told us at our first meeting that you were the elected leader of your people. It seems to me that such a momentous decision—either your plan or ours—should be brought before them to decide."

"I don't think that's…"

"Yes, Hakata! A town meeting!" exclaimed Paalova. "We've had them before for things far less important than this!"

"Stewart, calm down, we need to think this through before…"

"An excellent idea, Mister Paalova," said Chtak. "Can you start spreading the word? We need to move quickly."

"Sure! I'll get right on it!" Paalova turned and dashed out of the office.

"Stewart, wait!" exclaimed Carmichael, but the young man was gone. He turned a ferocious frown on Chtak. "You think you're pretty smart, don't you? You think you can come in here claiming to be from the League and expect us all to fall at your feet. Well, we don't owe anything to the League! Most of the people here know the League only as a legend. I can't stop this meeting, but don't you think my people are going to fall for your crazy scheme!" The man walked out.

"Nice going, Chtak," said Greg.

"At least it gives us a chance. I suspect that Mister Carmichael was not going to give us even that much."

"So what do we do now?"

"Start thinking of reasons why they should help us."

The only place big enough to hold the meeting was in the central atrium. It was a risk to bring everyone up from the basements, but a merc party had already been through once that day. Night was falling and the mercs tended to stay in their camp at night. Greg shuffled nervously as all the people assembled. He wasn't sure what to say or what to do. But he knew that somehow he and Chtak had to convince them. Eventually the crowd quieted and Hakata Carmichael came out in front of them.

"Friends, this meeting has been called because we face a difficult decision: One too important for any person or any small group of persons to make on their own. It is something that we must agree upon together."

Carmichael proceeded to explain the situation and their possible options. Greg had been steeling himself to interrupt if he slanted things or left out important information, but to his surprise, the summary was as even-handed and complete as he could have asked for.

"So, Hakata, you are telling us the options are to evacuate, stay here and hide, or try to help these people in their fight?" The question came from the woman doctor who had helped Rawlins. Greg couldn't remember her name.

"That's pretty much it, Marianne. As I'm sure you can see, there are advantages and disadvantages with all three plans."

"Which one do you favor, Hakata?" This question was repeated and seconded by a large number of people.

"I think I have to favor evacuation," he said slowly. Greg clenched his fist.

"Why?" asked the woman.

"If we stay here and hide, we are putting our fate into blind luck. If those mercenaries find us we'll be at their mercy and I don't expect them to have much mercy from what Lieutenant Sadgipour has been telling me. We could all be killed or carried off as slaves."

"And if we go with the Lieutenant's plan and fight?"

"We could all be killed."

"And if we evacuate and then come back later and find this place destroyed or completely stripped?"

"Then we start over. Build a new place to live. But at least we'd be alive."

"Not a very appealing prospect after all the work we've put into this."

"No, but at least we'd still be alive to try."

"Until the Skraks get us," muttered someone.

"I'm not saying any option is a very good one!" said Carmichael angrily. "But you asked which one I favor and I told you."

Greg stood up and came forward. "May I speak?" Carmichael glanced around and then nodded.

"We weren't entirely honest with you when we told you why we had come here." There was stir in the crowd and a number of people frowned at him. "The League is in a far more desperate situation than we told you. And our need for the equipment in that base is far more critical." Greg launched into an explanation of the disaster with the nano-chips and the dangers now facing the League. He was interrupted a number of times and Chtak added his own comments when appropriate. Eventually, he got through to the end.

"So you can see why we need your help. If we could do this alone and leave you in peace, we would. But we can't. We can't do this without you. The lives of billions of people are at stake. The entire future of the League is in your hands."

There was a long, long silence as the people digested all that Greg had told them. Finally, Carmichael stood up.

"That's quite a lot of news you've dumped on us, Lieutenant," he said. "But I don't see that it changes the situation any. We're still facing the same decision." Greg slumped in his seat. What was it going to take to convince these people? But apparently he had gotten through to some of them...

"I don't agree at all, Hakata!" said one man emphatically. "This changes things a lot! If it was just a matter of whether or not the League Navy had the latest model photon cannon on their ships then I'd agree with you, but this! This is different! The whole League might die without our help!"

"They didn't help us when we needed it," said Carmichael. "Maybe the League should die."

"Hakata," said the woman called Marianne, "we all know your family died in the first Skrak attack. But that wasn't the League's fault."

"That has nothing to do with it!" said Carmichael angrily. "I'm only concerned with what's best for all of us!"

Other people began shouting out their opinions and the discussion grew out of control. Greg looked around nervously. It was nearly dark now and some people had small lights. Could they be seen through the atrium roof? If the mercenaries caught them like this it could be very bad. They did have lookouts posted, but it would take time to get everyone down to the basements again.

But the debate continued. It seemed to Greg that the people were about evenly split for the three options. Was there anything more he could do to sway them? They had to decide soon…

"May I speak?" shouted a voice. The crowd quieted and Greg was surprised to see Stewart Paalova step out in front of everyone.

"You all know who I am," he said. "I've been the leader of the city scouts for the last four years. I've spent a lot of time outside, playing hide and seek with the Skraks. I was just an infant when the 'Nangs attacked here. I can't remember what it was like before. It's the same with most of the young folks. This city has been all we've known. You older ones told us stories about the old League. And you told us fairy tales for bedtime stories. You might not realize that for most of us there was no real difference."

There was some nervous laughter, but Stewart continued. "Most if us never really believed there was a League. It was just a fairy tale that the old folks would tell children. Oh, you had the books and pictures and the computer files, but it wasn't any more real to us than the fairy tales.

"Then these strangers came and we realized that all those things you told us were really true after all. There really are a thousand different worlds out there. Different people and different races." At this point he paused and pointed to Chtak. "We realized there was more than just our one broken down city on one broken down world. It really is out there—waiting for us.

"And some of you want us to turn our backs on it!" he shouted suddenly.

"Hide, you say! Hide here or run off to the badlands and hide there. And then maybe come back here and hide again! When I'm out on a scout I have to hide a lot. Any scout can tell you that's what we do. A scout who doesn't know how to hide doesn't last long out there. I hide out there and then I come back here to hide some more.

"Well, I'm tired of hiding!" His voice rang through the atrium and he turned round and round to look at all the people.

"I'm tired of hiding and I won't hide any longer! Whatever you decide here tonight, I know the strangers will try their plan anyway. I'll be going with them! I'll fight and maybe I'll die, but I won't hide! This world belongs to us. We should take it for ourselves and our children. And this world is a part of the Star League. That's ours, too! That's our heritage. I want it! I'm going to go and help take it! Who's coming with me?"

There was an immediate cheer from all the younger adults and they dashed out of the crowd to surround Stewart and shout. There were only a couple hundred of them, but their noise and enthusiasm was infectious. More people moved to join them. And then more. Greg was becoming alarmed at the noise…

Eventually they quieted. Hakata Carmichael looked very tired and old. He called for the vote and it went overwhelmingly in favor of the Star League. Greg breathed an enormous sigh of relief.

There was some further debate over how the whole thing was going to be organized and who would be in charge. Carmichael offered to resign as mayor, but that was shouted down. A military committee was formed with Greg as overall commander and Paalova as commander of the city troops. It wasn't an ideal arrangement but it would have to do.

"All right," said Greg. "First I want to thank all of you for this. I know what you are risking and you have my personal gratitude.

"Second, and as my first official order: let's all get downstairs before those mercs spot us!"

CHAPTER EIGHTEEN

"They are assembling a large device in front of the door, Greg," said Stewart Paalova. "One of my scouts took these pictures from the mountain." He handed Greg the imager.

"Looks like they gave up on using regular cutting torches on the door," said Greg. "They're getting impatient. Look at this thing, Chtak." The survey officer took it and sat there with his whiskers twitching.

"Interesting. It appears to be a shipboard point-defense laser. And they are setting up a portable power plant to energize it. How long do you suppose it will take them to get it operational?"

"I don't know. And how long will it take to burn through the door once it is operational? We can't let them get inside before we're ready."

"We could attempt to sabotage the laser, couldn't we?" asked Chtak.

"That would give the game away," said Paalova. "Surprise is our only hope for this."

"Yes," said Greg. "Well, the first strike team leaves in just a few hours. And then another forty-eight hours until we go into action. *Gilgamesh* is nearly ready to do its part. I don't think there's any way we can hurry this. We'll just have to hope the mercs are as lazy about setting the laser up as they were about digging out those rocks."

"We could have had it done in two days," said Doug Rawlins with pride.

"Even with all the extra stuff your little explosion brought down?"

"Well, okay, three days, then. And they've been at it nearly two weeks."

"I guess we're lucky you are on our side, Doug," said Greg.

"I've been telling you that for months."

"But how lucky do *you* feel? You've volunteered yourself for one helluva job, Doug. You're going to have about two minutes-—at most—to get it done before those droids are swarming all over you."

"Relax, I've been practicing on the door down below. I can get it done in ninety seconds flat. Plenty of time to get under cover when I'm done. It's you and Chtak—and Stewart here—who have the dangerous jobs."

"How are you coming along, Stewart?" asked Greg. "Got your teams pared down to where you want them?"

"Yes. I have the forty fastest runners among all of the scouts. They have all been getting practice at long distance runs when they place your communications relays."

Greg nodded. Some of Stewart's people were running thirty or forty kilometers to place those relays. "And their weapons?"

"We have nearly all the city's weapons. Hakata was not pleased, but he realizes it is necessary if the plan is going to work. My scouts are quite excited. We've never been allowed to carry the modern weapons outside the city like this before."

"Well, don't let them get too cocky," warned Greg. "They're going out as a lure, not to fight a pitched battle."

"They know that, Greg. Have no fear. They will do what has to be done."

"Sure wish I was going with you," said Rawlins with a frown.

"Why? Oh… because of Ensign Torres. I'm sorry."

"I just wish… well, I just wish we could do something now," said Rawlins sadly.

"Yeah," said Greg. Paalova stood and stared at the two young Marines.

"There will be a chance later, gentlemen," said Chtak gently. "Once we have dealt with the other challenges we can rescue Rhada and Claritta."

"It's just that it's been so long since they were captured," said Greg. "How long can they last in that place?"

"Worrying does no good, Greg. For now you must concentrate on your duty and the task at hand."

"Yes. Well, then, let's get to it."

The lower level of the city tower was filled with excited people milling about. But it was not quite as crowded as it had been for the past week. In spite of the decision to fight, they were evacuating the very young and those unable to fight and enough able-bodied people to look after them. Two hundred had already filtered out last night and another two hundred would be going tonight. But all the attention was on the forty young men and women who would be filtering out in the opposite direction. Stewart Paalova's scouts were the center of attention.

They all seemed terribly young, but the quiet confidence they had in themselves belied that youth. Every one of them had faced danger and death. In addition to their weapons and rations and water bottles, many of them were openly wearing their cherished necklaces of Skrak teeth. The necklaces they carefully hid from their parents so they would not know about the deadly games they played with the Skrak scouts. Most of those parents had known, of course, but had said nothing, in silent pride.

Chtak watched the scouts saying good-bye to those parents now. If the plan went as it was supposed to, those young humans should not be put in too terrible a danger. If they were lucky, every one of them might return to their parents again. But Chtak knew how rarely plans ever went exactly right. And luck was such a fickle thing to balance lives on.

He watched Greg and Stewart going over the plan one last time. The scouts would sneak out in groups of two or three and move slowly north. They would take a leisurely two days to make a forty kilometer circuit around the mountain. Their slow pace, with some random wandering thrown in would make them look like the native herbivores to orbital IR scans. Then they would rendezvous near their target. Greg and Stewart shook hands and then Paalova called his scouts together. While they were assembling, Chtak went over to Stewart.

"You appear to be all ready."

"Yes. Just about."

"I notice that of all your people, only you have not taken a modern weapon," said Chtak. Stewart changed color slightly.

"I'm more comfortable with my usual weapons," he said.

"I have spent a great deal of time with young humans in the last several years and I have become quite adept at spotting the signs when they are Up-to-Something." Paalova twitched slightly and frowned. But he said nothing.

"I wish you the best of luck, young human. And here, you might find this of some use." Chtak took his stunner out of its holster and gave it to Paalova. The man looked at him with wide eyes.

"Thank you." The man took the weapon and then was silent for several seconds. "When we first met, you spotted me in that bush.

How? I was being very careful."

"I could smell you."

"Really? If I had been approaching a party of Skraks I would have been careful to stay down wind. But with a band of humans, I did not." He laughed. "That is one of the first things we beat into the head of a scout: never underestimate an opponent. I believe I have underestimated you in several ways."

"I am not an opponent, I hope."

"No. Indeed not. You are a friend. Someday, perhaps, I can visit your world."

"Perhaps. I would welcome such a visit. But for now, we have a job to do."

"Yes." Paalova turned and led his scouts down the tunnel toward the exit door.

"Enough," hissed Sstrac, the weaponsmith. It was one of the words that Rhada had learned of the Skraknar language, and one of the most welcome. She let go of the crank for the grindstone and straightened up with a groan. It had been built for the low-slung Skraknars and for her to operate it was very hard on her back. The Skrak hissed out another string of words that she could not understand and then turned away with his newly sharpened spearhead.

"He says you are good slave," explained Sspara. "Do good work. Done for today. Come. You wash and rest."

She was led down to the lake and she washed herself. The daily routine was really becoming routine and she scarcely flinched at the icy water. In fact, she submerged herself completely and gave her hair as good a scrubbing as she could. Then it was back up the tunnel and around and down to her own little space. She used the pit and was then tied by her nest. She had convinced Sspau that she really was cold at night and they had relented and provided her with a large bundle of grass and leaves. It was almost comfortable. Sspara tossed her two strips of charred meat and a root-like vegetable that some experimentation had proved she could eat without problems. They were feeding her more, too, and that helped. She was not so tired or sore as she had been at first. Her muscles were becoming used to all the exercise. But she still moaned and groaned when they made her work. She had quickly learned the trick of not letting them know she was able to do more work than she was already doing. She shifted position slightly as she ate. Her back was healing, too. They hardly whipped her at all anymore. She knew what to do and did it quickly enough that they rarely needed to use their switches.

And Sstrac had said she had done good work today. She felt pleased at the compliment. She twitched her dripping hair back out of the way. It had not grown much in the time she had been here, but she wondered what she would do with it when it got a lot longer. Maybe they would let her use a knife long enough to cut it...

Rhada froze in mid-thought, a mouthful of meat forgotten. She began to shake. *Longer? Longer? How much longer? Oh God, no!* Without thinking, she was making plans for being here for years. For being here forever! As a slave! She turned and looked at Sspara. The creature was paying her no mind. *I'm thinking like a slave already! Pleased by my master's pat on the head! I've only been here a few weeks and it's happening already!*

She numbly spat the meat out of her mouth and took hold of her leash. She yanked on it, but there was no more give in it than there ever was. It was some smooth substance and she had no idea what it was made of. The knot around her neck had defeated her every attempt to untie it. It was as strong as steel. But she suddenly began yanking and pulling at it with all her strength.

"I'm not a slave! I'm not! I'm not!" she wept in frustration. Eventually she ran out of energy and sat there panting and weeping.

"Why you do this?" said Sspara. "Rest. Eat."

"I don't want to be a slave!"

"Fool. You slave. Forever. Never get free. Slave always. You slave. Your young be slaves. Young's young's young be slaves. Always."

Rhada stared at the creature with wide eyes. Then she burrowed into her nest and wept.

Charles Florkowski looked at the woman sleeping next to him and smiled. She was so beautiful when she was asleep. All the cares and all the fear left her face when she slept. He reached out and gently ran his finger down her arm and then across her ribs and back up between her breasts to the shoulder. Then down the arm again. Clara stirred slightly and cracked open an eye. She smiled and then stretched luxuriously.

"Hello."

"Hello."

"I could sleep all day," she said and then snuggled up to him. He put his arm around her and hugged.

"I wish we could," he said, "but I'm going to be going dirtside in a few hours. We start cutting through the door today."

"I'd like to see that," said Clara. "But I guess there's no way I could."

"No, probably not. I don't think you're allowed off the ship."

"No." She was quiet for a few minutes. Then she stared into his eyes. "Charles? Have you... have you talked to the Captain yet?"

"About buying you? No, I haven't."

She looked away. He tried to judge her expression. Hurt? Disappointed? Angry? "Clara, the situation is very complicated." He pulled her close and whispered into her ear. He had no doubt there were listening devices in his quarters. "The Commodore and all the other senior officers are playing power games. I don't want to be involved in them, but there's no way to avoid it. I'm sure they already know I'm fond of you, but if they knew how much; if they knew I wanted to buy you, they could use that against me. I'm sorry, but we just have to wait."

"It's all right. I understand." She pulled away slightly and wouldn't meet his eyes. He pulled her close again.

"Clara, Clara! I will free you, I promise," he whispered. "Here, I can prove it." He rolled over and grabbed his tunic off the floor. He reached into a pocket and pulled something out of it and concealed it in his hand. He rolled back and then pulled the sheets up over both them. Clara looked at him in surprise. He opened his hand to reveal a small electronic device.

"I bought this from one of the engineers," he said.

"What is it?"

"The key to your collar."

Her eyes got very big and then they filled with tears. She pressed against him and clung very closely. He held her for a long time. Finally she pulled back slightly. "Could... could you take it off now? Just for a minute?"

"No," he said shaking his head. "That would leave a record in the collar. Someone might notice. Please be patient, Clara."

"All right."

He put the device away and then drew down the sheets. It had probably been a stupid thing to do to buy the key. It might get back to Wolfe. But he was determined to free Clara—one way or another. Sooner or later they would touch at a real port and if he couldn't buy her, he would steal her. He leaned over and kissed her and she responded.

"Please be careful, Charles," she whispered. "The Commodore already knows you like me." Florkowski stiffened.

"How...?"

"He asks me about you when... when..."

"When he rapes you," he hissed. She nodded her head.

"Does he... hurt you?"

"It's not too bad. Not as bad as some of the others. But he plays mind games, tries to see how frightened he can make me. He's good at that."

Florkowski nodded. "I know."

"And he did do that," she said pointing with her hand to her back.

"What?"

"I thought you saw," she said and rolled over. She was pointing to a mark on her right buttock. He looked closer and saw that there was a tiny wolf's head etched into her flesh, cut there with a laser. It was a miniature version of the logo Wolfe used on his uniforms and all over the ship. Florkowski recoiled in shock. He had felt something there while they were making love, but he had not looked. It probably had not hurt her much when it was done, and any competent cosmetic surgeon could remove it without a trace, but still...

"All the slaves on the ship have them," said Clara.

"Damn him! Damn him!" He clenched his fists.

"Charles, don't."

He got control of his anger. Clara was right. He couldn't let himself be angry with Wolfe. It was just too dangerous right now. But he was angry. He cared about this woman and yet he had to share her with a half-dozen other officers who cared for nothing except their own pleasure. If only Ellsworth had let him bid on her at the auction! Then he and she... what? What would they have done? He would have stayed on *Gilgamesh* and Clara would have been one of the refugees. And she probably would have felt grateful to Ellsworth instead of him! No, it was all too complicated. But Clara's suffering was still Ellsworth's fault. He reached out to run his fingers along her collar.

She's the one who should be suffering! She should be wearing this collar instead of Clara!

The image of Ellsworth, naked and collared and lying here in his bed, seemed to float before him. *That would be justice!* It was such a powerful image, such a powerful thought, that his heart was suddenly pounding. He reached out and seized the woman in front of him and she gasped in surprise as he roughly pulled her to him.

"I think this is about as good as we're going to get it, ma'am," said Karl Bradley, pointing to the simulated tactical display.

"Yes, but we've still got major uncertainty nexuses here, here and here," said Jaq Ellsworth, pointing to three glowing spots along the ship tracks.

"I know, Skipper, but there are just too many variables. We can predict some of their actions but not all of them. And the further we travel along the elapsed time track, the worse it gets."

"Yes." Ellsworth leaned back and sighed. "Kind of like back at the Academy, isn't it? I can remember spending long nights trying to come up with a solution to the problems the tactical instructors threw at us."

"I guess so, but I can't remember any problems quite like this one. I think the commandant would have gotten a few protests from the cadets if they threw something like this at us!"

"That's for sure. But I'm still pretty happy with this. Unless they do something totally stupid, we can control the flow of the battle for at least the first hour or so. Unless they change their patrol pattern in the next few hours, that is."

"Not too likely. They've settled into a routine and hopefully they think we have, too."

"Right." Ellsworth checked the time. "Okay, we go with this plan. There's no time to come up with anything else, anyway. The ground teams will be in position by now and from what they tell us, Wolfe's people are going to start cutting through the door very soon. So let's get going."

She unbuckled the belt that was holding her to her chair and pushed toward the door. Bradley followed her. There was just time for one last inspection of the ship. They met up with Commander Van Rossum outside of Engineering.

"Everything set, Van?" she asked.

"As ready as we're going to be, Skipper. All the repairs have been completed and my damaged control parties are standing by."

"Good. What about our 'excess baggage'?"

"It's all secure, ma'am."

"What about the surprise packages?"

"They are in place, too, ma'am. We souped them up as much as we could and they should do the job."

Ellsworth nodded and then set out on her tour. She had about an hour and she was determined to see as many of her crew as she could in that time. It might well be her last chance. She paused when she spotted a man in civilian coveralls.

"Consul Brown, I wanted to thank you and your people for volunteering like you have. The extra hands in the medical parties and damage control teams will be very welcome."

"We wanted to help however we could, Captain. This is our fight now, too."

Ellsworth nodded. She had offered to cram all the civilians into the remaining shuttles if they wanted to take their chances elsewhere, but they had unanimously decided to stay with *Gilgamesh*. She held out her hand and Brown took it.

"Good luck, Captain,"

"Thank you, sir. And to you, too."

She continued her tour. A pang of sadness went through her when she inspected the Number Four photon mount. Ensign McClerndon should have been there.

She talked to as many of her crew as she could. A word here, a pat on the shoulder there. They all seemed nervous but eager. She found herself biting back her emotions on several occasions.

Well, Liu-Chen, I guess you were right after all, weren't you? You can't really command a ship and a crew without making that emotional commitment, can you?

She couldn't quite point to the moment when she had made the commitment, but there was no doubt she had. These were her people now and she would do everything in her power to keep them alive in the coming fight. She knew they wouldn't let her down and she was damned if she would let them down either. Finally, she arrived back at the bridge.

"Miss Terletsky, give me the 'all hands circuit', please," she said as she strapped herself in.

"You're on, ma'am."

"Attention, this is the Captain," she said. "In about an hour we will be engaging the enemy. I don't have to tell you how important or how difficult this fight is going to be. An awful lot is riding on us. But if we all stand fast and do our duty I have every confidence that we will win the day. Old *Gilgamesh* has seen a lot of action in her time.

She's given a lot of years to the League and has a record to be proud of. If we give her everything we have today then I think that maybe this coming fight will be her finest hour. Good luck to you all. Good luck and good shooting! Ellsworth out."

She looked around her bridge. Everyone looked very thoughtful. She took a deep breath.

"Miss Terletsky, is the transmitter in place?"

"Yes ma'am, it's holding position about a thousand kilometers directly ahead."

"Very good. Begin the transmission."

"Aye, ma'am, activating now." The woman pressed the button and they were committed.

"Commander Bradley."

"Yes, ma'am?"

"Clear the ship for action."

"Yes, ma'am!" He pressed a button on his console and the battle stations alarm howled through the ship.

She sat and watched the brisk but orderly activity around her. Then she glanced up as Chief Gossage floated in with her vac suit. He must have been waiting outside to have gotten here this soon.

"Thank you, Chief." She put on the suit and this time made the plumbing connections. It was going to be a long day.

"Will you be needing anything else right now, ma'am?" asked Gossage.

"I don't think so." She looked at the man and then held out her hand. He took it. "Good luck, Chief."

"And to you, ma'am. Have you given any though about what you'd like for dinner tonight?" Jaq blinked in surprise but then smiled.

"She probably won't be too hungry, Chief," said Karl Bradley. "Not after all the mercs she's about to have for lunch!"

She laughed. "I'll let you know later, Chief."

"Yes, ma'am." He gave a salute and then left the bridge.

The activity slowed and then everyone was waiting expectantly.

"All decks report at battle stations, Skipper," reported Bradley. "The ship is cleared for action."

"Elapsed time?"

"Five minutes, fifty-two seconds, ma'am," said Bradley with a grin. He gave her a 'thumbs up' gesture. She returned it with her own smile. After a moment, her smile became a shark-like grin.

"All right, people, let's go *get* those bastards."

CHAPTER NINETEEN

"There's another one of those things, sir," said the sensor tech aboard the destroyer *Mangudai.*

"Shit," growled Captain Zaccaria, "aren't those bastards ever going to get tired of this game?" He stared at the sensor display. A light was blinking near one edge of the gas giant's rings, about sixty thousand kilometers away. Another damn communications relay from that League cruiser. There had been about two a day for the last two weeks. And unfortunately, it looked like *Mangudai* was the closest ship to this one.

"Can we hit it from here?"

"I doubt it, sir. An awful lot of crap in the way. I'm afraid we'll have to get closer to it."

"Hell. Communication, contact *Huskarl."*

"Yes, sir," said the com officer. Several minutes passed. "I'm sorry, sir, they're not... oh, here they are." The com screen lit up and Zaccaria was staring at a rather disheveled looking 'officer'.

"Yeah?" he said.

"Zaccaria here. Is Captain Ramsey around by any chance?"

"Nope. Not sure where he is. Is it important?"

Zaccaria sighed. The frigate *Huskarl* was without doubt the worst ship in Norman Wolfe's little fleet. Far more pirate than mercenary, the discipline aboard was appalling. Half the captains had opposed bringing them into the organization, but Wolfe was obsessed with numbers. The more ships he had, the more impressive he would look—no matter if the ships were worth anything or not.

"Not important enough to disturb your captain from whatever he's doing, Lieutenant. Just another communications relay. If Ramsey should surface, please let him know we are moving to destroy it."

"Uh, sure, I'll do that."

"Thank you, Zaccaria out." He shrugged and turned to his helmsman. "Take us ahead at two-thirds, plot a course to that relay."

"Aye, aye, sir."

"We're going ahead alone?" asked his first officer. "Standing orders are for us to stay in our teams, sir."

"I know, but it would probably take Ramsey an hour to get his pants back on and I don't feel like waiting that long. And it will be safe enough. There's nothing showing on the scanners so if the Leaguie is around they're powered down. If they try anything we can blast them before they could get their reactor on-line. But get the weapons manned in any case."

"Yes, sir. Vac suits?"

"No, just man the forward lasers."

"Aye, aye, sir."

Mangudai moved toward the annoying com relay at an easy acceleration. The forward weapons were manned and the crews were taking bets on which mount would make the 'kill'. The range dropped, but the relay was in a dense cluster of debris and the weapons officer could not get a clear line of sight to it.

"Range is twenty-eight thousand klicks, sir. It should just be another minute or..."

"Sir!" interrupted the sensor tech. "I'm picking up energy readings, bearing three-one-two, by oh-four nine! Looks like a fusion plant in start-up mode!"

"Well, well!" said Zaccaria with a grin. "We might get more than one kill today! Full sensor sweep! Shields up! Weapons, stand by!"

"Aye, aye, sir!"

"Got 'em, sir! Range twenty-two thousand! A solid fix; matches profile for a *Hero* class cruiser. They're bow-on to us; passing targeting data to weapons!"

"Cold meat," said the first officer with a grin. "No power, no weapons, no shields."

"We've got a good lock on the target, sir," said the weapons officer. "Standing by to fire."

"Very well, open fire."

Mangudai's three forward lasers speared out. The range was point blank and it was hardly possible to miss.

"We hit them, sir!" crowed the weapons officer. "Three solid hits. Reading debris from the target."

"Good, maintain fire." The lasers fired another salvo and scored three more hits.

"More metallic debris," reported the sensor tech. "No air or vapor though. Power readings are getting stronger." Zaccaria frowned. At this range, with no shields, his lasers should be blasting deep into the target. Compartments would be ripped apart and opened to space. There would normally be air and water vapor escaping…

"We're still hitting them, sir!"

"Power reading has spiked, sir! Their reactor is on-line!"

"Hell, we should have gutted them by now! Are you sure of that fix?"

"Yes, sir. The power readings and the radar returns coincide exactly. Sir! The target has split into two readings! Only one has power, range now fifteen thousand!"

"What the hell…?"

LSS Gilgamesh cast off from the huge chunk of nickel-iron she had been shielding herself with and drifted upward on thrusters. It had taken a few days to find a rock that was about the same diameter as the ship and another few days to strap it in place, but the effort had been well worth it. Half the rock had been blown away by the enemy fire, but *Gilgamesh* was untouched. Her four forward photon cannons locked onto the mercenary ship and fired. The range was very short now and they blew through the enemy shields with ease and savaged the forward part of the lightly armored destroyer. One of its lasers was destroyed along with two dozen men and women who were exposed to vacuum without their vac suits.

Mangudai fired back in desperation—at the right target this time—but *Gilgamesh's* own shields were coming up and they blunted the fire sufficiently that it only gouged the ship's heavy frontal armor. *Gilgamesh* fired again, destroying another laser and most of the forward shield emitters. Captain Zaccaria finally realized he could not win this unequal duel and his ship veered away in hopes of escape. But it was far too late.

Gilgamesh leapt after him in pursuit and her two plasma torpedoes slammed into *Mangudai* amidships. Hull plates were blown apart, bulkheads shredded and the ship's fusion plant went down. The destroyer tumbled away without power; half her crew dead.

"Well done, people!" exclaimed Captain Jaq Ellsworth. "Helm, lay in an intercept course on that frigate. All ahead full. Commander Bradley, forward weapons on the frigate, everything else on that destroyer as we pass."

"Aye, aye, ma'am!"

Gilgamesh lunged forward, toward another victim, but as she passed, her broadside weapons broke *Mangudai* in two.

"Sir! *Huskarl* reports they are under attack!" Every eye on *Vindicator's* bridge darted to the tactical display. Charles Florkowski had been halfway out the hatch when the exclamation stopped him in his tracks. He spun around. Norman Wolfe was studying the display for an instant and then exploded.

"Where is *Mangudai*? They were supposed to be supporting *Huskarl*! If Zaccaria has gone swaning off somewhere, I'll have his head!"

"Uh, *Huskarl* is reporting that *Mangudai* has been destroyed, sir," said the com officer nervously. "The League cruiser ambushed them."

"Damnation! It's Ellsworth's head I'm going to have! And all the rest of her, too! Put all ships on full alert!"

"Aye aye, sir."

"*Huskarl* reports heavy damage, sir. They request immediate assistance."

Florkowski looked at the tactical display and it was instantly evident that *Huskarl* was not going to get that assistance—not before it was far too late to do any good. *Gilgamesh* was only a hundred thousand kilometers astern and overtaking her fast, in spite of the frigate's higher acceleration. How had those idiots allowed themselves to be taken by surprise like that? Even as he watched, *Huskarl's* icon flared brightly and then faded.

"They got her, sir. No energy readings and a lot of debris."

"That moron, Ramsey," snarled Wolfe. "No loss there. Communications! Order all ships to initiate pursuit. Captain Allen, prepare to take us out of orbit."

"Aye, aye, sir."

"Commodore, may I make a suggestion?" asked Florkowski. Wolfe swiveled his chair to face him.

"Why of course, Commander. Do you have some insight as to your former captain's intentions?" His voice was verging on the edge of sarcasm, but Florkowski ignored it.

"*Gilgamesh* still has three decoys left. I strongly suggest that you don't let her out of your sight."

Wolfe frowned and thought for a moment. "Yes. Yes, you are correct. Communications, order *Chu-Ko-Nu* and *Hardacre* to take positions above and below the planet's poles. At least a half-million klicks out. Make sure they have full sensor coverage and provide continuous updates on the enemy's position. Good thinking, Commander, we aren't going to let them break contact again." Florkowski nodded to himself. With those two ships, a corvette and a frigate, in those positions, they would be able to keep *Gilgamesh* in sight continuously. Ellsworth would have no hope of going back into hiding. On the other hand, that was two more ships effectively out of the fight. Ellsworth had already destroyed one in the first action. Now two more. With these two on sensor station, that only left seven to track her down. This could well become a very interesting fight, indeed.

"The drive is on line, sir," reported Captain Allen. "We can move whenever you are ready."

"Very good. Come to course one-four-two, by minus oh-two-seven. Ahead full."

"Aye, aye, sir."

Vindicator accelerated away from Tractenberg IIIc in search of prey.

"They are all on the move, ma'am," said Brevet Lieutenant (j.g.) Snowden from his sensor station. "The battleship is breaking orbit, too."

"Good. Lieutenant Terletsky, broadcast the execution signal," said Jaq Ellsworth.

"Yes, ma'am. Broadcasting now."

"And good luck to all of them," whispered Ellsworth.

"Stu! Stewart!" hissed Blaire Sujumi. "The signal! I'm picking up the signal!" Stewart Paalova sidled over to Blaire and looked at the tiny receiver. That was it all right. The signal that the mercenary ship was no longer sitting overhead, watching. Stewart took a deep breath and then made the pre-arranged hand signals to his scouts. Power cells were clicked into place and weapons activated. He sincerely hoped no one would suddenly get trigger happy.

He also hoped they had spotted all the Skrak sentries. For the last three hours his scouts had been slowly worming their way forward, through the thick scrub, into their attack positions. There appeared to be only four sentries on the ridge that overlooked the entrance to the Skraks' caverns. There would be more in the hills above the cave, of course, but he wasn't concerned about them just yet.

He gave the next set of signals and his people went into action. Near each of the Skrak sentry positions one of the scouts abandoned their careful secrecy and blundered through the brush noisily. As each Skrak sentry craned its head to see what was making the noise, another scout with a stunner picked them off. Then, his people were dashing forward. The quick strokes of a quartet of knives ensured that none of those Skraks would ever regain consciousness. Then a rapid, but careful scramble and the forty young humans were on the crest peering down at their target.

The sun was just rising over the mountain and the last shadows in the valley were being swept away. Blaire tugged on Stewart's arm and pointed. Perfect. A party of Skraks was heading toward the cave entrance, about four hundred meters away, after a night of hunting. A dozen of them, weighted down with their kills. Good. Just enough casualties to get them really angry...

"Blaire, are sure you know what you are supposed to do?"

"Sure. Fire for a while and when the Skraks start coming out, run like hell. You sure about your end of it?"

"Yes, I'm sure."

"Well, good luck. You're going to need it a lot more than the rest of us."

"Thanks. Okay, let's do it." He got to his feet, all thoughts of secrecy gone. "Scouts forward!" he shouted at the top of his lungs.

His young scouts rose up and poured over the crest. The Skrak hunting party froze momentarily and then dashed for the cave entrance, still carrying their burdens. The scouts stopped and shot them down. A storm of gauss rifle and laser fire ripped them apart before they got fifty meters. The scouts gave a cheer. There was movement on the slopes above the entrance and more fire was directed there. After a moment, the team with the Marines' rocket launcher was ready and they fired. A red streak leaped to the mouth of the cave and exploded. It was just a fragmentation round. They wanted to get the Skraks' attention, not seal them in the cave.

After that, there were no more targets for a while and the scouts whooped and hollered insults at the Skraks. A few minutes passed and then dimly seen shapes started boiling out of unseen holes on the slopes of the mountain. The scouts took a few shots at them, but there were no good targets. As expected, the Skraks were moving toward the flanks. They were not going to be so obliging as to charge straight into an arranged kill zone.

Blaire Sujumi glanced around. Stewart had already disappeared and it was time for the rest of them to go. To stay longer would risk being pinned in a fight and they couldn't afford that. He gave the signal and the scouts turned and vanished over the ridge in a moment. Blaire lingered for half a second and saw that a new wave of shapes was pouring from the cave mouth. He smiled as he broke into an easy run. He had less than an hour to cover eight kilometers. Piece of cake.

"It's time, sir."

Lieutenant Doug Rawlins, saw that Corporal Sabatini was correct: it was time. He got up and crept to the door of the storage compartment. Two men from the city crouched there with their precious plasma rifles. Beyond them was the main corridor that led to the south entrance of the base. In that corridor was a security droid. Rawlins and his men had followed their guides through a baffling maze of service corridors to reach this point. The inside of the south door, the door he had originally come here to excavate, was only a hundred meters down the corridor to his left. Unfortunately, the droid was only fifty meters to his right. The instant he stepped out the door, he would be gunned down. Rawlins stopped next to a third man who had a tiny spy-scope stuck through a crack in the door.

"What's the situation?" he asked.

"Hasn't budged. Still facing this way."

"Where's your other team?"

"Two compartments down. He's going to hit it from behind and when it turns our fellows will take it out."

"You hope."

"Yeah."

"When is he going to…?" Rawlins question was cut off by a muffled explosion.

"Now! Get ready! It's turning… Go!"

The door was pulled open and the two riflemen leaned out and fired. Doug got the momentary sight of the droid and then a dazzling flash and a loud explosion.

"We got it!" said one of the riflemen.

"Wait! It's still moving! Hit it again!"

Two more shots and another explosion. "Okay, that did it! Get moving, Lieutenant!"

"Come on, Corporal!" shouted Rawlins and he sprinted out into the corridor. He cast one glance back over his shoulder and saw the droid lying on its side and pouring smoke. Then he concentrated on covering the hundred meters to the door. His eyes scanned the wall, looking for a certain access panel. Where was it? He reached the door and stopped, panting. Where the hell was... There! He darted over to a panel set in the wall. There was a recessed handle which he grabbed and pulled.

It didn't open.

"Shit! It's stuck! Give me a pry bar! Come on! Come on!" The bloody droids would be here any second; they had no time to waste. The bar was produced and he rammed it into the joint and heaved with all his strength. The door popped open easily and he almost fell on his ass.

He tossed down the pry bar and looked into the compartment. Yes, it was just like the other door he had practiced on. With sure fingers he flipped open circuit boxes and clipped on cables there, there and...there. Okay...

"They're coming!" A cry from down the corridor. He forced himself not to look.

"Give me the power cell," he said to the Corporal. The heavy, type ten cell was put in his hands and he set it inside the compartment. Just one more connection. He saw a flash in the corner of his eye and the sound of an explosion rumbled down the corridor and past him. It didn't seem *that* close...

He took the power cable from the cell and slid it into the auxiliary port. Several lights came on in the control boxes. He hit one and a red light turned to green.

"Sir! Look out!" shouted Corporal Sabatini. But before he could look out, the Corporal had pushed him into the tiny compartment. There was another flash and Rawlins just had time to see Sabatini sliced in two by a plasma bolt. The flash left him dazzled and the thunderclap made his ears ring.

Here already? Oh, shit! Oh, shit!

The door swung out in the direction of the droids. They had not seen him yet. He reached out and pulled the door shut. The only light in his tiny coffin was from a few glowing buttons. He twisted around, being careful not to knock loose any of the wires he had just clipped in place, and looked for one particular button. There it was. He said a silent prayer and pushed it.

For a moment nothing happened and Rawlins' heart stopped beating. Then there was a loud screech of rusted metal and then a low rumble. It sounded like distant thunder...

...or like a very large door sliding open.

"Okay, Commander, it's all connected. All we have to do is fire this sucker up and you can start cutting."

"Damn well about time," said Commander Carol Nista, testily. Two weeks. Two bloody weeks on this bloody planet. All to open one stinking, bloody door. The metal the door was made of was one of the toughest alloys she had ever seen. Some League specialty, no doubt. Their regular drills and cutting torches would hardly touch it.

So they had decided to resort to more drastic measures.

The point-defense laser, which seemed rather dainty when mounted on a ship, now looked very menacing and businesslike sitting in its cradle, fifty meters from the door. In standard pulse mode she expected that it would blast a hole through the door in just a few minutes. It would take longer to make an opening someone could actually get through, of course, but she fully expected to be inside the base before the end of the day.

About bloody time.

She had been happy enough to get off the ship. Happy enough to get away from Wolfe's temper tantrums and posturings. She shook her head. She had been with Wolfe for fifteen years, ever since that abortive coup he had led back on Damerrung; ever since the League Navy had forced all the conspirators to flee. She had admired him back then. He had seemed like a great man to her. And those early years as raiders and mercenaries had been incredibly exciting. Watching Wolfe beard the Leaguies again and again had been heaven. But in the last few years he had changed. He was still experimenting with those damn drugs they had smuggled into Karatan and she could see the effects. And these latest schemes of his were going to take them all to perdition. First the 'fleet' and now this idea of his for empire. Crazy, just crazy. She had been glad to get off the ship for a while. But two weeks of riding herd on bored ground troopers and reluctant workers was quite enough for Carol Nista. Time to get this thing done with. *Unless there are more doors inside that need to be opened...*

Now *that* was an ugly thought. Oh well, there was no telling what they would find. It better be something good.

"Well, let's find out," she said aloud. She turned and headed for the generator. Time to get that cranked up and then they could...

A loud noise behind her made her spin about. For a horrible instant she thought maybe some more rocks were coming down from above or where they had piled them on either side and they would have to dig again. But no, no rocks were moving. What was causing that...?

The door was opening.

She stared incredulously as the huge metal door parted in the middle and the two halves began sliding open. All this work to get ready to cut and now it was opening on its own! Had they just forgotten to try "Open Sesame" or something? Nista was furious.

The mercenaries around her, however, were simply amazed, curious, or delighted. Several dozen of them began moving toward the door. Nista's anger vanished in an instant. This wasn't right.

"Hey! Stay where you are! Get back from there!" she shouted. A few people obeyed, but others continued to close in. But only for another moment.

"There's something here!" shouted one man. He unslung his weapon.

"What the hell is that?" said another.

"Look out! It's coming on!"

One man raised a laser carbine and before Carol Nista could stop him, he fired a shot into the dimly lit opening.

Apparently that was the wrong thing to do because a moment later the world exploded around her.

"Is it still there?" asked Greg Sadgipour.

"Yes, sir, it's still there," said Sergeant John McGill.

"Shit!"

"Gregory, I do wish you'd watch your language," said Chtak'Chr. "It has deteriorated alarmingly in the last few weeks."

"All right, we go to Plan B," said Greg, ignoring his former teacher. "Did any other droids go past the one that's out there?"

"Yes, sir, three, maybe four. It's hard to see from here."

"Good, maybe that's all of them. Get ready to move." Greg looked over his shoulder. All his Marines were in the compartment with him, along with a dozen volunteers from the city. They were in a storage compartment across the corridor from the one where he and Chtak had made their earlier, near-disastrous, attempt to deactivate the sentry droid. This compartment had the advantage of still possessing an intact door. Beyond the last volunteer in the room was another door. Greg knew that nearly three hundred of the city people filled the narrow corridors behind him, all of them eager to get their hands on the contents of the base armory.

But to get to that armory they had to get past that droid. He had hoped that once Doug Rawlins had gotten the south door open, all the droids might be drawn off. That hadn't happened. According to reports he had received Doug had gotten the door open, although Doug himself, was apparently missing, but this one droid had refused to budge. Greg had gotten word that the two surviving plasma riflemen from Doug's team were on their way to join him, but it would be a while before they could get here and he didn't have the time to wait—and two riflemen against one droid was not good odds in any case.

"Okay, signal Decoy One to go ahead," he said to one of the city squad leaders. The woman nodded and whispered into her communicator. A few seconds passed and then there was a faint noise from the corridor.

"Got him. Hit it dead center, sir. It's on the move," said McGill, peering through his spy-eye. "Hold your breath, everyone."

Greg and everyone else in the compartment froze. A volunteer had just shot a laser at the droid from a room further down the corridor. The laser wasn't powerful enough to hurt the droid, but it had done its job and gotten its attention. Hopefully, the droid would go down the corridor to investigate. Hopefully, the fellow who had fired the laser was getting the hell out of there. Most hopefully of all, the droid wouldn't decide to investigate this compartment on its way by or it would be a slaughter. Greg stood motionless and listened. All he could hear was his own heart pounding. An endless time seemed to go by.

"All right, it's gone past," whispered McGill. "It's almost to the other compartment. I hope Decoy Two is on time."

He was. As soon as the droid paused, another volunteer, another hundred meters down the corridor, fired a shot at the droid. Almost instantly, there was a loud 'bang'.

"Hell, the thing's at full combat mode," hissed McGill. "Took a shot back at Decoy Two almost instantly. Sure hope that bugger got under cover. Okay, it's moving again."

"Away from us?" asked Greg.

"Yeah, still heading down the corridor. It's past the next set of blast doors now. Decoy Three's turn."

This was the critical moment. Would it go far enough down the corridor so they could carry out their plan? There was another distant bang.

"Shot three fired," said McGill. "Those boys have got some guts. Yes! It's moving further, sir. Stand by on that door!"

"Right!" Greg signaled to the woman with the communicator and she nodded.

"It's about forty meters beyond the door... fifty... sixty... it's slowing... nearly stopped. Better do it, sir."

"Now!" said Greg. The woman repeated it into her com.

"Is it closing?" asked Greg anxiously to McGill.

"No... Yes! The doors are closing. Oops! Ol' Tin Head doesn't like it! He's heading back fast. Gonna be close!" There was a distant clang.

"Doors are closed!" shouted McGill. There was a restrained cheer in the compartment. McGill twisted his spy-eye around. "Nothing at all at the intersection now, sir."

"Okay, let's go!" McGill threw open the door and stepped out into the corridor. Greg was right behind. A hundred meters to his right a new set of blast doors had closed, trapping the security droid on the other side. A slightly greater distance to his left was the intersection. He trotted in that direction. McGill and another Marine were a dozen meters ahead of him, weapons at the ready. Greg paused briefly at the three lumps in the floor. The shattered, desiccated bodies were still there, but to his disappointment the plasma rifles he had been told they were carrying were not. Three more plasma rifles would have been extremely welcome at this point.

McGill and Private Friswell had reached the intersection and paused. They looked carefully either way and then McGill waved them on. Greg looked right and left himself when he got there, but there was nothing to see but the corridor defining the outer ring of the base curving away in either direction. As he stood there he heard a distant rumble to the left. Supposedly there was a hell of a fight going on by the south gate.

"Come on, Greg, we must hurry," said Chtak from beside him.

Greg nodded. "Yeah, we've still got a long way to go and there's no telling what's waiting for us."

* * *

"I think we've reached that first uncertainty nexus, ma'am," said Commander Karl Bradley.

"Nonsense, Commander," said Jaq Ellsworth, "We've got them right where they want us."

Bradley smiled a lop-sided smile. "Yes, ma'am."

Jaq returned the smile and hoped she was hiding just how nervous she really felt. Because the Commander was right: they had reached a critical decision-making point in the battle.

The first hour had gone as well as she could have hoped for. They had destroyed a frigate and a destroyer with no damage at all to themselves. Then they had led the other mercenaries on a merry chase around the gas giant, its rings and its moons. They had traded some long-range fire with the enemy on two occasions, but with no real effect on either side.

Now, however, the enemy had gotten their act together and were coming at them in a three-way pincer. *Gilgamesh* was headed back toward the gas giant and was about fifty thousand kilometers above the planet's rings. Coming around the giant planet from one direction was Norman Wolfe and his battleship; from around the other were the cruiser and a destroyer. And hot on their tail were three more destroyers and a frigate.

If she turned right or left, she would end up in a close range fight with a superior force. She couldn't afford that right now. It was still too early. The people down on that moon needed more time. A lot more time. She could bend her course around and head straight 'up' but that was no good either. All three groups would just follow her and it would turn into a stern chase. She couldn't outrun all of them and sooner or later they would overtake and overwhelm her.

So, I can't go right, I can't go left, I can't go forward, I can't turn back and I can't go up. Only one thing left!

"Commander van Rossum, are your toys still ready to go?" she asked.

"Yes, ma'am, they are just where we expected them to be and they are primed and ready."

"And you are sure they will do the job?"

"Forty megatons apiece, they *should* do it. But I will remind you again, ma'am, that this was *not* my idea."

"Noted, Commander. All right, let's find out if *my* idea was a good one. Helm, come to course oh-one-nine, by minus oh-eight-five."

"Aye, aye, ma'am," said Ensign Bartlett. Then he froze. "Uh, ma'am, did you really mean that?"

"Yes, Ensign, I did. Take us down—straight down."

"Well, Commander, it appears that Captain Ellsworth isn't quite as clever as you had thought, eh?" said Commodore Wolfe. "She's walked right into this trap and she is not going to get out of it again."

"So it would seem, sir," replied Charles Florkowski. As usual, Wolfe's tone irritated him, but he could not deny the truth of his words. Ellsworth's initial maneuvers had been masterful. She had deftly ambushed the two smaller ships and destroyed them. Then for the next hour she had skillfully avoided being engaged by a more powerful enemy. But now she had slipped up. There was no way for her to avoid the forces that were closing on her. *Gilgamesh* would fight valiantly, he was sure of that, but in the end she would take crippling damage and that would be it. Still, he had no doubt that *Old Gilgie* would give as good as she got. *Wolfe might not be so cheerful when he gets this butcher's bill.*

"We're nearly in effective range, sir," said the weapons officer.

"Good. Get ready to..."

"Sir! The target is changing course," said the sensor officer. "They... they... Sir, they're heading directly for the rings!"

"What?"

Every eye turned to the display. Florkowski stared along with the rest. It was true, *Gilgamesh* was bending her vector around and was now rushing on a collision course with the gas giant's rings.

"Heavens," said Wolfe, "we seem to have driven the poor woman to suicide. Pity. I truly wanted to meet her face to face."

Florkowski shook his head. He could not believe it. Ellsworth was a real bitch, but she never seemed like one to give up this easily. And to kill her whole crew at the same time! But trying to fly right through the rings at her current velocity truly would be suicide. Even with full shields the collisions she would suffer would pulverize *Gilgamesh*. There was just no way...

The icon representing *Gilgamesh* got closer and closer to the rings. Florkowski was tensing himself, almost like he expected to hear the crash from this distance. Then, without warning, a bright light appeared on the display, directly in *Gilgamesh's* path.

"Sir, I'm reading a large, correction, two large thermonuclear explosions. Inside the rings, sir," said the startled sensor officer.

"I'll be damned," hissed Florkowski. As he continued to stare, *Gilgamesh's* icon merged with the light and then a moment later emerged from the other side. She had passed completely through the rings and was apparently unscathed.

And all of Wolfe's ships were now on the wrong side.

"They blew a hole in the rings," said Captain Allen in astonishment.

"How?" demanded Wolfe. "They didn't launch anything! How could they have had two nukes there?"

"They must have planted them there earlier, sir."

"They planted them earlier and they were right where they needed them now? How could they have known that in advance?" Wolfe was turning a remarkable shade of red.

"They must have planned it..." Allen trailed off as the full meaning of his words sank in.

"They planned it? They planned for all of us and their own ship and those nukes to be right there at this moment? Bullshit!"

No one dared contradict Wolfe, but the implications could not be ignored: Ellsworth was still in control of this battle. Wolfe began snapping out orders to send his ships careening off in pursuit of *Gilgamesh*, but it would be nearly an hour before they could hope to engage her again—assuming Ellsworth did not have something else up her sleeve.

Concentrate you idiot, don't disperse again! thought Florkowski to himself as he studied Wolfe's new orders. Wolfe's handling of this situation had been flawed right from the start. He had two incompatible objectives: capture the base and destroy Ellsworth. He had tried to do both and that had led to the dispersed deployment that had allowed Ellsworth to do what she had done so far. He should have just concentrated his forces around the moon with the base and waited for Ellsworth to come to him. But he was too eager for anything so passive. So he had gone haring off after *Gilgamesh* and his ships were running in circles.

And apparently things were not going too well down on that moon, either. Only a few minutes ago they had gotten a message from Commander Nista that the ground party was under attack by some sort of automated security system from that base. Wolfe had told them to deal with it on their own. Florkowski wondered if they could.

* * *

Blaire Sujumi paused for a moment to catch his breath. The rest of the scouts caught up with him and stopped as well. The sounds of firing were very near now. Just ahead, beyond the series of small ridges that radiated outward from the gate. And there was a hell of a lot of shooting going on. Loud explosions punctuated the lighter rattle of small arms and a half-dozen columns of black smoke rose in the distance, smudging the clear sky.

A young woman trotted up and stopped next to him. "The Skraks are about three-quarters of a klick back, Blaire," she said between gasps. "Still coming on fast. A hell of a lot of them. We better keep moving."

"Right. Okay, take it easy up to the next crest. The mercs might be on the other side." He waved his people forward and they went up the slope, crouching low. As he neared the top, he slowed and looked around. Yes, the mercs had been here. There were empty ration containers and other junk scattered all over the place, but they weren't here now. Another loud explosion gave a good clue as to where they were. He cautiously edged forward a little more until he could see over the crest. Nothing. He knew that beyond the next crest was where the mercs had landed their small craft and beyond the crest after that, was where the gate—and presumably the battle—was. But there was nothing here now. The mercs had all pulled back to deal with the droids, just like Stewart and Gregory had planned. Now if he could just make sure that one more group of guests could be added to this party…

"It looks clear," he said to his people. "Come on."

He led them over the crest and down into the gully beyond, moving fast and staying low. When he reached the bottom he turned sharply to the east to parallel the ridge. There was no way he wanted to go over that next one! They covered three or four hundred meters and came to a patch of thicker brush.

"All right, everyone keep going. Circle around until you hit the old road. Stay away from that fight until you get new orders! I'm going to stay here to make sure the Skraks go the right way. I'll catch up when I can."

There were a few frowns from the scouts, but they did what he asked. In only a few seconds they had disappeared. Then he found a good spot to hide. Some bushes concealed him, but he made sure he had a quick route of retreat. He also had a clear route to make a dash up the next slope. He had to make sure the Skraks went over that ridge and if he had to use himself as bait, he would.

Several long minutes went by and then he saw the first Skrak slide over the hill. Then another. A half-dozen more. They followed his trail down to the bottom of the slope and then stopped. He held his breath as one Skrak pointed in his direction. But then there was another loud burst of firing off to the north and all the Skraks' heads turned in that direction. Some sort of discussion was going on with lots and lots of arms gesticulating wildly. His eyes darted to the left as more Skraks appeared on the far ridge. The first group made a last few gestures and then moved off—north.

Blaire breathed a silent sigh of relief. They were going the way they wanted them to. His breathing slowed again as a seemingly endless column of Skraks rolled down the hill and up the other ridge. Stewart had told him about the huge number he had seen, but it was still hard to believe. *My God, there's a lot of them!*

This was going to be very interesting…

Commander Carol Nista flinched as another explosion showered her with dirt. That was too close. Another one that was too close. There had been far too many already. She scrunched down in the small hollow a little more. She was a ship officer dammit! She had no business in a ground action!

She jumped as a squad of troopers scrambled into her hidey hole. They looked far more confident than she felt. The initial attack had come as such a complete surprise. One laser shot into the tunnel had been answered by a storm of plasma bolts coming back out. Most of the people standing close to the door had been cut down in an instant. And then those droids had come boiling out of the gate, shooting at everything. She wasn't quite sure how she had made it over the ridge to this dead ground, but she had. From then on it had been a matter of trying to stay out of the way.

She had to admit that the ground troopers had responded quickly to the sudden crisis. They were well trained and experienced in spite of their easy going discipline. They had fallen back to the ridge to meet with their reinforcements and engaged the droids with everything they could bring to bear. But the damn things were tough. Slug throwers and gauss weapons didn't seem to do much to them. It took a missile or a plasma bolt to do them any serious harm. And they were fast. A man with a missile launcher or a plasma gun didn't last long once he'd fired. The mercenaries had taken a lot of casualties.

But they were killing droids, too. From what she had heard on the tactical net there had been only about two-dozen of them to begin with and maybe half of those had been destroyed now. The remainder had fallen back to near the gate and were using the piles of boulders for cover. Still, finishing them off wasn't going to be easy. She looked to the pillars of smoke rising skyward. One of them was her damn cutting laser. All that work wasted! The others were the three assault shuttles that had tried to make strafing runs on the droids. The wreckage piled against the mountainside showed how well that had worked.

"How's it going?" she asked the squad leader.

"All right, I guess. Damn, those bastards are tough! But we've got the upper hand. We're getting the rest of our heavy weapons in position and in a few minutes we're going to start picking off those things one by one. Don't worry, commander, we know what to do." He rousted his squad out of the hole and trotted off with them.

Well, that sounded hopeful. She took off her hat and wiped the sweat out of her eyes. She was getting a lot more than she had bargained for on this trip! And that bastard Wolfe! When she had called up for fire support he had told her to 'deal with it'. Ha! She'd like to see him deal with it!

The firing died down a little and she got up. Maybe she could risk heading back to where the shuttles were landed. It would be a lot more comfortable—not to mention safer—back there. She headed down the slope.

She had not gone fifty meters when a half-dozen troopers came running over the hill in front of her at full tilt. The last one suddenly stumbled and fell. The others were shouting at the top of their lungs. What the hell was going on now?

An instant later she got her answer. A wave of gray-green shapes came rolling over the hilltop and down in her direction. She just stood and gawked for several long, fatal seconds. They looked like those weird creatures they had found in the rockslide!

She was clawing to get her laser pistol out of its holster when a dozen crossbow bolts riddled her.

CHAPTER TWENTY

Rhada McClerndon lay in a deep sleep and dreamed of Greg Sadgipour. He was there with her. Holding her, comforting her. He was making love to her and it was very, very nice. She lay on her back with her eyes closed and ran her hands up and down his spine. His skin was so smooth and his muscles so powerful. She felt warm and safe.

But then his motions became more urgent. Rougher. Harder. He was hurting her. She still had her hands on his back but it wasn't smooth anymore. There were strange bumps and rough spots. She slid her hands up to his neck and there was something tied around it…

In her dream her eyes snapped open.

There was a leash around his neck. There was one around hers, too.

Sspau and Sspara were standing on either side of them, their mouths partly opened with toothy grins. Each one was holding the end of a leash in one pair of hands and a switch in the others. They were lashing Greg unmercifully—urging him to greater efforts. His back was covered with welts and bruises.

She opened her mouth to scream but Greg was suddenly gone. Vanished. She lay there, propped up on her elbows, staring at Sspau and Sspara in confusion.

They were still smiling at her even though Skraks did not smile.

"Now you will serve the Great Masters, slave," said Sspau with perfect diction.

She shook her head. She didn't understand. Then Sspara pointed to her with her switch. Pointed to her belly. Rhada looked where she was pointing.

Her belly. It was growing.

As Rhada looked on in horror, her belly swelled up. It grew and grew. It was enormous, swollen to colossal size. And there was something moving inside it…

Sspau and Sspara scuttled down to stand between her outflung legs. Their smiles grew larger.

Then the pain came. Terrible stabbing pains in her abdomen. She writhed and moaned and wept. It hurt worse than anything she had ever experienced.

She screamed as the first baby popped from her loins. It was bloody and squalling. And then another baby and another. One after the other they squirted out of her.

Sspau caught each one. She handed them to Sspara who fastened tiny leashes around their necks...

No!

Rhada sat up with a shriek and clutched at her stomach. She looked around wildly and gasped for breath. It had been a dream, only a dream... But the pain and the horror had been so real; she clutched herself and rocked back and forth and wept.

"No, no, no..."

"What wrong? You ill?"

Rhada looked up and saw Sspara watching her from beside the fire. She was putting a few more sticks into it and had paused at Rhada's sudden movement. Rhada didn't answer and the Skrak went back to tending her fire.

Rhada was still breathing heavily and rubbing her stomach when the floor quivered ever so slightly and she heard a muffled 'boom' echoing through the cave. What was that? Sspara stiffened and looked around quickly. For a minute or two there was nothing, but then a growing clamor of Skrak voices could be heard out in the main passage. Then the clanging of weapons and the click of many clawed feet on stone. Sspara scuttled out of the chamber. Rhada just sat there, her mind a blank. Shortly, Sspara returned and seemed rather agitated.

"Humans attack cave," she said and Rhada's head jerked up. "No hope for you, slave. They flee already. Warriors make ready to chase. Maybe catch. Take many weapons. Maybe catch more slaves." She paused and seemed to be thinking. "Maybe catch mate for you. I must go tell Sslaskatar to try and catch male to mate with you!" Sspara dashed off and Rhada was alone.

The noises out in the corridor faded and there was nothing to hear except the occasional drip of water. What was going on? Humans attacking the cave? Maybe it was Greg at last! But they were fleeing already? What did that mean? She sat in the near-darkness and shivered. What would happen? Would there be a roar of gunfire and then would Greg rush in to save her? Or would she wait for hours and then see some naked stranger driven into the cave and forced to have sex with her while Sspau and Sspara watched?

The dream was still haunting her. And her earlier image of a whole race of human slaves returned. This time all the harnessed, groaning slaves had light brown skin and jet black hair, just like her. Each and every one was her descendant.

No. No, she couldn't let that happen. Her hand curled into a fist. The Skraks had whipped her. They had terrorized and degraded her. They had made her a slave.

But they hadn't defeated her. Not entirely. Not yet. There was still a part of her they had not conquered. A part that could remember being free. A part that still wanted to be free. And there was still courage inside her. They had not whipped that all out of her. There was a part that still dared to think of escape.

She looked around. She was alone in the chamber. Almost all the Skraks were gone, out chasing the humans. Sspara was gone, too—chasing Sslaskatar apparently. She might never have a better chance.

She took hold of her leash. It was too strong to break, but would it cut? She had thought about that often. She bent over and felt under the grass of her nest. A few days earlier she had found a hard, smooth stone. She had hit it with another stone. Again and again until she had gotten a shard with a sharp edge. She had hidden it under the grass. Now she found it. It was sharp, no doubt about that: she cut her finger on it as she grasped it.

She held up the stone. Did she dare to try? If she cut the leash and was then caught again, she would never be given another chance. They would beat her and tie her and watch her. And Sstrac was already experimenting with making chains. If they caught her, he would forge a steel collar and chain for her and she would never, ever get away again.

But they might do that anyway. This was the best chance she would ever get. She mustered her courage and pressed the stone against the leash and sawed at it. Back and forth, back and forth. She stretched the leash taut and sawed at it.

Nothing.

After a few minutes of intense effort there was nothing to show for it. Maybe a tiny rough spot where she had been working. It had to cut! She went at it again with frantic energy. She cast anxious glances to watch for Sspara's return. She sawed until her finger were cramping.

Nothing.

Tears of bitter frustration ran down her face. It wouldn't cut! All that hope, all that effort, wasted! She bowed her head and wept. It wasn't fair! She couldn't escape. She would be a slave forever and so would her children.

No. She stopped her tears and took a deep breath. She would not be the mother to a race of slaves. She looked at the cutting stone in her hand. There was another way to escape. And the Skraks had taught her that there were worse things than dying.

She was shaking as she brought the edge of the stone to her wrist. She bit hard on her tongue and drew the edge across her flesh. She could feel it cutting her. She held her wrist up to the light. There was a small cut and a little blood, but it was not gushing out by any means. She'd have to press harder and do it again.

She was shaking almost uncontrollably now. She squeezed the stone tightly and brought it to her wrist again...

...and gasped when it squirted out of her hand and fell in the grass of her nest.

Shit!

Where had it gone? How long until Sspara returned? She carefully felt around in the grass for the stone. She couldn't find it. She bit back her panic and kept looking. The fire blazed up and she had a little more light to see by. There! She could see the firelight reflecting off the smooth stone. She reached for it... and froze. Her gaze drifted up to the fire.

It won't cut. Will it burn?

She stretched and tried to reach the fire. She had been forbidden to have anything to do with the fire. But there was a log there. It was as thick as her wrist and a half-meter long. One end was in the fire, burning, and the other end was pointing towards her, propped up on one of the rocks. Her hand flailed far short of it. She turned around and stretched out her leg. Still short. She pulled on her leash and stretched as far as she could. Her toes waved mere centimeters away from the log. She pulled and pulled until she was choking herself with the leash, but she still couldn't reach.

She gave up and pulled back, gasping for breath. Maybe she should just try to strangle herself with the leash...

No, dammit! She knelt there, thinking frantically. The end of the log was up in the air. What if she tossed a stone…? She felt around and found a good stone. She weighed it in her hand and then lobbed it in the air. It missed. About five centimeters to the right. She winced at the noise it made when it hit the floor. She found another stone and tried again. Another miss. To the left this time. Again. This time she hit the log but only grazed it. She cursed as it moved a few centimeters. If it rolled away… One more try…

Come on, girl! You were the best shot in your entire class…

She hit it. The stone came right down on the end of the log and flipped it into the air with a shower of sparks. It turned end over end three times and clattered to the floor of the cave. It was much closer. She lunged out to grab it, but the leash pulled her up short. She twisted around and tried with her foot. She had it! Her toes reached it with centimeters to spare. She dragged it toward her until she could reach it with her hand. She had it!

The fire had gone out but the end of the log glowed with hot coals. She quickly brushed away the grass to make a clear spot and then piled up a small clump and put the end of the log in it. She bent over and blew on the coals. It only took a moment for the dry grass to flare up. Now, how to get the fire to the leash? She didn't have enough slack to get the leash down into the fire—not without burning her face off. And the grass was too short and fast-burning for a proper torch. She would have to get the log burning again. She fed in more grass and soon the end of the log was aflame.

She twisted around and put the flame up to her leash. She held the burning end down so that the flames would not run out of fuel and she turned the log to keep it burning. The leash was in the center of the flame. At first nothing seemed to be happening, but slowly the leash started to darken. She pulled on it, but it seemed as strong as ever. Damn! And where was Sspara?

The flame flickered out and she had to rekindle it in the grass. She was running out of time. This was taking far too long. The log was burning again. Back to the leash. She pulled on it and turned the log and gently blew on the coals all at the same time. The glowing flame was right in her face and she could feel the heat. The leash was turning black. She pulled on it as hard as she could. Was anything happening at all? Maybe. Was the leash starting to stretch a little? Yes! It was a tiny bit thinner right where the fire was. She braced her foot against the rock wall and pulled.

It was stretching! She put all her strength into it. Her muscles were knotted with the effort. And then, suddenly, it melted like a bit of taffy and hung limply in two pieces.

She stared at in wonder. She had done it. She had...

"What you do?"

Sspara! Oh no!

"What you do?"

She had her back to the entrance to the chamber. Sspara had come back and she had not heard her! No! Not when she was this close!

"What you do?" demanded Sspara again.

Rhada slowly turned around and draped the loose end of her leash behind her. She didn't flinch when the hot end burned her back. She pressed herself against the stone. Maybe Sspara had not seen. The junior clutchmistress flowed over until she was only two meters away. She gestured with her switch.

"What you do?" She was pointing to the burning log and the smoking grass—not the severed leash.

"I... I was cold," said Rhada.

"Bad! Bad slave!" She moved closer and hit Rhada with the switch. "Bad! Fire forbidden! You know! You disobey! Bad!" She hit her again and again. Rhada warded off the blows with her left arm.

"Up! Get up! Turn round! I punish!" Sspara continued to rain blows on Rhada, but she wanted her to get up and turn around so she could do a proper job of it.

I can't! If I turn around she'll see the broken leash!

"Up! Turn round!"

No! This couldn't be happening! She had been so close and now she would be caught! They would beat her and tie her and chain her and breed her and breed her and breed her! No! No! *No!* A long-smoldering fire inside her seemed to burst into flames.

"Up! Get up!"

Rhada got up.

She grasped the burning log in her right hand and sprang at Sspara with a scream of pure rage. The Skrak was taken completely by surprise and knocked on her back by the larger human. Rhada landed right on top of her. She rained a series of savage blows to the side of Sspara's head with the log, reducing one eye to a ruin.

Sspara squealed and tried to twist away, but Rhada was straddling her. Rhada's feet and knees were pinning both pairs of Spara's legs and she had no leverage at all to move. Rhada continued to beat her with the log, but Sspara was fighting back now. The Skrak's tail lashed at Rhada and the four arms clawed at her, tearing skin and drawing blood. Sspara bared her fangs and struck at Rhada's throat.

Rhada rammed the burning end of the log into Sspara's gaping mouth.

The Skrak made a horrid noise and tried to twist away. Two hands clutched the log but Rhada drove it in with all her strength. The fire sizzled out with a puff of steam. But still Sspara fought back. Her tail continued to pound Rhada and the claws raked her. Rhada shifted her weight slightly and rammed the log in deeper, breaking off Skrak teeth as she did so.

Out of the corner of her eye she saw that Sspara's lower right hand was pulling her knife out of its sheath. Rhada grabbed for it with her left hand and caught Sspara's wrist. But in an eye-blink Sspara's other right hand snatched the knife free and slashed at her. Rhada twisted and felt the blade score along her ribs with a pain like fire. Sspara drew back for another strike and Rhada caught the wrist again and then slid her hand up and closed it around Sspara's, pinning the knife.

Now. She had to finish it now. Rhada reared up and rammed the log home, twisting it savagely. Sspara thrashed madly and then blood was gushing out of her mouth. Rhada pushed again and there was more blood, splashing hot on her hand. A shudder ran through the Skrak's body. The tail stopped hitting her. Sspara's arms fell away limply.

Rhada was shaking and gasping for breath. Her tormentor was lying there, and her hatred for the Skrak was burning as hotly as the pain along her ribs. Sspara's remaining eye stared at her and there was still a flicker of life in it. Rhada bent over until her face was only a few centimeters away.

"I lied," she hissed. "I lied, Sspara. I lied to Sslaskatar. The war is over. All of your Great Masters are dead! *Dead!*"

Sspara's eye widened slightly and for the first and only time Rhada saw fear. The body twitched again and then lay still.

"Dead!" said Rhada loudly. "Dead!"

"Dead!" and her voice was a shriek that rang through the cave.

She pried the knife out of Sspara's hand and plunged it into the Skrak's throat up to the hilt. Again and again. Blood oozed out. "Dead! Dead! Dead!" She stabbed and slashed. She tore Sspara's belly open and blood and gore splashed all over her thighs and ran down her legs. She shrieked and laughed hysterically.

"Bottom rail on top now!"

She laughed and cried until she couldn't anymore. She heaved herself up, off Sspara's body and collapsed in her nest, shaking uncontrollably. She lay there but her befuddled brain told her to get up. Someone would hear, someone would come and catch her. *Get out! Get out!*

She crawled over by the fire and found the water skin and drank. Her cuts and scratches were burning and she splashed some water on them. The slash along her ribs hurt like hell, but did not seem too bad. The blood was clotting already. She pressed some of the grass to it. She ate a strip of meat. It was raw. She got her shakes under control and she stood up. She had to get out. Now.

She slung the water skin over her shoulder and took the knife. Rhada started to walk away but then paused. She stooped and picked up Sspara's switch from where it had fallen. She looked at it and then snapped it in two and tossed it in the fire. Then she headed up the passage to the main corridor. She looked to the left. She was sure that was the way out, even though she had never seen the exit. But there would surely be more Skraks on guard near the entrance. She would never get by them. As she stood there, trying to decide what to do, she became aware of a faint clanging noise. *Sstrac. Working at the forge.* Apparently he had not gone off with the warriors, He was still working to make more weapons.

Weapons.

Rhada turned to the right and moved silently down the passage.

Sstrac worked the bellows and then pulled the blade out of the fire and set it on the anvil. He would be glad when Sspara brought the slave to work again. It was a great help to him. It would be wonderful when they had more slaves to help with the work. He had labored for many years to arm the warriors, but it would be wonderful to have the proper tools and resources to prepare this world for the Great Masters.

As he hammered, he sensed movement behind him. He turned his head slightly, but the glow from the forge had dimmed his night vision and he could see nothing. Then he caught a strong whiff of scent. It was Sspara's odor. He felt a twitch of pleasure. She would not be making a smell like that unless she was interested in mating. It was amazingly strong…

He turned his head a bit more and saw a brief flicker of firelight reflecting off one of his sword blades—an instant before it cut through his neck.

Rhada looked down at the body of Sstrac. She felt none of the hysterical glee that she had felt when she killed Sspara. Sstrac was just an enemy to be killed. Sspara had been...

She turned and went back to the weapons racks. She found a sheath and belt for her sword. The belt was designed for a Skrak body, but by looping part of it over one shoulder she was able to make it work well enough. She found a shield that she could use and then picked up a short spear. It had a long blade that could be used for hacking and a wicked looking point for thrusting. She briefly considered one of the crossbows, but without the time to practice with it, she doubted it would be much use.

So now she was armed. She felt a little more confident, but not much. What now? She could head back up the passage and try to make a break for it. Her chances were terrible and she knew it. Even two or three Skrak warriors would have no trouble killing her. But what other option was there? If she took the passage the other way it would only lead down to the lake or to the...

Rhada twitched as another thought struck her. She would dearly love to get out. She wanted to live very much. But if she couldn't... What then?

She stood there quivering for a long time. Then she turned to the right and went very quietly down the passage. She had only been this way once before and she almost missed the turn. With all the Skraks gone the fires and torches were burning down and it was darker than usual. She went slowly now. She knew that at the very least Sspau would be somewhere up ahead. Hopefully alone.

Rhada reached the entrance to the chamber and halted. She listened, but could hear nothing but her own breathing and pounding heart. She edged around the corner and looked hard. There. She could make out the shape of a Skrak a few meters ahead. She took a step forward and the shape suddenly moved. There was a loud hissing and then Sspau came leaping toward her. Rhada gripped her spear and prepared to fend off an attack, but Sspau dodged to the side and tried to get past her. Rhada realized that the elder clutchmistress was trying to escape, not fight.

She almost did escape. Had she been as young as Sspara, she

would have, but she was old and slow. Sspara had told Rhada several times that Sspau would not live much longer and then Sspara would be in charge of the eggs—and the slaves. When Rhada realized what Sspau intended, she leapt after her and came down right on Sspau's tail. Sspau was stopped short and Rhada thrust her spear into the Skrak's body. Sspau thrashed violently, but another thrust finished her.

Rhada stared at the remains of the other one who had tortured her so and found that she couldn't feel anything at all now. Her mind and her emotions were bouncing around so wildly she didn't know how she felt. She could only feel an ever-heightening tension inside her. She was being wound up tighter and tighter.

She shook herself and walked to the edge of the egg chamber. The thousands of eggs stretched away into the distance and she felt an incredible sense of power flow through her. She was there, all by herself, and she had a sword and a spear.

The Skraks had brought her here to give life to a generation of slaves. Instead, she would bring death to a generation of warriors.

She put down her shield and took the spear in both hands. She stepped forward and drove the point into the first egg. The shell was rubbery and flexible, but once punctured, it split open easily. A clot of ichor spilled out along with a tiny horror that splashed about weakly for a few moments. Rhada did not stop to look, she just thrust her spear into the next egg and the next and the next. When she had murdered all the eggs in one nest she stepped to the next and did the same.

Up, down, up, down, with the spear. Over and over. She started counting to herself. One, two three, four... He arms began to ache and her wounds were burning, but she didn't stop. Thirty-three, thirty-four, thirty-five... She didn't know how much time she would have before she was caught, but she was determined to make the full use of every moment she had. Ninety-seven, ninety-eight, ninety-nine, one hundred, one, two, three...

Some of the eggs didn't puncture on the first try and others popped rather messily, splattering her with gore, but she ignored it, except for when it splashed in her eyes. Then she wiped it off with the back of her hand and went back to work. Sometimes her spear would impale the tiny Skrak and she would have to shake it loose or even push it off with her foot. She tried using the sword, just for a different type of motion to give her muscles a break, but the sword didn't work as well and tended to splash a lot more, so she went back to the spear.

Finally, after counting to one hundred at least ten times, she had to stop and rest for a few moments. As she did so, she heard a faint noise from near the entrance to the chamber and she froze, barely daring to breath. She looked back in that direction and then took a few tentative steps and froze again. She could make out a number of dim shapes. They seemed smaller than the Skraks…

The hatchlings! Oh, God!

The young Skraks who had killed Ritta on their very first day here. Rhada was terrified of them. They seemed to roam around the caves in groups more or less at will. Once, she had awakened to find three of them sniffing at her. She had screamed and screamed until Sspau had come and shooed them away. As long as there was an adult Skrak around to restrain them they were not too terribly aggressive. But there was no adult around now…

She couldn't tell how many there were, but if there were as many as had been when Ritta died, she couldn't possibly fight them all off. She gripped her spear and wished she had her shield, but she had left it near the entrance. The shapes moved down from the entrance passage and disappeared among the egg nests. Rhada looked around frantically and backed away, expecting to be attacked at any moment. Long seconds passed, but there was nothing.

She waited and listened again and she thought she could hear something. Mustering her courage she went forward a dozen meters and stopped again. She could hear a horribly familiar slurping and eating noise. She took another few steps and realized what she was hearing. The hatchlings were eating the ruined eggs! Her stomach heaved in revulsion, but there was no doubt. The small Skraks were gorging themselves.

Rhada was shaking again, but she sighed silently in relief. The horrid little things must know that she was there, but apparently they could not pass up this unexpected feast. Still, there was no point in tempting them any more than necessary. Rhada quickly retreated to the far end of the egg chamber. She would resume her destruction here and work back toward the entrance. She paused. She could faintly hear the hatchlings in the distance, but they did not seem to be coming after her. All right then.

She took her spear and started thrusting it into eggs again. Up, down, up, down, shift the feet and then up, down, again. Egg after egg was destroyed. She resumed her counting. One, two, three, four... On and on for what seemed like hours.

She had counted to a hundred twenty more times (or was it twenty-one?) when she had to stop and rest. Her arms were incredibly sore. Even more than after a day of turning the grindstone or working the bellows. She leaned on her spear and closed her eyes and listened to the silence.

Silence...

She jerked erect and listened. There was no sound beyond the drip of water. No sound from the hatchlings. A chill of fear ran down her back. Where were they? She walked a short distance toward the entrance and listened again. Nothing. There were a few beams of sunlight entering the cavern far above, but not enough to see clearly or very far. The hatchlings could be anywhere. They could be creeping up just a few meters away and she wouldn't see them. The first she would know they were hunting her would be when razor sharp teeth closed around her legs. Then they would pull her down and start tearing her open. Just like Ritta...

A tiny noise made her spin around, spear at the ready. Nothing. She looked one way and then another, the hair on the back of her neck standing up.

There is a limit to everything. Even something as unquantifiable as courage cannot be infinite. Rhada had been burning her courage in prodigious quantities for far too long and now she came to the end of it. She felt her legs shaking and she knew she had to get out. There were still thousands of undamaged eggs around her, but she had to get out of these caverns. She looked up at the sunbeams. She had to see the sky again. Feel the wind and the sun on her face. Right now she would have given her soul for one glimpse of the sky. Even if it was for the last time. Even if she fell at the entrance of the cave hacked and sliced and punctured with Skrak weapons. She had to get out of here or die trying.

She moved to the chamber entrance, scooped up her shield and hurried up the passage as quickly as her quivering legs would carry her. Past the forge, past the tunnel that led to her little nest, past the training area for the warriors, and past Sslaskatar's chamber. She met nothing; heard nothing except her own gasping breath and pounding heart.

Now she was in unknown territory. She was sure this was the way out but she had only ever been here when she was brought in and then she had been blindfolded. The corridor continued to lead up, but there were a lot of other tunnels branching off. She tried to stay on the one that looked the most traveled. Then she came to a section where the fires had died. It was completely dark and she edged forward, keeping one hand on the wall of the tunnel. She almost turned down a side passage by mistake, but when it started to go down instead of up she retraced her steps and found the main tunnel again.

After what seemed a terribly long time she saw a faint glow ahead of her. She turned another corner and the light was brighter. And it was sunlight! Not firelight! The sun! She began to hurry forward…

…and stopped short. There was a loud hissing and snarling from just ahead.

She had found the hatchlings.

As she stared in horror, at least a dozen small shapes rose up from the floor of the tunnel and started coming toward her. She gripped her spear in both hands.

"End of the road," she whispered.

CHAPTER TWENTY-ONE

"All right, get back everyone!" commanded Gregory Sadgipour. The two-dozen people in the compartment obeyed and moved away from the bulkhead where he and one of the engineers had placed their cutting charge. It was directional, of course, but you could never be sure where pieces might go flying. Greg looked around and was satisfied. Then he nodded to Corporal Chilnik, one of Doug Rawlins' engineers.

"Fire in the hole!" he said and pressed the button on his detonator. There was a ringing explosion and smoke billowed through the compartment.

Greg started forward almost immediately to look over the results. The smoke cleared and he could see that a clean hole had been blown through the wall. "Okay! Let's go!" he said. Sergeant McGill led his point team forward to scout the next compartment. After a moment he stuck his head back through the hole.

"All clear, sir."

"Good." Greg stepped through into the next compartment. It appeared to be an office of some sort. The cutting charge had shredded several cubicles, but it was obvious that there had been more mayhem unleashed in here than their unauthorized entrance had caused. Many of the partitions had been torn apart of knocked over. A lot of the furniture had been smashed, too. And there were a half-dozen mummified bodies amidst the debris. Greg paid no attention to them. As they neared the core of the base they were finding more and more evidence of the desperate fighting that had gone on twenty years ago.

As he worked his way across the room, Sergeant McGill came back to him. "The next door's sealed, too, sir."

"Hell. Bring up another charge."

"We've only got a few left, sir," said the engineer as he hurried past him.

"I know. Hopefully we won't need many more." Greg glanced to his side as Chtak came up.

"We should be almost to the inner core of the base, Greg," said the survey officer, consulting the layout of the base on his computer. "In fact, the main corridor around the periphery of the core should be on the other side of that wall." He pointed.

"It damn well better be," said Greg with a frown. "We've spent far too long getting this far."

"Agreed. Three hours, eight minutes since the execution code was given."

Greg nodded. It had taken them only a few minutes to get past the first sentry droid and it had been clear sailing for a while after that. They had moved up the main corridor without a hitch. As they did so, they came to appreciate just how enormous the base really was. The inner core was a kilometer across and each of the outer rings was another kilometer wide. And the middle ring was three levels thick and the inner core five. There had been dozens of tantalizing signs along the way telling them what was to be found on either side of the corridor. Factories and machine shops, repair bays and storage compartments. It would take weeks to explore.

But right now there was no time for exploring. They had to reach the Marine armory and reach it quickly. Unfortunately, they were not reaching it quickly. The first two kilometers might have been crossed in less than fifteen minutes, but the next hundred meters had taken over two hours. They had reached the intersection with the main corridor that circled the base's inner core only to find another blast door sealing them out. It was shut tight and if there was an access panel to get at the controls, it must have been on the other side. They had nothing even remotely capable of cutting or blasting a way through it, so the only alternative was to find a way around. The diagram of the base had shown them a possible way, but it meant going through a number of adjoining compartments. Most of the doors to those rooms had also been sealed and the only way through had been to blast holes in the walls.

Now they had reached the wall separating them from the main ring. Once through that they would be near their goal. But how many other walls or doors were still in the way? Greg watched the engineer place the cutting charge on the wall. It was just an innocent looking plastic tube, but it was filled with a special explosive compound that would direct nearly all of its force in one direction. The engineer was being very careful to keep the red side of the tube against the wall and the green side facing outward. It was easier since only the red side was sticky.

Greg tapped his foot impatiently. They were getting sporadic reports from *Gilgamesh* and the other teams. Old *Gilgie* was doing a great job of keeping the mercenary ships occupied. Doug Rawlins had gotten the south door open and Stewart Paalova's scouts had brought the Skraks from their cave. Apparently, a tremendous three-way fight between the security droids, the mercenaries and the Skraks was going on.

But how much longer would any of that last? Everyone was depending on Greg and his people to get into the core of the base and get those weapons. If they failed—or simply took too long in succeeding—it could ruin everything.

"Ready, sir," said the engineer. Greg nodded and then backed away. At his signal he pushed the detonator and there was a loud explosion. When the smoke cleared Greg went forward to investigate but to his annoyance the cutting charge had not done the job completely.

"There are a few places it didn't cut through all the way," said the engineer. "Do you want me to try again, sir?"

"No, we may need those last two charges later," said Greg. "Let's see if the plasma rifles can finish this." The two men with plasma rifles who had gone with Doug Rawlins had caught up with them an hour ago. The story they had to tell had not held out a great deal of hope for the survival of the combat engineer. Greg felt very bad about that. He had liked Doug in spite of his raucous personality. He didn't know what he was going to tell Ritta Torres if—when!—they rescued her and Rhada from the caves.

Now Greg directed the riflemen to use their weapons to finish cutting through the wall. "Aim right here first," he said indicating a scorched point on the wall and then stepping back. "Both of you together."

The men took aim and fired. Greg shielded his eyes from the dazzling light. Then he went over and checked the results. "Good. That cut through all right. Now do it again here."

They fired again and then again. Greg and the engineer directed their fire and they slowly cut through the points the cutting charge had not. They had to stop and replace their power cells once, but finally it was just about done.

"I think if we gave it a good shove it might go, sir," said the engineer.

"Okay, let's give it a try." Greg put his shoulder against the wall and then heaved with all his strength. Somewhat to his surprise, the section of wall moved easily and with a screech of tearing metal fell away with a loud clang. Sergeant McGill tried to lead the way but Greg beat him to it this time. He stepped through and looked around. It was a large, empty corridor that curved away in both directions.

"This is it," said Chtak excitedly when he stuck his head through. "The entrance to the armory should be about four hundred meters down to the left."

"Good," said Greg. "Come on, we can't waste any more time."

Blaire Sujumi looked down on the battlefield and whistled silently to himself. There was still a hell of a lot of firepower in action, in spite of all the casualties. He had caught up with the rest of the scouts as they skirted the battle. Now they were in the rocks on the mountainside above and east of the south gate. It was a good position to watch what was happening.

Even though they had not seen the opening stages of the Skrak assault, it was pretty obvious how it had gone just from where the bodies were lying. They had overrun the area where the mercenary shuttles had landed very quickly. Almost all the merc ground troops had gone off to fight the security droids and the shuttles were nearly unguarded. With scarcely a pause the Skraks had surged onward against the rear of the mercenary lines. The mercs had seen them coming soon enough to turn some of their considerable firepower against them and hundreds of Skrak bodies littered the far ridge. But then the Skraks had gotten in among them along the eastern end and it had gotten very bloody indeed. The mercs probably could have prevailed except for the fact that the Skraks were able and willing to pick up the weapons of the slain mercenaries and knew how to use them. That had evened the odds enormously. The mercs' line had been broken and the remainder of them fell back to the western edge of the ridge and the lower slopes of the mountain. The Skraks were still pressing them, although they were showing much more caution than they had during their first headlong charge.

And there were still a few of those droids left wandering around, too. They seemed to be shooting at anything that moved. Hundreds of bodies, wrecked droids, and burning shuttles covered the battlefield. Blaire had been happy to keep his people out of it.

"Blaire, look," said Gina D'Angelo from beside him. He looked where she was pointing and frowned. A group of about a hundred Skraks was working its way east along the ridge. They were coming in their direction. If they were trying to get up on the mountain so they could move against the mercs' eastern flank, they would come right through where the scouts were waiting. He looked hard and could see that at least some of the Skraks had modern weapons. Not good. His orders were to avoid combat.

"Pass the word to get ready to pull out and head east," he said. Gina nodded and moved quickly away.

He continued to watch the Skraks. They were about four hundred meters away in a straight line, although considerably farther by the route they would have to take to get up here. Then they halted. Motionless, they were very difficult to see, their skins blended into the background almost perfectly. After a few moments they started moving again—but not towards him. They had changed direction and Blaire felt a sudden shock when he realized they were heading for the gate. Gina had just returned and she immediately noticed it, too.

"We can't let them get inside!" she said urgently. That was something every scout was told again and again: do nothing that would allow the Skraks to get inside! Even though they meant the city, it still held true for the base.

Blaire nodded. "Okay, let's try to intercept them." He made the hand signals to advance and in a moment his people were slipping from rock to rock down the slope toward the gate. They had not gone fifty meters when there was the distinctive sound of a plasma rifle and a small explosion. Blaire froze when he saw the shape of a security droid emerge from the rocks at the base of the mountain. He was very chagrined that it had been there all this time and he had not seen it. A fine scout he was!

Fortunately it was interested in the Skraks instead of the young humans.

Its initial shots had felled several of the Skraks and the others had scattered and taken cover. The machine advanced on them and continued to fire, picking them off. They returned fire, but they only seemed to have lighter weapons. When the droid reached about a hundred meters from them the Skraks rose up and charged with a snarl that Blaire could hear from where he was. The droid cut down at least half of them, but then it disappeared under a mass of Skraks.

Blaire shook himself and motioned his scouts forward again. They neared the base of the mountain and took cover.

When Blaire looked out he was only slightly surprised to see that the Skraks had somehow managed to wreck the droid. It was lying on its side and not moving. There were only about thirty Skraks left, milling about it. Blaire made another motion with his hand and then shouted:

"All right! Take them!" The scouts rose up and opened fire. The range was less than two hundred meters and a few seconds later all the Skraks were down. There had been almost no cover and they had not had a chance. You *never* gave a Skrak a chance if you could help it.

Blaire looked around. Now what? He had no doubt that there were other surviving Skraks up on the ridge who had seen them fire. Their concealment was lost. He didn't like the position they were in. There were several directions they could not see far that would allow an enemy to sneak up on them. They could just go back up the slope to where they were before. But that would leave the gate uncovered again. They had spotted the larger group of Skraks, but a smaller group might make it in unseen. Blaire wrestled with the problem for a moment and then made his decision.

"We'll go to the gate," he said. Gina's eyes widened slightly, but then she nodded. The word was passed and then the scouts slipped from their concealment and skirted along the edge of the cliff to the gate. Halfway there Blaire suddenly realized that if there was another one of those droids inside the gate they were going to be in very serious trouble. He halted the group just short of the entrance and peeked inside. Nothing. He breathed again. Then he waved his people through.

There were two wrecked droids just inside and evidence that a lot of fire had been directed this way, but nothing else. There was also no cover at all. Anyone firing into the gate from outside would have an easy shot. Was there any way to close the gate again? All the droids were outside now—or were supposed to be. There was no real need to keep the gate open, was there? Presumably that Marine engineer had gotten the gate open, there must be a way to shut it again.

"Take a look around," he said. "See if you can find controls for the gate or anything we can use to build a barricade." The scouts scattered, except for a half dozen on lookout.

"Blaire! Over here!" shouted someone after only a moment. He trotted over and saw Ray Donovan holding open a mangled access panel. Something fairly powerful had punched a hole right through it. He stopped and blinked when he saw that there was a body wedged inside the tiny space. He blinked again when the body moved.

"He's still alive! Give me a hand here!"

Gently they lifted the person out of the compartment. Blaire saw that it was Doug Rawlins, the Marine engineer. He seemed to be burned on the face and arms, but he was definitely still alive. He groaned and opened his eyes as they lay him down on the floor.

"Why am I always the one who gets hurt?" he mumbled.

"Are you all right?" asked Blaire.

"Oh, just dandy. Where's that slacker Sadgipour? I'm gonna kick his ass when I see him."

"He's not here yet, sir. None of the others have gotten here yet. We're just the scouts."

"The hell you say. Well, from the sound of things they better get here quick," said Rawlins motioning toward the roar of battle.

"All the droids have gone outside," explained Blaire. "The mercenaries and Skraks and droids are all fighting. Can we shut the gate to keep them outside?"

Rawlins shook his head and pointed to the wrecked electrical panels inside the small compartment they had found him in. "Not a chance. Looks like you folks are going to have to hold the gate on your own."

"I need those damage reports and I need them now!" said Captain Jaq Ellsworth though clenched teeth.

"Working on it, Skipper!" said Commander Van Rossum.

"Captain, I'm afraid this is going to hurt a bit," said the medic standing beside her.

"Just do it!" she snarled. She vaguely realized that either the medic or Van Rossum could think her comment was meant for them, but she didn't really give a damn right now.

"Yes, ma'am," said the medic. He took hold of the metal splinter that was pinning her right forearm to the command chair and pulled. It did not come loose with the first try and he had to wiggle it a little, sending waves of agony along her arm in spite of the painkillers he had given her. On the next try it came loose and he pulled it out of her arm. Bright red blood oozed out through her vac suit, The medic immediately sprayed more of the medical gel and Numbitall into the wound. Then he turned her arm over and did the same thing to where the splinter had emerged from the other side.

"I don't suppose I can persuade you to come down to sick bay, ma'am?" She just glared at him. "Okay, I'll patch you up here. You were lucky: no broken bones or major blood vessels severed."

The medic bandaged her arm and then put patches on her vac suit and deflated the automatic tourniquet at her shoulder. The bridge had lost pressure briefly and might possibly do so again.

"I've got that report, Skipper," said Van Rossum suddenly. His own station had been smashed and he had been reconfiguring another station to damage control. "We've lost three of the main turrets and four of the secondaries. I doubt we can get any of them back on line any time soon. The number two torpedo launcher is out, but that might be repairable. We've lost a number of the shield emitters and overall strength is down to about seventy percent. It's worse on the port side: about sixty percent strength there. Three drive modules are out and acceleration is down by twenty percent. Miscellaneous sensor clusters are gone, but we still have full coverage. It could have been a lot worse."

Ellsworth nodded grimly. She checked the time and saw that nearly four hours had gone by since she started the action. She had dodged, dazzled, and baffled the enemy for the first three and a half, but then their luck had run out. They had unexpectedly encountered the enemy cruiser and a destroyer on a reciprocal course around the gas giant. There had been no way to avoid them and they had exchanged fire at very close range for five harrowing minutes.

"Commander Bradley, estimates on damage to those two ships?"

"I think we dished it out better than we took, Skipper. The cruiser was bleeding air and water from a dozen holes. Their firepower and acceleration was down by at least thirty percent before they went around the planet. The destroyer was about the same. We hammered them pretty good."

Yes, but *Gilgamesh* had lost at least twenty-five percent of her overall fighting abilities. Another exchange like that last one would leave them crippled.

"Van, what about the main display?" she asked. The monitor at the front of the bridge was blank.

"The problem's in CIC, Skipper," answered Van Rossum without looking up from his own console. "They should have it back in a few minutes."

Ellsworth nodded and looked at the bustling damage control parties. One of the hits had blasted through all the way to the bridge. There was a freshly patched hole the size of a dinner plate in one bulkhead. The armor had stopped most of the hit, but when it failed in that one spot, it had sent metal splinters tearing across the bridge. One had skewered Ellsworth's arm, another had wrecked Van Rossum's console and another had sliced half of Jeremy Snowden's head off. Ellsworth looked at the blood splattered on the deck near the sensor station. She was very glad she had given Snowden that brevet promotion. It was just a shame that he had not had longer to enjoy it. She touched a button on her chair and then frowned when nothing happened. That splinter had shorted out half her controls.

"Svetlana, get me Sick Bay."

"Yes, ma'am. You've got them."

"Doctor, casualty report, please."

"I have about thirty wounded here, ma'am," said Doctor Twiggs. "Still more coming in. A whole range of injuries, some pretty serious."

"Thank you." Thirty wounded. There could easily be that many more dead. Space combat typically left more dead than alive. Ellsworth sighed. Her ship was hurt and her crew were dying. And it had not even gotten really bad—yet. She looked up as the main display screen came back to life. She put on the tactical display.

Gilgamesh was completing her swing around the gas giant and would soon be heading outbound toward the planet's moons again. The enemy cruiser and destroyer were out of the picture for a while and Wolfe's battleship was still a safe distance away. She had to stay away from that ship! In fact, it was her dodging the battleship that had thrown her into the fight with the cruiser. Now where were the rest of his...?

"New contact!" said the replacement sensor operator excitedly. She was an ensign who seemed incredibly young to Ellsworth. What the hell was her name?

"Looks like trouble, Skipper," said Bradley.

She studied the display and had to agree with her executive officer. Four contacts blinked on the screen in a tight formation. Three destroyers and a frigate and they were coming right at her. Damn. This was not what she had wanted. *Gilgamesh* was heading outward and only a few minutes would put them above the planet's rings. The enemy was coming at them, but they were still sixty thousand kilometers beyond the outer edge of the rings. No matter if *Gilgamesh* dodged up or down, the enemy could easily match her and force a combat. And a close range combat would leave them crippled. The only other option was to run for it, but that would end up with that stern chase she was trying to avoid. To top it off, it was time to start heading back for Tractenberg IIIc. The ground parties should nearly be ready and *Gilgamesh* needed to get there. But the enemy ships were blocking her path.

Ellsworth continued to stare at the screen hoping for inspiration. She had used all her tricks. There was nothing left to do except…

"Well, I think we would have gotten at least an 'A-minus' on this one," sighed Karl Bradley.

Jaq Ellsworth shook herself and gently rubbed her aching arm. "The test's not over yet, Brad."

"No, ma'am," said Bradley, but his expression showed what he was thinking.

Gilgamesh passed over the inner edge of the rings. The option to even try and dodge was gone. And there were no more nukes waiting in the rings to give them an escape route. Ellsworth was thinking frantically. They would be in range in another few minutes. Individually, she outclassed any of the enemy ships, but their combined firepower would be enough to hurt *Gilgamesh* badly. Badly enough to wreck any chances of carrying out the rest of the plan.

Use your strengths against the enemy's weaknesses, the instructors told us back at the Academy, she thought. *I've used our strengths: mobility, initiative, a central position, is there anything else I've overlooked? What other weaknesses do these mercenaries have?*

Ellsworth jerked erect. *Mercenaries!*

"Helm!"

"Yes, ma'am?" said Ensign Bartlett.

"Ensign, I want you to steer a course directly toward that middle destroyer."

"Yes, ma'am. An intercept course?"

"A *collision* course, Ensign."

"Uh, yes, ma'am." Bartlett looked startled, but apparently he decided that if the skipper wanted to try and commit suicide twice in one day that was her prerogative.

"Brad, concentrate all fire on that same ship."

"Yes, ma'am." Bradley hesitated for a moment. "Skipper, we have longer ranged weapons than they do. A zero-range engagement like you are ordering is going to be awfully... bloody."

"I know that, Brad." She pointed at the icons on the display. "They know that, too."

Her face was set like it was carved of granite and her eyes glinted. "Let's see if they have the belly for it!"

They didn't.

The destroyer swerved from side to side but Ensign Bartlett matched every move. *Gilgamesh* had only fired off a single salvo at extreme range when the destroyer changed its course again: downward, to go under the rings instead of over them.

"Shift to the right hand DD, Ensign," commanded Ellsworth. "Same as before."

"Aye, aye, ma'am!"

It only took a moment before that ship ducked down just like the first one. Jaq didn't even have time to tell Bartlett to go after the third destroyer when the last two enemy ships changed course as well. A minute later they were past the edge of the rings and out of the battle for the moment.

"They blinked!" shouted Karl Bradley. "You stared the bastards down, Skipper!"

Ellsworth took a deep breath and slumped in her chair. "Couldn't face the cold steel," she whispered. She had gambled and won. She had sent a clear message to the mercs: 'No matter what else happens I am going to kill *you!*' and they couldn't take that. The sure knowledge that the enemy was not going to flinch no matter what you did had broken more armies and won more battles than any other factor in history. She had been counting on that and it had worked.

Her arm was throbbing as she sat up straight again. A few minutes had changed the situation completely. The destroyers and the frigate were stuck beneath the rings and heading the opposite direction. It would be at least an hour before they could turn around or swing round the planet. The cruiser and destroyer were also out of the picture for a while and the battleship was a good ways off, too. Time to make a move.

"Helm, steer for the moon IIIf. We'll swing around it and head for IIIc. Our people should be about ready by now."

"Aye, aye, ma'am!"

* * *

"Those cowardly bastards!" screamed Norman Wolfe. He was staring incredulously at the tactical display where four of his ships had just veered away from the League cruiser. Charles Florkowski looked nervously at the Commodore. He had been getting progressively more agitated as the battle proceeded. Florkowski could scarcely imagine what he would do now.

"They had them and they ran away! Communications! Get me *Viper*! Immediately!"

"Yes, sir!" A moment later Captain Hardunna appeared on the monitor. He did not look any happier than Wolfe.

"Hardunna! What the hell do you think you're doing?"

"What I had to do, Wolfe. What you'd have done if you'd been here in my place instead of on that fat battleship of yours!"

"You had her, you idiot! She was headed right for you and you let her escape! You miserable coward!"

"Easy for you to say! You didn't have her trying to ram that cruiser down *your* throat! But then your mouth is big enough it might have fit!"

"Hardunna, you are relieved! Turn your ship over to your second in command and place yourself under arrest!"

Captain Hardunna laughed at the screen. "Oh really? And just how are you going to make me do that, Big Man?"

"You son of a bitch!" snarled Wolfe. "I'll blast you out of space!"

Hardunna laughed again. "As the old saying goes: you'll have to catch me first. So long, Wolfe. I wish I could stick around to see Ellsworth hand you your head, but I think my welcome has worn out here." The screen went blank.

"*Viper* is altering course, sir," said the sensor tech nervously. "It looks like they are heading for the gravity well boundary."

"Damnation! Communications, tell Captain Jurgens on *Mangonel* that she is in command of that squadron and to blow *Viper* to hell!"

"Uh, there is no response, sir," said the com officer after a few moments.

"*Mangonel* is altering course now, too, sir. Looks like they are heading out as well."

"Deserting! Those filthy traitors!" Wolfe began a long, profane rant against his former subordinates. Florkowski just looked on in wonder. Ellsworth had cost Wolfe two more ships—two of his better ones—while hardly firing a shot. He hated to admit it, but Ellsworth's performance was bordering on the miraculous. She had used the 'terrain' of the gas giant, its rings and moons to prevent Wolfe from concentrating his forces against her. And when she had finally been cornered, she had used her enemies' greatest weakness against them.

They were mercenaries.

Mercenaries could be as tough, as brave, and as disciplined as any regular troops. More so than a lot of them. But they were still mercenaries. They fought for themselves, not for a nation or a planet or a cause. Regular troops were willing to die, if need be, to assure their nation's victory. But for a mercenary there could be no victory without survival. They would take the risks of combat for the chance of pay and plunder, but they had no incentive to sacrifice themselves so other mercenaries could split their share of the loot. Ellsworth had realized that and when she sent Hardunna the clear message that he was going to have to die to secure Wolfe's loot, it had just been too much for him.

So now what? *Gilgamesh* was heading outbound toward one of the moons. From there Ellsworth could swing around and head off in almost any direction. Wolfe's counter options had just shrunk, too, because of his temper. With the loss of the two destroyers and the damage to his cruiser, he was going to have to combine all his lighter ships into one group to have something that could beat *Gilgamesh*—assuming he could convince them to fight.

Wolfe was giving orders to that effect now and he was ordering *Vindicator* onto another course he hoped would allow him to catch *Gilgamesh*. Florkowski did not see much hope for that.

Unless…

"Commodore?"

"What?" snapped Wolfe. He fixed a burning stare on Florkowski that seemed to be saying: 'You brought me on this fool's errand. You cost me five of my ships. Why shouldn't I blow your head off this instant?' Florkowski almost quailed before that gaze.

"Commodore, when you make your next moves, I suggest you keep in mind just what brought Captain Ellsworth to this system in the first place."

For a moment it looked like Wolfe was going to ignore his advice and possibly go ahead and shoot him, but then that bizarre transition from foaming madman to calculating commander took place yet again and Wolfe nodded.

"Yes. Helm, bring us about. Set a course back to that moon. Full ahead."

* * *

Blaire Sujumi squinted through the powerspecs at the distant ridge. The mercenaries had taken up a position and dug in over there. They were about two kilometers from the gate and did not look like they intended to go anywhere soon. The Skraks, on the other hand, were roaming all over the place. Blaire knew they had taken heavy casualties, but there were still hundreds of them left and most had managed to acquire a modern weapon. If this whole plan did not work out, it would be very risky going outside the city for a long time.

He zoomed in the view and saw that there were a lot of Skraks ringing in the mercenaries' position and there seemed to be a lively firefight still going on. Good, the more ammo they burned up the better. But there did not seem to be anything headed toward the gate just at the moment. Blaire moved back from the edge of the door and then walked the twenty meters back to the barricade. They had found a compartment full of storage containers in one of the rooms on the west side of the corridors—one of the rooms they had never been able to get to because of the droids—and dragged them out to form a barricade in the main corridor. He climbed over it and sat down.

"Anything happening?" asked Gina D'Angelo.

"Not that I can see. I sure wish the reinforcements would get here."

"Me, too." They had gotten some reports that Lieutenant Sadgipour's team was making progress towards getting to the armory, but that had been nearly an hour ago. Blaire had sent several runners to try and make contact with them and get some help. He also wanted to get Lieutenant Rawlins some medical attention. He looked to where the Marine was resting and then went over to him.

"How are you doing, Lieutenant?" he asked.

"Not too bad. The painkillers are helping." They had used the items in their first aid kits to treat his wounds, but the burns looked pretty bad. Several gobbets of molten metal had drilled right into him. They had to hurt like hell. "So what's going on?"

"The battle is still being fought out there. We have not had any new word from Lieutenant Sadgipour. For now we seem secure enough here."

"Yeah? Well, I hope you are..."

A shout and then a roar of gunfire cut off Rawlins' statement.

Blaire spun around to see a dozen Skraks dropping down from above the top of the open gate. It was a four meter fall, but they were up and firing in an instant. Several of Blaire's scouts went down and then the rest were kneeling behind the barricade and firing back. He pushed Rawlins down and then scrambled on hands and knees back to the barricade, drawing his pistol at the same time.

Even the few seconds it took him to reach the barricade had been enough for the fight to end. There was no cover in that corridor and the Skraks had been massacred. The scouts fired a few more bursts into the heaped bodies in front of them and then the firing stopped. The silence was punctuated with moans from the wounded. Someone was crying.

"Who's hit?" shouted Blaire. Several answers came back and people moved to help the wounded.

"Sam! Connie! Check out those bodies!" he commanded. "Bring back the weapons. The rest of you cover them, there could be more!"

He was cursing himself for carelessness. The Skraks had gone up onto the mountain and then come right down above the gate and then just jumped. He was going to have to post some lookouts up there to warn them of any more attempts—assuming there weren't more of them already up there.

"Blaire! Come here!"

He looked up and he saw two scouts waving at him. They were on either side of someone who was down. He crawled over and stopped.

Gina! Shit!

Gina D'Angelo was lying on her back, staring at the ceiling, He came closer and saw that there was the end of a Skrak crossbow bolt sticking out of her chest. The weeping boy next to her was trying to staunch the flow of blood but without much success. As Blaire came closer Gina seemed to see him.

"G-got hit, Blaire..."

"Take it easy, Gina," he said, but his voice was shaking and his eyes were blinking back tears. None of the scouts was any stranger to death, but it was still nothing you could get used to. And everyone liked Gina...

She reached up a twitching hand and he took it. Her eyes were wandering. Then she coughed harshly and blood splattered out of her mouth and nose.

"F-fun while it lasted…"

"Hang on, Gina, we'll get help."

"Blaire?"

"I'm right here, Gina."

"D-don't let them get inside."

"We won't, Gina. We won't let them inside."

And then she was gone. Her eyes closed and her breathing stopped and her hand went limp in his.

Blaire Sujumi gently put her hand down and then turned away.

Where were those damn reinforcements?

"Just about ready, sir," said Corporal Chilnik as he finished placing the cutting charge.

"That's our last one," said Greg Sadgipour, "it had better do the job."

"I can't promise anything, sir," said Chilnik, "this is one hell of a tough door. We may have to do some burning with the plasma rifles."

Greg cursed under his breath. This was taking far too long. They had gotten into the main ring around the core area and then found the entrance to the security headquarters which contained the Marine armory. He had breathed a sigh of relief when the outer door opened without a problem. But then after a ten meter corridor, they had come to another door that would not open. And this time there was no way around it. On the other side of these walls was solid rock. The door was the only way in and it was a heavy one. The first cutting charge had left some deep gouges in it, but had not gone through at all. The engineer corporal was carefully placing the second charge to go exactly where the first one had been in hopes of finishing the job. It was now over four hours since operations had begun and they were running out of time.

"Ready, sir," said the corporal.

"Okay, everyone move back," he commanded. The corridor was only four meters wide and they would have to get entirely out of it to stay away from the blast. When a charge failed to cut through there was a lot of stuff that ended up coming the other way. After a moment, everyone had backed out into the main corridor. He was just about to give the go-ahead to the engineer to fire the charge when there was a shout from down the corridor.

"Lieutenant! There's a messenger here from the gate!"

There were over two hundred people filling the corridor so it took a few moments for the man to make his way through. It was one of Stewart Paalova's scouts.

"Report," snapped Greg and then remembered the man wasn't a Marine. "What's happening?"

"I've got a message from Blaire Sujumi," gasped the man. "We've been trying to radio you, but the reception through all this rock is terrible. Our scouts are holding the main gate. The controls are damaged so we can't close it again. We have it barricaded, but we could sure use some help."

"What happened to Paalova?"

"He... he didn't come back with us. But we found Lieutenant Rawlins by the gate. He's hurt and needs some medical attention."

Greg was simultaneously relieved and concerned. It was great that Doug was still alive, but what did he mean that Paalova had not come back? Was he dead, hurt, captured? No time to wonder.

"We're just about to get into the armory, so help should be on the way very soon. Chtak, isn't there an infirmary around here close by?"

"Yes, another two hundred meters further around this ring," answered the survey officer.

"Can some of you folks get over there and see if it's operational or if there are any grav stretchers?" A dozen volunteers headed off in that direction.

"All right, Corporal, let's get that door open."

"Yes, sir. Everyone clear the entrance." This was done and a moment later he pushed the detonator. There was an explosion and a good deal of smoke gushed out into the main corridor. But had the charge done the job? Greg hurried into the corridor with a small crowd following him.

"Damn!" The door was still intact. Or at least mostly so. The cutting charge had done some good.

"You can see where it cut through here and here and over here," said Corporal Chilnik, pointing to several spots on the door. "But we're going to have to do some serious cutting in a few spots to get all the way through."

Greg turned away and waved to some of his people. "Okay, bring up those plasma rifles and get ready to..."

The door exploded.

No warning, nothing. The door just exploded outward and Greg was flung against the wall. Chilnik, right in the path, was reduced to a mangled corpse and thrown into several other people who were sent sprawling by the impact. Shouts and screams rang through the corridor. Greg was stunned and slid to the floor trying to figure out what had happened.

A moment later he got the answer as a security droid floated through the hole in the door. It hovered almost directly over where he was lying, no more than a meter away. *Oh, God, it'll slaughter everyone!* The only thing that could stop it were the plasma rifles and Greg saw that both the riflemen had been knocked flat by the blast. The droid would kill them before they could possible get the weapons. In fact, the droid was training its weapons to begin the massacre as he watched.

"Everyone, get back!" shouted a high pitched voice. Greg's eyes widened when he saw that it was Chtak. The Kt'Ktr native was standing in the corridor, facing the droid. Its weapons zeroed in on him.

Then Chtak moved.

Greg had come to realize on this expedition that his teacher was far faster than a human, but now he saw just how fast. In an eyeblink Chtak was three meters to the right of where he had just been. The droid shifted its aim and suddenly Chtak was somewhere else. Back and forth across the width of the corridor Chtak dodged for a few priceless seconds while the humans scrambled out of the way.

But it could not go on forever and finally the droid fired.

There was a bright flash and Chtak was thrown against a wall, his fur smoldering from the near-miss. The droid shifted to finish the job…

"No!"

Greg surged up from the floor and seized the droid's anti-grav sled and heaved with all his strength. He slammed the machine up into the corner next to the door, pinning it against the ceiling. The anti-grav unit compensated automatically for this unexpected motion so by the time he had the droid against the ceiling, he was supporting its entire weight—all five hundred kilograms of it.

The droid twisted and tried to bring its weapons to bear, but it was jammed into the corner and could not. Greg's muscles were knotted with the effort and the propulsor field from the droid made if feel like a million bugs were crawling on his skin. But he would not let go.

There was a loud bang and a dozen sharp pains peppered his arms and legs. The droid had fired off an anti-personnel round from its torso. The blast could not hit him directly, but the ricochets off the walls could. It hurt, but he refused to let go.

"Someone get those plasma rifles!" he shouted. The droid continued to squirm and he could not look to see if anyone had obeyed his order. He braced his legs and pushed with everything he had. He was gasping with the effort and his arms were starting to quiver. How long could he...?

There was someone next to him, crouching low. It was Sergeant McGill and he had a plasma rifle. With a steady hand McGill thrust the weapon around the curve of the anti-grav unit and jammed the muzzle into a joint in the droid's armor. He pulled the trigger. There was a flash and a muffled explosion. The droid still continued to fight him.

"Let's try that again," muttered McGill. There was another flash and another bang and then suddenly the tingle from the propulsor field was gone.

"I think that did it, sir," said McGill.

"Make sure!" gasped Greg. He wasn't going to let go until he was sure the thing was dead.

"Right." McGill shifted his weapon and fired again. There was a brighter flash and a shower of sparks and the noise of power cells shorting out. That really did it.

"Stand back, I'm going to drop it!" McGill did so and then Greg sprang back and the droid fell to the floor with a crash. It didn't move.

"Nice work, sir," said McGill, looking at the wreck. "Never heard of anyone fighting a droid hand-to-hand before—not and live to talk about it."

"Well, thank you, Sergeant," said Greg. He stood there quivering for a second and then remembered Chtak. He spun around and was relieved to see his friend sitting up on the floor a few meters away. He went over to him.

"Are you all right?"

"A few burns, I'm afraid and I'm a bit dizzy, but I think I will recover, Greg. Thank you for your concern."

"Chtak, that was incredible what you did! I didn't realize how fast you are. You probably saved a dozen lives."

"Your own performance was very impressive, too, Gregory. I did not realize how strong *you* are."

"Sir? The way seems clear now," said McGill, reminding Greg of what they were there for.

"Right. Let's take a look. Chtak, can you move?"

"Yes, I think so. But you are injured, too, Greg," said Chtak pointing to several bloody spots on Greg's uniform. "Do you need medical attention?"

"I'll live. My body armor kept anything vital from being hurt. Come on, let's go."

McGill led the way, plasma rifle at the ready. Greg and Chtak and the rest of the Marines followed. Greg stepped over the remains of the droid and then through the shattered door. Inside was another corridor running left and right. Directly opposite them was a glass-walled checkpoint. An ancient body was sprawled on the floor inside.

"The main security station should be this way," said Chtak, pointing to the right. They went that way and came to an open door. Inside was a large room filled with dozens of control consoles. They all seemed to be working, with glowing monitors and flashing lights. There were half a dozen bodies on the floor, but their eyes were all drawn to a single body in a chair by the central console.

Greg walked over and saw the mummified remains of a man wearing a Marine colonel's uniform. There was a large hole burned through the right chest area. One hand was still propped up next to the keyboard on the console. The other was hanging down with a pistol lying on the floor below it. Chtak came closer and studied the display above the keyboard.

"I believe we are in luck, Greg."

"How so?"

"I was concerned that we would not have the proper security codes to access the computer here. But this man, apparently the commander of the Marine detachment, is still logged on using his own codes. See? The last two command lines are orders sealing the doors and activating the security droids. The computer is still waiting for the next order."

"I wonder who he was? And which side he was on when he gave those orders?" asked Greg. The name tag on the uniform was burned away but he supposed the colonel's name would be in the records. But had he done what he had done as a helpless pawn of the Darj'Nang overlords or had he done it to stop others who had already been taken over? Was he a hero or an involuntary traitor? They might never know.

"Can you open the doors to the armory and shut off the droids?"

"I believe so." Chtak gently pushed the chair with the body away from the console. Greg winced when the body's left arm fell out of the uniform sleeve. Chtak went to the keyboard and carefully typed in a command. Then he nodded.

"Very good. There are still eight operational security droids—including four still here inside the base—and I've changed their instructions to only fire upon Skraknars or humans who are firing on the droids."

"What about the doors?"

"I am working on that now... yes. The door to the armory is right there. It is now unlocked."

"Great! Come on, Sergeant let's see if the prize is worth the candle."

They quickly went to the door Chtak had indicated and pressed the entry button. The door slid open immediately. Greg stepped through and halted with an intake of breath.

The prize was worth it.

Racks and racks of gleaming weapons stood there. Plasma rifles, missile launchers and all manner of mayhem makers. He walked forward and saw the lockers full of power cells, grenades and other ordnance. He took a plasma rifle from a rack and a power cell from a locker and fit the cell into the receptacle. The weapon came to life at his touch and he went through the check-out without a hitch. It was fully functional.

"All right! Let's get those people in here and fitted out! We need to get reinforcements up to the south gate on the double!"

The word was passed and soon a stream of volunteers from the city were filing in and having weapons handed out to them. They already had their own squad organizations set up so as each squad was ready, they moved out.

"Sir?" said McGill suddenly from beside him.

"Yeah?"

"Sir, you might want to have a look over here." The Sergeant was smiling and motioning toward another door. He followed him over and then just gawked.

Power armor! Star League power armor, the nastiest bit of ground combat gear in known space. Oh yes!

Row after row of the armored suits hung in their ready racks. Small tell-tale lights glowed from the status panels.

"Do you think they are operational, Sarge?"

"They look that way to me, sir. One way to find out, of course."

"There sure is. Marines! Over here and prepare to suit up!" The heads of his troopers jerked up at the old command they thought they might never hear again. In seconds they were in the compartment, picking out suits to try on. Greg looked on in envy. The suits were fairly flexible as far as the size of the people who were wearing them went, but he doubted there was one for his particular build. Heavy gravity worlders generally had to have a special model...

"Lieutenant?" said McGill. "There's a suit over there that might fit you."

He looked where McGill was pointing and saw a suit that was much broader than the other ones. A huge grin split his face as he walked over to it. Yes, this would do just fine! He supposed that with enough suits for an entire battalion there was bound to be one or two made for people like him.

With a small effort, he recalled the procedures for entering and activating a suit of power armor. These suits were of an older model than he was used to, but they did not look that much different. He punched a few buttons on a control panel next to the suit and the back of it opened up like a flower. He stripped off his body armor, wincing slightly at his wounds, and then stepped into the suit. His legs slid down into the suit's legs and then he pushed his arms into the servo restraints. The way the massive suits were constructed would not allow a person's arms to actually go into the suit's arms— not without ripping the person's arms out of their sockets—but the suit was able to adapt for that. Greg pressed a button and the suit closed around him and firmly snugged him into place.

He quickly ran through the power-up routine and was relieved when the suit came to life just as it was supposed to. He stepped backwards out of the rack and turned. The suit was massive, but it felt almost like a second skin. The rest of the Marines were already suited up and getting their weapons armed. Greg did likewise. It felt a little awkward at first, especially the arm movements, but it was all soon coming back to him.

"I think we're ready to move out, sir," said McGill. Greg nodded and then led the way back into the control room. There was another door that led out of the suit room, but Greg wanted to talk to Chtak.

"Well, you seem to have grown a bit, Gregory!" said Chtak when he saw him.

"Yeah. We're heading out to the gate. Are you going to be okay here?" Greg stared down at him through the open helmet visor.

"I believe so. We need to get one of the fusion plants on-line and then the other systems up and running. *Gilgamesh* should be arriving shortly and we must be prepared."

"Do you have all the help you need?"

"I am hoping that I do. If you can send Lieutenant Rawlins back here, he could be of some use if he is not too badly injured."

"Will do. Okay, we are going now."

"Good luck, Greg. I will try to get the base's internal com system operational as soon as possible. That should solve our current communications difficulties."

"Good. See you later." Greg turned to his Marines.

"All right! Let's move out!"

CHAPTER TWENTY-TWO

Stewart Paalova wormed his way forward through the icy water and cursed when his 'armor' caught on another snag. He never usually wore the thick leather trousers, arm pieces and heavy vest when he went on a scout, but this time was different. This time he fully expected to encounter Skraks at close quarters and the extra protection might make the difference.

He had nearly reached the base of the cliff where the spring emerged from the mountainside. It had taken him longer than he had hoped. After the scouts had opened fire on the Skraks, Stewart had found a good hiding spot—one he had discovered years earlier—and waited for the hoard of enraged Skraks to go by. There had been at least two thousand of them and he sincerely hoped Blaire could keep ahead of them. As he had expected, the Skraks had left a new group of sentries behind when they left, but just as he had planned, they took position on that same ridge where the others had been and he was left inside their perimeter.

The Skraks had all been looking outward, but it still took him over an hour to make his way down from his hiding place to the small stream. Then more time to work his way through the stream to the cliff. But he was there now. With a little luck he could get up the cliff and into the cave through one of the smaller entrances. He had been here once before on a scout. That other time it had been just for the thrill of it. This time he had another purpose.

He could still scarcely believe he was doing this. The chance that he could rescue the two captives was exceedingly small and he knew it. But he also knew that even if Greg and Doug got the weapons out of that base and then came here to wipe out the Skraks, the chance of finding the two women alive was almost nil. The Skraks would certainly kill them rather than allow them to be rescued. Even so, just why he was risking his neck to save those women was a question he could not really answer. He liked both of the young Marines and he felt very sorry for them. But that still didn't explain what he was doing here.

Just an idiot, I guess.

He reached the spring and then lay there very quietly. There did not appear to be anyone close by. There were at least twenty Skraks off on the far ridge. There were probably at least a few further up the mountain and probably a couple in the cave mouth, but with any luck none of them would be looking in his direction right now.

Taking a deep breath he rose up out of the water and scrambled up the cliff face from handhold to handhold. There was a way in about twenty meters up and he reached it in less than a minute. He crouched down in the entrance and listened. Nothing. No cries of alarm, no rattle of weapons. He closed his eyes and sat there for two full minutes to try and develop a little bit of night vision and then he eased himself into the crack in the rock and crawled forward.

This was the trickiest part. If he ran into a Skrak now he would be at a terrible disadvantage. But he met nothing and after about thirty meters the passage opened out and he was able to draw the stunner that Chtak'Chr had given him. Another twenty meters and the tunnel tilted down. Stewart had an excellent sense of direction and space. He could tell that this tunnel would meet the main passage very shortly. And so it did. He dropped down silently and looked around. He froze when he saw two Skraks silhouetted against the light of the entrance about forty meters away. He hesitated for a moment, but then decided he better secure his rear before proceeding. He took careful aim with the stunner and fired. The silent beam took the one Skrak and before the other knew what had happened, Stewart got it, too. They would be out for hours and he decided not to use his knife on them. Skrak blood made a noticeable scent and it would carry. Best to leave them for now.

He turned and slowly proceeded down the passage, keeping very close to the wall so *he* would not be silhouetted against the light. He was in unfamiliar territory now. As he went further, he began to realize just how hopeless his task was. The caves were probably enormous. He could wander for hours without finding where the prisoners were kept—assuming they were even alive after this amount of time. Did he dare shout for them? Surely there were a few Skraks still about who would hear.

He was paused, frozen in indecision, when he heard a sound from just ahead. There was a snarling and hissing that was all too familiar. Skraks. He peered forward and could see a number of small shapes moving in the faint light. He instantly realized that these were the young ones he sometimes saw accompanying the adults on their hunts. They weren't likely to have weapons, but in a group they could still be very dangerous. They must have heard or smelt him. He raised his stunner.

But then he saw that they were not coming toward him. They were all moving away, deeper into the cave. What were they…?

He saw the woman. She was just a faint shape in the gloom, perhaps twenty meters away, but he could not mistake her for a Skrak. It was her the Skrak young were going after! Without a second thought, he took aim with the stunner and fired. One of the Skraks twitched and curled up into a ball. He shot another one and wished he had a heavy stunner that could fire on continuous beam. At his third shot the Skraks had noticed him. They turned, forgetting the woman, and charged back at Stewart. He shot down two more. The creatures all seemed to have swollen bellies and were not moving as fast as they usually did. Stewart took advantage to stun another one, but then they were on him. There were still at least a dozen of them and they attacked savagely.

Jaws clamped around both of his legs. Claws were pulling at his thick trousers. He stunned another one, but then one of them was hanging from his arm, weighing it down. Another leaped up and was clawing at his face. He flung it off with his free hand, but then another set of jaws closed around that arm. He had to protect his throat and his eyes! They were climbing up his chest. They were pulling him down…

Then he heard a scream. It was a woman's scream. But it was not a scream of fear or pain. It was a shriek of anger. Of pure rage. A battle cry.

He looked up to see the woman charging the Skraks from behind, shield on one arm, spear drawn back to deliver a thrust. The Skraks hardly had time to notice her when she drove the spear into the milling throng just in front of Stewart. It went completely through two of them and imbedded itself in a third. The Skraks convulsed violently, pulling the spear out of her grasp. The woman screamed again and drew a sword and chopped at the Skraks. The ones who had latched onto Stewart did not let go, but the others turned to face the woman.

She hacked right and left. Skrak heads and limbs went flying. Two of them sprang at her and she interposed her shield. They sank their teeth into it and hung on. She dropped it and took the sword in both hands. She lunged a step forward and chopped the Skrak clinging to Stewart's left arm in two. Hot blood splashed over both of them. The jaws loosened and his hand was free. He grabbed his knife from its sheath and plunged the point into the eye of the Skrak hanging from his other arm. He stabbed and slashed at the others clinging to him. The woman was still screaming and hacking at the miserable creatures.

By the time he had freed himself, she had killed the others. As he watched, she went back to the ones he had stunned and hacked them to pieces with a maniacal energy. She kept chopping and chopping long after it was necessary. He pulled himself upright and took a few steps in her direction.

"T-they're dead," he gasped.

The woman whipped her sword around to face him and he stopped in his tracks and stared at her. The feeling that went through him was indescribable. The sight of her there: Stark naked, covered from head to foot in blood and gore, dripping sword poised to strike, was the most incredible, the most frightening, the most *magnificent* thing he had ever seen. He would never forget this instant as long as he lived. *And I thought I was rescuing her!*

"They're dead," he said again. The woman's eyes glinted in the light from the entrance and her lips drew back in a snarl.

"Dead!" she said suddenly. Her voice was like rusty steel.

"Uh, yes, they're dead. W-where is the other woman who was with you?"

"Dead!" she screeched again, her sword point not wavering a centimeter.

Stewart didn't know what to say. Was the other woman dead or was this one just babbling? But as he watched, the fire left her eyes and the sword point drooped.

"S-she's dead," she said in a tiny voice.

"I'm sorry. But we better get out of here." He gestured toward the mouth of the cave. He wasn't sure how they would get past all the sentries, but they had to try. The woman nodded. She took hold of her spear and he helped pry the bodies of the Skraks from it. Then she picked up her shield.

"Come on, this way."

"Wait." He looked back and the woman was standing with a strange look on her face.

"What's wrong?"

"There are eggs."

"Eggs?"

"Skrak eggs. Back in the cave. Thousands of them. We should destroy them."

"I... I don't know," said Stewart in surprise. "We really need to get out of here."

"They are unguarded. We need to destroy them. Or there will be thousands more of... of those." She pointed at the dead hatchlings. Without another word the woman turned around and headed back into the cave. Stewart stood with his mouth hanging open and then hurried to catch up.

She led him down and down. They came to a stretch of tunnel where it was completely dark. He had a small flashlight but she just kept going and he followed along without using it. Then there was some light again and they passed a number of branching tunnels on either side. Stewart realized he never would have found her on his own. She came to a side tunnel and paused.

"You will need a spear," she said.

She led him into another large chamber. It was an armory of some sort. A fire burned in one corner. Racks held hundreds of weapons. He noticed a dead Skrak by the forge. It was one of the largest he had ever seen—even without its head.

"Did you kill this one?"

The woman just handed him a spear. "Dead," she said.

She walked out of the chamber and he followed her. Down and down again. They came to the entrance to a large chamber and the woman stopped to stare at another dead Skrak. Stewart just looked at her. He remembered that one of the women had been blonde and named Claritta and that Doug was her lover. The other had been dark haired and named Rhada and Greg was in love with her. In the dim light he could not honestly tell which this one was. Her hair, like all the rest of her, was totally covered in blood and dirt. He couldn't tell what color it was.

"My name is Stewart. What's yours?"

The woman looked up from the dead Skrak to stare at him. Then she looked down again.

"My name is Rhada," she whispered. Greg's girl. Stewart felt a pang of sorrow for Doug Rawlins.

"My name is Rhada McClerndon," said the woman more loudly. She kicked at the body of the Skrak. Then suddenly she screamed:

"My name is Rhada! *Rhada McClerndon*!" Then she took her spear and drove it into the body of the Skrak. Again and again, screaming out her name the whole time. Stewart looked around in alarm. Her voice was echoing through the cavern. Were all the Skraks dead?

Finally, the woman stopped. The Skrak body had been ripped apart. She walked past him. "The eggs are in here. Come on."

He followed her and then, again, stopped in amazement. The egg chamber was enormous. A shudder of fear ran through him at the thought of all those eggs hatching. Thousands and thousands of eggs. Each one could hatch a Skrak warrior that would someday threaten him and his people.

But a great many of the eggs had already been destroyed.

The remains lay in great pools of nauseating slime. Stewart tried to pick his way around them, but the woman just waded right through it without flinching—in her bare feet. He sheepishly splashed after her. They soon came to eggs which had not been destroyed and Rhada began thrusting her spear into them, one after the other. Stewart watched for a moment and then did the same. It was disgusting, but he told himself that each one he destroyed now was one less they would have to face later. If Greg and Chtak's plan worked out, it would not make any difference, he supposed, but if the plan failed, this might be what ultimately saved his own people from destruction.

As he progressed through the chamber he was amazed at the number Rhada had already destroyed, apparently on her own. Easily half of them. Five thousand or more at a rough guess. And she had done this on her own. Somehow she had escaped, armed herself, killed those Skraks and done all this. All on her own! It was unbelievable...

After what seemed a very long time his arms were aching. He stopped and checked the time. Over four hours since the scouts first launched their attack. It seemed like centuries. He looked up as Rhada splashed over to him.

"I think that's all."

He looked around. They had, no doubt, missed some of the eggs in all this mess, but they had gotten the bulk of them. They were both coated in slime and the stench was becoming unbearable. And they had definitely pushed their luck as far as they dared. He still did not know how they would make it past the sentries. He was exhausted and the woman was almost reeling with fatigue.

"We better go," he said. She nodded.

Back the way they had come. Stewart breathed the fresher air gratefully. But the woman paused again when they reached the entrance to the armory. Without a word she went back inside. Now what?

She set down her shield and spear and walked over to the far side of the chamber. She picked up a basket of black stones that Stewart recognized as coal. What was she…? She took the basket over to the fire and dumped it in, basket and all. She went back for another basket. Stewart, baffled, offered to help, but she stopped and actually snarled at him and he stepped back. Three more baskets went on the fire and the wicker flamed up. Stewart did not know much about blacksmithing, but it seemed like there was far too much coal on that fire. He looked around nervously. How much time did they have? How could he get this incredible woman out of here?

Rhada now took hold of the bellows and began to pump it. Up down, up down. Again she refused his help. She pumped with a frantic energy that he could not imagine how she was maintaining. The wicker baskets were long gone when the coal suddenly blazed up. A red light filled the chamber.

Satisfied at last, Rhada stepped back and looked at the fire for a few moments. Then she went over to the racks of weapons and grabbed an armful. She brought them back and tossed them into the fire. Spear shafts and sword grips flared up immediately. The metal blades were not going to burn, but Stewart supposed that this might ruin their temper. He went and grabbed an armful himself and this time she did not object. Load after load was tossed on and soon it was spilling over the sides of the forge. The shields burned particularly well, along with the wood stocks for the crossbows. Soon there was a veritable bonfire in the chamber.

The bellows caught fire and blazed up. This seemed to delight the woman and she danced around squealing with childish giggles. Then she stopped suddenly and went over to the grindstone. She started tugging it toward the fire, but it was too heavy for her. Stewart went over to help.

"I don't think this will burn," he said, but the look on her face told him that she didn't care. The fire was putting off in incredible amount of heat now. They got as close as they could stand and heaved the grindstone into the flames. The wood parts caught fire immediately. Perhaps the heat would crack the stone… Rhada danced about with new cries of glee.

Eventually, they had everything that would burn thrown in the fire. The heat drove him back, but she stood much closer and he didn't see how she could possibly stand it, naked as she was. He stared at her. The fire was reflecting off her body and it made her seem like a bronze statue. He found her incredibly beautiful despite the filth covering her and the terrible cuts and claw marks on her skin. He supposed he should try to get her some clothes, but the only thing of his own he could take off in a reasonable time would be his vest. It would fit her slender form like a tent and there might be more fighting to do anyway. So he stood and stared at her. He was surprised and ashamed at the desire that flamed up in him. He remembered the time he and Peg Ryan had snuck to within a few hundred meters of the cave entrance and made love there. It had been incredibly dangerous and exciting. But it paled in comparison to what he was feeling now. He wanted this woman like he had never wanted anything in his life. But he also knew that she was not his to have. Not because she was Greg's girl. He could not think of this woman belonging to anyone. She might offer herself to a man, but no man would ever take her.

He shook himself. This was crazy. They had to get out of here. He looked up and saw that the smoke had filled the upper parts of the chamber. He could feel a cool breeze on his back. The cavern was acting like a chimney; the hot air and smoke was going up and out through the opening above and fresh air was being drawn in...

The smoke!

The smoke would be pouring out! The Skraks outside would be sure to see it!

"Come on! We have to get out of here!" He reached out to touch the woman's arm. She stood and stared at him for one moment more and then nodded. They headed to the entrance of the chamber and she paused and looked around. In her frenzy she had thrown their two spears and her shield in the fire along with everything else. She shrugged and went on.

Up and up they went now. Suddenly, he heard noise from ahead. He grabbed the woman and pulled her back. Her skin seemed like hot metal in his hand. They froze and listened. There were hissing and sputtering Skraks headed their way!

Rhada turned and dashed down a side tunnel, pulling him after her. They came to a small chamber. There was yet another dead

Skrak in here, lying next to a dimly glowing fire. This one was more badly mangled than any of the others. She pulled him over against one wall. In the distance they could hear a number of Skraks hurrying past. Heading for the fire apparently.

But then they heard a closer noise. Stewart had the stunner out and ready. As he watched, a Skrak came into the chamber, crossbow cocked and wary. It hissed when it saw the body. Then it saw Stewart, but he shot it before it could turn. Carefully he edged out and looked back up the tunnel. Nothing. The others had gone past. He took a few steps and then heard something behind him. He looked back and saw that Rhada had used her sword on the stunned Skrak. He motioned for her to come on. With all the Skraks he had heard go by, they must have pulled in almost all the sentries from outside. If they could just get out, they might have a good chance of escaping. But they would have to hurry—and at the same time not be spotted.

Then they were back in the main tunnel. They made it through the dark section and then he slowed as they got closer to the entrance. He peered around the bend and he could see at least eight Skraks silhouetted against the light, just like the first two had been. Damn, there was no way he could get them all. He stepped back and looked up. The small tunnel he had used to get in was still there. He pointed to it and Rhada nodded. The woman was nearly exhausted and he had to boost her up. In spite of the danger he was incredibly aware of his hands on her body as he helped her. Her skin was still hot, but there was nothing soft about her. Her muscles were like steel cables. Once she was up he followed. They crawled through the tunnel and squirmed out into the daylight. Rhada blinked and blinked and just stared upward. To his amazement she began to cry. Tears ran down her filthy cheeks.

"Thank you. Thank you," she whispered. "Thank you for getting me out."

He felt incredibly good about her words, but the tears bothered him enormously. He had not thought she was capable of such a thing.

"We're not home yet. We've got a long way go."

"It doesn't matter now," she said. "I've seen the sky."

CHAPTER TWENTY-THREE

Lieutenant Gregory Sadgipour soared down the corridor, taking thirty-meter strides. Sergeant McGill and the rest of the squad were right behind him. He'd almost forgotten what it was like to wear power armor. The suit's anti-grav unit could nullify his apparent weight or in this case, almost nullify it, and allow him to take these long gliding motions along the corridors. Even though the ceiling was only four meters high, he could go about thirty kilometers an hour in this fashion.

They had already caught up with, and passed, the squads of city volunteers they had sent off to the gate, even though they had a fifteen-minute head start. Up ahead he could see a pair of utility scooters carrying the medical team he had dispatched even earlier. And just coming into view now was the south gate. He switched on his powerspecs and zoomed in. He was relieved to see that the scouts were still holding their barricade. It was only another minute before he and his Marines bounced to a halt among them. Immediately Blaire Sujumi came up to him.

"What's the situation?" asked Greg.

"The Skraks have tried to get in twice. We drove them off both times. But I've got three dead and six wounded. Where the hell were you?" The young man was clearly angry and Greg winced when he saw the dead and wounded. Just a few seconds later, the first scooter arrived with the medics.

"I'm sorry we're late, but we had a lot of trouble getting into the armory. Droid trouble, too. We lost some of our own people. We got here as quickly as we could. You did a good job holding this position, Blaire." Sujumi seemed slightly mollified, but still not happy.

"There are Skraks ranging around all over out there. I think there are a bunch of them right above the gate. I lost two of my people when I sent a party out to check."

"All right. You've got two hundred armed reinforcements on the way. They should be here in about ten minutes. In the meantime we'll go out and secure the immediate area. What about the mercenaries?"

"They're holed up in a position about two klicks west of here. The Skraks have them penned in. Be careful out there! The Skraks have picked up all the weapons they could get their hands on."

"Thanks, we'll be careful." Greg was about to order his Marines forward when he noticed Doug Rawlins propped against the wall. He headed over to him.

"How are you doing, Doug?"

"Not too bad," answered the engineer. He looked Greg up and down and scowled. "Guess I'll have to wait until you get out of that tin can before I kick your ass. About time you guys got here. I've been holding off these Skraks all by myself."

"Well, you did a good job of it. Here, the medics will get you back to the infirmary." As he spoke, two people from the city came over to Doug and helped him toward the scooter. Greg turned back to his Marines.

"Sergeant McGill, leave two men here to help secure the gate. The rest of us will clear out the immediate area."

"Yes, sir! Hammond! Tanner! Secure this area and wait for orders. The rest of you prepare to advance. Full combat mode, people, the Skraks are right outside!"

The Marines stepped over the barricade and moved toward the gate. Greg was right behind. He armed his weapons and put his scanners on active. The heads-up display in his helmet flowed with information.

McGill made his dispositions and then Greg gave him the go-ahead. The squad bounded out of the entrance and then spun to cover every direction. Almost instantly, fire started raining down on them from above. Fortunately it was just lighter stuff and a half second later the Marines were returning the fire. Greg followed them out, ready to fight. His scanners immediately picked up a number of power sources on the slope above the gate, but as Chtak had warned weeks ago, there was very little IR signature to pinpoint the enemy. The targeting reticule on his HUD followed his eye movements, but he could not see anything specific to fire at. That wasn't stopping his Marines from firing, though. Plasma bolts and pulse laser fire blanketed the slope, kicking up dust and debris. The enemy fire had almost completely stopped.

"First section, up and at 'em!" ordered McGill. Immediately, four troopers leaped up the cliff. Their anti-gravs allowed them to go forty meters almost straight up in a bound. They were firing as they soared upward, their new position revealing targets as they went. They landed on the cliff face and then jumped again, rising even higher. Plasma and laser fire flashed and winked and Greg saw bits of stuff flying away that was not rock or dirt. His troopers were finding the enemy. The first section bounced around on the slopes for a few more minutes, firing occasionally, and then reported the area secure.

"Hold them here, Sergeant. I'll be back in a minute," said Greg.

"Yes, sir," said McGill.

Greg went back through the gate and up to the barricade. The scooters had left and Doug Rawlins with them. About two hundred meters up the corridor he could see the first of the volunteer squads approaching. A few minutes later they arrived. Greg called Blaire Sujumi and the squad leader over to him.

"Blaire, the slopes above the gate have been cleared out. If you could send a few of your scouts out to form a picket line, we can send the new folks up there to secure it completely. More squads will be arriving at intervals—in fact, here comes the next one now. You should be able to set up a secure perimeter."

"Right, but what are you going to be doing?"

"Skrak hunting."

"Okay, have fun."

"Right."

Greg closed his helmet and went back outside. It took a few minutes for Blaire to get his people in place and the fresh squads into position, but then Greg and the rest of his Marines headed south in a broad skirmish line. For the first half a kilometer they saw nothing except for bodies and wrecked equipment. Greg noted with some amusement that the point defense laser they had worried about so much had been completely smashed. As they bounced up the first ridge they started to take some fire from small groups of Skraks. Once again, it was only light weapons and posed no danger to them. As each group was spotted, two or three Marines would close in on them and wipe them out. It soon became obvious that the Skraks did not know how to deal with the power armor and they began to fall back in front of them. It also became obvious that there weren't all that many of them left in this neighborhood—not that were alive anyway; there were hundreds of bodies. He directed his sensors toward where the mercenaries had set up their position and saw why: there were still plenty of Skraks over that way. Several hundred at least that he could spot and probably as many more that he couldn't.

The question now became what to do about them? Both the Skraks and the mercenaries were enemies and it might make sense just to let them kill each other. As he pondered, a Skrak rose up out of a small crater and fired a laser at him. He dodged aside and fixed his targeting reticule on the creature. It was only seventy meters away and he blew it in half with the first shot from his plasma gun. Then he inspected his suit where he had been hit. The laser had drilled a centimeter-deep hole in the armor. Another half a centimeter and it would have gone through. He'd have to hope he did not get hit in that exact spot again.

"Sorry about that, sir," said Sergeant McGill through the com. "Hard to spot the blighters in all this mess."

"No problem, Sarge. Let's start heading west and see how the mercs are making out."

"Yes, sir."

Greg had made up his mind. He did not want to let the Skraks withdraw or get away. They would head back to their caves and that would make it all the harder to rescue Rhada and Claritta. He very much wanted to head for those caves this instant, but he had duties to perform here. He would have to wait.

They bounced about a kilometer west and then began to draw some fire from the Skraks who had the mercenaries hemmed in. Greg launched a miniature sensor drone and sent it high above the battlefield, trying to get a better picture of what was going on. He was a little shocked when the IR scan only showed about fifty heat sources from the mercenary position. He had not realized they had been so badly chewed up. The heat and energy readings from the Skrak positions were less reliable, but there seemed to be three or four hundred of them ringing the mercenaries. He shifted to a wider angle and was relieved to see that there were very few other contacts in the vicinity. A few isolated parties here and there, but the Skraks facing the mercenaries seemed to be the bulk of them.

He hesitated for another few seconds and then keyed his communications to a general wavelength.

"Attention, any soldier from Wolfe's Free Mercenaries please respond. This is Lieutenant Gregory Sadgipour from the Star League Marines." No response. He tried again. On the third attempt, he got an answer.

"All right, Leaguie, what the hell do you want? We're kind of busy right now."

"Who am I speaking to?"

"This is Major Hannahs from the cruiser *Fenris*. Now what do you want?"

"Major, I'm about a klick away from your position. I've got twelve troopers in power armor and I wanted to discuss your situation."

"Our situation? Our situation stinks, as you bloody well know! You led those damn things here! Them and the droids. Three-quarters of my people are dead thanks to you!"

"This is League territory and you came here with hostile intent, Major. I don't think you have any cause for complaint."

"The hell I don't!" Greg suddenly heard a loud burst of firing in the background and some urgent shouts. There was a long pause before Hannahs came back. "But if you can see my situation you see we could use some help. If you're offering, I won't turn it down."

"Well, actually, Major, I had something else in mind."

"Like what?"

"I think we should talk about your surrender."

"We're in high orbit, ma'am," said Ensign Bartlett. "Holding station right over the base."

"Very good," said Captain Jaq Ellsworth. "Svetlana, try and make contact with our ground party."

"Yes,. ma'am."

"Skipper, we've got torpedo tube two working again—I think," said Commander van Rossum. "Getting a few strange telemetry readings, but it should work."

"Good. What about the rest of the repairs?"

"Nothing beyond what I reported a few minutes ago. We're still working on the other things."

"All right. Miss... ah... Wells, please launch a sensor drone and have it stay opposite us in orbit. With the planet here we can't afford to let anything sneak up on us."

"Uh, yes, ma'am." The replacement sensor officer looked over her controls in a small frenzy. After a moment Commander Bradley leaned over and pointed out the right button. "Drone launched, ma'am," she said, blushing a nice pink.

Ellsworth smiled in spite of her anxiety, but the smile faded quickly. Well, they were here, in orbit around Tractenberg IIIc. They had bamboozled the enemy for five solid hours and now they were where they wanted to be.

But did they really want to be here? Wolfe's battleship would be in weapons range in only another ten minutes. Ellsworth planned to keep the planet interposed for as long as possible, but even decelerating as it was, the battleship would reach orbit in forty minutes at most. Wolfe's other ships had regrouped and they would be here thirty minutes after that. What then?

They couldn't win. Not on their own. They needed help, but was there any help in the offing? She looked at the sensor display showing the planet. There were a few faint energy readings, but the same low-level glow from a fusion plant in stand-by mode had not changed since their first day here. What was happening down there? Could they do the job in the time remaining? And if they could not, what should she do? It was already too late to run. From a dead stop, she could not outrun Wolfe's ship this time. They would catch her and that would be the end.

"Ma'am?" said Lieutenant Terletsky, "I've got Lieutenant Chtak'Chr, putting him on the monitor."

The screen lit up and she was facing the Kt'Ktrian Survey Officer. She was surprised to see several bandages on him.

"Greeting, Captain, it is good to see you."

"And you, Lieutenant. Have you been injured?"

"Nothing serious, ma'am. There has been some fighting down here, but we are now in possession of the Marine armory and the central control area."

"Excellent, Lieutenant! But I'm not reading an active fusion plant on sensors. Are you going to be able to get that installation ready for our guests?"

The alien twitched his whiskers in a rather distracting fashion. "That is proving to be harder than we had hoped, Captain. Would it be possible for you to send down Mister Haussler and the other technicians you have aboard? They could be of considerable use in this situation."

A twinge of panic went through her. They didn't even know how to fire up the fusion plant! "Uh, yes, we were getting ready to send down three shuttle loads of Marines, I'll pull some of them and send the technicians instead."

"Very good. I will have scooters waiting for them at the South Gate."

"Lieutenant, that battleship is going to be right overhead in forty minutes. If you aren't ready down there we are going to be truly and royally screwed." Chtak's whiskers twitched again.

"We shall do our very best, Captain. I have people checking out all the necessary equipment and we shall try to be ready."

"All right, I'll be sending down those people right away. Ellsworth out." She looked to her executive officer.

"Brad, you heard that. Get those people to the shuttle on the double. Helm, take us down. Hold station right above the atmosphere."

"Yes, ma'am," said Bradley and Bartlett in unison.

She frowned and looked at the pulsing icon for the battleship getting closer by the minute. This was going to be close.

Too damn close.

Greg Sadgipour took another thirty-meter leap and smiled to himself. They were heading for the caves. Heading for Rhada! At last!

The mercenary ground commander had reluctantly agreed to surrender. Greg had led his Marines, supported by a hundred of the city volunteers, and smashed through the Skrak lines. The Skraks had drawn back and the battered, dispirited mercs had come stumbling out of their holes and allowed themselves to be escorted away. They had been disarmed and were now under guard in a storeroom in the base. They looked to be in no shape to cause any more trouble.

The Skraks seemed to have had enough for one day as well. The power armor was just too much for them. After losing half their number, they were retreating west through the foothills, heading back to their caves. Greg and his troopers were going to get there first. The volunteers and a dozen scouts were pursuing them, but Greg had taken his Marines and swung around their flank at full speed and were going to be waiting for them at the cavern entrance. It would be much easier to deal with the Skraks out in the open. They should get there at least thirty minutes before the Skraks and Greg fully intended to make use of that time to find and rescue the girls. Nothing was going to stop him this time!

"Lieutenant," said McGill, "there's something up ahead, doesn't look like Skraks."

Greg looked at his sensor display and spotted the IR signature McGill was talking about. Nine hundred meters ahead and a little to their right. He altered his course slightly and closed the distance. At five hundred meters he spotted two human figures and zoomed in on them with the built-in powerspecs…

…and nearly fell on his face.

"Rhada!"

He was so startled that he simply forgot to jump again. Fortunately his suit was smart enough to bounce him to a gentle halt instead of letting him plow a furrow in the ground with his armored body.

Rhada. She was alive. She was here. He started bouncing forward again. He was soon close enough to see her clearly. It was really her. He could also see who was with her: Stewart Paalova. Stewart had rescued her. That was what Blaire Sujumi had meant when he said that Stewart had not come back with them. He had gone into those caves and rescued Rhada. His sense of incredible relief was mixed with a swirling sense of jealousy. He mentally slapped himself. *At least she's safe! But where is Ritta Torres?*

A moment later he skidded to a halt in front of them. They had both stopped when they saw the Marines coming. Greg threw open his visor and then froze in shock.

"My God, Rhada, are you all right?" She looked like she had fallen into a meat grinder! She was battered and cut and bruised and covered with blood and filth from head to foot. Tears had made muddy little tracks down her cheeks. She looked mortally weary. Paalova was half carrying her. And she was practically naked. She was wearing Paalova's vest which was far too big and yet still covered very little of her. She looked up at him.

"Hello, Greg." That was all. Nothing more.

"Where's Ritta?" He had to ask even though the answer was completely obvious. Rhada just dropped her eyes and shook her head.

"I'm sorry," said Greg. Then he looked at Paalova. He had an arm around her. His feelings of jealousy flared up, but he was an honest man. He had to say it, no matter how hard it was.

"Thanks, Stewart. Thanks for getting her out."

Paalova snorted a tired laugh, shrugged and shook his head. "Don't thank me. She saved both of us. I don't know what sort of medals your Star League Navy gives out, but she's earned every one of them in the book today."

"I, uh, I think she needs medical attention more than medals right now, Stewart." Paalova nodded.

"Sir," said Sergeant McGill, "why don't you take her back to the base and see she gets the proper care. The rest of us can secure those caves." Greg hesitated, but Paalova brought Rhada over to Greg.

"Sounds good to me," he said. "I can go with the sergeant and point out the entrances. There are only a handful of Skraks left in the caves right now."

Greg still hesitated—this was his command—but McGill slapped an armored hand against his armored shoulder. "Go ahead, sir. She needs a doctor. We can handle things here."

"All right," said Greg finally. He carefully lifted Rhada into his arms. He took one last look around and then headed back toward the base. He set the anti-grav for almost complete nullification of their weight and took long, hundred meter bounds. It wasn't a good thing to do in a battle, since it left you a sitting duck for seconds at a time, but it was the gentlest possible ride for Rhada. He set his course to go further south in an arc that should take them clear of any Skraks. He could not afford to come under fire with this precious cargo! He radioed Chtak and told him to send a scooter to the gate and to have a doctor ready. Chtak sounded very pleased to hear that Rhada was alive. He assured him that one of the doctors from the city was already getting the infirmary up and running.

During those seconds in the air on each bounce he looked at her. Close up, her injuries seemed even worse: Ugly bruises and nasty tears in her skin scabbed over with blood. But she was alive! She stared up at him and smiled weakly.

"I'm sorry," he said. "I'm sorry I didn't come for you. I tried, but they...." no, no he wouldn't blame anyone else. "I tried, but I couldn't get there."

"It's all right," she said. "The worst of it was all done before you could possibly have come. They killed Ritta in the first two hours. After that... after that..." she trailed off.

"Stewart said you saved both of you."

"I... I got loose when someone attacked the cave. We bumped into each other and we got out. I'll tell you the rest later. I'm kind of tired right now."

"You rest, we'll be there soon."

She just lay there in his metal arms, looking up at the sky. In spite of her wounds and the filth she seemed very beautiful to him. The wind blew the vest open and she was virtually naked, but she did not seem to care. He had dreamed of seeing her naked, but not quite like this. Paalova had seen her naked, too...

He reached the gate just as a trio of shuttles touched down.

"That did it. The reactor is coming on line. We should have power in about fifteen minutes."

Chtak'Chr looked up in considerable surprise. He moved over to the control console and stared at where the man was pointing. It was true. Chtak had been trying to get the auxiliary reactor started for over half an hour without success. This Mister Haussler had only been here for five minutes and he had succeeded!

"That is wonderful, but how did you do this?" he asked in amazement.

"Tricked it," said the human in obvious satisfaction. "It's following the orders someone gave it twenty years ago and without the proper codes it's not going accept new orders."

"I know that," said Chtak. "So how did you manage this?"

"If you can't go through, you go around. This thing was programmed to fire itself up every ten months to recharge the base's batteries and capacitors. It was scheduled to do that again four months from now. I figured we couldn't afford to wait for four months so I just made a few little adjustments to the internal clock. It thinks it's four months later than it is and so it's coming on line. Now all we have to do is get down there and engage the manual overrides once it's up to keep it from shutting itself down again."

"Amazing, I never would have thought of that," said Chtak in admiration.

"That's because you critters aren't naturally sneaky like us apes."

"Perhaps not. But in addition to the reactor, we are going to need several other items activated." Chtak pointed to the huge engineering schematic that covered one wall of the central control room. He checked off the items he was referring to. "We have to get power to them, we have to get them working, and we have to do it in the next twenty minutes."

Haussler looked and then shook his head. "No way. Can't be done. The reactor will come on line in fifteen, but it will be another ten before we can start drawing power from it. As for those other things, I'll have to take a look."

Chtak twitched his whiskers. "The enemy battleship will be overhead in twenty minutes. We must be ready."

"You should have gotten started on this sooner, Lieutenant. There is no way to do this faster."

Chtak's whiskers twitched even more rapidly. "Then we must find a way to delay the enemy."

Jaq Ellsworth closed the connection with her survey officer and turned to her exec. "We need to buy some time, Brad."

"Yes, ma'am."

"The question is: how?"

Ellsworth pulled up the tactical display and studied it. Wolfe's battleship was continuing to decelerate, but it was less than twenty minutes away now. Its course had taken it out beyond the moon's orbit, so from where *Gilgamesh* was hovering over the base, the enemy was still hidden. But in eighteen minutes they would come curving around the planet and they would be here.

"The only thing I can think of is to try and convince Wolfe to chase us around the planet the other way. If we were to slip around to the opposite side and get him to chase us back this way—the long way around, we could pick up another fifteen or twenty minutes."

"Yes, that could work, ma'am," said Bradley. "But how do we get him to do that?"

"Bait, Commander. We must be the bait."

"If you say so, Skipper."

"I do. Mister Bartlett, bring us about. A quick trip around to the other side of the moon, if you please. All ahead two-thirds."

"Aye, aye, ma'am."

"Brad, get the crew back to their battlestations."

"Right, Skipper."

After they had eluded the enemy ships, Ellsworth had let the crew stand down from General Quarters and get something to eat. Only the damage control parties had to keep at it. She hoped the break would allow the rest of them to keep their fighting edge.

Because they were surely going to need it.

"Sir, the target is moving around the planet and coming toward us. We may have a line of sight to them in just a few minutes," said the sensor operator on the battleship *Vindicator*.

"Probably hoping to take a few potshots at us and duck back behind the planet," said Norman Wolfe. "Captain Allen, I want your weapons crews on full alert. Bring the shields up to maximum. If Ellsworth does poke her nose out, I want you to be ready to chop it off!"

"Yes, sir, we'll be ready."

Charles Florkowski watched the activity on the bridge around him. He still had no official job. He just sat at an unused control console and observed.

He did not like what he was seeing.

What was Ellsworth up to now? She had maneuvered so skillfully up to this point. Why was she going to accept battle at such horrible odds? When she had headed back to the moon, he had assumed it was to try and pick up her stranded ground party. She had plenty of time to do that and still get away. He had suspected that her people down there had secretly gotten into the base and collected enough nano-chips, plus the software instructions for making more, and she was going to try and make a run for it back to Leavitte and leave this world to Wolfe. That's what he would have done in her place. But she was still here. Had she run into some unexpected snag? He could only hope so.

In another few minutes they would have her. Or so it seemed. He reminded himself that twice before it had looked like they had her only for her to pull another trick out of her hat.

But what trick could she pull now? Florkowski wished they had a better sensor picture. Since the mercenaries' troops on the ground had gone silent they were dependent on getting information relayed from the two ships Wolfe had stationed above the planet's poles for that purpose. But they were nearly a million kilometers away from here and the information was sketchy and always at least seven seconds out of date. Wolfe should launch a few sensor drones, but the mercenary was so damn stingy with any sort of expendable resources. He had not even allowed his ships to employ their nuclear missiles during the fighting. Granted, they wouldn't be very effective against *Gilgamesh's* point defense, but you could still get lucky. Clearly, Wolfe's long years as a raider and mercenary had made him very leery of wasting resources. Except this time it would not be a waste.

"Looks like they are moving… there they are!" exclaimed the sensor tech.

"Fire!" commanded Captain Allen. An instant later the ship shook slightly with the impact of enemy weapons.

"Two blast-throughs forward," said the damage control officer. "Minor hull damage; sensor twenty-two is out."

"They are back down behind the curve again, sir."

"What did we do to them?" demanded Wolfe.

"At least eight solid hits. Probably a few blast-throughs. I'm reading a few bits of debris, sir."

"Good. Watch sharp. She'll probably do it again as soon as her damn torpedoes are recharged."

And indeed she did. A minute later *Gilgamesh* appeared in front of them and the ship shook again. "Laser fourteen is out of action, sir," reported the DC officer.

"We hit them again, sir," said the sensor tech. "Some air and water vapor this time."

"Good shooting, Captain," said Wolfe. "But I'm getting annoyed with Ellsworth again. Change course to go directly after her, Captain."

"Aye, aye, sir."

Florkowski twitched. Wolfe was going to ignore his advice about heading for the base? He was going to start chasing Ellsworth directly again? Hadn't he learned anything?

"Commodore, if we continue to head for the base, Ellsworth is bound to engage us. She certainly would have run already if she planned to."

"Perhaps, Commander, but if I go on around the planet the way you suggest, it will give her a perfect opportunity to chase *us* and put a couple of torpedoes up our ass. I have no intention of letting her do that. Our stern armor is a lot thinner than on the bow. Even if she continues to play hide and seek with us like this, our other ships will be here soon and catch her between us. Then we can squash her like a bug."

"I see, sir." Florkowski frowned. What Wolfe said was true, but he still did not like this.

And he really wished he could get an accurate sensor read on that base!

"Good news, Mister Haussler," said Chtak'Chr. "The Captain has managed to draw the enemy away for a while. We should have an extra twenty minutes or so."

"Well, I wish I had better news for you, Lieutenant," said Haussler in reply.

"Oh dear, what's wrong now?"

"Not everything. We have the fusion plant up and running. The manual overrides are in operation and we have power. I should even have it routed where you want it in a few more minutes."

"That sounds very good. So what is the problem?'

"These other things you want on-line. It's not going to happen. At least not quickly. The shields are out of commission altogether. Someone purged the controlling computers completely."

"That probably happened during the battle years ago," said Chtak. "The Darj'Nang were having their pawns sabotage things down here."

"Well, whatever happened, the shields are out. Now these sensor stations you had called for have all been trashed, too. Looks like they got blasted, so there's no hope there."

"Perhaps we can get a sensor feed from *Gilgamesh*."

"Maybe, but it wouldn't matter, because the fire control computers have all been purged, just like the ones for the shields. We couldn't use the data even if we had it."

"Surely there must be a back-up copy of the software," said Chtak in growing alarm.

"No doubt there is, Lieutenant, but there is no way in hell I'm going to find it and get it reloaded in the next twenty-five minutes!"

"I see." Chtak thought furiously. They could not have come this close to fail just at the end!

"I'm sorry, Lieutenant," said Haussler. "As much as I hate to admit it, I can't perform miracles. So I sure hope you've got an alternative idea."

Chtak stared at the human for a moment as an idea struck him.

"Perhaps I do, Mister Haussler, perhaps I do."

Rhada McClerndon sat on the exam table in the infirmary and stared at the pale green wall. It was a very soothing color, really. A woman doctor and a medic hovered around her saying cheerful things that she really wasn't listening to. She was very, very tired. And she was in pain, although they had given her something for that.

They had carefully peeled off Stewart's bloody vest, reopening several of her wounds in the process. They had also tried to cut off the sword belt that she had still been wearing. She had woken up enough to forbid that. The belt and the sword were sitting on a table a few meters away. She had made them promise they would not lose it.

So she was sitting on the table wearing nothing at all. A medical gown was piled nearby, but there were so many cuts and scratches, gouges and bruises on her that they had not been able to put it on her yet. They were carefully cleaning her a bit at a time and treating her injuries as they went. Rhada had suggested they just toss her in a shower for an hour or two, but they had only laughed. She had been completely serious... She *really* wanted a shower.

"Rhada! Rhada!" She heard someone calling her name. She looked up and an icicle of dread shot through her. Doug Rawlins was standing in the door of the exam room. His tunic and shirt were off. He had bandages and medical gel all over his chest, arms and part of his face. He was staring at her with wide eyes. She could clearly see the question in those eyes and she didn't know what to tell him.

"Lieutenant, do you mind?" asked the doctor tartly. "I'm trying to treat the ensign, and she should have some privacy. And you should be in bed!"

"Rhada, I just heard you were here! Where's Ritta?" Doug ignored the doctor and came into the room and stood only a meter away from her. The look on his face was so fearful and anguished, she found herself crying.

"I'm sorry, Doug," she said, shaking her head. "I'm so sorry." The man visibly drooped. He seemed to have shrunk by half a meter at least.

"Hell, hell, hell..." he muttered.

"She... she was very brave, Doug. She was so brave. Braver than me. She wouldn't give them anything. She wouldn't give in... so they killed her. I'm still alive because I gave in. Ritta wouldn't. She was very brave."

He just stood there shaking his head until the medic led him away. Rhada was still crying.

"I'm sorry about that, Ensign. You don't need that right now. Here, let me give you something to help you relax." Rhada felt a hypo at her neck briefly. "My God, you've taken a beating! Could you raise your arm? I want to take a look at this wound on your side."

Rhada did as she was asked and tried to stop crying. She felt so sad for Doug. Would he hate her after this because she was alive and Ritta wasn't?

Little by little the doctor worked her way around Rhada's body. Cleaning and medicating and patching. At the rate she was patching her, she wasn't going to need any clothes after all. Rhada looked up as the door opened again. In spite of her gloom she smiled when she saw Chtak.

"Chtak! You are a sight for sore eyes! I've missed you."

But Chtak was not a sight for the doctor's sore eyes. "Lieutenant, I am treating this patient! Will you please get the hell out of here!"

"I'm sorry, Doctor, but this is very urgent; I must speak to Ensign McClerndon. And Rhada, I am very glad to see you, too."

"Lieutenant, whatever it is will have to wait until…"

"I'm sorry, ma'am, but it cannot. I must insist." Rhada's eyes widened slightly. For Chtak to have interrupted someone like that was almost unheard of. It must be pretty important.

"What's up, Chtak?" she asked.

"I'm sorry to do this to you, but we need your help. Rather urgently."

"My help?" she said in surprise. "What can I possibly do to help anyone right now?"

"There is not much time, but I will try to explain. *Gilgamesh* was attacked by a number of mercenary spaceships."

"Yes, I heard a bit about that from Greg on the way here."

"All right. *Gilgamesh* has managed to draw the enemy off for a while, but they are now returning. In about twenty minutes a battleship will entering orbit and coming right over our heads."

"That doesn't sound too good," said Rhada. She was having trouble concentrating on what Chtak was saying. The painkillers and whatever the doctor had just given her and her fatigue were catching up with her. She felt lightheaded and almost giddy. She felt a strange urge to laugh at the way Chtak's whiskers were twitching. "But what can I do to help?"

"We would like you to destroy that battleship for us."

"What!? Are you crazy?"

"I hope not," said Chtak earnestly. "We have activated some of the facilities here at the base. In particular, we have managed to get part of the defensive armament operational. Rhada, we have a 200 centimeter, Mark XXIV particle cannon ready to fire."

"Cool."

"No, we are warming it up now. The capacitors will be at full charge very shortly." Rhada bit back a giggle.

"But, Rhada, the base sensors and fire control systems are not operational. We are going to have to fire that cannon using only the weapon's emergency optical sights. Through a rather embarrassing oversight, you are the only person we have here right now with naval gunnery experience. There's no time to bring another gunner down from *Gilgamesh*. And in any case..."

"...I'm the best damn shot on the whole ship," finished Rhada.

"Indeed. Are you willing to try?"

"Sure. I'll try." She slid off the exam table and nearly fell when her legs refused to support her. Chtak helped hold her up. His fur felt very nice and warm; not at all like Skrak skin. The doctor was furious.

"Ensign! Get your tush back on this table right now!"

"Sorry, doctor, duty calls."

"It's calling you right here! You're in no shape to do anything except let me treat you!" Chtak steadied Rhada and then stepped in front of the doctor.

"I'm sorry, ma'am, but I really must borrow your patient for a while. I don't mean to be melodramatic, but everyone here is counting on her to do this. If we fail it isn't going to matter whether she gets proper medical attention or not."

The woman frowned and shook her head. "Look at her, she can't even stand up on her own!"

"You're going to have to give me something, Doc," said Rhada. "Something to keep me going for a while."

"I just gave you a sedative! I can't give you a stimulant right on top of it!"

"I don't like it either, Doctor," said Chtak, "but there really isn't any choice. In about fifteen minutes that battleship is going to start dropping bombs on us."

The woman's frown grew deeper, but she suddenly turned away and started rummaging through her equipment. A moment later she returned with a hypo. She was muttering under her breath as she injected Rhada.

"This is pretty powerful, ensign, so be careful. And it will probably counteract the painkillers."

For a minute or so nothing seemed to be happening and Rhada swayed slightly back and forth. But then she could feel her heart beating faster. Her head, which had been all slow and fuzzy, started to clear. And, as she had been warned, the pain from her wounds was suddenly back, full force.

"Ouch," she said. It hurt, but she could stand and she could think.

"Isn't there anything you can do for her pain, doctor?" asked Chtak.

"I don't dare give her anything else on top of what she's already got in her. It could send her system into shock and then she couldn't fire your damn cannon."

"It's all right, Chtak, I can go for a few minutes more."

The doctor fitted the gown over her carefully. It seemed to tug at every cut and scrape. Sometimes it was definitely better not to have to wear clothes. She got her some soft slippers, too. All the while, Rhada was mentally evaluating the problem.

"Chtak, how close is the target going to be? How fast will it be moving?"

"I cannot predict exactly, but it should be in a fairly low orbit, and not moving too much faster than orbital velocity. So the range should be two or three thousand kilometers and the speed between fifteen and twenty kilometers per second. But that is just a guess. Do you think you can do that?"

Rhada's mind was suddenly working at high speed. The drug was kicking in. She quickly did some calculations, estimating the time it would take for the particle beam to reach the target and how far the target would move in that time. She smiled when she realized that the enemy ship would only move a few hundred meters. She would hardly have to lead it at all.

"Not a problem, Chtak," she said. She walked over to the table and picked up her sword and fastened the sword belt on over her gown. Her smile drew back into a feral grin.

"It'll be like smashing eggs in a nest."

"The number two tube is out again, Skipper," said Commander van Rossum from his damage control station. "That last hit shook something loose. DC teams are on the way."

"Understood," said Ellsworth.

"We've got more casualties than the SickBay can handle, Skipper," reported Karl Bradley. "They are setting up a triage in the mess hall. We're getting hit pretty bad."

Jaq nodded and gritted her teeth. Her ship was being wrecked. She was dishing it out pretty good, too, but the odds were just too great. The enemy battleship had heavier shields, heavier armor and a lot more weapons. Each time *Gilgamesh* popped up from around the curve of the planet to take a shot, they took a lot more shots in return. Nothing crippling yet, but they could not take a lot more. But they had to keep Wolfe interested and keep him coming.

"We'll be over the base in seven minutes, ma'am," said Lieutenant

Pliskin. "The target should be within range of the base about two minutes later."

"Commander Bradley, this is going to be very tricky. The base is not going to have any shields. If Wolfe were to spot the cannon and get a shot off first, or if one of his other ship spots it and he starts sending missiles ahead of him, we could lose our chance."

"Yes, ma'am, I suppose that's true. But what can we do about it?"

"We need to provide Mister Wolfe with something even more interesting to keep his attention."

"I was afraid you were going to say that. What do you have in mind?"

Ellsworth smiled a grim smile. "Mister Bartlett, reduce our speed. Let them catch up with us a bit."

Rhada sat on the scooter and watched the walls of the corridor zip by. They must be doing nearly forty kilometers an hour and the wind was trying to whip her hair around. But it was so filthy and matted that it just flapped half-heartedly. She still felt a bit dizzy and the zipping corridors were not helping. It seemed so very strange being here. After weeks—had it only been weeks?—in the Skrak caves, the sudden transition to the clean and well-lit corridors of the League base was very jarring.

She could not really believe she was out of there. The nightmare in the caves; the incredible scramble out into the sunshine; the wary trek away from the caverns; being found by Greg. It was all so…she didn't have a word for it. But she was so glad to be out. She had a sudden memory of Stewart and her hiding from that small party of Skraks who were dragging a terrified and naked man—one of the mercenaries, apparently—toward the caves. Sspara's message had gotten through. Rhada closed her eyes and shuddered. If she had not gotten away that man would be with her right now and…

"I was so glad to learn that you were alive, Rhada," said Chtak, suddenly. She opened her eyes and looked at him. He was driving the scooter in a fashion that made her want to laugh again. The drug the doctor had given her was doing weird things to her emotions.

"It's good to be alive."

"Greg was frantic. We nearly had to stun him to keep him from charging after you. I was quite worried myself."

Rhada felt a warm glow of affection both for Greg and her teacher. Then she thought of Ritta and Doug and she was nearly crying again. She bit on her tongue and forced herself to think about nothing but the task at hand.

As if in answer to her thought, the corridor came to an end and Chtak braked the scooter to a halt. A large, armored door was standing open.

"We must hurry, Rhada. There is very little time."

She slid off the seat with a groan and hobbled through the door with Chtak close beside her. Damn, she was sore. On the other side she stopped and looked up in amazement. She had been expecting something pretty big, but this was just... incredible.

"Wow," she whispered. The particle cannon mount towered over her. A huge armored sphere with an ugly looking muzzle projecting from one side sat in the middle of an enormous chamber. The roof was high overhead: a heavily reinforced and retractable dome. A number of people were scurrying around while others stood with their heads poked into access panels along the side walls. Chtak directed her to the control chamber which seemed tiny next to the mammoth weapon.

As she stepped inside she was relieved to see that the layout was entirely familiar. Much newer than her gunnery station on *Gilgamesh*, but remarkably similar to what she had trained on at OCS.

"Can you do it?" asked Chtak.

"I think so." She sat down and started flipping switches.

"The enemy has reduced speed, sir," said the sensor tech on *Vindicator*. "We should have a clear shot in just a few seconds."

"It looks like we've brought them to bay," said Commodore Wolfe in anticipation.

"All weapons are standing by, Commodore," said Captain Allen.

"Good, but I think we may have an opportunity here, Captain. Ready the tractor beams. If the situation allows I want to try and capture that ship. It would make a nice prize and I do so want to meet Captain Ellsworth. After all the trouble she's caused me, I have a lot to say to her."

"Yes, sir."

Charles Florkowski looked on at what he expected to be the last moments of the League cruiser *Gilgamesh*. Ellsworth really was finished this time. With all the damage she had already taken, another close range encounter would end very quickly. She had managed to do considerable damage to *Vindicator*, but nothing that was going to change the outcome of this. But he rather doubted that Wolfe was going to get his wish and capture either the ship or Ellsworth. Surely she would blow herself up rather than face capture. His gaze shifted briefly to that other glowing spot on the tactical display. There was still no new information on that base. It worried him, but it probably made no difference now.

"Target in sight!" said the sensor tech.

"Fire!" commanded Captain Allen.

The battleship's massed lasers lashed out at the much smaller opponent. The ship lurched as *Gilgamesh* responded with a single plasma torpedo and three photon cannons. New damage reports flowed in, but it was nothing critical. *Gilgamesh* was spouting debris, air and water vapor as Wolfe's lasers raked her.

"They are not trying to disengage, sir," said Allen.

"Good. We have them. Pour it on, Captain, and stand by on the tractor beams."

They had to batter the target's shields completely down with a continuous rain of laser fire to get a tractor lock, but that was not going to take long. *Gilgamesh's* next salvo was only two photon cannons strong. They were clearly hurting her. Florkowski expected Ellsworth to turn enough to bring some of her other weapons to bear, but she did not. This made some sense, since it kept the ship's heavily armored bow to the enemy and protected those critical items like the power plant and drives, but she was rapidly losing her only forward firing weapons.

"Target's shield is down!"

"Engage tractors!"

"We've got them, sir! A solid lock!"

"Good work, Captain!" exclaimed Wolfe. "Now pull her teeth."

"Yes, sir! Weapons, precision fire on the enemy turrets."

Gilgamesh was caught in *Vindicator's* tractor beams. She was stuck. She could not dodge at all and her captor could now aim at precise points on the enemy ship. It only took one more salvo to reduce their foe to helplessness.

"I think that's it sir," said Allen. "Do you want to pull them in?"

"No, I think Captain Ellsworth might be desperate enough to scuttle her ship and try to take us with her. Leave them where they are and get the boarding parties to the shuttles."

* * *

"They've got us, ma'am," said Bradley. He did not look particularly happy about it.

"Helm, try and break us free," commanded Ellsworth.

"Skipper, there's no way we're going to break that lock," said Bradley.

"I know, but the bait should wiggle on the hook a bit, just to keep them interested."

"If you say so, ma'am. What do we do now?"

Ellsworth looked at her first officer. She ran her gaze around the rest of her bridge officers. They were all glancing at her nervously except for Ensign Bartlett who was vainly trying to pull the ship free from the enemy tractor beam.

What *was* she going to do? In a little over four minutes their orbit would bring them in sight of the base down on the planet. Wolfe's ship would take another minute or so. Then if everything went according to plan, the people down there would blow Norman Wolfe and his flagship to hell.

But what if that didn't happen? What if the cannon didn't fire? What if Wolfe destroyed it before it could fire? What if the plan did not work? The last hope of the Star League was out the airlock. If that happened, what was her duty then? Right now she needed to preserve her ship in a functional condition so if things did go right she could transport the nano-chips to where they were needed. But if that hope was lost, then what should she do? Blow up her ship? She had used both of her scuttling charges to blow a nice hole in the gas giant's rings a few hours ago, and she had no other nukes aboard. But she could still put the fusion plant on maximum and then shut down the containment field. That would wreck the ship just as thoroughly, although it probably wouldn't kill everyone.

A nice, quick, clean death would be preferable to what Wolfe and Florkowski had planned for them. Torture, rape and eventual sale into slavery for her crew. Probably a lot worse for her personally. But did she have the right to kill herself—or get herself killed resisting capture? Once her ship and her crew were gone, there was no hope whatever for the League. If she was still alive there was still a chance.

How far did duty demand she go? Was she expected to submit herself to a living hell for the one-in-a-billion chance that someday she might be able to turn the tables? What should she do?

The light on the sensor display that represented the base was crawling closer and closer. She would know for sure in a very few minutes. In the meantime…

She reached into the pocket of her vac suit and pulled out an antique gauss pistol. It felt very heavy and reassuring in her hand.

"Commander Bradley, pass the word to all hands: Prepare to repel boarders."

"Rhada, we have about four minutes until the enemy is in sight," said Chtak.

"I know; almost ready." She flicked a last few switches and all the lights on her board were green. All except the normal targeting displays which were still blank. The capacitors would be at full charge in another ninety seconds. She pulled the optical targeting unit down so it hung in front of her. The two joysticks were in her hands. The trigger on the left joystick was the safety, and the one on the right, the actual trigger. She shifted the joysticks and the cannon began to move. She could see it moving through the small window in the control booth and she could feel the faint rumble as the massive weapon started to traverse.

A thrill ran down her spine. The controls were virtually identical to what she had used on *Gilgamesh*, but somehow she could sense the incredible power of the weapon. The cruiser's weapons had been designed to fight ships her own size. This one was meant to slug it out toe-to-toe with superdreadnoughts—and win. The power felt good in her hands. It felt like… like… it felt like having a sword in her hands.

But what if I miss?

The thought came out of nowhere and it rocked her to her core. What if she did miss? The enemy ship would return fire and without shields it would not take much to disable the cannon. Then the enemy would capture *Gilgamesh* and this base. If she survived the destruction of her weapon they might capture her, too. The image of that girl at the auction on Freeport flashed into her mind. *I wonder where she is now?* But then the image changed and it was her on the auction block. It could happen…

No. No it won't. Her hands tightened on the controls and she banished her doubts.

I'll never be a slave again.

"All right, Chtak," she said. "You can open the dome."

"Yes, opening now."

He hit a switch and there was a terrible squeal of metal and then dirt and small stones began raining down from the roof. The roof split into twelve, pie-shaped sections and retracted out, toward the walls. A shaft of bright sunshine streamed in.

"Clear the area and seal the control chamber."

"Yes, ma'am." A moment later the people were sprinting for the armored door. The heavy door to the control room shut and the noise stopped abruptly.

"We are ready to fire."

Gregory Sadgipour bounced through the foothills at the head of twenty-four power-armored Marines. Just ahead were the city volunteers who were pursing the Skraks. After delivering Rhada to the medics he had cooled his heels for twenty anxious minutes at the South Gate while the Marines who had come down on the shuttles had gotten suited up in power armor. Then it was only a matter of catching up with the Skraks.

Which they had just done. The city volunteers were scrambling over the rocks and small hillocks and trading a long range fire with the fleeing Skraks. Greg had been in contact with Sergeant McGill. His squad was at the cave entrances and waiting for Greg and the volunteers to chase the enemy into their arms. Greg had decided to reinforce the volunteers instead of making another flank run to get to the caves. The power armor support should allow the volunteers to avoid any unnecessary casualties.

Greg bounded up to one of the volunteer officers and flipped his visor up. "How's it going?" he asked.

"Okay," said the woman. "They aren't really trying to fight anymore, just to get away. But we're pressing them. With your help we should be able to—what the hell is that!?"

The ground was suddenly shaking and a terrible screeching noise filled the air. Greg looked up and saw that the small hillock they were next to was moving! Dust was boiling up and several dark, straight cracks had appeared in the ground. What was going on? In a flash, Greg knew what was going on.

Holy shit! It can't be!

He quickly called up the tactical map on his heads-up display. Dozens of blue and red icons crawled over it. Then he ordered the computer to superimpose a diagram of the base on the map. A large, circular object appeared, almost centered on his current position. It looked exactly like the large, circular object that Stewart Paalova had pointed out two weeks earlier.

Oh, my God! Greg keyed the general circuit and then turned on his external loudspeakers.

"Clear the area! Everyone get out! As fast as you can!" His amplified voice boomed across the hillside. He looked and saw that the hillock was disappearing and a large, nasty-looking tube was emerging from the ground. The end of it had a shimmering ionization glow forming. He scooped up the awestruck volunteer and bounced away.

"Come on, people! *Move!*"

"The boarding parties will be ready to shove off in just a few minutes, Commodore," said Captain Allen.

"Good. But tell them to be careful. They will have to approach from the front or the target might be able to shoot at them. They still have some broadside weapons. It would probably be best if they entered through some of the hull breaches rather than at an airlock. The Leaguies will be waiting for them there. Make sure they have the materials to build some temporary locks if need be. Sensors, I want a radar map of their forward hull right away."

"Yes, sir."

"Captain, tell your people they can use whatever force they need to secure the ship, but let them know I'll pay a double bonus for any officers they can capture and a triple bonus for Ellsworth."

"Yes, sir."

Charles Florkowski watched the activity around the bridge of *Vindicator*. It looked like this really was the end. In a few minutes the boarding parties would leave and eventually *Gilgamesh* would be captured and the prisoners would start coming back. He was really dreading seeing Ellsworth face to face. All of his fantasies for revenge seemed more like nightmares now. He was sincerely hoping she didn't allow herself to be taken alive. And the others, his former shipmates, how could he possibly face them?

A new light appeared on the sensor display on his console and his head jerked around. One of Wolfe's other ships was now close enough to get a good read on that base and was forwarding the data. His eyes widened when he saw that the energy levels from that faint contact had now multiplied a hundredfold. *They've got the fusion plant on-line down there!* And now there was a second strong energy reading about four kilometers to the southwest of the first. What did that mean? He was afraid he knew exactly what that meant! He looked up at the other officers. They were all busy preparing to board *Gilgamesh*. The sensor tech was getting the radar map of the hull Wolfe wanted and was paying no attention to this new reading.

"Commodore..."

"Not now, Mister Florkowski, I'm busy."

"Commodore, I really think..."

"I don't really care what you think right now, Florkowski. Shut up or I'll make you wait a month for your turn with Ellsworth."

Charles Florkowski rocked back in his chair and stared at the back of Wolfe's head. *That arrogant son of a bitch.* In that instant he knew he could no longer serve Wolfe. Just as he had known it with Ellsworth months ago, he now knew it was the same with Wolfe. He was even less worthy of his loyalty than Ellsworth had been!

He looked at the new contact. It would be in sight in less than five minutes. He was sure Wolfe would really like to know about that new contact, but now he had absolutely no responsibility to report it to him. His time with Norman Wolfe was fast coming to an end.

Without a backward glance he stood up and left the bridge.

Four minutes. He had about four minutes. As soon as he had come aboard he had made sure he knew the location of all the emergency equipment on *Vindicator*. He could get to one particular piece of equipment in less than thirty seconds. But he had to make a very important side trip first.

He broke into a run.

Rhada McClerndon stared into the targeting scope. The ships should be appearing over the horizon very shortly. But would she be able to spot them? The sky glare was very bad in spite of the powerful telescopes and filters she was using. She could not see any stars at all. The ships would be a lot brighter, but would she be able to spot them?

"*Gilgamesh* should be in sight now. Rhada, the enemy ship has them in a tractor beam, so be careful," said Chtak from beside her. He was in radio contact with the ship.

"I don't see it... wait, that must be it." A very faint, fuzzy blob of light had moved up over the horizon. It was really hard to see. The enemy ship would be a few seconds behind it. She hurriedly wiped the sweat out of her eyes and stared hard. Damn, this was not good.

She had not counted on…

The sky began to darken.

As she watched in amazement, the glare faded and the stars started to come out. What was happening? She pulled her head away from the eyepiece and looked out the small window. The shaft of sunlight coming down into the gun bay was gone.

"What's going on?"

"The gas giant is eclipsing the sun. It is nearly local noon," said Chtak.

She shoved her face against the eyepiece again. The sky was black now, but the ships would still be in the sunlight for a few seconds! She zoomed in on that first moving star and could clearly see the familiar shape of *Gilgamesh*. The thirty-centimeter telescopes were very good. She zoomed back out and looked again.

There!

A second star appeared on the horizon. It was much brighter than the first. She zoomed in on it. It was blurred and shimmering through the thick atmosphere, but she could easily see the shape of the enemy battleship. In fact, she could make out the huge head of some sort of animal that had been painted on the bow of the ship. She zoomed back out a bit and activated the targeting reticule. She moved the joysticks and began tracking the target. Out in the gun bay the cannon followed her motions.

The stereoscopic range finder was giving her the distance to the target. Twenty-five hundred kilometers and dropping fast. She moved the reticule so it was just in front of the target and then slid it along, following the target's motions. She would fire at two thousand.

Rhada was sweating and her heart was pounding. She would get only one chance.

That's all I need.

Twenty-two hundred… twenty-one hundred… closer and closer… almost there…

She adjusted the reticule a bit and squeezed the left-hand trigger. The reticule turned from green to red. One more tiny adjustment and her finger tightened on the right-hand trigger.

"Firing… *Now!*"

Greg was gliding through the air, a volunteer under each arm, when the landscape turned white. A glare brighter than a thousand suns blotted everything out as a man-made lightning bolt tore the sky in two.

A moment later he grunted with an impact on his armor and the volunteers twitched like rag dolls in his grasp as the concussion slammed into them. The blow nearly sent him sprawling, but he managed to land on his feet. He gently put down the stunned volunteers and looked up.

The incredible glow was fading, but there was still a sparkling trail leading up into the dark sky. It was pointing to a new star that was blossoming just to the side of the gas giant's gleaming rings.

Rhada's aim had been perfect. The beam blew through the battleship's shield; blew directly through the center of the painted wolf's head on the bow; blew out the other side of the ship and through the other side of the shield as well.

Then the ship's own motion dragged it through that beam of annihilation like a piece of wood through a buzz saw, slicing the battleship *Vindicator* in half, from bow to stern. Several thousand tons of the ship's structure and contents were instantly converted from a solid to a gas in the process and the resulting explosion blew the two halves into very tiny bits.

A half-dozen assault shuttles were just pulling away from *Vindicator* when it happened. Their occupants had one horrifying instant to realize that something had gone terribly wrong before the blast hit them. Five were so close they were torn apart completely in an eyeblink. The sixth survived, more or less in one piece, but the impact still killed everyone aboard. The shuttle, and its occupants, were just a slightly larger bit of debris in the rapidly expanding cloud that swept around the planet.

One other object had left the battleship prior to its destruction. This one survived intact, but acted as inert as all the rest of the debris.

The jolt nearly threw Jaq Ellsworth to the deck.

"We're loose!" exclaimed Ensign Bartlett. Jaq's eyes darted to the tactical display. The icon for Wolfe's ship was fading away. She looked to the small visual monitor and froze in amazement and relief.

"What the hell happened?" asked Bradley. Jaq touched a button and the visual display was put on the main monitor. It showed a fading explosion and a glittering cloud of debris.

"They did it," she whispered. Then in a louder voice: *"They did it!"*

It was suddenly deafening on the bridge as everyone there, including Jaq Ellsworth, cheered and shouted at the top of their lungs.

Rhada stared, without blinking, into the eyepiece at the remains of the target.

"Rhada!" exclaimed Chtak. His voice had always been high-pitched, but it was now reaching the edge of hearing. "Rhada! You did it! The ship is saying the enemy battleship has been destroyed! You did it!"

She leaned back and let go of the controls. Her hands were shaking. She looked at Chtak. "I know."

"Well done, Rhada! Well done!"

"Are we finished here?"

"I think so. For the moment."

"Good. Catch me."

Rhada passed out and slumped into Chtak's arms.

When the cheers died down enough for her to be heard, Jaq Ellsworth got the attention of her helmsman. "Mister Bartlett, bring us about and hold station over the base. Same as before."

"Aye, aye, ma'am!"

"So what now, Skipper?" asked Bradley. "There are still those other ships out there."

"We'll stick close to the base and that cannon. I have a feeling that the rest of Wolfe's people aren't going to want to tangle with us as long as that's around!"

Nor did they. The remaining ships of Wolfe's Free Mercenaries bent their courses to keep the planet between them and *Gilgamesh*. Their vectors brought them very close to the planet, but they were able to stop short of it. A spirited discussion between the captains was in progress when it was noticed that there was a radio beacon amidst the cloud of debris that was once the battleship *Vindicator*. The cloud's orbit brought it close to the ships and it was soon evident that the signal was coming from an escape pod. One of the ships extended a tractor beam to snag it.

There was great anticipation among the mercenaries. Had the legendary Norman Wolfe managed to cheat death once again? The disappointment among the crews (and the sighs of relief among the captains) were considerable when the pod only proved to contain a man and a woman: an engineering lieutenant and a power tech. Their explanations for how they, of all the crew, had managed to escape was a little odd, but no one really cared at this point; Wolfe was clearly dead. And engineers and power techs were always in demand so they were signed up to the crew of the ship who had rescued them and that was that.

A half-hour later, the captains agreed that no agreement could be reached on further cooperation and they officially disbanded Wolfe's Free Mercenaries. Shortly afterward, each ship set out on its own to look for greener pastures.

CHAPTER TWENTY-FOUR

Captain Jaqueline Ellsworth of the Star League cruiser *Gilgamesh* sat in her chair in the enormous conference room and stared at the tiny object sitting in the palm of her hand.

"So this is what it was all about," she said. "All the worry, all the effort, all the deaths. I sure hope it was worth it."

"I'm sure it will be, ma'am," said Karl Bradley. "The factories are coming on-line and we can produce all the nano-chips we need now. We can get our equipment operational and put the Star League back on its feet!"

"At least in theory," said Lieutenant Chtak'Chr.

Ellsworth frowned. "Lieutenant, when you start tossing out quali-fiers like that, I break out in hives." She glanced around at the other people in the room. They were meeting in the base with most of her senior staff, representatives from the city, and Consul Brown. "Is there something else we haven't thought of?"

"Well, ma'am, we can now start replacing the chips themselves, but there is still the issue of the software. We can repair a fusion reactor or a fire control system but without the actual software to make it run, it won't."

"Surely there must be copies, Lieutenant!"

"Not necessarily, ma'am. Many of these programs can be several million lines of code. Hard copy printouts are rarely made in those circumstances. And any electronic copies would have been destroyed along with the original nano-chips."

"What about in the computers here at the base?"

"Yes, that is what will save us, I think. All of the software here is twenty years out of date, but at least it gives us a starting point. Very little software these days is written completely from scratch. Most of it is just a modification of existing software. The operating instruc-tions for a new fusion plant is probably ninety-nine percent identical to the instructions for a plant thirty years old. We will have to make modifications to those programs in a lot of cases, but we should be able to provide substitute software for most of our equipment."

"I'm glad to hear that, Lieutenant. And since you are our computer expert, I'm going to put you in charge of seeing that it gets done."

"My pleasure, Captain."

Ellsworth leaned back in her chair. "All right then, I think we have the makings of a plan. Mister Carmichael, you and your people, along with some of our technical personnel, will be getting the factories operational. I know you don't have a lot of people to do the work, but with the robots you should be in pretty good shape."

"Yes, Captain," said the 'mayor' of the local population. "My people are eager to get going. For years we've been hiding here, afraid of the Skraks and afraid to do anything that would point out our presence. But now we are free to grow and build. Once we have the factories running, we plan to get the mining operations in the Rings going again and start building an orbital station. Then shipyards and everything else. We're all very excited."

"Wonderful. We'll be leaving some of our Marines to make sure you are secure. I doubt we got all of the Skraks, but they should not be able to bother you again for a long time. I'll also be leaving enough people to man the planetary defenses. With the shields working and those cannons in place, there's not much that could really bother you now."

"And that's a wonderful thing to know, Captain," said Carmichael. "After all those years of fear, security is a marvelous feeling."

Ellsworth nodded and then turned to Consul Brown. "You'll be staying here, sir?" He nodded.

"It seems the sensible thing, Captain. Under League laws, Mayor Carmichael and his people are the sovereign inhabitants of this planet. A League representative is a must. And if I and my people stay here, it will allow you to carry that much more equipment with you when you go back to Leavitte."

"Yes," said Ellsworth, "as soon as repairs are completed on *Gilgamesh* and we have our cargo loaded, I intend to hyper out and return to Leavitte. Commodore Shusterman gave me discretionary orders, but I believe the proper thing is to go back there. We know we have a stable base and it is not too far to Flemington. With these chips we can get those other ships in operation and try to get the fleet base working again. That would give us some substantial resources."

"But you will be coming back, won't you, Captain?" asked Carmichael.

"If we can. Certainly someone will be coming back. It might not be us. There are just too many unknowns at this point to plan very far ahead."

"Too many unknowns, and a hell of a lot of work," said Karl Bradley.

"True, Commander, very true. But we've made a good start and with a bit of luck we may just pull this off." Ellsworth stared at the people's faces. They all looked as hopeful as she felt. It might work. It really might work. At least they had a chance now.

"In any case," she said after a moment, "we are all going to be kept busy for a long, long time."

Rhada McClerndon sat on a large rock and watched the sky.

"The clouds are so beautiful, aren't they? I could just sit here and watch them all day."

"They are nice," agreed Gregory Sadgipour. "This is a nice world. Or at least it will be. How are you feeling, Rhada?"

"Oh, not too bad. Still pretty tired. Most of the cuts and bruises are nearly healed. A little sore here and there, but not bad."

"You had a rough time. You've earned some rest."

Rhada was silent. She was thinking about things she really did not want to think about.

"I've lost you, haven't I?" asked Greg suddenly. She stared at him but didn't know what to say.

"We never really had a chance and it's over before it even began," he said sadly.

"Greg... Greg, I don't know," she said after the silence became unbearable. "So much has happened to me. All the things they did to me. All the things I did. The things I didn't do. It's all swirling around in my head and I don't know what it all means. It... it's like everything that I was before has been burned away. My soul is floating naked on the wind. It's going to take a while for me to figure out who I am now. What I am. What I want. Please be patient with me."

"I... sure. I can do that." He looked down at the ground. As he did so, the sun was obscured by the gas giant and the shadow swept across the world and them. Rhada was fascinated by the transition. She came up here every day to watch it. But this time she was watching Greg. She didn't want to hurt him, but she could not describe what she felt toward him now. Everything was fuzzy and undefined. She slowly reached out and touched his hand. He looked up at her.

"But whatever happens, I'll always need a good friend." He nodded and smiled.

"You've got one."

Stewart Paalova stood on the hillside and watched the two people sitting a hundred meters below him. Years of scouting made him keep a careful watch around, too. He doubted there were any Skraks in the area. The few survivors of the Massacre at the Caves were scattered and probably heading for more hospitable regions. But old habits died hard and there was no point in taking chances. They didn't know he was there, Rhada and Greg. What were they talking about? A part of him felt very jealous that she was with Greg instead of him. But it was a small part. He thought back to those incredible moments in the caves when he had wanted her so much. It seemed like a dream now.

He had talked with Rhada a number of times since then. He liked her a lot, but that intense desire was gone. At that moment, in the cave, she had been an impossible fantasy. A warrior goddess that he could worship. It was so bizarre. He'd never felt anything like that. Now he knew that she was not a goddess. She was a woman. A very, very brave woman. He could admire her. Someday he might come to love her. But he did not worship her. And that was fine.

They would be leaving soon, those two. They would be getting on their starship and heading out. Out to the League. He looked up at the glittering ring of the gas giant and the distant stars. There was a civilization out there. It was in trouble, he knew. It was falling into ruins as he stood there. But it could be rebuilt. Stewart had spent his entire life among the ruins of this world. The thought of a galaxy full of ruins did not daunt him in the slightest.

He wanted to see that galaxy. Be a part of it. Help to rebuild it.

He looked down the hill at Rhada and Greg. Their captain was leaving a lot of the ship's crew behind. A lot of them had been killed in the battle, too. There must be quite a few empty berths on that ship.

And they owed him a favor.

He took his spear and started down the hill to talk with his friends.

The End

Author's Note:

One nice thing about self-publishing is that I can be as indulgent as I want to be and put in stuff like this, which a real publisher would chop out in an eyeblink.

This was the second novel I wrote, but the first that I'm publishing. There is nothing wrong with my first novel and it will join this one in print before too long, but *War Among the Ruins* (originally titled just *Ruins*) is probably the better story of the two and I wanted to start out strong. It certainly has received the more favorable reactions. Writer Eric Flint was actively pushing my first novel on his own publisher when he read this one. He immediately suggested that he try to interest his publisher in this one instead. Sadly, his efforts were not successful, but we both kept trying to find a buyer. One small publisher actually made an offer, but had to retract it after suffering a financial setback. But even the rejections were all very encouraging. It seemed like I had written a story that people would like to read—even if the publishers weren't willing to buy.

Eventually, after several more years of frustration and no sales—despite an agent and seven finished novels—I decided to self-publish. It wasn't an easy decision. I had never thought much of self publishing, or those who went that route. But after being told by publisher after publisher that they liked my work but it did not fit into their current marketing schemes, I realized that self-publishing was probably my only course of action. The only other choice was to let my stories languish on my hard drive until I died and they were lost forever. That seemed a shame, because they are good stories. If self-publishing gets them into the hands of even a few dozen people then it will be worth it.

And if you are reading this, then it *was* worth it! Enjoy!

Scott Washburn
Philadelphia
2007

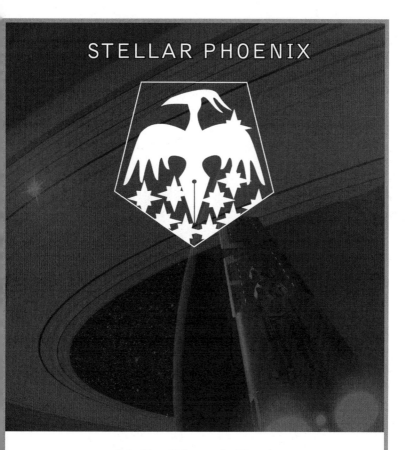

Made in the USA